Within the Space of a Second

A note from the author

This book contains explicit content and elements that may be triggering for some.

For a full list of warnings, please turn to the end of the book or visit my website: www.elisehelliwell.com.

Within the Space of a Second

The Mark of the Time Traveler: Book I

Elise Helliwell

ATRIA BOOKS
New York   Amsterdam/Antwerp   London   Toronto   Sydney/Melbourne   New Delhi

ATRIA BOOKS

WITHIN THE SPACE OF A SECOND
First published in Australia in 2025 by
Atria Books Australia, an imprint of Simon & Schuster (Australia) Pty Limited
Level 4, 32 York St, Sydney NSW 2000

10 9 8 7 6 5 4 3 2 1

New York Amsterdam/Antwerp London Toronto Sydney/Melbourne New Delhi
Visit our website at www.simonandschuster.com.au

For more than 100 years, Simon & Schuster has championed authors and the stories they create. By respecting the copyright of an author's intellectual property, you enable Simon & Schuster and the author to continue publishing exceptional books for years to come. We thank you for supporting the author's copyright by purchasing an authorised edition of this book.

No amount of this book may be reproduced or stored in any format, nor may it be uploaded to any website, database, language-learning model, or other repository, retrieval, or artificial intelligence system without express permission. All rights reserved. Inquiries may be directed to Simon & Schuster, 1230 Avenue of the Americas, New York, NY 10020 or permissions@simonandschuster.com.

© Elise Helliwell 2025

All rights reserved. No part of this publication may be reproduced, stored in a retrieval system, or transmitted in any form or by any means, electronic, mechanical, photocopying, recording or otherwise, without prior permission of the publisher.

ATRIA B O O K S and colophon are trademarks of Simon & Schuster, LLC.

This book is a work of fiction. Any references to historical events, real people, or real places are used fictitiously. Other names, characters, places, and events are products of the author's imagination, and any resemblance to actual events or places or persons, living or dead, is entirely coincidental.

 A catalogue record for this book is available from the National Library of Australia

ISBN: 9781761635953

Cover design and illustration: Libby Sparks
Typeset by Midland Typesetters, Australia
Printed and bound in China by RR Donnelley

For Katharine.

Prologue

Mariella

I've dreamed of my death every night since I was seven years old.

I tried to explain the dreams to my mother—the volatile tension twisting through my body, and the cold shadows slithering beneath my skin. But there were no words for a terror so consuming it stole the breath from my lungs and left me paralyzed. She'd find me perched on the top stair of our porch, slick with sweat, stammering about being so small I was scared I might disappear.

"It's only a nightmare, Mari," my mother would whisper through the darkness, rocking me against her chest as electrical current licked my fingertips. "Everyone gets them."

The strange symptoms peaked when I was twelve. This time, my mother wasn't there to reassure me, and I soon learned the other girls at boarding school weren't like me. They didn't wake at night screaming, bodies scalding, electricity whipping through their limbs.

My isolation worsened after my mother died, but when I was seventeen it stopped. I finished school and found medication that made everything—the nightmares, the paranoia, and the symptoms—go away, smothering my oddities like a weighted blanket.

At seventeen, my life began.

1

Mariella

"Ella, wait up." Anna's high-pitched voice carries across Harvard Yard. Her hot pink dress billows as she leaps over a puddle with the elegance of a dancer, rather than a freshman psychology student in platform wedges. Passing students turn their heads before hurrying to their morning classes.

I double back to meet her, the college's imposing sandstone buildings towering over me. Craning my neck, I trace the slabs of windows, each reflecting a sliver of the sky's miserable, stony gray.

"Good morning," I say, stifling a yawn. "Love the dress."

"Thanks," she says, shifting onto the tips of her wedges to smack a lip-glossed kiss on my cheek. "I'll forgive you for making me chase you across the lawn. I was calling you for *ages*."

I groan. "Feels like I'm still half asleep." I don't mention my pills, or that I took them too late last night. My savior medication, designed to stop my paranoia, vivid nightmares, and waking with strange electrical tingling in my limbs. I shouldn't complain, even if they do dampen my senses and memories. They're working, but the sedative side effects have been . . . an adjustment.

"Lucky you have me." Anna bats her false lashes and hands me a coffee.

"You're the best." I wrap my hands around the cup and take a sip. "*Ugh*, how much sugar is in this?"

"Whoops. Sorry, that's mine," she says, swapping the cups around. We mosey forward, each gust of wind pushing us along as if to mock our measured pace.

"I forgot to tell you," Anna says, "they announced the date for the psychology ball last night." Her sandy blonde hair bobs as she hops over another puddle. "We'll get ready together at my place with the girls. I can't wait!" She lifts her shoulders and squeals, then nudges me with her elbow. "Why aren't you shrieking like a teen at a boy-band concert?"

"Anna." Her name comes out with an exhale.

"Nope." She lifts her manicured hand in front of my face. "You promised. You're not getting out of this."

I *did* promise. But that was . . . *before*. Silas's stormy gaze flashes across my mind, eliciting an ache deep in my chest. "You know balls aren't my thing."

"That's what she said." She quirks a brow at me, and I try to muster a smile. Her glossy lips pull down into a frown. "Is this because of the police officer?"

"You don't need me anymore."

I push Silas's words away. Leaves flutter to the ground around us, bathing the yard in vivid hues of crimson, burnt orange and golden-brown. At a distance, it must look like the yard is on fire. "I have no idea what you're talking about."

Anna exhales. "Ella, I agree it was a bad . . . situationship, but you broke up months ago."

"We never dated," I remind her.

"Exactly. It's time to move on. You should try this new

dating app," she says, pulling her phone from her dress pocket. "Look. I matched with the new guy from work this morning." She flashes me a profile picture of a blond man. Every inch of his skin is covered in dark ink, multiple piercings hanging from his ears and nose.

"His name is Christiaan," Anna says. "Hot, right?"

I study the man's tongue, pressed against his teeth to profile the silver ball of his tongue piercing.

Anna's green gaze narrows. "What?"

I pinch my lips together to suppress a grin. "Nothing. It's just—" I gesture to her phone. "I've never understood why people do things like that."

"Like what?" Anna asks. "Body piercings?"

"Piercings. Tattoos. It's as if their sole purpose in life is to stand out." If anything, I applaud him for being so daring. Maybe he's a good match for Anna.

"Being the same as everyone else is boring," Anna says, linking a goosebump-covered arm through mine. "Being different is exciting."

It couldn't be warmer than fifty-three degrees and she's dressed for a bottomless brunch. I shrug off my favorite brown leather jacket and drape it over her bare shoulders.

She wraps it across her chest and sighs. "I love how warm this jacket is, but I despise everything else about it."

"You're welcome, Anna." I don't take her comment personally. She never wears the same thing twice or anything that isn't a designer brand.

We stroll past grand brick buildings with wrought-iron gates, the quiet morning broken by a hawk's sharp screech. John Harvard's statue lacks the habitual group of tourists crowded at his bronze feet.

Anna throws her head toward the sky. "I'm *so* not ready for our midterm, which is the only reason I'm coming to this stupid lecture."

"You'll be fine," I say. "We have a new guest lecturer today. He has a specialty in . . ."

My mind blanks. I scrunch my eyes shut and search through the medication-induced fog that's inhabited my brain for the past seven months. I read through our lecture notes twice last night. *Why can't I remember?*

"You okay?" Anna asks.

"Psychoneuroimmunology," I finally cry. "Which studies the relationship between our emotional state and the immune and endocrine systems. Isn't that interesting?"

Anna laughs. "No. Come on, Ella. You know it's weird to study the lecture slides *before* the actual lecture, right?"

My hand finds its way to my throat, clutching the rose-gold, heart-shaped charm on my necklace. "This is the most prestigious psychology school in the state. I'm willing to bet half the class has read today's slides."

Anna wraps her arm around my shoulder. "Whatever gets you to sleep at night, nerd. That clever brain's going to get us both through this degree."

We arrive at our lecture hall and filter in among our peers. My chest tightens at the sea of heads filling the tiered amphitheater. We squeeze between two groups and sit, Anna still hounding me about the psychology ball in February.

A middle-aged man with round glasses appears at the front of the room. He strides toward the lectern and connects his laptop to the overhead screen. Conversations diminish to a low hum. "Good morning. My name is Professor McGregor, and I'll be guest lecturing for the next two sessions."

"Shh, Anna," I whisper when she starts talking about ball gowns.

She arches a perfectly shaped eyebrow. "Give me a break. He can't hear me from all the way back here. Besides—"

I ignore Anna, absorbed in Professor McGregor's introduction, but the moment he finishes each sentence, the words fall away like grains of sand from a dune.

Anna stops talking mid-sentence and smacks my arm. "Ella." I jerk my arm away and sink lower into my chair. "*Ella*," she repeats.

"What?" I whisper, focusing on the overhead screen.

Anna's acrylic nails dig into my chin, and she forces my head toward a blond man sitting to the front left of the lecture hall. "Would you look at that fine specimen? He's hotter than flambé."

I yank my face from Anna's grasp. "Stop pointing, Anna. I'm trying to listen."

"But how've I never seen him before?" she asks without taking her eyes off him.

"Because you never come to class." I stifle my grin behind my hand. I'm being unfair. The honest answer is because he isn't *in* this class. Unless this is his first time attending, which I doubt, given we're months into the semester.

"*Because you never come to class*," Anna says in a mimicking tone. "You're so funny."

"Which brings me to my subspecialty. Psychoneuroimmunology," Professor McGregor says, and my attention snaps to the front of the room. "Has anyone heard of it before?" he asks, glancing around the lecture hall. "Any guesses as to what it might mean?"

Anna's elbow nudges me, but I'm already sitting up in

my seat. *Answer the question.* As the course advances, only the top students will be selected for the psychology honors program and taking part in class discussions is the first step. My chest tightens. *Put your hand up.* And I almost do, before Silas's mantra plays in my mind: *Keep your head down and don't draw attention to yourself.* And my limbs turn to lead, my throat so tight each breath is strained. I can't let boarding school repeat itself. I won't become another target.

"Anyone?" Professor McGregor repeats.

Anna's elbow strikes me again, this time in my ribs and somewhat more violently.

"What?" I whisper.

Anna's eyebrows crease. "You know this. Why aren't you saying anything?"

Heat rushes to my cheeks and I shake my head. Another student answers Professor McGregor's question and Anna slumps back in her seat.

I release a breath and my eyes sweep over the hall, halting on the man Anna pointed out earlier. He's relaxed back in his chair, hands tucked into the pockets of his chinos. His long legs are extended, ankles crossed as if he doesn't have a care in the world. I frown at the heavy shadow of his blond beard, concealing the strong jawline beneath. *Wait. How could I possibly know that?*

The corner of his mouth curves upward into a sexy, tight-lipped smirk, as if he's heard something amusing. A dimple appears in his cheek and a wave of heat races through my body, an image of a hand trailing up my thigh flashing in my mind. Cheeks on fire, I tear my gaze away, but within seconds I'm biting my lip and scrutinizing the tanned skin on the back of his neck. Why does he seem so familiar to me?

"You're drooling, babe," Anna says out of the corner of her mouth. "I told you he was a baddie."

I let out a small laugh, and more than one classmate turns in their seat. I clamp my hand over my mouth with a sharp inhale. "Sorry," I mumble, returning my attention to Professor McGregor, who's now going over key points for our upcoming exam.

Concentrate, Mariella.

But my eyes pull back to the man, like a compass needle to magnetic north. He's sitting next to a dark-haired woman I've also never seen in this class. Her black sweatshirt brushes the man's shoulder each time she leans over to whisper in his ear.

She's strikingly beautiful despite the dark crescents under her eyes and her gaunt face. The harsh scowl on her olive skin's a mere distraction from those prominent cheekbones and full lips. There's something dangerous about her allure, reminding me of a leopard stalking its prey. Strands of dark hair frame her face and her onyx eyes prowl the room, frequently dropping to her dated analogue watch as her slender leg jitters underneath the fold-out desk.

I focus again on the overhead screen and my stomach twists. The class is almost over and for the first time in my life, I haven't typed any notes. *At least I can copy Anna's.*

I stifle a smile. Anna's asleep, her head resting on her desk with saliva creeping from her mouth.

"Good luck with your midterm," Professor McGregor concludes.

The lecture hall swells with activity as students gather their things to leave. Anna jerks awake, her precisely drawn eyeliner now smudged along her temple. As we wait for the crowd in front of us to file out, I locate the man I've been watching, still seated and surveying those around him. His roaming gaze passes over me at first, but then his head snaps back and our eyes lock, his widening. He rises to his feet, mouth slack, hands falling by his sides.

My immediate instinct is to look away, but something holds me in place.

"Ella, get your shit," Anna says, startling me.

I bend down and shove my laptop into my satchel. A wall of my chestnut hair blocks the man from view, yet I can still sense him watching me.

Don't look! my brain screams.

I look up. He's definitely still staring. And it's—*rude*. Body rigid, he scrutinizes me. I wait for him to move. To blink. Do anything other than gawp at me with wide eyes. A jumble of emotions flicker across his face before his chest rises with a deep inhale, as if he'd forgotten for a moment that he needs to breathe.

My heart rate spikes. Does he recognize me from somewhere? *Where?* Maybe he knows someone from boarding school? Has he heard the rumors?

He slips his hand into his pocket, and the corner of his mouth kicks up into a slow, disbelieving smile, emphasizing the dimples in his cheeks.

Could this line move any slower?

My gaze drops to my feet and, when I look up, the man is gone.

2

Rose

"Rose, wait," Parker calls behind me.

I storm out of the lecture hall, swearing under my breath. My head's pounding. I shove two painkillers into my mouth and swallow them dry. *Ugh.* How is *this* what I've become? Popping painkillers like an addict. Taking uncalculated risks. Crashing a lecture full of people. What if someone recognized us? I've never been this stupid before.

You've never been this desperate before.

"This was a dumb idea," I mutter, more to myself than Parker, who's trailed out behind me. "Why do I listen to you?"

Lips pressed together and eyes vacant, he only shrugs. I grit my teeth.

Now he's lounging on the concrete stairs to the building's entrance, leaning back on his arms so casually he could be on vacation. Don't get me started on his preppy shirt and chinos. A panicked laugh builds in my throat, but I swallow it down and re-scan the perimeter. Are we making a mistake trusting McGregor's past self? Parker says we aren't, but a whisper in the back of my mind chants *Trap. Trap. Trap.*

He drags a hand through his unkempt hair, a gesture so uniquely Parker it may have been involuntary. Catching me staring, he offers an easy smile that doesn't reach his eyes.

"What's taking him so long?" I pull out my vape and inhale.

Two students amble past, both glaring at the white vapor curling from my mouth. I flip them off with a dirt-rimmed nail. If this headache would ease for five fucking minutes, I could—

"Stop pacing, Rose," Parker says. "You're making me nervous."

I scoff. "You *should* be nervous. You know there are people looking for us, and if they find us?" I lower my voice. "Have you forgotten your oath?" *The one we lived our life by before we got into this mess.*

He pushes off the step and strolls toward me. "Stop being dramatic." His large hands splay over my shoulders, holding me in place, and his light brown eyes bore into mine.

I jerk away from him, hot tension unfurling in my chest. Parker frowns. "I'm still not convinced we can trust him," I say.

"Have a little faith, Rose. There are good people in the world"—*there aren't*—"and I have an offer that he won't refuse. Trust me, he'll help us."

But what if he doesn't? What if he turns us in?

My breathing picks up, my head pounding with each forced inhale. Parker's tall form blurs and suddenly I've slipped into my past and I'm standing within Neurovida's walls, reaching toward the recruit who's just fallen flat on her ass.

Her delicate hand wraps around mine and I haul her to her feet.

"I'm Flame," she says.

"Rose." Parker yanks me from my memory, his eyes searching mine. "Are you okay?"

I turn away from him and rub my throbbing temples. "I'm fine. Just tired." I bite the inside of my cheek. Maybe he's right about us traveling again so soon. And if we leave now, I'll be stuck with his unbearable presence for even longer. My skin prickles. I've waited six months for this meeting with McGregor. He'll fix Parker, and we'll go our separate ways. *I'll be free.* I check the time on my new analogue watch and glare at the wooden lecture hall door.

"Who knows? McGregor might be expecting us," Parker says.

Trap. Trap. Trap.

My stomach turns. If he's right, it's possible Matthews— the person we're running from—might expect us, too.

Parker eyes me. "Remember, we need to gain his trust so he'll help us."

"He might not help us, whether he trusts us or not," I mutter, scanning the maple-lined path.

"This is what I love about you, Rose," Parker says, stretching his tanned arms above his head. "You're the face of positivity in a crisis."

Before I can reply, the lecture hall door opens, and McGregor steps outside. I take him in, his features no longer dulled by the dim lecture theatre lighting. Although leaner than his future self, he still wears his gray hair combed over to conceal his receding hairline.

He halts before us, his blue gaze darting between Parker and me from behind his round glasses. "Can I help you?" he asks, his aristocratic English accent clipped.

Parker pushes off the wall and strolls toward us. "Actually, we're hoping you can," he says with his most charming grin. "I'm Parker, and this is—"

"Rose," I say in a low voice. I step forward, trapping McGregor between us and the door. "Can we speak somewhere private? In your office or . . ." I trail off at McGregor's deep frown.

I know what he sees. He's staring at my tight set jaw and the holes in my sleeve like he can see right through them. Growing up on the streets not only alters who you are, it changes your appearance in a way no amount of food, money or clothing can fix. The brutality, the crime and the disadvantage settle underneath your skin, dimming the light in your eyes, and leaving a permanent harshness to your face. It's a hardship people like Parker and McGregor will never understand.

McGregor edges backward, peering at us over the top of his glasses. "What is this regarding?"

"We want to offer you an opportunity to further your research on immune cells," I say, trying to mimic Parker's easy smile, but the muscles in my face feel tight and wrong.

McGregor waves us off and turns to leave. "Submissions for research proposals closed last month."

"It's not a research proposal. Not for us anyway," Parker calls to McGregor's back and clears his throat. "You would be the one doing the research."

McGregor turns toward us with an incredulous chuckle. "Thank you, but I'm not taking on any new projects at this time."

I jump forward. "But—"

"I can't help you," he says with a finality that has my hands clenching into fists by my sides.

Heat rises in my chest, and I stride toward him. "Just fucking *listen*."

"Rose." Parker's hand snakes around my biceps, his firm grip halting my steps. "Professor, you once told me the only difference between a proven and unproven theory is persistence."

Brows raised, McGregor gives a quick, scoffing laugh. "You must be mistaken. We've never met before."

Parker takes another step toward McGregor. "What if I told you *we* are one of those unproven theories?"

McGregor shakes his head, a deep crease between his gray, bushy brows.

"You've been researching time travel for over a decade," Parker says, his voice barely above a whisper.

McGregor's spine straightens. "Time travel's impossible," he says in a soft, rushed voice.

Parker arches a brow. "Are you sure? Or do you want to look at our blood and see?"

3

Mariella

I trail out of the lecture hall in a daze, the stranger's face burned into my mind.

"Hello, anybody there?" Anna asks, grabbing my shoulder.

"Sorry. What?" I turn to face her. Her head's tilted to the side, her button nose scrunched.

"Why didn't you answer Professor McGregor's question?" she asks.

My arms lace around my torso, hot shame spreading through my gut. "I didn't want to get it wrong."

"But you knew the answer. You told me before we went in." Lines crease Anna's forehead. "Girl, what are you afraid of?"

"Nothing," I blurt, but I avoid Anna's narrowed glare by staring at my muddy shoes.

Anna's phone beeps, drawing her attention. "I'm going to meet some friends for coffee," she says, typing a reply. "You should come."

"Thanks, but I'm meeting my school friend and then I have a shift at the library."

"Ugh, *my school friend*," Anna mimics. "What's her name again?"

"Sarah Walker," I bite out.

"That's right. Tell her I want to meet her." Anna's eyes widen. "Wait. Does she party?"

"Have fun at coffee," I say with a small smile, and she rolls her eyes.

We part ways and I wander toward the river, plonking down beneath the brilliant carmine leaves of a flame tree. My left wrist twinges at my awkward descent, and I massage the bone beneath my surgical scar. I broke it three months ago and it still aches daily.

I pull my sketchbook from my satchel and flip through its pages, my stomach growing tighter with every half-finished drawing of Silas staring back at me. Whenever I draw, I never *intend* for him to be my subject, but my pencil automatically forms the familiar angle of his square jaw, shades beneath his sculpted cheekbones, and marks the subtle dimple in his chin, often hidden beneath dark stubble.

I pause on my last sketch, drawn four months ago. Conflicted emotions dance behind Silas's gray-blue eyes. Even with his subtle scars, he's the most beautiful man I've ever seen. I could spend hours perfecting the crease in his brow or the curve of his top lip, yet the sketch always feels incomplete. Now more so than ever.

Flowers flutter down around me, creating tiny ripples at the river's edge. I turn to a blank page and submit to the golden gaze that has consumed my mind since the morning lecture. By the time the stranger's face stares back at me from the page of my sketchbook, my wrist's throbbing, and I'm still perplexed. *Who are you?*

The crunching of leaves pulls me from my thoughts. I hold my breath, hoping the person's just passing by, but they sit. *Damn it.* I track a sailboat as it glides past, water rippling in its wake.

After fiddling with the corner of my sketchbook for several minutes, I throw my pencil down and lean forward to glare at the person intruding on my leafy sanctuary. I clutch the book to my chest.

It's the man from my lecture, his broad shoulders lazing against the tree trunk. His head's tilted back, eyes closed, dark blond brows pinched together. The baffling sense of familiarity I experienced in the lecture hall comes rushing back. *Where have I seen him before?* The answer feels just out of reach, like a misplaced word playing on the tip of my tongue.

A crew of rowers glide past, the coxswain's bellow shattering the quiet morning air. The man's amber eyes shoot open and catch me staring. He jolts forward, his eyebrows raised as he surveys every inch of me. I should look away, but I'm frozen like a second-hand laptop. His gaze lifts to my heated cheeks, and a subtle, knowing smile creeps across his lips.

My sketchbook slips, and I fumble it back against my chest. "I'm sorry. I was just leaving." I throw my drawing utensils into my satchel and jump to my feet.

"Wait," he says. It's only one word, but his warm voice vibrates through me, both familiar and foreign, like the melody of a long-forgotten song.

He runs his hands through his messy hair, throwing my brain into another déjà vu flurry. I take a step toward him. "Do I know you from somewhere?" The moment the words leave my mouth, the tips of my ears grow warm. *Shut up and leave, Mariella.* I shake my head. "Sorry, I'm—" *Deranged.* "Sleep deprived."

He puts his hands behind his head and leans back against the tree. "Is that why you were stalking me in the lecture hall back there?" He cocks a brow.

"*What?* I wasn't—" Is he enjoying watching me squirm?

"What were you drawing?" he asks, his eyes flicking to the sketchbook still clutched in my hands.

"Nothing." My grip tightens and he tilts his head. "Why are you looking at me like that?" I demand.

"Like what?" he teases. "Are you going to let me see your sketches or not?"

"Of course not. I don't even know you."

"I thought you said you did?" he says, and I smile despite myself, my hand rising to my mouth to cover it.

He tilts his head to the space beside him, a silent request. I eye him and sit, leaving a solid yard between us. "So . . . what were you doing in Professor McGregor's class?"

"Who says I'm not a student?" he asks in a taunting tone.

I search his tanned face, his blond, windswept hair. "Are you?"

"No. I was there to meet with McGregor."

I note the casual way he speaks of Professor McGregor. It's not uncommon for fellow academics to drop in on each other's lectures, but something nags in my gut. "Why?"

"So inquisitive," he murmurs.

"So evasive," I fire back, and a surprised laugh bursts from him, melting the tension in my chest.

He leans toward me. There's a daring glint in his eyes, his mouth curving into a wicked smile. "So, how long have you been preying on innocent men in dark lecture halls, stalker?" he says.

I tighten my lips to suppress a smile. "It's Mariella—Ella."

His eyes widen and the smile on his lips falters, but it's so quick I might have imagined it.

"It's a pleasure to meet you, Ella. I'm Parker." When he says my name, it's as if he's savoring the sound, triggering another memory I can't place.

"And you're sure we've never met?" I ask again.

"People always say that to me. I must have one of those faces," he says, pushing his hair away from his eyes. "What drew you to psychology?"

There's a flash of navy scrubs and green linoleum floors. White coats and black Velcro bed restraints. A shiver curls down my spine. *The fear of ending up like her.* "I want to develop a new framework for the early diagnosis and treatment of mental illness. And eventually, I'd like to become a clinical psychologist."

He nods. "You want to help people."

"I'd like to try."

His head cocks to the side. "So, Mari. Tell me—"

The word knifes through me. "Don't call me that." I swallow the lump in my throat. "Please," I add with far less fire.

His brows shoot up, and he studies my face. "I'm sorry. I didn't mean to—"

"Parker, where are you?" a husky voice calls from behind the tree.

His head snaps toward the voice and, for a split second, his body stills. She calls him again and he abruptly stands. Every nerve in my body tingles as he drags his gaze over me once more, as if committing me to memory. "I wish I could stay. Goodbye, Ella."

Then he slips his hands into his pockets and strolls away.

4

Rose

"At least McGregor agreed to meet with us," Parker says later, as we trudge toward a college bar to kill time until our evening meeting.

No thanks to Parker, who'd bailed halfway through our conversation. "A meeting doesn't guarantee his help," I say, clenching my fists to stop hacking at my clean nails.

After cornering McGregor, we'd snuck into the college gym to clean up. Thank the academic gods for gym bathrooms and communal soap. I haven't been this clean for weeks.

"Stop staring at me," Parker says, running his hand across his head. He'd exited the men's bathroom clean-shaven, hair buzzed to a number three or four.

I press my lips together to suppress a laugh. Parker self-conscious is a rare treat and there's no way I'm going to ease his insecurity. "I'm sorry, Jimmy. It's a massive change."

A muscle tenses in his jaw. "When are you going to stop calling me that? And it's not like I can drop into a barber whenever I want."

"Are you okay?" I stare at him flatly. "Do you want to talk about it?"

"I hate you," he says, sauntering ahead of me, but not before I catch the dimple in his cheek.

"Should we contact the press? Get ahead of this so *we* control the story?" I call to the back of his head.

We enter the campus bar overlooking the river and weave past wooden tables filled with students reeking of body odor, stale beer and privilege. I shout our drink order over the dim bar, competing with club chanting and drunken banter. The moment our drinks are in my hand, Parker and I head outside where it's quieter and I won't cop judgment for vaping. He leads me to a small bench overlooking the water, and I sit beside him in silence.

Tones of red, burnt orange and indigo are smudged across the sky behind the remnants of storm clouds. I let out a deep breath. Is this what life's supposed to be like?

Perhaps if my parents hadn't abandoned me, I'd be one of these advantaged students, drinking after class with my friends, my only worry passing my next exam. I push the thought from my mind. That will never be my reality.

I turn to Parker, who's swirling the whiskey in his glass. My head throbs. "What if McGregor won't help us?" I ask. *If he doesn't, I'll be forced to choose between Parker and the one thing I've spent my entire life chasing: safety.*

His light brown gaze flickers to mine, and he tilts his head so we're eye to eye. "He will. Everything will be okay, Rose." His confidence is almost believable.

"You don't know that," I say, unable to stomach the hope brimming in his eyes. There's something else there, too. Something that hints at camaraderie, because we're riding out this storm together. And I need to shut it down. Because Parker isn't my ally or my friend. I'm helping him to repay my debt to a friend, and then I'm done.

I turn toward a small rowboat floating past, creating

tiny ripples in the water that blur as my eyes lose focus. "Remember, the second McGregor helps us, we go our separate ways."

"I know," Parker says, and for the first time since we fell into this mess, he sounds tired.

Silence stretches between us until our glasses are empty and we're sitting in darkness.

"Are you okay?" Parker rests his arm on my shoulder.

My stomach clenches and I shrug him off. "Get off me. I'm fine." I turn to face him, and snort. "I *am* worried the yacht club will replace you as their poster boy once they see your new haircut."

The crease in his brow eases. "You're unbearable."

"Am I?" I ask, pushing my face toward his until we're nose to nose. "Am *I* the unbearable one, Jimmy?"

Parker laughs and shoves me away. "Go get me another drink."

"Yeah, yeah." I turn away with a wave of my hand.

My moment of reprieve vanishes the moment I reenter the bar and line up to order. I gnaw on the inside of my cheek, surrounded by tables of lively students in matching team colors. Even if I swapped my Doc Martens and black clothing for the college sporting jersey or a bright sorority top, I'd never fit in. Not like Parker. It's not in my blood.

The couple in front of me shuffles forward to order and I glimpse a young woman sitting at the end of the bar, chatting to one of the female bartenders. *It can't be.* My stomach does an awkward somersault. I should turn and run, but my feet stay rooted to the spot.

The young woman has the same high cheekbones and small chin. The same strong nose, spattered with freckles.

Her wavy brown hair's shorter, but her mannerisms haven't changed—legs crossed, ankles tangled together as she fiddles with the cuff of her sleeve.

A heavy weight pulls on my heart. She's still humbly unaware of how everyone who steps into her orbit is drawn toward her. Her unique blue-brown eyes are cast downward at her hands, fiddling with her sleeve. A sad smile creeps across my face. She's the only girl I've ever met who'd describe partial heterochromia as a curse.

The bartender passes her a jacket and she slips it on, her shoulders dropping as if she was missing a small part of herself without it. She slips off the stool and grabs her bag. I take a step toward her and stop, my heart pounding. *What am I doing? We swore to stay out of each other's pasts.* I need to go. Now.

I turn to flee and collide with solid muscle. *Parker.* We can still leave before any damage is done.

"Parker, let's go," I say, pulling him away, but he resists me. His eyes are glued to the woman, his face twisted in regret. I glance between him and the woman at the bar, and a prickling heat spreads across my chest. "Did you know she was going to be here?" Not waiting for his answer, I yank him toward the door.

Parker convinced me to come here to meet with McGregor. Did he have an ulterior motive this whole time?

I let go of him and storm toward the closest exit, throwing myself into the cool night air. The door swings open behind me.

"Rose, stop."

I whip around and draw in a ragged breath, my heart thumping in synchrony with my hammering head. "Why?

So you can waste another six months of my life lying to me? Admit it, you brought us here for her."

Parker's broad chest expands in a slow breath. "It's not like that."

"Then tell me what it's like, Parker." I shove my hands into his chest, my full body weight behind my assault, but he barely moves. "*Ugh*, I'm such an idiot. Do you have any idea what this is like for me? Holding you in this time with me, twenty-four seven, for six fucking months." I gesture to my pounding head. "Stuck with this relentless headache. I thought you had a plan."

I storm away from him and find myself staring at the Charles. The city lights reflect off the dark water, a reminder of the world that cast me aside. My heart sinks. It feels like only yesterday that Matthews turned on us, and now here it is again—the pain of utter betrayal. I was a fool for helping Parker. His hand closes around my wrist and I rip my arm out of his hold, as if scalded.

"Wait," he says, his voice gruff. "I knew McGregor would be here *because* of her. He's one of her lecturers. It's how I knew to come here, to this time. So, I mean, I knew we might see her, but that's not why—" Parker drags a hand across his freshly-shorn hair. "Our plan is solid. This changes nothing."

Parker's a terrible liar.

"This changes *everything*. Us being here puts her in danger. What were you thinking?"

I draw in heaving breath after breath, my pounding headache now a vicious stabbing. *Parker's just using me to get what he wants. I mean nothing to him. Why am I even doing this?* I bring my hands to my temples, trying to silence the barrage of thoughts swarming my skull. *Send him back home. Be done with him. Then I'll have what I want—to be safe and alone.*

"Rose?" Parker's voice sounds miles away.

With only myself to count on, the way it's always been. The way I like it. The thrashing in my head builds to a crescendo and I turn away from him, a strangled cry ripping from my throat. I drag my hands down my face.

"Rose? What's going on? Rose!"

Parker's plea fades. A door materializes before me, and I walk through it into my bedroom.

"What's going on?" I ask, shutting the door behind me. Flame's in bed, leaning against the headboard. She turns toward me and I tense. Her left eye is swollen shut, the surrounding skin a deep purplish black.

She flinches as she pushes herself upright. "I made a deal with Matthews. I said I'd help him with his shield if he trains us in the gym every morning."

"Us?" The word sounds foreign on my tongue.

She nods, brows arched, a tiny smile on her face. "You and me."

"You know we're competing against each other, right? I could use what he teaches us against you."

"I know. But I trust you." She glances down to her hands, the white bedsheet looped around her fingers. "And if anyone's going to make it to the final test, I'd hope it was one of us."

"But—how will I repay you?"

"Rose, wake up!" Parker shouts.

I'm thrown back into the crisp night air, knees buckling from my crushing migraine.

"What are you doing?" Parker's hands grip my shoulders, hauling me upright.

Saliva floods my mouth and I keel over, vomiting onto the grass. Parker supports my body as I heave until there's nothing left inside my churning stomach. I catch my breath and straighten, blinking at him. Something's wrong. My eyes can't seem to focus. I squint through his translucent torso, to the illuminated elm trees beside the footpath. *Fuck. FUCK.* He looks like he's about to travel. The blood rushes from my limbs. *What am I doing?* I lurch toward him and grab his forearms, snatching him back into this time with me. His body reappears and sharp bolts of pain tear through my head.

He hauls me against his chest, cutting off my groan. I almost let him go, sending him to his assured death. And that memory with Flame . . . *What's happening to me?*

"Fuck," I mutter, enveloped in Parker's arms.

"You're okay," he says, holding me tighter. I breathe in his familiar woody scent and my stomach drops. I yank out of his hold.

Parker's brows twitch as he slips his hands back into his pockets. "What's going on?"

I square my shoulders. "Nothing."

"Bullshit. The same thing happened outside the lecture hall this morning, didn't it? Your eyes glazed over, and you were mumbling to yourself."

I hold his stare. "It's nothing. I—slipped into a memory for a second. It's not a big deal."

"By accident?" Parker scoffs. "Jesus, Rose. You nearly lost your hold on me. Another few seconds and I'd be gone."

And there it is. "Of course you'd make this about you."

Parker's mouth drops. "He'll kill me, Rose. If you don't have this under control, I need to know."

"It was an accident, alright?" I snap. "It won't happen again."

"It's happened twice in one day. What if next time I can't pull you out?" He drags a hand over his short hair. "When we meet with McGregor tonight, we tell him the truth. He can't help us if he doesn't have all the facts."

I want to argue, but Parker's right. Whatever just happened, I can't control it. What's the point in everything we've been through if Matthews kills Parker before McGregor's even had a chance to help us? I draw in a deep breath. "Fine. We tell him the truth. But I want you to promise me you won't see or talk to *her* while we're here." Parker nods his head, but it's not enough. "Promise me. *Say it.* Tell me you *know* you can't start anything with her."

"I know," he mutters, his gaze sliding to the dark river behind me. "I promise. From here on out, it's just you and me."

5

Mariella

I turn onto my block, my shoes scraping along the concrete path. My house is midway down the street, nestled between grander, two-story homes with freshly painted picket fences and manicured front lawns. It may be old, with faulty electricity and peeling paint, but it's the only home I've ever known.

The stairs groan as I climb to the porch. The bottom keyhole on my front door unlocks with a reassuring *clunk*; the three above sit rusted from neglect. Inside, I kick off my shoes and dump my satchel on the dining table, the wood marked from the week my mother dabbled in sculpting. She's been gone for ten years, and yet most of the books on my shelves are her annotated classics, the throw on the couch she once wore as a shawl. Her memory clings to every crevice of this house.

My phone chimes in quick succession, Anna's trademark messaging pattern.

> you HAVE to come to bromley house tonight
> pleaseeeee
> it's going to be the best. night. EVER.

I want to hang out with Anna, but the half-dozen friends orbiting her? Not so much.

> Sorry, I have plans with Sarah tonight.
> Have fun!! xx

I put my phone on silent and sink into the couch with a contented sigh.

✧

My lungs are burning, every breath ripping through me like I've inhaled shards of glass. Coughing and gagging, I roll onto my side, and my hand grazes damp concrete. Cool night air bites at my bare feet. I'm . . . outside?

Not again.

A chill skitters down my spine, and my hands move from my jacket to the front of my dress. *At least I'm not naked this time.* And there isn't a boarding school full of witnesses.

I'm lying between parked cars, concealing me from the empty street. I wait for my coughing to ease and sit up, the high-pitched wail of a siren amplifying. Getting to my feet, I wrap my arms around my torso and scamper toward my house.

Police are diverting cars past a huge fire truck, while spectators watch firefighters spray water at the side of my house. The world around me slows as I take in the white smoke billowing from my smashed bedroom window, tainting the clear night sky. An ambulance pulls up somewhere behind me and the piercing siren cuts off, accentuating the pounding of my pulse in my ears.

I push through the crowd of people watching my house burn as if it's some sort of sick entertainment.

"Mari! Thank heavens." My elderly neighbor, Mrs Bensen, rushes toward me and her bony hands grasp my forearms. She's lived in the house behind mine for as long as I can remember.

"What's—*happening*?" I ask, my words a croaky plea that scratches against my throat. *I must be dreaming.* Any second I'll wake up, safe on my sofa, and find this has all been a horrible nightmare.

"Fire's almost out, I'd say," she says. I tear my eyes away from her face, unable to stomach the pity in her glassy blue gaze. "Oh, Mari. They got here as quickly as they could. I only heard the alarm when the fire truck pulled up."

I look past her to my family home, illuminated in red and blue from the fire truck's lights. My safe place. I clamp my hand over my mouth. Everything I have is in that house. *Everything.* What if it's all gone? What will I do? Where will I go?

No. No. No. I break away from Mrs Bensen and sprint toward my front door, blades of wet grass clinging to my feet.

My trembling hand is inches from the wooden banister of the porch when two arms clamp around my waist, and I'm hauled backward.

"Are you deaf? You can't go in," a firefighter yells, carrying me away from my house. He plonks me down with the other spectators and storms toward the fire truck, muttering under his breath.

Mrs Bensen wraps her arm around my shoulders, and we stand in silence while the firefighters work, their uniforms a bright, blurry haze cutting through the dark night.

Within five minutes the smoke eases. Many of the workers congregate beside the truck. I leave Mrs Bensen and head toward them.

"When can I go back in?" I ask a burly firefighter with a thick mustache.

"Is this your place?" he asks in a Southern accent. His alert gaze moves from my bare feet to his colleagues trudging past, as if he's looking for someone else to deal with me.

"Is there someone you can call? To come pick you up?"

Silas. I should call Silas.

"You don't need me anymore."

"Don't you need me?" I push the words past the sob building in my throat. A subtle shake of his head is enough to tear my heart open.

"Not enough, Mariella."

I swallow the lump in my throat. "Please just tell me when I can go back in," I say, my lip trembling.

His face softens. "You can't. Not until it's been assessed structurally. You'll need to stay somewhere else for a while." He's recording my personal details when there's a crackle and a distorted voice blares through the two-way radio attached to his navy and yellow tunic. He tilts his head to reply and turns back to me with a leveling stare. "Stay here." He storms away, leaving me on my front lawn.

Before long, the fire diminishes and the spectators disperse. I should leave too, but my limbs are numb, my mouth dry. I sit on the curb while firefighters trudge in and out of my home like some sort of sad open inspection. *It can't be that dangerous if they're still going in, can it?*

I stride back down the street and turn a corner, stopping at Mrs Bensen's house. Her gate creaks open, my feet silent on the damp grass. I sneak down the side of her house toward the backyard. The fence between the two properties is broken from a storm last year, and I squeeze between it, the rough wood catching on my dress.

My backyard is empty of firefighters, and the overgrown grass brushes my calves as I dart toward the open back door. I pause briefly in the doorway and release a breath. The living room is hazy with smoke, but intact. *Maybe it's not that bad?* I move past the undamaged sofa on light feet, my footsteps slowing in the hallway leading to the bedrooms.

Thick, dark smoke hangs in the air, and scorch marks creep along the walls like black claws summoning me. Rubbing my stinging eyes, I creep forward, water seeping from the hall runner beneath my feet.

I cover my mouth with my sleeve and halt outside my mother's bedroom, the wooden door open for the first time in a decade. The once cream curtains are now spines of tattered fabric, floating in the icy breeze stealing through her broken window. My stomach coils at the memory of my mother peeking through a slit in those curtains, her wary gaze glued to the street outside. I can still see her weight shifting from foot to foot, her olive dress swishing at her calves.

I step into the room and drag my hand along the blackened brick wall, as if the contact might stop the room from swallowing me whole. The metal frame is scorched, the blue and cream floor rug sodden and black, the corners curling inward like the legs of a giant dead spider. A heavy feeling settles in my stomach as I frown at the square of flooring peeking out from beneath the rug. From the doorway, I study the subtle gap around its perimeter, demarcating it from the other long, wooden boards. I step into the room and fold the rug over itself to expose the now prominent rectangle of wood and its gapped edge.

"What'd ya say?" someone shouts from the living area, probably a firefighter speaking through his two-way radio.

My head snaps back to the floor, and I shove my nails into the cracks and lift the wooden block. I reveal a hidden compartment the size of a large shoebox, much of its space taken up by a rusted metal box. I ease the box from its hiding place and pry off the lid.

Inside, a dozen or so books are stacked side by side, their spines crinkled with age. My mother's journals. I pull one out and crack the spine. My mother's tidy, slanted scrawl fills the page. *Mari and I went to the park after work today, she's getting so—*

A hard mass forms in my stomach. I snap the journal shut and slide it back into place. I've gotten through the past ten years without these journals. I didn't need them when she left me, and I don't need them now. I shove the box back into the hidden compartment and stand.

Heavy footsteps thump by the front door.

I'm halfway along the hallway when my feet jerk to a halt. The image of my mother's aged journals flashes through my mind, a bitter taste filling my mouth.

Leave them, like she left you.

I should be grabbing clothing or toiletries—things I need for the next twenty-four hours—but I race back into my mother's room and fall to my knees. Water seeps into the fabric of my dress. I seize the metal box and hurry back along the corridor, grabbing my phone and satchel from the dining-room table and scampering away from my family home with the dated ramblings of a dead woman.

6

Rose

"Quickly, come in," McGregor says, skittering into the old brick building Parker and I have spent the past ten minutes waiting outside. McGregor beelines down a labyrinth of door-lined corridors and disappears inside his office. Parker and I follow him, Parker pausing at the threshold and gesturing for me to enter before him.

I roll my eyes and step into the stuffy room. My throat tightens. Bookshelves line the walls, crammed with aged textbooks and journal articles that leave barely enough space for the dark, mahogany desk and the two chairs before it.

McGregor sits behind his desk, staring at me as if I'm a disobedient student. Holding back my own scowl, I cross my arms over my chest and lean against one of the bookshelves.

"May we sit?" Parker asks, as if he's about to schmooze McGregor over a lavish lunch.

The slight incline of McGregor's head is stiff. I pick up a mound of papers resting on one of the sad fabric chairs and plant my ass down. I keep my face blank but, hidden by McGregor's desk, my left foot twitches like I'm an addict in withdrawal. Parker reclines in the seat beside me.

McGregor clasps his hands on top of his desk and leans forward, his beady eyes darting between Parker's face and mine. "I want you to tell me absolutely *everything* you know about time travel," he says in a sharp tone.

"You taught us everything we know," Parker says. "Anchors and shields and theories—*your* theories really. All of the research was conducted by you."

McGregor's stern expression gives nothing away. "When do we meet? What year?"

"In—"

"Parker," I say. I'm not hand-feeding McGregor from a silver spoon until I know he'll make it worth our while. "All you need to know is that we'll meet in the future at a time-traveling institution."

"Run by whom?" McGregor asks.

"We were never told," I say, shaking my head. "We weren't the first time travelers to live there. But we were the first group to be formally recruited."

"Why?" McGregor asks Parker.

"To stop—"

"Next question," I snap, and McGregor's lips pull down at the corners.

"I want to hear it from the beginning," McGregor says, eyes flicking to Parker. "From him."

I grit my teeth as Parker launches into conversation with McGregor before I can stop him, beginning with Neurovida, the time travel training institution where we first met McGregor's future self. As they speak, Parker weaves in personal recollections of the time he and McGregor shared at Neurovida, cementing the close relationship I never knew they had. I keep waiting for McGregor to chuck us out, or for Parker to say the wrong thing but . . .

He won't. Because Parker is . . . Parker. And I may have

bad luck, but if life's a hand of cards, he was dealt a royal fucking flush. *Dick.*

"I was hoping you'd take a look at our blood, see if anything stands out," Parker says.

"I'm willing to study your blood under a microscope, but I won't promise anything else," McGregor says, adjusting his glasses.

Parker releases a breath. "Thank you. You told me the key to time travel is in our white blood cells." His eyes dart to mine. *Don't do it, Parker.* "I want you to look at mine because . . . I've lost my ability to travel," he says, and I huff.

"How?" McGregor asks.

"A drug. Injected into my neck." His fingers brush the puncture site as if he can still feel the sting of the needle. "You created it, in the future. And I'm hoping if a drug can be given to take someone's powers away—"

"One can be created to restore it," McGregor says, his blue eyes twinkling.

"Exactly," Parker says. "Rose's powers are intact. I'm hoping you can compare our blood and see what's different with mine. Then figure out how to reverse it."

I study the dust-lined bookshelf while Parker pulls out his trump card, making an offer we knew would have McGregor eating out of the palm of our hands before we even entered the building.

My head pounds as Parker and McGregor rise to their feet and shake hands, McGregor sporting a deep, troubled frown. He wanders toward his office door, scratching his jaw with an unfocused gaze. I throw Parker a questioning look. His answer is an indifferent shrug.

"Follow me," McGregor calls from the corridor, and he leads us to a nearby lab. Inside, he glides past rows of metal benches and collects numerous items from the cupboards above an industrial-looking sink. Parker shadows his every move, but I hover by the doorway until I'm called forward to surrender four small vials of blood.

"I'll look at the samples and let you know what I find," he says to Parker. "How will I contact you?"

Parker grimaces and scratches the back of his head. "That ties into the other favor we need to ask you. Do you have anywhere we could stay? To lie low until we hear from you."

"I might be able to find an unoccupied residence," McGregor says, rubbing his forehead. His sharp eyes land on me. "Until then, I want you to stay out of sight."

"Finally, we agree on something," I mutter, looking at Parker.

"We'll take anything you can give us," he says, with an infuriatingly charismatic smile.

"Wait here. I'll see what's available," McGregor says, and he leaves the room.

The moment the door closes, Parker pulls me into a hug, lifting my feet off the ground. "Didn't I tell you he'd help us?" he says.

Our bodies are pressed together between rows of metal benches, Parker's chest firm and warm against mine. My breath hitches and I claw at the strong forearms wrapped around my waist. "Put me down before I take you out."

Parker stiffens and releases me, relaxing back against one of the workbenches with his arms stretched out on either side of his body. "You can say it."

"Say what?" I ask, eyeing him.

"That I'm a genius and I was right."

I laugh. "I'm *never* saying that to you, Jimmy. Your head is gigantic."

Parker only grins and slips his hands into his pockets. The movement shifts the fabric of his shirt over his biceps, and I look away.

The minute McGregor develops Parker's cure, I'm going to put years of distance between us.

7

Mariella

I creep across campus toward Bromley House in bare feet, avoiding the broad columns of shadow cast by towering elms and oaks. Sandstone gargoyles leer above the building's entrance, as old as the campus itself. Lungs burning, I haul myself up the staircase to the second floor, and find Anna drinking with friends in a cozy communal living room. Warmth and laughter spill from the room, where students laze on sofas and beanbags. I hover in the doorway, clutching the metal box filled with journals to my chest. The chatter dies and seven curious pairs of eyes land on me. The muscles in my upper body stiffen. *Don't cry.*

"Ella, you came," Anna says, rushing toward me, the charms on her bracelet jingling. She's still in her work outfit, her miniskirt a band of fabric beneath her sheer, overhanging top. She glances at my bare feet and her face falls. "Are you okay?"

I smooth my hands over my crumpled dress. I must look like . . . well, like I've escaped a burning building. The moment she reaches me, my façade crumbles. "There was a fire at my house."

"What?" she cries, wrapping her arm around my shoulder.

My voice wavers. "Can I please stay here tonight?"

"Of course," Anna says. She leads me away from the common area and we pause outside a door halfway along the corridor. Tongue pressed to her hot pink lips, she jostles the handle, jimmying the key left and right until the door budges with a loud groan. "This is me."

Leaving me in the entrance, she breezes past a small, garment-strewn sofa. Her heels click on the polished floorboards as she waltzes around the room and flicks switches. The heater rumbles to life, and mushrooms of orange-hued light spill from numerous fabric-draped lampshades. She pauses at the far end of the room and draws the curtains covering a grand floor-to-ceiling window, framed by exposed brick.

"What happened?" she asks, crossing the room and ushering me further inside.

"I don't know." I trace the woven, gray fibers in the floor rug beneath her sofa. "I was asleep and then—" There's a flash of ravenous flames escaping my bedroom windows. "I was outside, and my house was on fire." More tears burn behind my eyes and Anna rushes toward me. "I think I just need to go to bed," I mutter.

"Yeah. Of course," Anna says, releasing me. She guides me toward two doors leading off the small living area, and points to one of them. "This is my room." She opens the door to the right of her bedroom. "And this is the spare. Lucky my roommate Jamie dropped out last week or you'd be on the sofa."

I nod in agreement, but nothing about my situation feels lucky. Anna flicks a switch, illuminating the room with warm light. There's a single bed pushed against the wall to make space for a small desk. I step inside and dump the journals and my satchel on the floor.

Anna turns toward me, light reflecting off the glitter in her dark purple eyeshadow. "Are you sure you're okay?"

"I'm fine," I say, but I avoid her pitying gaze by studying the oversized black-and-white prints hanging on the wall. "I just want to go to bed."

"Okay . . . I'm here for you, Ella. Whatever you need." She hesitates for a moment, then flings her arms around me and crushes me against her short frame.

Arms hanging limply by my sides, I close my eyes and let her hold me. "Thanks, Anna."

She releases me and cracks a sad grin. "God, you *reek* of smoke."

I sniff the collar of my leather jacket, but I can't smell anything. "I didn't have time to get any fresh clothes."

Anna inclines her head toward the wardrobe, a sequined sleeve pinched between the closed doors. "I've been using this room as a second wardrobe. Take anything you want. I'll just grab you some pajamas." She ducks into her bedroom and returns with a purple and gold set.

"Thank you," I say. "I'm only staying tonight. I'll find somewhere else tomorrow."

Anna scrunches her nose. "Why? The room's empty, and it's been *super* dull since Jamie dropped out." She gestures her head toward the front door. "The place opposite's empty too. Please move in?"

"I could never afford it." My throat constricts. I don't have property insurance, and until my house is assessed structurally, I'm homeless. *What am I going to do?*

"Don't worry about that. My dad owns the building." Anna's face lights up. "I know, you can tutor me in exchange for board. Dad's been begging me to get my grades up."

She places her hands on my shoulders. "Stay as long as you need."

✧

My body's tingling, a buzzing energy radiating heat beneath my skin. My fingers extend through clear air, toward a wall of sparkling white light. The sun warms my skin, but above me is more of the shimmering light, each dense ray refracting away from me, encasing me inside an iridescent dome.

Closing my eyes, I inhale salty air, tinged with coconut sunscreen. Waves break against the shore and seagulls screech somewhere in the distance. I move forward, and the light-free circle moves with me, its diameter increasing with each step to reveal a tiny playground beside the beach.

A girl skips past me.

"Mari, come here."

The soft, familiar voice startles me, the speaker obscured behind the wall of light. I step toward the voice, and the rays bounce backward.

A woman sits on a wooden bench at the playground's edge. Chest aching, I stare at her, my mother. Her wavy chestnut hair is pulled back into a messy bun, and love and adoration burn in her blue-brown eyes.

Ten years on and our similarities have only grown.

The young girl bounds toward my mother with the same exuberance that swirls within my own chest, despite the silent tears sliding down my cheeks. I search for any signs of illness, but my mother's face is healthy, a ripe blush in the apples of her cheeks.

"Mommy," my younger self squeals. She hugs my mother, and her fresh, citrus scent floods my nostrils. I close my eyes and inhale deeply, savoring the smell. How had I forgotten?

"Happy birthday, Mari. I've missed you," my mother says, stroking the girl's head. Somehow, I can feel her cool hands on my forehead, as if it's my hair she's brushing away from my face.

"Mommy, when are you coming home?" the girl asks.

My mother places her hands on the girl's cheeks, cocooning her round face. "The second I can, sweet girl."

The little girl's mouth pulls to the side, a slight frown on her face. "Sarah Walker and the girls at boarding school said you're crazy. They said you tried to run away." Tears pool in her eyes. "Promise if you do, you'll take me with you?"

My mother dips her head to bring their gazes level, hands still holding her tiny face. "I'd never leave you, Mari. Never." She pulls the girl toward her, her head nestled over my mother's heart. "You're the light of my life," my mother whispers, her voice wavering with emotion. "Oh, I almost forgot." Releasing the girl, my mother unclasps a rose-gold, heart-shaped necklace from her own neck and secures it around the girl's. "Happy birthday, special girl."

I'm oblivious to the reapproaching wall of white, but it's upon me in seconds, encasing me in a tunnel of blinding light. My mother's muffled words fade away. A cool breeze ripples over my skin and voices sing out in the distance, strange and distorted, like a recording in slow motion.

Eyes watering, I squint through the impenetrable beams, but they're no easier to discern than the blinding rays of the sun. I close my eyes and exhale, switching my focus to the voices.

A man's deep chuckle echoes around me, growing sharper as he approaches. My eyes snap open and the wall of light has regressed, as if repelled from my body by an invisible force.

Smoke laces the frosty air, stinging my throat after the humidity in my previous dream. I walk forward and my boots sink into thick snow. The light-reflective circle moves again with me, expanding to expose numerous tall pines.

An adult version of myself steps inside my circle of clarity, and my legs halt. Unaware of my presence, my dream-self walks past me with confident, purposeful strides. Long, wavy hair hangs past bony shoulders, her physique slight compared to the fullness of my own.

I touch the small single stud in my left ear. The "other" Mariella's ears hold many more piercings—dainty, feminine jewelry, some pieces spotted with tiny diamonds.

She's holding a black flask, and her gaze is focused on something outside the perimeter of light.

A man steps through the wall of white and I jolt.

Parker.

He runs a hand through his messy hair, shorter at the sides and longer on top to give the appearance of a model who's just rolled out of bed. Butterflies swirl in my stomach as he prowls toward this dream version of myself, yet she steps away in a slow, tentative dance.

She extends the flask toward him, flashing him a flirtatious smile. "Did Nickol kick you out again?" she asks, her tone light and taunting.

Parker reaches toward her and his hand wraps around her wrist, making her pause. "Do you have any idea how long I've waited to be alone with you?" he murmurs, holding her gaze.

He moves closer still. One more step and his body will touch hers. They stare at each other, breaths mingling in the cool air, fingers threading together. His gaze flickers to her lips, and I shudder.

My palm tingles from the graze of his fingertips, the warmth of his touch transferring to my skin. Is it her knees shaking? Her heart pounding? Or my own? He lowers his head, and my breath quickens as he brings his mouth to hers. Brushing my tingling lips, I close my eyes and it's as if Parker's soft lips are pressed to mine. His hands move to my waist, pulling my body against his, and his tongue slides into my mouth.

Erratic, warm energy flares inside my chest, and I stumble backward with a startled breath. The heat intensifies, spreading through my body. I clutch my hands over my racing heart and my body begins to shake, a light tremble that strengthens until every cell in my body is vibrating.

Doubling over, I gasp for breath, but it feels as if the air entering and exiting my lungs is pulsating. Pressure builds within my chest, and I cry out as the energy explodes.

✧

I jerk awake in Anna's spare bedroom with electricity flooding my body. The blood drains from my face at the too-familiar sensation. One I haven't experienced for seven months. *My medication. I didn't take it last night.*

Waves of residual current race down my arms, the energy dissipating through my fingertips in miniature, heated zaps. I flick my hands to will it away, and the old injury in my wrist protests in sharp stabs of pain. I need to get more medication from Dr Williams. *Today.*

My dreams of Parker and my mother replay in my mind. They seemed so real, almost like memories. And my mother—she was well. Lucid. Nothing like a woman contemplating suicide. Nothing like the woman I remember. No signs of her demons, hiding beneath the surface.

"I'd never leave you, Mari. Never. You're the light of my life."

My mother loved me.

The realization leaves me breathless. Guilt bubbles up through my chest. How had I forgotten?

Another surge of current races through my fingers and I flick it away. My mother knew about my dreams and my symptoms. She told me to ignore them. Is that what she did with her own demons? Suppressed them until they consumed her? The dream replays in my mind. I remember the day well—my eighth birthday. She'd been healthy. Adamant she would return home. And yet she died three months later. How had her mind failed her in only three months? Were there warning signs?

My attention snaps to the metal box beside my feet and I leap off the bed, knees sinking into the plush sage rug. I pull the journals out, arrange them in chronological order, and devour the first from front to back. There's a brief mention of my nightmares, but the rest of my mother's journal is—mundane. She writes of daily activities and general life stressors.

By the time I reach the third journal, I'm skipping pages, skimming my mother's neat, curling scrawl. I turn through page after page, searching for signs of poor health or paranoid thoughts, but my mother's life seemed . . . *good*. Healthy. She'd enjoyed being a mother.

I grab the last journal, flicking to the back, and a crinkled piece of paper flutters into my lap. The frail paper wavers in my hand, the folded seam crackling when opened to reveal an intricate drawing of a bizarre clock. I trace its outline with a trembling finger: a large circle with a rippled edge on one side. At the center, it has not two but six unique hands, and above and below the clock are long vertical lines of varying length, some broken. *What does it mean?*

I pick up the journal and turn to the last page, which contains only one sentence: *Let the current carry you.* My fingers find their way to the charm on my necklace, and my thumb brushes the same worn inscription on its back. My mother's necklace. The one she fastened around my younger self's neck in my dream.

I read the sentence again. Her last entry. Written on—

I lurch forward, scrutinizing the date from ten years past. *December 25.*

The day *after* my mother died.

8

Mariella

I jump to my feet and drag my fingers through my tangled hair. I need to—I don't know what I need to do. My mother's diary must be wrong. No length of time or medication could suppress my memory of the day she died. It was Christmas Eve and I was sitting at Mrs Bensen's dining table. Meager red and green tinsel was draped around the room, and the tips of my shoes barely kissed the dark wooden floorboards.

People think children live in their own heads, oblivious to the world around them. But when Mrs Bensen lowered the phone, her mouth settling into a firm line, brows rounded and eyes dim, *I knew*.

The crushing sensation in my chest had begun even before she'd eased to the floor on stiff knees and taken my hands in hers.

"Mari, your mother is gone."

Why is there an entry in her diary after that day? I fan my pajama top against my chest. Was there a mix up between my mother and another patient? Did my mother not die? I shake my head. She's dead, I'm sure of it. Maybe the hospital got the date of her death wrong? Or was my mother confused the day she wrote her last entry? But who would mistake any other day for Christmas? *This is insane.*

I reopen the journal and stare at the date, my hands tugging on the roots of my hair. My mother was unwell. *I know this.* I've known this since I was eight years old. Why did she seem perfectly healthy in my dream?

"I'd never leave you, Mari."

Clutching the journal against my chest, I storm into Anna's living room. I'm hit with blaring music, and the strong scent of golden toast, melted butter and sizzling bacon.

"Morning. How did you sleep?" Anna calls from her makeshift kitchenette. She's piling food onto two plates with her back to me. She spins around, golden pants glimmering, the waist concealed by an oversized, vivid purple sweater. Our eyes meet and the smile on her glossy red lips falls. "Ella?" She grabs her phone and the music ceases. "You're shaking. When was the last time you ate?"

"Last night . . . I think." Food isn't important. Nothing matters except uncovering how it's possible my mother left a note in her diary the day *after* she died. "I have to go."

Anna inserts herself between me and the front door, and I'm inundated with a whoosh of sweet, floral fragrance and strawberry lip gloss. I'd forgotten just how much my medication dampened my sense of smell.

"But—I made breakfast," Anna says. "And you're still wearing pajamas. Come and sit down for a second." She plants her hands on my shoulders and forces me to sit at her small dining table. "Tell me what's going on while you eat," she says, sliding two plates of food onto the table. She sits next to me and crosses her legs, her wide green gaze flickering from my face to the journal still clutched against my chest.

I've kept the details of my past a secret since the day I left school. What if I tell Anna the truth and I lose her? Isn't that what happened with Silas? I inwardly cringe.

"My mother died in hospital when I was eight." Anna's eyes widen, her lips parting to draw in a small gasp. "But after the fire last night, I found some of her old journals. I was reading them this morning, and her last entry was *after* the date I was told she died."

I open the journal to the last entry and slide it toward Anna. She picks it up and her contoured face momentarily dips behind the pages. "Let the current carry you," she mutters, turning the page as if it's fragile. "Is it possible you remembered the date wrong?"

"No. She died on Christmas Eve."

"I'm so sorry," Anna says, flipping to the front of the journal. She pauses on a sketch of my mother with my younger self. "*Oh*, Ella. She was beautiful." Her eyes scan my face and drop back to the sketch. "You could be twins."

I swallow the lump in my throat. "I think the hospital must have confused her death with another patient's or something."

"I'm sure there's an explanation," Anna says, returning the journal to me. "Have you checked her death certificate?"

I shake my head. "I never saw one."

"You know, when my Aunt Gaye was searching our family tree, she entered some details into a website and all the information just came up."

"Really?" My fork clangs on the tabletop. "Can we look up my mother?"

"You eat," Anna says, and she jabs an acrylic nail at my plate. "I'll get my laptop."

While she ducks into her bedroom, I take a bite of food and groan. Did food taste this good before? "What's in this?" I ask Anna when she returns.

"It's just scrambled eggs and bacon," she says, placing her laptop on the table. She pulls up a chair beside mine, finds an ancestry page, and tilts the screen toward me. I type *Evelyn Adams* into the search field.

"Hmm," Anna says, frowning at the screen when the search comes back empty. "Try another one."

I return to the search engine and open another ancestry site. Re-entering my mother's details, I hit the return key. "It's not here," I say after another three attempts.

Anna huffs at the screen. "I don't understand why it's not showing up." She leans her shoulder into mine. "I'm sorry."

"It's okay. Thank you for helping me."

"Of course." There's a wrinkle between her brows, and she's biting her lip.

"What?" I ask.

Anna's gaze finds mine. "How did she die?" she asks softly.

There's a flash of white walls and sterile floors. Nurses. And light glinting off sharp, beveled needle tips. A bead of sweat forms over my brow. *She killed herself. Say it.* The words huddle on the tip of my tongue. *Don't lie about this.*

Anna stares at me, waiting.

"She had a heart attack," I blurt. The lie burns the back of my throat.

Tears brim in Anna's eyes. "I'm so sorry, Ella," she says. "I can't imagine losing a mother so young."

"Thanks," I say, lowering my gaze to the table.

"Wait a sec." Anna's fingers fly over the keyboard. She

pounds the return key and leans forward, the light from the screen reflecting in her green irises. "It says here if someone dies in a hospital, the attending doctor issues the death certificate. What's the name of the hospital?"

"Massachusetts General," I say, already on my feet. I'll go to the hospital and request a copy of my mother's death certificate. Then I can deposit my memories of my mother back in the past where they belong.

Anna clears the plates from the table and follows me to the front door.

"What are you doing?" I ask.

"Coming with you," she says, bending over to fasten the buckles on her cream ankle boots. "Obviously." She grabs her handbag from the entry table and shifts her weight to one side, eyeing me up and down. "You'd better get dressed, nerd."

✧

The beige, knee-high boots I borrowed from Anna click against the shiny hospital floor. We cross the spacious foyer, passing under a large red sign pointing toward the ER, and my pulse jumps. It's warmer than outside, but the heated space is tinged with bitter antiseptic and lavender air freshener.

"Are you okay?" Anna asks, and I'm thrown back in time. Silas is carrying me through the same hospital doors as if I'm dying.

"Are you okay?" Silas asks.

"Yes. And I can walk, Silas," I say, shifting in his arms to reach up and brush the deep groove between his dark brows. "Hey. I'm fine."

He pulls away from my touch. "You're not fine. Nothing about this is fine," he says through gritted teeth, a subtle tremble in the strong arms cradling me. "I did this to you."

"Don't say that. We were messing around, and I fell. Please don't blame yourself."

He shakes his head and my heart sinks. Why did I have to trip and ruin the most perfect day of my life?

We enter the ER, and I suck in a breath, but my lungs expand less with each inhale.

Silas lowers me onto a plastic chair in front of the triage nurse and spots cloud my vision. My uninjured hand reaches out to grip his strong forearm and his muscles tense beneath my fingers. "I—I don't like hospitals. After everything that happened to my mom." There's a flash of limbs secured to bed rails and my heart jumps. "Don't leave."

Silas's large, warm hand slips into mine, his touch firm. "Never."

"—Ella?" Anna pulls me from the dormant memory, awakened in the absence of my medication. I'd forgotten. *All of it.* The strength in Silas's arms as he'd carried me into the hospital. The tension in his clenched jaw. His pained stare.

Why did he push me away? I scrunch my eyes shut. I'd always believed the amnesia-like side effects of my medication were a curse. Now they seem like a cruel blessing.

I clear my throat. "I'm fine," I say to Anna, feigning a smile.

We turn right and line up at the front desk in silence. The hairs on the back of my neck rise, and my head whips from the hospital entrance to the mezzanine overhead. My arms wrap around my chest. *No one is following you.*

"Next," the receptionist at the front desk calls, and adrenaline pulses through my veins. Her spectacled gaze is fixed to her computer, fingernails tapping on the keys.

Anna and I step toward the glass partition, and I hunch to speak into the circular patterned holes. "I'd like to request a copy of my mother's death certificate." My voice seems to reflect off the glass, the sound dampened. "She died here, ten years ago."

"Okay," the woman says, eyes trained on her computer. I mutter my mother's name and date of birth, and the woman types something on the keyboard. The printer behind her hums to life.

"That was easy," Anna whispers in my ear.

The woman's arm flings over her head to the printer behind her, and she snatches the freshly printed paper from the tray. "There you go," she says, sliding the paper through a rectangular opening in the bottom of the glass.

I pick up the paper. "Request for access of medical information," I read aloud.

"Complete this form and submit to the records department with photo ID. The requested information will be sent to you in six to eight weeks." The woman's attention slides to the elderly couple waiting behind us. "Next."

Six to eight weeks? "But—"

"Records is on level four," the receptionist says, gesturing to the people behind us.

My shoulders slump and I turn, but Anna clutches my forearm and leans toward the glass.

"Surely there's something we can do to fast-track the process?" she asks in a sickly sweet voice. "A donation to the hospital or—"

"Six. To. Eight. Weeks," repeats the lady, with a forced smile. "Next."

✧

"Thanks again," I say to Anna in the car park outside Bromley House.

"That's okay," she says with a sad smile. "I'm sorry you didn't get any answers."

We exit her black Jeep and dawdle toward her building. The frigid air stirs behind me and my pulse jumps. My gaze scurries across the leaf-strewn lawn, settling on the broad trunk of an elm tree.

No one is following you. I shake my head. Without my meds, my paranoia was bound to return. *Was it this bad before?* The fire probably obliterated the remaining supply of pills on my nightstand. If I want more, I'll need to make an appointment with Dr Williams. Soon.

I find the charm on my necklace and run my thumb over its worn inscription. *Let the current carry you.* I didn't understand the phrase when I was eight years old, and I don't understand it now. *What happened to you, Mom?*

I follow Anna up the stairs to her floor. She reaches the first landing and her head whips to me, her eyes wide and mouth pulled into an ecstatic grin. "New neighbors," she whisper-shrieks. Flicking her sandy blonde hair over her shoulder, she struts forward and calls down the corridor, "You have to push the door in while you jimmy the lock."

"Thanks," says a husky, female voice.

"I'm Anna. I live opposite."

I trip on the top step. Anna's standing beside Parker and the frightening woman from Professor McGregor's lecture.

Parker's leaning against the wall opposite Anna's apartment, hands tucked into the pockets of his emerald chinos, with a bored look on his face. He's cut his hair since I last saw him, yet the same sense of familiarity washes over me, as if I've known him in another lifetime.

I step onto the landing and his eyes lift to me, his back straightening.

"Oh, and this is Ella, my roomie," Anna says as I approach, pointing a dainty finger toward me.

The woman's face falls, her onyx eyes narrowing, while Parker scours me from head to toe.

I edge back until I'm leaning against Anna's apartment door.

"Aren't you going to tell us your names?" Anna asks with an easy smile.

"Rose." She jerks her head to the right. "And Parker." She turns back toward the door and rams her key into the lock. Anna shoots me a quizzical look. Meanwhile, Parker's still drinking me in as if I'm a warped figment of his imagination.

Say something. Anything. Talk, Mariella!

My head snaps up to catch the ghost of a smirk on Parker's lips, and I'm back at the riverside after McGregor's lecture, that taunting grin heating me from the inside out. "Parker and I have met before," I blurt. "After Professor McGregor's guest lecture."

"How nice," Rose says through her teeth, still trying to unlock the door. Parker shifts on his feet and slips his hands back into his pockets.

In my periphery, Anna glances between Rose, Parker and me with an arched brow.

"What the fuck is wrong with this door?" Rose grumbles, ramming her shoulder into the wood.

"Let me help you," Anna says, moving forward. The bright colors in her outfit pop beside Rose's faded jeans and black hoodie.

Parker prowls across the hallway and leans his shoulder on the wall beside me. "It's good to see you again," he says in a low, warm voice so only I can hear.

"Why are you staying here, if you're not students?" I ask.

A soft grin creeps across his face, his eyes glued to mine. "Still inquisitive I see."

"Still evasive I see," I reply.

Parker's brow kicks up. "You still stalking, too?"

Heat floods my cheeks and I look to Anna, but she's still assisting Rose with the door. My gaze swings back to Parker. "*You* were staring at *me* in the lecture, not the other way around—and you're the one moving into my building. So, I'd say the untoward behavior lies with you."

"Untoward?" He says the word like it's our own private joke. His grin morphs into something predatory and he edges closer. How have I not noticed the small freckle near his top lip until now? My gaze drifts lower. There's something undeniably sexy about his mouth, something tempting that draws my mind to shadowy, inappropriate places.

"Is *this* untoward, Ella?" he says in a deep, warm voice, inching closer.

A shudder races through me and I swallow the lump in my throat. He's so close, I'd just need to lean in a little and I'd be touching him. He's staring at my mouth, as if he can sense the reply caught in my throat.

Across the corridor, Rose rams her shoulder into the door

and the wood budges with a tired groan. "Thank fuck," she cries and storms inside.

"Well, it was great meeting you," Anna calls to Rose's retreating back.

"*Parker*!" Rose calls from inside the apartment, and his head whips in her direction, releasing me from his trance.

His focus shifts to Anna. "Nice to meet you, Anna." His gaze returns to me. Lingers. "Ella," he says, as if the word holds impossibly more than just my name. Then he turns and slips inside.

I follow Anna back into her peony-scented apartment, breathing a little too heavily.

She sits on her cream sofa, crosses her legs, and explodes. "You met Mr Hottie and you didn't *tell* me?"

"We met briefly." I sit beside her, tugging a tasseled cushion against my chest.

"Do you think they're fucking?" Anna asks.

My head snaps toward her. "I don't know. Do you?"

"Well, that's a one-bedroom apartment," she says, tilting her head toward the front door.

I shouldn't care. *I don't care.*

Anna taps her acrylic nails on her bottom lip. "I don't know, though. I was struggling to get a read on them." Her phone chimes, and she pulls it from her handbag. She sulks at the screen. "*Ugh*, I have dinner with my family tonight. You should come. I'd love someone to take the attention off me."

I avert my eyes and pull my knitted sleeves over my knuckles. "Sorry, I have plans with Sarah."

Anna exhales. "All good." She smooths her palms down her hair and tugs at the ends.

"What's wrong?" I ask, following her vacant stare toward the TV.

Her green eyes snap to mine. "Nothing," she says with a weak shrug. "I'm just not looking forward to it. I know Dad's going to grill me about my grades. He has this dumb rule that I can't join the family business unless I complete a degree. This is the second time I've done this course." She bites her lip. "I can't fail again, Ella."

I stare at the beautiful woman before me, who's never shown me anything but kindness. Who invited me to live with her when I had nowhere else to go. Who literally gave me the clothes on my back. "Get out your lecture slides," I say. "You're not going to fail."

I'll make sure of it.

9

Rose

Head throbbing, I lie motionless in bed, a large crack in the ceiling looming over me. One agonizing week has passed since McGregor took our blood. How much longer will the old man take? I grab my vape from the bedside table, inhale slowly, and blow vapor in Parker's direction.

He's comatose on the single bed opposite mine, the repetitive clenching and unclenching of his hands the only tell he isn't asleep. His fist tightens, the thick tendons in his forearm contracting underneath his tan skin.

I look away, a bitter aftertaste from my vape bleeding through the sweet, artificial flavor. He's acting weird lately. In his own head. I should check in with him, but I'm still livid he hid his impromptu meeting with Ella. He promised it was before he swore to stay away from her, but . . . Parker's keeping something from me. I'd beat it out of him if I wasn't so paranoid about blowing up and slipping into another memory.

A knock at the door has us both on our feet: McGregor, wearing his usual khaki slacks, glasses and a frown. Time won't be kind to his receding hairline. Chewing the inside of my cheek, I let him in. My gaze lowers to the briefcase in his hand. *This is it. He'll have the cure. We can get the hell out of here, and I'll finally get a break.*

"What did you find?" Parker asks before he's closed the door.

McGregor adjusts his glasses and sits at the dining table. "It's impossible you two are alive."

"What?" My stomach seizes.

"I wasn't able to study any of the samples, because the blood appears to be years old." He launches into a boring explanation of the multitude of tests he couldn't carry out using words like flow cytometry, electron microscopes and protein expression. Although the concepts are foreign, the problem is clear: the moment our blood cells leave our bodies, they die.

"So that's it?" Parker asks, placing his hands behind his head. "Isn't there anything more you can do?"

"Not without a live sample. Analyzing deceased cells would yield inaccurate results. But I'd like to continue working with you." He retrieves a fountain pen and a small black journal from his briefcase and opens it to a fresh page. "I still have many questions. What was the exact date we first met?"

His pen hovers over the blank paper for a beat before his sharp gaze darts between Parker and me. We stand in silence and McGregor raises his brows. "The date?" he repeats.

Parker opens his mouth.

"Parker," I growl, silencing him. I want to scream. Break something. Six months of hiding with relentless headaches. Six months torturing my mind and body for *nothing*. McGregor can't help us; he wants to *use* us for information. Cash in on our bargain without holding up his end.

"This meeting is over," I say, striding toward the front door.

"Wait," McGregor says. He gets to his feet. "Rose, if I could please—"

"Get out." I rip open the front door.

McGregor exhales through his nose and places his journal back in his briefcase. "If you change your mind, you know where to find me," he says, and he steps out into the corridor.

I slam the door shut and storm toward the bedroom.

"Rose," Parker calls to my back.

"What?" I reply, rubbing my eyes.

"McGregor can't use *our* blood, but it doesn't mean he can't use someone else's," he says, speaking quickly. "We need a blood sample from someone else. *Someone here.*"

"No," I say immediately, turning to face him. "No way."

Parker splays his hands out by his sides. "We have no other option."

"It's too dangerous," I say. "We agreed not to mess around in each other's past. Plus, it breaks our oath."

"We'll be careful. Approach her when she's alone, ask for her blood and leave. No harm done," he says with a shrug, as if his words aren't dripping with desperation. "She'd want to help us. If we just talk to her—"

"I said no, Parker." I clutch my head, willing my breathing to slow.

Parker strides toward me, and I edge backward. "Then we leave," he says in a raised voice. "Go home and wait for Matthews to find us. Is that what you want?"

His chest is almost touching mine, cramming me against the wall beside our bedroom door. My pulse jumps and I thrust my hands into his chest, shoving him away. "There is no *us*," I yell.

"Fine," Parker yells back, throwing his hands in the air. "Send me back, then. If you hate being around me so much."

He disappears into the bedroom and I grimace, his words stealing the tension from my body. I rub my hand over the thickness in my throat and step into the room after him. He's sitting on his bed, leaning back against the wall, shoulders slumped and eyebrows tight.

"Stop being so dramatic," I say.

He lifts his head. "I'm serious," he says, the fire in his voice replaced with icy defeat. "Send me back. Without her blood, I'm as good as dead anyway. Unless you want to carry me around for the rest of our lives."

I bite the inside of my cheek. We both know I can't do that. And it's only a matter of time before my brain takes another impromptu vacation in my past. *Fuck*.

"Fine," I say. "We'll ask her for her blood. But we do it my way, with minimal impact. We'll be a tiny blip in her timeline."

"Miniscule," Parker says with a shit-eating grin.

10

Mariella

"You look cute," gushes Anna two weeks later, surveying my high-waisted jeans and beige coat. "Is that mine?"

"Everything I wear is yours," I say, passing her laptop over the bar at Tilly's.

"Thanks, I want to study during my dinner break." She tucks the computer away and mindlessly wipes the bar with a cloth. "Hey, are you okay? You were calling out in your sleep again last night."

I fiddle with the large buttons on my coat. "Yeah. Sorry." I force a laugh. "I've always been a vivid dreamer."

I rub my eyes. Every night since stopping my medication, I've dreamed of my mother on my eighth birthday, and of me kissing Parker. I rouse multiple times a night. Heart racing. Body humming. Volatile electricity emanating shockwaves toward my periphery. Each morning I promise myself I'll make another appointment with my psychiatrist, Dr Williams, to get more medication. But as the sun sets, I long for those minutes wrapped in my mother's arms while she's alive and lucid and healthy. She'll tell me how much she loves me, and I'm not ready to let go. *I can't.*

I need to understand what happened to her, and I know

in my gut I won't uncover answers while I'm sedated by my medication.

Anna places a cocktail on the bar between us and I peer toward the bouncer at the door. He only let me inside because Anna slept with him last semester.

"Are we allowed to drink in here?" I ask.

"Course not," she says, lifting it to her lips and taking a healthy swig.

She forces it into my hand and I take a sip. Sweetness and citrus and *alcohol* saturate my taste buds.

"Any word from the hospital yet?" Anna asks, stealing another sip.

"Not yet." I'd filled out the forms and returned them the day we visited the hospital. "They said it might take a while, though." I slump down onto the bar. "I did hear back from the engineer. Can you believe I paid him six hundred dollars to tell me the bedrooms in my house are not structurally sound and I should not, under any circumstances, enter it?"

"I'm so sorry," Anna says and I feign a smile.

"Thanks." With property taxes and utility bills I could barely afford my house *before* the fire. There's no way I can pay to fix it. *What am I going to do?*

"Ella," Anna whispers, tipping her head toward the door, where Parker and Rose have entered. I sit up and take another sip of my cocktail.

"I still can't get a grasp on their relationship," Anna says, watching them find a table. "Maybe they're hate fucking?"

I choke on my drink. My eyes track Parker as he takes a seat at an empty table in the corner while Rose orders drinks from Christiaan.

"She looks sick," Anna says, once Rose rejoins Parker.

The rings under Rose's eyes grow darker by the day, and her black jeans are hanging off her. She sits beside Parker, their heads lowered in a seemingly intense conversation, despite the loud, squealing cheerleaders wedged around the table next to them.

"She looks worse every time I see her," I say in a low voice.

Anna's eyes flicker toward them. "I think they're arguing," she says.

I subtly glance toward their corner of the bar. Rose throws back her drink and storms toward the bathrooms, leaving Parker frowning at the amber liquid inside his tumbler.

"I'm going to go," I say, sliding off my stool.

"Okay. Thanks again for bringing my laptop. See you at home later?"

I nod and beeline for the exit, but as I pass the women's bathroom, a strangled cry has the hairs on my arms rising. I immediately turn and follow the noise inside.

Rose is muttering to herself, leaning over the sink as she splashes water onto her face. Her black hoodie lies discarded on the bathroom floor, and her elbows jut out beside her body, nothing more than skin and bones.

"Hey, are you okay?" I ask.

Her head snaps up, wild eyes searching beyond her own reflection. "Is that really you?" she whispers.

"What?"

Rose whips around, the tense lines around her face easing. "I'm so glad you're here. I can't keep doing this without you."

"Rose, it's Ella. I live in the apartment opposite yours." I edge toward her.

She's staring directly at me, but her gaze is unfocused, her face bathed in a sickly green hue from the restroom lighting. Tears well in her large eyes. "Fuck, I've missed you," she says, flinging her arms around me, and I'm inundated with notes of sweet green apple, jasmine and musk.

I stiffen and gingerly pat her back.

"Rose? Is everything okay?" Parker's voice rings out from the other side of the door, startling Rose. She pulls away from me, shaking her head. "Rose, please come out," Parker calls again.

She wraps her hand around the door handle, her onyx eyes glistening. "I'll kill him for what he did to you," she whispers over her shoulder, then she flings open the door.

I grab her hoodie and chase her into the bar where Parker is waiting.

Rose crashes into his chest, muttering under her breath. He wraps his arms around her, and I notice a few small, rounded Band-Aids spotting his forearms. He turns to me and my heart stutters, but his gaze is focused on the patrons behind me. "What did she say to you?"

"She—Nothing. She was confused." Why is he more concerned with a restroom conversation than the state of his—friend? Girlfriend? "It's okay," I mouth to Anna, who's watching us from behind the bar.

Parker picks Rose up, the muscles in his arms shifting to easily accommodate her weight. In his arms, her tall frame folds into something tiny and fragile, like a bird fallen from a nest. "I'll take you home, Rose," he says, stepping past me.

I chase him to the door. "She needs help, Parker."

"If you want to help her, then help me get her back to our apartment." He shifts on his feet beside the door, his rigid arms encasing Rose. "Can you get the door?"

I hesitate. "She needs to see—"

"Trust me, she'll be fine after she rests," he says, and I tense.

He's talking as if I'm overreacting. As if Rose's turn isn't concerning. As if—

"Has this happened to her before?" I ask.

He slowly turns toward me, almost unwillingly. His golden gaze settles on mine and the air vanishes from my lungs. "Ella, please help me?"

I want to refuse, but my skin's crawling at the number of people staring at us. "Fine." I open the door for him. "I'll help you, but tomorrow you need to take her to a doctor."

We step out into the brisk, clear night, the drunken chanting and conversations fading with each step from the door. I wrap my coat around my chest, and jog to keep up with Parker's long strides.

Rose is mostly silent in his arms, but with each sharp inhale or incoherent mumble, his head drops to her face.

How did I get myself into this situation? I should excuse myself and go back to the bar, but Parker asked me for help and there's no way he'll be able to get the apartment door open while holding Rose. Plus he'll need someone to enter the code to get inside the building.

I sneak a glance at him. His mouth is tense, eyes focused on something in the distance.

"How long have you known Rose?" I ask, breaking the silence.

"About three years," he says in a rough voice.

We cross the road and walk between two buildings. Campus is littered with Halloween decorations. Carved pumpkins with evil faces track our steps as we pass. "She's lucky to have you. To take care of her like this."

"Yeah, well, it's easy when she's this docile. Normally she's a colossal pain in my ass," he says, his tone lifting despite his harsh words.

"Does this happen to her often?"

"Sometimes." His brows draw in and he scans Rose's face. "Trust me, she'll be back to her old, *charming* self soon enough." His eyes flicker to me, as if he can't quite look away.

"What?" I ask.

"I'm sorry for ruining your night."

"You didn't. I was about to leave anyway."

"Didn't want to stay and party with the cheerleaders?" The corners of his mouth twitch.

I cringe. "The whole party cheerleader thing isn't really my scene. You?"

"No, the skirts never fit right."

My laugh breaks the quiet night air and I brush my fingertips over my lips. "You know, I still don't know anything about you."

I catch his smirk—a cat playing with its meal. "What do you want to know?"

"I don't know. Where are you from?"

"Such a generic question," he says. "I'm disappointed. Come on, Ella, ask me something unique."

"Fine." I purse my lips, studying the shadowed columns stretching across the sidewalk, broken by rings of amber streetlight. "What makes you happy?"

He stares at me for a moment, and the smile on his face dissipates. His gaze drifts somewhere over the buildings in the distance. "The ocean. Anything in water, really," he says eventually. "Swimming, sailing, surfing. There's something about it that makes me feel . . . free."

"That's how I feel when I'm reading. I love the escape. Being able to jump out of my head and into someone else's. Or drawing by the river. It's peaceful. It's like, I can shut everything else out and just focus on one minute detail at a time."

He nods in agreement. "What do you like to draw?"

Silas's dark brows flash through my mind, the tortured intensity in his blue irises. "People. Their features. If I don't understand something about a person, I'll try and capture it." I laugh. "But if I can't perfect it, I get really frustrated."

"Is that your favorite place? The river?"

I nod. "Beneath the flame trees. You?"

"There's this place I—"

Rose mumbles something and Parker winces, our brief reprieve broken. We continue the rest of the walk in silence, only stopping beneath the spiderweb-draped archway of Bromley House while I select the entry code.

"There's a key in her back pocket," Parker says once we're standing in the corridor between our apartments. He shifts Rose's weight. "Can you grab it?"

I pull the key from her black jeans and spend five minutes trying to unlock the door. Finally, it opens and I step aside for Parker to enter. Their apartment's smaller than Anna's, and it lacks warmth—empty of personal objects, no books filling the barren shelves or photos on the walls. There's an empty space where a lounge should sit, and aside from some papers stacked on the dining table, the place appears unoccupied.

I follow Parker to the sole bedroom and hover in the doorway. Two single beds are positioned on opposite sides of the room, separated by a small desk bearing a clunky laptop. Parker eases Rose onto one of the beds as if she's made of glass and brushes the dark brown hair from her face.

"Okay, thanks. I've got it from here," he says, ushering me back into the living room. He hovers in the bedroom doorway and glances back to Rose.

My cheeks flush. I'm being dismissed, but now's my chance to confront him, or at least try to understand my abnormal dreams and unhealthy infatuation while Rose is indisposed. I doubt I'll get another opportunity.

I sit at the dining table and turn to catch Parker exhaling. "What kind of work are you doing with Professor McGregor?" I ask. He crosses his arms over his chest, and my eyes snag on the bulge of his biceps. "Is it for your PhD or something?"

"No. I'm not studying." Parker moves toward the front door, but I'm not leaving without answers.

"Why were you in McGregor's lecture the day we met?"

Parker smiles, but his gaze darts back to the open bedroom door. "I told you. Professor McGregor is helping us with something."

"What?" I'm fiddling with a loose piece of paper on the desk when it dawns on me—Rose must be a psychology patient of McGregor's. My stomach clenches. It'd explain why the topic makes him so uncomfortable. And here I am pressing him like an insensitive idiot.

I push my chair away from the table, disturbing the papers littering its surface. My own neat handwriting pokes out from the bottom of the pile, and I freeze. Lowering my head toward the table, I push the papers aside and frown at a photocopy of—

"My schedule?"

"I can explain that." Parker steps toward me, his eyes wide.

Why would Rose and Parker have a photocopy of my class schedule?

He runs a hand through his short, dark blond hair, and an unnerving feeling of déjà vu courses through my body. I abruptly stand. "I've met you before, haven't I? I mean, before McGregor's lecture."

"No, you haven't," he says, but his smile is strained.

"Why are you lying to me?" I ask.

He turns to look me square in the eye. "I would never lie to you, Ella."

My heart kicks into a gallop. "Then tell me why you have my class schedule," I say, searching his eyes. "What aren't you telling me?" My stomach twists and something clicks—Parker and Rose appearing everywhere I go. My paranoia. The feeling of being watched. "Have you been following me?"

Parker links his hands behind his head and tilts his face to the ceiling. "Can you please wait until Rose wakes up? Then I promise she'll explain everything."

"Explain it to me now."

Parker doesn't move any closer. "It's difficult."

I take a step toward him, my trembling hands tucked into my armpits, arms crossed over my chest like armor. "It shouldn't be. Why can't you ever give me a straight answer?" He looks back to the bedroom where Rose is resting, as if willing her to wake. "Parker. Answer me." My voice is louder now, my pulse pounding in my ears.

"Because I don't want to mess this up."

"What are you talking about?" *At what point did I start yelling?*

He turns back toward me. "This," he says, and he gestures between us. He opens his mouth as if to elaborate further, then snaps it shut.

"Parker, talk to me," I beg.

"I can't." His eyebrows furrow, and he turns away from me. "Fuck!" he shouts. "I can't do this again."

"Again?" I march toward him, not stopping until my face is inches from his. "I knew it. We've met before. That's why you're in my dreams."

He sucks in a sharp breath, his body still. "You need to leave. Now."

"Parker, please." I edge closer still and reach for his forearm, but he jerks away, as if my touch is toxic.

A thick vein pulses over the strained muscles in his neck. "Ella, you're acting crazy," he says, and I flinch.

Crazy. Mad Mari. Hearing those words from his mouth cuts much deeper than I care to admit, ripping open the tender scars I'm forever trying to mend.

"Go!" he yells.

Tears welling in my eyes, I fling open the door and run from the room.

11

Rose

I awake in darkness with a cool hand pressed to my pounding forehead. A stifled groan leaves my throat and Parker mutters something, pulling his hand away.

I roll onto my side, and my stomach churns. Why do I have no memory of returning home from the bar? I bite the inside of my cheek, tasting copper.

"Parker?" I whisper. I push myself up and flick the light switch beside my bed. Light fills the room and I flinch, drawing my hand up to shield my face. Parker's sitting on the floor, back resting against the desk, and his head in his hands. "Parker?" I repeat.

He raises his head, and hollow, bloodshot eyes stare back at me.

My throat constricts. "What is it?"

"There's no way she's going to help us now," he mutters.

"What do you mean? What happened?" I groan. "What did you do?" I demand, and I'm hit with a flashback of Ella edging away from me, her eyes wide and shoulders tight. I suck in a sharp breath. "How much damage have I done?"

"Do you mean when you went mentally AWOL in the bathroom?" He lets out a sober laugh. "I think me calling her crazy and yelling at her to get out did more damage."

I rub the bridge of my nose. "Wait, what? Why did you yell at her?"

"She was helping me get you home and saw her class schedule on the table. She started asking questions. I panicked. I didn't know what to say."

I clutch my head, still aching like I've been sucker punched. "Couldn't you have made something up?"

He gets up, lies on his bed and stares at the ceiling.

My pulse booms in my ears. "Parker?"

"I won't lie to her," he says.

I grit my teeth. We've spent the past two weeks arguing about the best way to approach Ella but have yet to agree on anything. My patience is wavering. "What's your plan, then?"

"We tell her the truth," he says, as if it's obvious.

"We've been over this. Why do you want to tell her things that will scare her? Besides, it's not lying if we choose to leave certain things out."

"Yes, it is," he says, hands clenched by his side.

"No. It isn't. Can't you see I'm protecting her?" I hack at my nails. It's obvious he's blinded by his feelings for Ella. "There's no other way." I whip my head toward him. "I can't stop blacking out and slipping into my memories, which means it's only a matter of time before I lose my hold on you." I square my shoulders and look him dead in the eye. "Either you want to live and we do it my way, or we split and you're on your own. Which is it?"

Parker glares at me. "I won't lie to—"

"Yeah, I heard you the first time," I snap. "You won't lie to her."

But I will.

12

Mariella

I'm saturated in white light, sparkling rays reflecting off my skin like shooting stars. I edge toward muffled voices, but with each step the surrounding light fades. The high-pitched notes of a music box echo around me and an icy shiver races down my spine. The last rays of light wane, plunging me into darkness, but the song reverberates, each off-key tone twisting my stomach into tight knots.

A deep rumble begins in the distance, cascading toward me until the ground below my feet is quaking. The noise doubles in intensity, threatening to burst my eardrums. I turn to run, the sound waves pulsing across my skin and vibrating through my chest.

I stumble forward on trembling legs, swallowed by a roaring, unrelenting abyss. Pain erupts in my abdomen, and I scream, hunching over. Wet warmth coats my hands, and my heart falters, fluttering like a bird trapped inside a shrinking cage. I gasp for breath, but the deafening noise is compressing the air within my lungs. Clutching at my bleeding torso, I fall to the floor, legs burning as the skin scrapes off my knees.

Lost in the darkness, suffocating, I wait for death to take me. Time slows. The pain fades, and I slip away. I'm floating in deafening silence.

I love you, Mariella.

A sharp whisper cuts through the calm—the speaker's deep, smooth voice a gentle symphony as I take my last, shallow breath.

✧

I wake gasping for breath, electricity flooding my body and those words echoing in my ears.

I love you, Mariella.

I'm clutching my necklace in my trembling hand, my heart racing beneath my clenched fist. I'm half asleep, still trapped in my nightmare, the unrelenting roar crushing my chest. Another shiver races down my spine and my eyes snap open.

Morning light pours through Silas's living room window and recollections of last night rush through my head: fleeing Parker's apartment. Flagging a passing taxi. Mumbling Silas's address to the driver before my brain caught up with my mouth. I'd texted Anna, houses and streetlights flying past in a blur, spaced further apart as we drove closer to the edge of the Middlesex Fells Reservation. I banged on the door for several moments before retrieving the spare key hidden above the porch light. Letting myself in, I called out for Silas, but the air in his cottage was still, the fireplace in the living room unlit. With heavy eyelids, I collapsed onto his couch and passed out moments later.

I sit up, rubbing my neck as Parker's departing words ring in my head.

"You're acting crazy."

I draw in a tense breath and scan Silas's living room, silent except for the steady ticking of the clock beside his record player. His once subtle scent is now powerful in the absence of my meds, minty yet masculine, mingled with remnant smoke from the fireplace, and lingering traces of soap from his bodywash. I rub my hands over my face. Coming here was a mistake. *Thank God he's away for work.*

I reach for my phone and sigh at the dead screen. Surely Silas has a phone charger somewhere? I roll off the sofa and edge toward his bedroom, drawing in a breath before I enter his room. His clean, minty scent lingers, yet his room's unchanged from the last time I was here—spotless aside from a stray shoe on the floor and a small box sitting beside his nightstand. I walk over and peer inside. It holds a sweater and a half-empty bottle of my sleep medication that I must have left here. I open the top drawer of his nightstand and my mouth drops.

It's overflowing with half-dispensed pill packets—codeine, oxycodone, diazepam, tapentadol. The list goes on. The packets scrape against one another as I rifle to the bottom of the drawer, discovering a collection of old soccer cards and a brass key. Silas told me he took pills for headaches, but this is something else entirely. This is an addict's candy store.

I rub my brow. I shouldn't be surprised. Silas kept his life wrapped in secrets, and peeling one back will only reveal more. We were inseparable for five months, and I learned nothing of his friends and family, only that he's married to his job. I laugh dryly. Does he have a work wife locked in that study of his?

My head shoots up, looking to the office door handle gleaming through the open bedroom door.

"Never go in there, Mariella."

Before I can breathe, my fingers are curled around the cool metal. I twist the knob, releasing a breath when it doesn't budge, locked. I press my ear to the door and a faint ticking filters through. Perhaps the key in his bedside drawer—

Someone pounds on the front door, and my heart jumps into my throat.

I creep along the hallway and peer through the peephole. My heart drops. Rose stands outside, clad in black, white vapor curling from her mouth. She brings her knuckles to the door and pounds again. Gone is any sign of the vulnerable woman from last night.

"Ella, are you there?" she says, her voice taut.

I pause, clutching my charm. I'm not ready to talk to her, but if I don't, I'll never understand why I feel this familiarity toward Parker, or why they've been following me.

"How did you know I was here?" I call through the door.

"Your roommate."

Damn it, Anna.

"Open the door and I'll explain everything. Starting with this." Something drops through the mail slot, falling at my feet with a soft *tink*. Picking up the necklace, I brush my thumb over the writing inscribed into the worn gold. My fingers fumble to the heart-shaped charm resting between my collarbones. How does Rose have an exact copy of my mother's necklace? *And why?*

"It's not a replica," she calls.

This doesn't make any sense. I press my eye back to the peephole. Parker stands a few paces behind Rose, leaning against the porch railing with his hands tucked into his pockets. His words from last night flicker through my mind. *"I can't do this again."*

Do what again?

Rose's gaunt face moves in front of the peephole. "Let us in and I'll explain everything."

I shouldn't let them in, but I want answers. *I need them.* With a deep breath, I open the door, the necklace still clutched in my hand. Rose steps forward, but Parker remains still, watching me.

"You have five minutes," I say.

"Thanks." Rose barges past me to enter Silas's cottage, her boots thumping on the wooden floor. She snatches the necklace from my hand on her way past and secures it around her own neck, pulling her dark, thick plait free from the chain.

"Are you coming in too?" I ask Parker. He's still relaxed against the balustrade, despite the tense muscles in his forearms. He offers me a small smile, but something about it feels wrong.

"Jimmy, get the fuck in here," Rose calls from the hallway.

Jimmy?

Parker pushes off the railing and steps inside, avoiding my gaze. We all linger in the tight corridor.

"Can we sit?" Rose asks, her full eyebrows raised.

I cross my arms over my chest. "Why do you have that necklace?" I'm doing my best to keep my voice stern.

"Can we please sit?" repeats Rose.

I lead them to the kitchen table and pull up a heavy wooden chair. Rose grabs the chair directly opposite while Parker stands at the end of the table, hands still tucked away in his pockets. His gaze flickers to me as I sit, but he immediately looks away.

Rose's sharp eyes survey the room, pausing on the soccer magazine lying open on Silas's coffee table. "Will he be home soon?" she asks.

Wouldn't I like to know. "I'm not sure," I say, and Parker smirks. *What exactly did Anna tell them?*

"In that case, I'll make this quick. I'm sure you have questions and, to save time, I'll give it to you straight." She lifts the duplicate of my mother's necklace from underneath her black hoodie. "This necklace isn't a copy of yours. It's the same one. You'll give it to me in the future, because you know I'll need it to prove you can trust us. I know how important it is to you."

I glance between Rose's hard stare and Parker's averted one. He shifts on his feet. I'm waiting for them to laugh. *Do they think I'm an idiot?*

I force a smile. "Right. The future. Got it."

Rose's face is deadly serious. "In your future, you're recruited to a place where we'll meet."

"And what is this place?"

Rose hesitates. "I'd rather not go into specifics."

It's hard to go into specifics when you're messing with someone. These two are unbelievable. I never should've let them in the front door. I go to stand, but Rose grabs my arm.

"Wait." She exhales. "Fine, it's called Neurovida, and it's a place where you'll train to develop—special skills."

I narrow my eyes. "I don't have any special skills."

Rose and Parker exchange a quick glance. It's as if they have a way of knowing what the other's thinking without needing to speak.

"Not yet, but you will," Rose says.

I laugh. "Is this the part where you tell me I'm one of the X-Men?"

Rose's mouth twitches. "The skills you'll learn to develop at Neurovida solely involve the act of time travel."

"Get out," I say. I've been tricked before, too many times to count. The girls at boarding school practically trained me for moments like this.

Rose lets out a deliberate breath. "Ella, if the roles were reversed, I wouldn't believe me either. But I'm telling you the truth."

"Then prove it," I say, raising my chin. "Show me. Time travel."

"It's not a fucking parlor trick," Rose says, shaking her head. "Even if I wanted to, my precision sucks. I can't risk losing our footing on this specific moment in time. We might end up in last month or—"

"Last year," Parker adds. It's the first time he's spoken since they arrived.

"If you're not going to help me then shut up, Parker," Rose snaps in his direction and turns back to me. "I can't prove it to you—you'll just need to trust me."

Trust her? What reason have either of them given me to trust them? Rose, with her spiteful glances, and Parker . . . He's frowning, eyes downcast. I want to trust him. My heart tells me I can, but I'm smarter than that. I straighten in my chair. "I want you to leave."

Parker's head shoots up, his golden eyes alight. "Wait. There might be a way we can convince you." He's speaking to me, but his eyes are fixed on Rose. She shakes her head. "Her sub-t," he says.

What the hell is going on?

"Yes." Rose's eyes widen. "Parker, you're a genius."

"I know," he says, tucking his hands into his pockets. Rose scoffs.

"You two are impossible," I say.

Parker turns to me and my breath hitches in my throat. His gaze scours my face. "You're probably time traveling already, but you aren't aware of it." He rubs the back of his neck and stares down at the table. "You told me last night you've seen me in your dreams, right?"

Nerves shoot through me, and I curse my past self.

"Sometimes we time travel in our sleep," Rose says. "We call it subconscious traveling. An untrained traveler will mistake it for a dream, but you can tell the difference because when you time travel, you get this sensation, like—warmth in your body. Tingling." She turns toward Parker. "Are you just going to stand there? Help me out."

"Electricity," Parker murmurs, a distant look sweeping across his face. "She always described it like electricity."

"Thank you," Rose says, jabbing her hand toward Parker. "It's like electricity. Running through your body. Have you ever experienced anything like that after you've woken from a dream?"

The blood drains from my face, and I lean back in my chair. *This can't be real.*

"Tell me about a dream with us in it," Rose says. I glance at Parker and avert my stare, but Rose misses nothing. "Jesus Christ," she mutters, rolling her eyes. "*Or* specifically, Parker." Heat rushes to my cheeks. "That wasn't a dream, but a glimpse into your future. Why don't you tell us how it starts, and Parker can tell you what happens next?"

I turn to face Parker. His intense, honey-hued eyes are focused on me, his mouth drawn into a straight line.

A glimpse into my future. His fingers wrapped around my wrist, pulling me toward him. The taste of his lips. Our bodies pressed together.

The heat in my face intensifies. She wants me to recount my intimate dream with Parker. *Out loud.*

"Anything you can remember," Rose says.

This is ridiculous, but what if Rose is telling the truth? Wouldn't it explain the familiarity I feel toward Parker and the reason behind my fiery dream? I shut my eyes and force the words out. "I have a dream, and in it I'm holding a flask."

"A matte black flask?" Rose asks. My eyes snap open and I nod. "That's Parker's flask. Were there any other people around? Any buildings or landmarks?"

"No. We're outside. We might be in a garden or a park. I'm not sure. I can never see past the wall of white."

"That's okay. What else can you remember?" Rose asks.

I curl the fabric of my jumper around my fingers. "Well, I'm there with Parker." My stomach churns. He's now frowning at his large hands, the muscles in his neck tense. *Why is he nervous? It's not like it's* his *subconscious sex dream.* "I have the flask in my hand, and as I pass it to Parker, I say—"

"Did Nickol kick you out again?" Parker says.

My head snaps up, my hands falling to my sides. I search his face, his dilated pupils boring into mine.

This *can't* be real.

"Holy shit, Jimmy." Rose smacks the tabletop. "How do you even remember that?" She leans forward, resting her forearms on the table. "What happened next?"

Parker's eyes are glued to mine, stripping me bare. Is he, too, remembering the events that transpired? I've experienced this dream every night for the past two weeks.

"Do you know how long I've waited to be alone with you?"

His hand on my jaw, his tongue slipping into my mouth . . .

He looks away and shrugs, leaning back against the wall with his hands tucked into his pockets. "Nothing memorable."

I flinch at the sting of his words. Is Parker embarrassed about what happened between us? Maybe it was a one-time thing? *Of course it was.*

"So, you're saying every time I wake up with electricity in my body, I've been . . . time traveling?" I ask.

"Subconscious traveling. It's a form of time travel. You're there as an observer, and the people you're observing don't know you're there. Think of it like watching a movie of yourself while dreaming. Your body stays where it is, but your mind travels to another place and time. It's always within a personal experience, normally from your past."

"And when you aren't subconsciously traveling, can you go further back or forward than your own life?"

"No," Rose says. "I mean, I did once by accident, but no one's done it since."

"How many different types of time travel are there?" I ask.

"Two," says Rose.

My gaze slides between her and Parker. "Are you both asleep right now, in your own time?"

"No. Of course not. You can't communicate with people in your sleep." She gestures to her chest. "This is communicative travel, because you can see and hear us—" She cuts herself off and clicks her tongue. "It doesn't fucking matter. There are two different types of time travel, the intricacies of which you'll learn when you get recruited."

The void in my stomach deepens. *When I get recruited.*

I swallow the lump in my throat, but it's as stubborn as the information Rose is asking me to digest.

Time travel.

I don't want this. I refuse to believe it. I don't need another thing that makes me different. Something else impeding the ordinary life I'm fighting to build. The life my mother never had.

Oh my—

Coldness blooms in my gut. My mother was a time traveler. She must have been. It would explain the incorrect date in her journal.

My head shoots up. "Is this genetic?" I look from Parker to Rose. "Are your parents time travelers?" I demand.

"I don't know," Rose says, her lips twitching.

"How can you not know?" I lean forward, and the table digs into my torso.

Rose's lips pull back into a snarl. "Were your parents time travelers, Ella? How can *you* not know?"

"Rose," Parker warns.

She releases a breath and studies the wall behind me for a moment, picking at her nails. "I've never met my biological parents," she says through her teeth.

"I—I'm sorry. I didn't mean to pry."

"It's fine." Rose's head snaps to Parker. "Parker?"

"It's not genetic," he says. *They must be wrong.*

Rose turns back to me. "Not genetic. Happy? Now, is that enough to make you believe us?"

As much as I want to deny what they're saying, the evidence is there—the tingling in my limbs when I wake, Parker recalling my dream, Rose having my necklace, but . . .

"Why would I give you my necklace instead of coming back here myself?"

Rose watches Parker as he walks away from the table and

drops onto Silas's leather sofa. "Interacting with your past self can be messy, so you sent us instead. To find McGregor."

"Why are you working with Professor McGregor? Is he a time traveler?"

"No." Rose clears her throat. "Parker can't time travel anymore. McGregor might be able to help us because in the future, he works at Neurovida. He needs to study the blood of a time traveler. He tried using ours, but because we aren't from here, the samples are useless."

"If Parker can't time travel, then how is he here?" I ask.

"I'm holding him here. Another skill you'll learn at Neurovida. One I'm obviously shit at." She hesitates. "It's also the reason I was so messed up last night. It takes an enormous toll to time travel with another person, and it turns out staying in the wrong time makes it worse. I'm trying to keep it under control, but sometimes . . . well, you saw."

She rubs her fingers over the dark rings beneath her eyes, blood caking her nail beds. Is this the effect time travel has on a person? *Time travel isn't real!*

I glance between Parker and Rose. "So . . . you want a sample of my blood?"

"Yeah," Rose says. "Which is why we have your class schedule in our room. We've been trying to catch you alone, but you're always with Anna or working at the library. We gave up and knocked on your door this morning, and she told us you might be here."

Explains why they were showing up everywhere I went. "And after I give you my blood, you'll leave here?"

"Eventually, yes. You won't see us again until you're recruited, and our younger selves won't know we've met." She leans toward me, her onyx eyes narrowing. "It needs to stay that way, Ella. You can't tell anyone about this. And just tell Anna we needed help with something at the library. Got it?" Her mouth pulls to the side, and she gnaws on the inside of her cheek.

"Why can't I mention I've met you before?" I ask.

"Because Neurovida has rules. Time travelers aren't allowed to just gallivant around in the past," Rose says, wringing her hands. Her gaze briefly flickers to Parker.

"What aren't you telling me?" I turn to stare at the back of Parker's head. "Parker, how did you lose your ability to time travel?"

"I told you last night I would never lie to you, so please don't make me now," he says, face glued to Silas's blank TV screen. I shudder, the despondence in his tone squeezing my heart like a tight fist.

Rose's sharp eyes land on mine. "You tell anyone we were here, even our younger selves, and we become traceable. That puts all of us in danger. We've told you much more than we ever should have. Just trust us."

There's that word again. *Trust.*

"I . . ." My gaze pivots between Rose and Parker. It's not that simple. Trust is earned. It took me months to open up to Silas. Even Anna is unaware of the details of my past. "I can't."

"I told you this would be a fucking waste of time," Rose growls in Parker's direction. She slams her palms against the tabletop and abruptly stands.

"Wait." Parker gets off the couch and closes the distance between us, his amber eyes piercing my soul. "Ella, you can trust me." His warm voice is like a calming wave drenching my skin. *He's right.* I feel as though I've known him for years, and it makes no sense, but I trust him. "I hate to ask you to do anything for us, but we—*I* need a sample of your blood. And I promise we'll stay away from you after this. I don't want to meddle in your life."

But I *want* him to meddle in my life. My dreams may explain the familiarity I feel toward him, but they don't negate this burning need to know him.

I turn back to Rose, now hacking at her nails. If time travel's making her sick and I don't help them, she'll get worse. "How much blood do you need?"

"A few vials," she says.

It's not as if I'll miss it. And if my blood will help them—help Parker—I can't say no. But maybe they can give me something in return. "You said your precision was always poor with time traveling." I incline my head toward Parker, who's now standing behind Rose. "What about his?"

Rose tilts her head, her eyes narrowed as she takes me in. "Why do you want to know?"

"I'll give you my blood. But once Parker has his powers back, I want him to take me into the past. To see my mother."

"Absolutely not," Rose says.

I lean back in my chair. "Then you can't have my blood."

Rose grits her teeth. "You don't even know what you're asking. Wait until you're recruited and understand the implications of interacting with your past before you do it. By then, you'll have the skills to time travel and visit your mother yourself."

My throat constricts. "I'm not going to Neurovida."

"What?" Parker says, staring at me like I've wounded him.

I avert my gaze to my hands. "I'm not going. I don't want to be a time traveler, and I don't want any special skills. I just want to see my mother and move on with my life."

"You can't change it," Rose says, scolding me like I'm a child demanding a different toy. "It's already done."

"Do they force you to go?" I ask.

"No," Parker says. "We went by choice."

"Then I choose not to go. I'll only give you my blood if you promise to take me to see my mother."

Rose opens her mouth to argue but Parker cuts her off. "I'll do it," he says.

"Parker," Rose says.

"Do you promise?" I ask him.

He dips his head, and his golden eyes lock with mine. "Yes," he says, as if Rose isn't here. As if we're the only two people in the world.

I tear my gaze to Rose, who's gritting her teeth. "Then you can take my blood," I say.

Muttering under her breath, she pulls a small case from the front pocket of her hoodie.

"You—want to do it right now?"

"No time like the present," she says dryly, unloading the contents of the case onto the wooden dining table. Parker steps away, content to study Silas's record collection.

"*Okay.*" I pull up my sleeve and hesitate. "You've done this before, right?"

"Yeah." An evil grin breezes across her face. "I've been practicing on Parker."

I hesitate, recalling Parker's arms covered in plasters at Tilly's, before extending my exposed arm toward Rose. She secures a tourniquet around my biceps and my pulse spikes. She rips open a packet and rubs an antiseptic wipe over my skin. I scrunch my eyes shut.

The sting of the needle is brief, a dull pain remaining as Rose takes the vials of my blood. Before long, she removes the needle and I wince, pressing a cotton bud over my punctured skin.

Rose packs away her supplies and gets to her feet. "Where's the washroom?"

"By the front door," I say, pointing down the hallway.

Her head snaps to Parker, her thick plait swinging down her back. "Keep your mouth shut, Jimmy," she says, leaving Parker and me in silence.

It's surreal. Parker, standing here in Silas's cottage. *It feels wrong.* The man before me is nothing like the man in my dreams. Where's the man who was dying to get me alone?

"Did you mean it?" I say before I lose my nerve.

He's still perusing Silas's records with his back to me. He doesn't turn. "Mean what?"

"That nothing *memorable* happened?"

"No." I wait for him to elaborate, but he's silent, the muscles in his neck tense.

"Is it because of Rose?" I ask, rising from the table.

Parker runs a hand over his head. "I don't want to get into it right now."

He can't even turn to look at me. I suppress the urge to cry, scolding myself for getting caught up in a fantasy. Regardless of the inexplicable way I feel about him, he's a stranger.

He finally turns, and something like pain flashes across his face. He strolls toward me, slipping his hands into his pockets. "Sometimes the past is better kept in the past, you know?"

I nod, but I *don't* know. How can I? It may have been his past, but it's still my future. Or would've been, if I went to Neurovida.

The sternness in his face softens and, for a fleeting moment, I think he might reach out and touch me. "Ella, there are *so* many things I want to tell you, but I—"

"Parker, let's go." Rose's heavy footsteps echo along the hallway. She appears behind us with her hands tucked into the pouch of her hoodie, and her sharp, onyx gaze snaps to mine. "Remember, not a word to anyone about us, or that you've ever met us before." She hesitates. "And thank you," she spits out before striding away, boots thumping toward the front door.

Parker releases a deep breath, his dark blond brows creased together. His lips twitch as if he wants to tell me something but can't find the right words.

"Jimmy, come on," Rose yells.

"Take care, Ella," he says, and with one final glance, he follows Rose outside.

I wait for the front door to close and scamper after him, peeking through the narrow window beside the front door. Rose's quick strides have taken her halfway down the street, a trail of vapor billowing in her wake. Parker strolls after her, hands still tucked into his pockets as if he has all the time in the world.

Their retreating figures disappear beyond the street corner, and I slump against the wall beside Silas's door. The past hour feels like a surreal dream. I've just exchanged my blood for a chance to time travel into the past to visit my dead mother.

And yet my mind can't seem to stop swinging back to the same thought.

Everything in my dream was real, for Parker at least, and he'd acted as if it meant nothing.

13

Mariella

"There she is," Anna yells over the upbeat music blaring through her apartment. She struts toward me in a minidress and black thigh-high boots, swigging champagne straight from the bottle.

"Hey," I say, slipping off my shoes. "Are you going out?"

"No. I just got home from another *charming* family dinner." She tugs my satchel off my shoulder and pulls me toward her living area. "So *we* are going out, and we're getting lit." She tips the bottle toward me in a toast and takes another mouthful of champagne. "You must've made an impression on Parker and Rose, because they were here this morning looking for you. Did they find you?"

"I wanted to mention that," I say, collapsing onto her sofa. "Please do not give Silas's address to strangers."

Anna snorts, perching beside me. "*Pfft*, with that face? Parker's not a stranger, he's a God. Plus, I've seen the way you stare at him." *Am I that transparent?* "I think the words you're looking for are *thank you.*"

"Thank God Silas wasn't there," I mutter.

"Wasn't he?" Anna asks in a high-pitched voice, but her grin resembles the Cheshire Cat's. "Shame. Would've served him right for what he did. So," she says, placing the bottle of champagne on her coffee table and crossing her legs. "What did Parker and Rose want?"

I fiddle with a cushion tassel. "Nothing really. Help browsing the journal database at the library."

Anna's shoulders drop. "Riveting." She takes another sip of champagne and hands me the bottle, but I shake my head, craving the comfort of a warm shower, a romance novel, and her plush spare bed.

"Come on, Ella," Anna whines. "Let's go out. There's a new nightclub in town that opened last week."

A new song begins, the bass on Anna's speaker vibrating with each incessant beat. "Sorry, I have plans with—"

"Invite Sarah." Anna tips the neck of the champagne bottle toward my face. "I'd love to meet her."

"I don't think—"

"Ella," Anna says, an uncharacteristic finality in her voice. "We're going out." She forces the bottle into my hand and surveys her sparkling purple nails. "And I hate to pull this card, but you owe me one."

I owe her more than *one*. I'm living in her apartment, rent free, with her clothes on my back. How many times have I turned down her requests to go out since I moved in? To join her for family dinner? I've lost count. I stare into Anna's wide green eyes, the champagne bottle chilling my hand.

"One drink," I say, and Anna squeals. Bringing the bottle to my lips, I sip before I change my mind. Before I accept that I've failed to be good enough for Silas, or for Parker to acknowledge kissing. Or the fact that I am a time traveler, and no matter what I study or how I change my clothes, I'll always be different.

"Wow, slow down," Anna says, plucking the bottle out of my hand. "I need to do your hair and makeup. And then we need to try on outfits."

✧

Over the next hour, Anna smooths my hair into thick waves, and applies my makeup, enhancing my eyes with a smoky, dark purple eyeshadow.

"Are you sure I should wear this?" I cross the living room, my skintight dress creeping up my thighs. Stopping at the floor-length mirror beside the front door, I tug it back down to my knees. "It shows . . ." I turn and crane my neck. The sparkling black fabric clings to my ass like a second skin. "Everything."

"Exactly," Anna calls from her bedroom. "You look hot." She struts out of her room in a colorful, bejeweled one piece with a plunging neckline and high-rise jeans. Her face drops when she sees me slipping on my brown leather jacket. "No *way* are you wearing that jacket. It ruins my styling."

"I'll take it off inside the club." *If I'm there that long.* "It's freezing."

"Fine," she says through her pristine white teeth, and hands me a glass of champagne. Her phone dings and she pulls it from her back pocket, frowning at the screen. "Uber's still fifteen minutes away. Should we sit?"

I nod and follow her to the sofa, my dress riding higher with each step. "How's tongue-ring dude?" I ask.

Anna's face breaks into a wide grin. "Who, Christiaan? *Meh*, he's fun for now." She grabs her handbag and rifles through it, tossing aside lipstick and old receipts. She pulls out a bottle of pills and shakes two into her open palm.

"You take medication?" I ask.

"Yep," she says, throwing the pills into her mouth and washing them down with a swig of champagne. "Helps me concentrate. Or at least, it's meant to." She leans toward me and lowers her voice, as if she's telling me a secret. "To be honest with you, my psychiatrist's a bit of an idiot."

Anna's never seemed the type to see a psychiatrist or take medication. She's the most put-together person I've ever met. And she speaks about her mental health in the same manner as the rest of her life, with unabashed confidence. I envy her. "I don't like my psychiatrist either," I say. The moment the words leave my mouth, I want to stuff them back in. But there's no judgment on Anna's face. Instead, she's nodding, her pink glossy lips pulled to the side in a soft, understanding smile.

"Did you ever think of changing?" She laughs. "Not that I'd recommend mine."

I shrug, twisting my champagne glass in my hand. "Silas set up the appointment, and I didn't have the heart to see someone else." And I'd rather suffer than voice my issues aloud to *another* stranger.

"I still don't understand what happened with Silas," Anna says.

Vivid, gray-blue eyes flash across my mind and the muscles in my chest seize. "Truthfully, neither do I. You know we were friends and he was weird about the age gap, but I thought we'd worked past that. He was so worried when I broke my wrist. He stayed with me for days. I thought—" I plant my elbows on my knees and slide my fingers through my hair, nails scraping along my scalp. "I don't know."

Anna offers me a reassuring nod, waiting for me to find the words.

"The last time I saw him, I thought he was going to ask me out. I thought that's what we were building to." A pit opens in my stomach. "But he didn't. He said, 'You don't need me anymore,' and he cut me out of his life, like I meant nothing to him."

The memory's a hazy, depressing dream.

Anna shakes her head. "Asshole. I dated a guy like that once. He came over every night. For months. Then one night, he fed me that 'you're too good for me, I'm doing you a favor' bullshit." She motions with her champagne flute as she speaks, the golden liquid sloshing against the glass. "But I told him he owed me the truth and I wasn't leaving until I got it. He said I was too loud. Too opinionated." She gestures to herself with a laugh. "Too *me*, I guess. So, I told him how tiny his dick was, and never spoke to him again."

"Well done, Anna," I say, but my chest stings like I'm battling a lingering cold. Was that the problem with Silas? Was I too different? Too broken, with too many problems? *Too . . . me?* I push the thought away. "You know, I'd kill to be *too you*."

A slight flush creeps up Anna's neck. "Thanks, Ella. You should confront Silas. I'm serious," she says when I shake my head. "You need closure."

"Maybe." But what if I don't want to know? My whole life, I've never fit in. At school I was picked apart for everything from my unwell mother down to the wedge of brown in my right eye. But those girls were strangers. Cruel nobodies who didn't *know* me.

Not like Silas. He knew me down to my core. Knew my story, my fears and my dreams. He came into my life at precisely the right time, helping me with the transition into college, booking my first appointment with my psychiatrist, and setting me up with ways to protect myself from the world. Something about being in his presence had felt so *right*, like the comfort of your own bed after an all-nighter or a sliver of sunshine on a cold winter's day. Deep down, I'm grateful for the heavy blanket of fog that hangs over our memories. Because hearing how messed up I am from Silas's mouth would break me.

"I don't think I'm ready to hear what he has to say." I clutch my mother's charm in my hand. "I think . . . it might hurt too much."

"It might. But never knowing might hurt you more, long term. You know?" Anna chews on her bottom lip. "Oh, what did Sarah say?" I stare at her blankly, and Anna tilts her head. "Your school friend. Is she coming?"

"*Oh*." I check my phone. "She didn't write back."

"Boo. I want to meet her." A notification chimes on her phone and she shrieks, jumping to her feet. "Uber's here."

I follow her to the front door, tripping in my borrowed stilettos. Taking one last glance in the mirror, I adjust the stretchy fabric over my torso, grab my clutch and follow Anna into the night.

✧

Wet grass tickles my feet as I stagger toward our apartment, my high heels swinging from my hand. I dart past a lone figure sitting in the dark beside Bromley House without a second glance. *I guess liquor has its perks.* I stumble up the steps leading to the building's entrance. I'll pay for this tomorrow.

Beside the front door, the numbers on the keypad split into blurry doubles, chasing each other around the screen. *How many shots did I have?* Four attempts later, I enter the building, climb to the second floor, and sink onto the rough, brown carpet outside Anna's apartment.

"Where are you, Mr Keys?" I murmur to myself between hiccups. I tip my clutch upside down, littering the floor with lipstick, tampons and debit cards. *No key.* I burst into giggles, broken by my back thudding against Anna's front door. My eyes drift shut.

"Ella?" says a warm voice from behind the door opposite mine.

My eyelids snap open. Even in my drunken state, Parker's voice sparks shivers along my skin.

"Can you open the door?" he asks from inside his apartment. "It's unlocked."

Leaning forward on my knees, I grasp the handle, twisting it back and forth until it budges open. Parker steps out into the communal corridor. "And they say chivalry is dead," I murmur, laughing as I slump back against my door.

Parker's tall frame towers above me. He drags his thumb along his bottom lip, his mouth curving into a dimpled grin.

"What?" I ask, struggling to focus on his translucent skin.

"You look beautiful," he says, his voice almost pained. He sits opposite me, lazing against the wall with his forearms resting on bent knees.

"All Anna's"—*hiccup*—"doing."

An easy smile flitters across his face. "Have you been drinking, Ella?"

"A bit." *Wait. Why is he transparent?* "Why do you look like that?"

"I'm not sure." He studies his large, faded hand. "It gets worse the further I am from Rose."

I push myself more upright. "Do you think she's losing her powers?"

"No," he says, a little too quickly, and looks away. "She's just exhausted."

"Where is she?"

He tips his head to his apartment. "Sleeping."

I press my lips together and nod, but I can't stand the silence stretching between us. "Are you really going to take me to see my mother when you get your powers back?" I ask.

The tension in his shoulders ebbs. "I promise," he says, staring me directly in the eye. "You're my first stop the second I can travel again." He leans toward me, squinting at the side of my face. "Hey, did you get your ear pierced?"

I beam. "Anna pierced it at the club with the back of her earring."

"Sounds sanitary," he says, shaking his head at the ceiling, but there's a wide grin on his face.

My heart squirms. I want to make him smile again, large enough for those dimples to appear.

"How did you meet Anna?" he asks.

"She came to class on the first day drunk and sat next to me. She thought I was someone else—her friend, Janice." I snort. "She spent the whole hour calling me Janny-Wanny." Parker's warm laugh mingles with mine. "She's been hounding me to go clubbing with her pretty much every day since. That and get a tattoo or more piercings." I gesture to my ear. "She swore it wouldn't draw attention, but you noticed it, so . . ." I shrug.

"There isn't much you could change without me noticing," he says, and something flutters in my stomach. "It looks great."

Why is he giving me compliments? I doubt Rose would approve. "Is Rose your girlfriend?" I blurt.

"What?" Parker says, all emotion leeched from his voice.

I fiddle with the hem of my dress. "Well, I mean, you're always together. And you were so avoidant about my dream. I thought she might be the reason. You're different when she's around."

"I'm sorry, Ella, I'm trying to—" He runs a hand through his hair. "Interacting with the past can alter your memories when you return to the future. We call it memory splitting. Your original memory overlaps with a new one, and once it's done, you'll never remember which memory was real."

"So, you change the past, but you can't remember how?" I ask.

"That's the thing. Changing the past isn't possible. I mean, you can make small ripples by interacting with it, but nothing will change *long term*. McGregor used to say it was nature's way of balancing itself out. For example, you can stop someone getting on a plane, but if they really want to go, they'll get on the next one." He shrugs. "Or they won't. Either way, it won't change the grand trajectory of their life. Meddling in the past won't achieve anything other than splitting your memories, and I don't want that to happen to me. It's easier for me if I keep my distance. And as for Rose, she's like—an annoying sister."

A knot of tension releases in my chest. But—a *sister*? I tilt my head to the side, but my whole body follows, and I catch myself before I slump over. "Why are men so clueless when it comes to women?"

"You're the psychology major, you tell me," he says, another grin playing on his lips.

"I'll let you know once I figure it out. Which I will, once I'm a boss clinical psychologist with my own private consultation rooms."

"Okay, Ella," he says with a low chuckle. "Time to go to bed."

"Can't. Lost my keys," I say, my eyelids drooping.

"Where's Anna?"

"She went home with tongue-ring guy, but it's okay." I gesture to the floor. "I'm going to sleep here."

"What a great idea," he murmurs.

"I'm a clever woman." I smile, closing my eyes, and Parker sighs.

"I know. Come on."

I open my eyes and he's on his feet.

"You can sleep in my bed. Just be quiet because Rose needs her sleep."

Looking up at him, my head lolls back against my door and the corridor spins.

He suppresses a laugh. "Okay, Ella. I need you to get up." I stand and trip, giggling. "You need to be quiet, remember?" he whispers. "And don't forget your jacket."

"Okay." I follow him through his half-furnished apartment to the bedroom. The light from the living area spills over Rose, lying on her side on one of the single beds.

Parker gestures to the empty bed against the opposite wall. "Sleep there. I'll be in the living room."

"Okay. *Wait*," I say as he turns to leave. There's no sofa in the living room, only a hard wooden floor.

"What?" he whispers, pausing inside the doorframe.

"I can't let you sleep on the floor"—*hiccup*—"after you've given up your bed to stop me from doing the very same thing." But what's the alternative? I stare at the single bed and nerves flood my vodka-soaked body. I've never shared a bed with a man. And his bed is *tiny* and he's *enormous*. My eyes crawl up his expansive chest and over his defined jaw, hitching on his lips. I won't be able to sleep knowing he's on the cold floor because of me. I finally reach his eyes, a deep bronze in the dim light. "We'll share the bed."

"Are you coming on to me, Ella?" He arches a dark blond brow, that adorable dimple appearing in his cheek, and heat floods my face.

"Stop being"—*hiccup*—"an idiot." I stumble into the room, place my things beside the bed, and lie down, trying my best to be quiet. Parker watches me from the doorway, relaxed against its frame with his arms crossed and one ankle hooked over the other.

"Okay, I'm going to sleep out here now. Goodnight," he whispers.

"Parker," I whisper-yell.

"*Shh*," he says, glancing at Rose. "Okay. Just . . . keep it down." He straightens and walks toward the bed and my heart rate escalates with each step, until his broad frame towers over me.

I shuffle over, and he lies on his back next to me. He tucks his hands under his head, eyes fixed on the ceiling.

He takes up so much space, my back is flush against the wall for the both of us to fit without touching.

I study the profile of his face, the swell of his lips, his straight nose and dark blond lashes. I trace his silhouette, the rise and fall of his chest. He must sense me staring again, because he turns his head toward me, our noses less than an inch apart. His dilated pupils lock with mine, stealing my breath. I'm suddenly one hundred times more sober.

My breathing quickens as I observe him. Even in his translucent state, tiny flecks of brown fill his amber eyes, and freckles spot his cheeks. I focus on the freckle above his top lip and an image of my tongue sweeping across it, tasting him, flashes across my mind. My pulse spikes, but I don't break his unwavering stare.

He studies my features in turn, as if memorizing them. Under his penetrating stare, awareness ripples through my entire body, every skin cell scorching.

"You know, you never told me your favorite place," I whisper, breaking the silence.

His mouth curves into a gentle, nostalgic smile. "There was a beach I used to visit with my family. It was my favorite place in the world," he says, his voice deep and soft. "The dirt's so red it bleeds into the sand, and it has these massive, red sandstone cliffs that hang over the ocean. And the water is the most vivid, turquoise blue. I'll never forget the first time I saw you—that little wedge of color in your right eye." His gaze hasn't left mine, tracing my features as he speaks. "All I could see were those red rocks, jutting over the sea." He shifts and places his transparent hand on top of mine. "God, I've missed you."

I stare at his large hand resting over mine, yet I feel *nothing*. No weight or warmth. Only air, as if he isn't touching me at all.

"It's impossible," I say.

A sad smile plays on his lips. "Another downside to losing my abilities and being in the wrong time." His eyes lock with mine again. "But I'd give anything to touch you, one last time."

Rose stirs in the bed beside us, partially rousing, and I swallow my reply. My heart's in overdrive, my fingers aching. I've never wanted to touch anyone in my life more than in this moment. Is it a cruel blessing that I can't? I've dreamed of the warmth of Parker's skin, the passion in his embrace. Would it differ in real life? What would life be like at Neurovida with Parker's younger self? Am I accepting this bizarre fate? Giving up any hope of the normal life I've been fighting to create? And if I do, when will that be? How many more nights will I have to wait until our times align?

I ignore the tiny voice of reason in the back of my mind, muddled by darkness and vodka, whispering that I'll never throw it away—everything I'm working toward—to be a time traveler. That I can't have Parker *and* a normal life.

But just for tonight, I'll let myself pretend.

"Go to sleep, Ella," Parker whispers, but his greedy gaze stays trained on me.

I'm unsure whether we lie there for minutes or hours, silently staring at one another, my heart pounding in my chest. But at some point I fall asleep, and when I wake, both Rose and the man from my dreams are gone.

14

Rose

I yank Parker into the corridor outside our apartment. "What the fuck were you thinking, having Ella in there?" Is he trying to torture himself? I need to get him out of here before it's too late. Before he does something reckless. I drag on my vape and take off along the corridor.

"She was locked out. What was I supposed to do, let her sleep in the corridor?" he asks, easily keeping up with my brisk strides.

I suppress the urge to hit him. *Typical, arrogant Parker, never admitting his mistakes.* "Yes, you should have. The more time you spend with her, the higher the chances our memories will split when we get back. Plus, being around her puts her in danger." I bring my hand to my pounding head. "I shouldn't need to spell this out to you."

"She *was* in danger." His mouth twists, and he gestures to the worn hallway carpet. "Look at this floor."

I yank him into the small rec room by the stairs, feeling like a bomb with a faulty switch, ready to explode at any second. "This isn't a fucking joke, Parker." I jab him in the chest. "You need to leave her alone."

"You're the one wearing her jacket. It looks good on you, by the way." He reaches up and adjusts my collar, his bulging biceps encasing my face. "Who knew you could wear anything but black and not combust into flames."

I smack his hands away. "Don't change the subject. Put an end to this. Tell her you won't see her again."

His smile falters. "I promised I'd take her to see her mother."

"So? She'll get over it. We aren't here for her. Jesus Christ, Parker, we're here to fix your powers, not play house in the past." Parker's expression hardens, but I step forward, my face an inch from his. "You need to hear this. You're deluding yourself if you think you can have a life here with her."

"I know that," he says, stepping away from me, but I match him step for step.

"I don't think you do."

"I said, I got it." Parker turns away from me, running his hand through his hair. "Shit, how many times do I have to say it?"

I want to trust him, but when it comes to Ella, Parker's judgment has always been clouded. A knot forms in my stomach. What if Parker only wants to get his powers back so he can stay here with her? Would he do that? I shake my pounding head. It doesn't matter. Once his powers are restored, Parker won't be my problem anymore. "Good, because McGregor emailed me, and he wants to meet."

Parker's head shoots to the desk dividing our beds, and the ancient, second-hand laptop we use to communicate with McGregor. "Already?"

"Yep." I take off, but Parker's hand snakes around my arm.

"Wait." His eyes search mine. "Rose, I need to talk to you."

"Later," I bark. "McGregor's waiting." I shrug him off and run down the stairs.

✧

I hold my breath and open McGregor's office door. *Please tell me he has good news.*

He's silent as we enter, remaining seated behind his large oak desk. On its surface, a pendulum of metal balls swings back and forth. *Click. Click. Click.*

The silence between each click is deafening.

"Please sit," McGregor says, gesturing to the chairs before his desk.

I tiptoe between piles of coffee-rimmed papers—many with notes scribbled in the margins—and sit among the organized chaos.

I can see Parker's reflection in the shiny pendulum, a dark blur shifting on his feet behind me.

Click. Click. Click.

I look away. I've been too hard on him. If this doesn't work, he has a lot more to lose than I do. "Please tell me you have something, McGregor," I say, leaning so far forward in my chair I'm in danger of falling.

He considers us. "I analyzed the blood from the sample you gave me, and I found cells I've never seen before. They must be the key to your time-traveling abilities, albeit a small component of a much larger signaling pathway . . . I'll need to conduct more studies to further my understanding."

There's excitement in the professor's voice. He's as intrigued as we are desperate to discover what was done to Parker. He wants answers.

Join the club, buddy.

"Does this mean you can find out what's wrong with me?" Parker asks.

"I can tell you what's different about this person's blood from a normal individual. But to tell you what's happening in your body, Parker, without a sample of your blood, would be quite impossible."

Click. Click. Click.

I suppress the urge to grab the pendulum and hurl it across the room. "That's not what you said before," I say through gritted teeth. "You know we can't get that for you."

When did I stand? I clench my shaking hands into fists. I can't believe we're back to square one. *What the hell are we going to do?*

Professor McGregor is also on his feet. "I'm sorry. But if you can get me another sample of blood, I—"

My mind goes blank, McGregor's words fading to white noise. The clicking of the balls on his desk reverberates through me. *Click.* McGregor can't help us. No one can. *Click.* Everything that brought us to this moment has been a complete waste of time. My pulse pounds in my ears.

Click.

I want to scream. I want to lunge across the desk and throttle McGregor. Parker's hand touches my shoulder, pulling me from my trance. His face is as dark and empty as the pit in my stomach.

"Rose, let's go. We'll find another way," he says, turning toward the door.

"Wait," McGregor says. "There must be research behind the drug given to Parker. Scientific articles or future literature?"

I pause, halfway between McGregor and the door.

I should follow Parker, but my feet won't budge. Can I even get access to that sort of information? It goes against the oath I live my life by. And it's risky. If it doesn't get us killed, it's going to take an incredible toll. But what's the alternative? If we don't fix Parker, we're stuck. I can't carry him in a different time forever. McGregor's our only hope.

I shake my head, but find myself staring at Parker, waiting for me by the door.

I will risk my life to save him. Repeatedly. I swallow the bile rising in my throat. "And that's what you need, to fix Parker?" I ask McGregor.

He nods. "It's the only way I'll be able to try."

"Rose," Parker says. "We need to find another way."

Ignoring him, I speak to McGregor in a low voice. "Then I'll get it for you. Everything I can about the drug given to Parker. And when I bring it to you, you'll fix him." McGregor's blue eyes narrow as I extend a trembling hand toward him. A cold sweat breaks out over my skin. "Deal?"

Parker's firm shoulder presses against mine. "Rose," he warns under his breath.

"Deal?" I repeat to McGregor, arm still extended.

"Deal," he says, and his burly palm slides into mine.

The moment our fingers part, I check my watch and plant my hands on Parker's broad shoulders. Energy flares beneath my sternum, lashing against the walls of my chest like a tiger's claw through the bars of its cage.

Parker grips my hand, still clutching his shoulder. "Rose, stop."

Head hammering and body vibrating, I close my eyes and push the volatile energy into him. Every cell in his body pulsates alongside mine, as if his blood and flesh are an extension of my own. Pain rips through my head, but I grit my teeth and muffle the cry building in my throat.

Parker's grasp on my hand is almost painful. "Rose, don't do this. Let me see her one last time."

He doesn't believe we'll return. Which means he's guessed where I'm taking us, or he thinks I'm too weak to bring us back. *Maybe I am.* Either way, Parker's words are my ammunition, fueling the shaking of every single cell in my body. I suck in a breath and the energy in my chest explodes, engulfing us both.

15

Mariella

My body's on fire. My limbs are shaking, my heart pounding. I'm naked, my chest pressed against skin, warm and firm. My fingertips ripple over the muscular ridges of a strong, broad back. Eyes clamped shut, tension builds between my thighs as hands explore my body, roughly caressing and teasing, guiding my hips as they rock.

Each breath abandons my lungs in a short pant, quickening when soft lips and coarse stubble press against my neck. With each passing second, I'm closer and closer to shattering. The palm on my thigh glides upward, over the skin of my bare abdomen to rest over the wild thumping of my heart. And beneath it, chilling energy flares to life, a contrast to the euphoric heat between my thighs. Starting as a tiny ball, the power wells, snaking through my body, and ricocheting against my rib cage, searching for the path of least resistance.

I push the feeling away. I want to focus on the lips trailing down my neck. But it only grows until my entire body's pulsating with current, radiating from my chest to the tips of my fingers and toes. A stubbled cheek presses to mine, and a sharp whispering fills my ears.

✧

I jolt awake, unfulfilled and gasping for breath, the words dissolving into hazy wisps that will forever be out of reach.

I'm lying on Parker's bed, alone and hungover, my body buzzing with electricity. I bring my hand to my face and stare at the pads of my fingertips, the sparkling current racing along my skin. Closing my eyes, I focus on it, and electrical energy combusts within my chest, jolting my heart into a frantic rhythm. Power inundates my body, shooting down my arms and legs. I cry out and force it away, shaking my hands like they're crawling with eight-legged insects.

My heart's still racing when I sit up and the room spins. *Did it look like this yesterday?* I rifle through my hazy recollection of last night. Parker's heated gaze flashes through my mind and every muscle in my body clenches. I have a sudden urge to capture the moment in my sketchbook.

Clutch and shoes in hand, I exit the bedroom, my chest sinking when Parker isn't in the living room or anywhere else in his apartment. Neither is Rose. Every scrap of paper has been removed from the tiny dining table. No dishes await cleaning in the kitchen sink. No toothbrushes or soap sit beside the spotless bathroom sink.

I lock the door from the inside and pull it shut behind me. "Shit." I stop outside my own door without a key. Shivering in my dress, I knock on our door.

"Coming," Anna calls, answering the door still dressed in last night's clothing. "Just getting home, are we?" she asks with a knowing grin.

If only she knew the half of it. "I lost my key."

"I just got in myself." I enter her apartment and we both collapse on the sofa. "Where did you sleep?"

Think of an excuse, Mariella.

My stomach rolls and I groan. I lower my pounding head onto a sofa cushion and flinch from the sting of my new piercing.

"Ella?" Anna says.

I'm too hungover for this.

"In Rose and Parker's room," I say, my words stifled by the pillow.

Anna gasps, sitting up. "You didn't. Where?"

A slow smile pulls at my mouth, and I brush my knuckles across my lips. "On Parker's bed." My cheeks flush and I cover my head with another sequined cushion. "They only have one bedroom, so Rose was in there too. I slept there, that's all."

"And Parker slept where? With Rose?" Anna asks, yanking the pillow away.

I peek up at her. "Actually, they're just friends."

"*What?* Are you kidding me? This whole time he's been single? I could've sworn they were together. Wait, you didn't answer my question. Where did he sleep?"

Parker's intense gaze flashes through my mind and my blush deepens at the memory of his dilated pupils and the moisture on his parted lips. *I'd give anything to touch you, one last time.* A thrill races through me.

"*Mariella. Katharine. Adams.* You little hussy," Anna squeals, whacking me repeatedly with a cushion.

I hold out my hand to prevent a blow to the face. "Nothing happened. We just . . . fell asleep."

"Sure. Sure." Anna's grinning from ear to ear. "When are you seeing him again?"

The smile on my face falls. I may have entertained the possibility of a future with Parker last night while drunk, but now I'm sober, reality's set in. I clear my throat. "Parker's not my type."

"Please," Anna says, rolling her eyes. "With that face? He's everybody's type."

I hesitate, then relent, knowing I'm not telling Anna anything I shouldn't. "When I woke up this morning, their place was empty. Completely empty. Besides the furniture. It's as if they don't live there anymore."

The smile on Anna's face wavers. "What? They weren't there?"

"No. They must've left before I woke up." It's even stranger when I say it out loud.

"Maybe they changed apartments? Or . . ." Anna's brows crease.

"Or what?" I ask, a chill sweeping down my arms despite the warm air blowing from Anna's heater.

She winces. "Well, the other day when they were here looking for you, Rose mentioned they weren't staying long."

I tear my gaze from Anna's. *This is for the best, right?* Parker will never be a constant in my life. He's from a different time. A different world, really. One I can't be part of, unless I enter Neurovida and become a time traveler. A hard mass forms in my stomach. *I won't.*

The mail slot on the front door squeaks, and a thin envelope drops onto the floor. Anna hops off the sofa and picks it up. I expect her to tear it open, but her mouth drops and she extends it toward me. "Ella," she whispers.

I reach out and take the sealed envelope, addressed to me and bearing the hospital's teal logo. The paper trembles in my hands. Holding my breath, I tear it open.

16

Parker

Gravel crunches beneath my feet, two walls of dense forest encasing me as I sprint along Neurovida's long, winding driveway. Under the cover of darkness, I can barely make out my own hands, let alone Rose, who's somewhere ahead of me. Lungs burning, I push forward. It's been seven months since my powers were taken and Rose carried me into the past. Seven months since solid ground pushed back against my feet, now aching with each stride. How strange to forget the pull of gravity on my body and cool air on my face.

If being away has affected Rose, I can't tell. When we first appeared inside Neurovida's tall, wrought-iron gates, she swore, clutching her hands over her temples. But within seconds she'd taken off, gravel and dust flying. Now she's in her element.

Probably because I'm not weighing her down. She could've left me the moment I lost my powers, but she stuck by me, regardless of the immense mental and physical toll it's taken on her. I owe her my life.

I come to the edge of the forest, the driveway widening to encircle a large, gushing fountain. Neurovida's outdoor lights are on, bathing the grand home in warm light. The lush gardens surrounding the immediate vicinity of the house remain pristine, each perfectly trimmed hedge lit from below. I follow Rose around the side of the home, her back flattened against the bricks. I slump against the wall beside her, each ragged breath breaking the eerie silence.

She turns and presses her index finger to her lips. Unable to speak, I only nod. We barely escaped here last time. If we're caught again, I doubt we'll be so lucky.

After a moment, Rose gestures with her head and takes off down a small pathway leading to the back of the home. I glance at my left wrist and follow her, forgetting that the watch once permanently glued there has now gone. Seven months and I'm yet to kick the habit of checking it at least fifty times a day. I'm guessing it's past midnight, with only the stars to guide us as we sneak further inside Neurovida's walls.

At the back of the property, the ground slopes downward toward miles of thick, untouched forest. We climb down the slope to a wooden landing with a metal door, partially hidden from the upper levels of the home by its multiple grand balconies. Rose grips the door handle and I hold my breath, praying Neurovida's staff haven't discovered its faulty locking mechanism. The door opens with a loud click, and we slip inside.

I don't ask her where we're going. Even in the dead of night, I know Neurovida like the back of my hand. I've lost blood, sweat and tears training under this roof. Made and lost best friends. Fell for the love of my life, all here within these walls. This was home. Now it's an execution chamber. Matthews made sure of it the day he took everything from me.

I try not to think of Ella, but every door I pass leads to a room bursting with her memory—her gentle laugh, her peaceful presence, her soft curves. There are so many things I wish I'd done differently. Too many words left unsaid.

Rose stops in front of another door, and I frown at the small keypad to the right of the handle.

"Was that there before?" Rose whispers, her voice unusually high.

"No. They must've brought in tighter security measures since we left," I say.

"There's no way we're getting in. Let's go," she says, grabbing my arm.

"Wait." I examine the keypad. "I'll get us in."

Rose's head whips back and forth, surveying the empty corridor. "Parker, if you get this wrong, there might be an alarm. We *can't* be found here. Let's go back and work on honing my skills. I'll travel us directly into the room."

"We're here now," I say, eyes glued to the keypad. "I need to try."

Footsteps echo along a connecting hallway and I hold my breath, a bead of sweat dripping down my temple. *Calm down, it's only a cleaner.* Or do they already know we're here?

"Parker," Rose begs.

"Get ready to travel." I take a deep breath and enter five digits into the keypad, each responding with a small beep.

Rose's fingers dig into my shoulder, tiny prickling sparks emanating from her contact point. The footsteps grow louder and her hand trembles. Another thirty seconds and we'll be discovered. I enter the last digit, earning two short beeps. The light above the keypad flashes red and my heart palpitates.

Fuck. Maybe I don't know McGregor as well as I thought.

"Parker, please," Rose repeats, voice trembling.

"Wait," I mutter. Electricity races into my body, collecting in my chest; Rose readying to travel at a second's notice. The footsteps draw closer.

"If we get caught, I'll kill you myself, Parker," she growls.

I roll my shoulders, take another deep breath and press my finger to the panel. The steps are louder now, and close. Too close. We have ten seconds at best. I enter the fifth digit and my finger blurs, like thousands of tiny pixels jumping from my skin—the effects of Rose exerting her power to travel us to safety.

"Hold it, Rose," I order. Not daring to blink, I enter the last digit, earning a longer beep from the keypad, a green flashing light and a small click. I rip open the door, haul Rose inside and shut the door behind us. Breathing heavily, we wait behind the door until the steps recede.

"Told you I'd get us in," I say with a smug grin and turn toward the room, drawing in a breath of leather, coffee and old books. A wave of nostalgia warms my chest. McGregor's pushed his computer to the edge of the desk to make room for the stacks of papers scrawled with his looping handwriting. His cardigan's draped over the back of his chair, probably left behind in his preoccupation with another impossible theory. A photo of the son he lost still sits on the shelf beside his desk, between volumes of encyclopedias and scientific journals. It's as if no time's passed at all.

I cross the room and run my hand along the dark timber desk. "What date is it?" I ask Rose, still standing by the door.

"I don't know, my watch doesn't Wi-Fi update like the—" Rose's jaw drops, her focus on the tall figure materializing in the space between us.

The one man in the world I hate. The man who took everything from me.

"Matthews," I say, the word tasting like ash on my tongue. He takes a step forward on mismatched feet. "Nice choice of footwear. Still having trouble, are we?"

A muscle tenses in his jaw. "Not as much trouble as you."

A growl leaves my throat, my sight condensing to tunnel vision, lined in red, Matthews at the center. I don't know why he's holding his hands up in front of his chest. And I don't care. He's a dead man. Suddenly, escaping here with McGregor's journal isn't as important as wrapping my hands around Matthews' neck. I want to hurt him like he's hurt me. I want to *kill* him.

Matthews takes another step toward me, his deep voice filling the room. "Parker, listen to me."

Not a chance. I swing at him but he vanishes, reappearing just out of arm's reach.

"Parker—" he says, but his words are clipped short as I lunge again.

I'm left holding nothing but air as Matthews materializes behind McGregor's desk. *Fuck, how's he doing that?*

Matthews' dark brows draw together. "I've been trying to find you two for—"

"Why did you do it?" Rose asks, her voice filled with thick, rare emotion. "I trusted you." Her hands curl into fists. "*She* trusted you." Her voice cracks and the sound claws at my insides. "And you sold us out. *Why?*"

Matthews turns toward her, and I have my chance. I grab a glass paperweight off the desk and hurl it at him. It strikes his cheek with a satisfying crack and he crumples to the floor, hand pressed to his eye. Blood spurts between his fingers.

Twisted pleasure balloons in my chest at the sight of him on the floor, but before we can grab him, he vanishes. Rose and I wait with rapid breaths, watching the space where he disappeared.

"Holy shit," Rose says, her wide eyes like two black coins. "He knew we were going to be here. Let's find McGregor's research notes and get the hell out of here before he comes back."

"I still can't believe we're doing this," I say. "I can't believe *you're* doing it. After all your lectures about keeping the oath and lying low." Rose has always been a stickler for rules, and after all the grief she's given me about Ella . . .

"It's not like we're stealing. It's *his* work. We're just . . . giving it to him early."

I open my mouth to argue when someone bangs on the door.

"Fuck," Rose says.

"Start looking." I shoot to McGregor's desk while Rose beelines to his computer. "It won't be on there. He's old school. We need to find his research journal. It's handwritten."

I yank the top drawer from its hold, rummage through the contents and toss it into the corner of the room with a loud crash. There's no point in being quiet now. Whoever's on the other side of the door might not have access, but it's only a matter of time before someone shows up who does. Or Matthews reappears.

"What does it look like?" Rose yells, rummaging through piles of papers stacked on top of the desk.

"It's an A4, brown leather-bound book. I've seen it here so many times." I tug open another desk drawer, adrenaline pulsing through me. More people are shouting from behind the door now.

"We need to go," Rose says.

"We can't come back. We get it now." I yank the bottom desk drawer, but it's locked.

"Parker," Rose repeats. The noise outside grows, and the banging on the door continues.

"It's in the bottom drawer." I flip the heavy wooden desk upside down. The computer crashes to the floor, papers and pens following. "Help me."

We shove the desk against the door, and I kick the locked drawer, over and over, swearing each time it doesn't budge. My chest numbs at the faint beeping of a code being entered into the keypad.

I grab a trophy from one of the office shelves and smash it into the base of the drawer. The wood splinters, fragments biting into my skin as I rip them away. My heart lurches at the sight of brown leather. *McGregor's journal.* "Rose, get ready," I say, yanking it free.

The office door bursts open, launching the desk toward us. We jump backward, Rose's hand grabbing my shoulder. Her influence, scorching me from the inside out, wavers as Matthews steps into the room. His face is unharmed, and he's flanked by guards with their weapons drawn.

I shove Rose behind me, but my foot catches on something and we both stumble. Her power hits me like an explosion, engulfing my body and traveling us from the room. But not before the gun fires. Or before the bullet slices through my skin. And somehow, we are simultaneously falling and ripping through time.

I tense for impact, but when I open my eyes I'm standing in a sunken garden, and Rose is unconscious on the ground beside me.

17

Mariella

I open the typed letter from the hospital and read the contents with wide eyes.

"What's wrong?" Anna asks.

I swallow against the tightness in my throat. "It says—" I release the letter, and it flutters down onto the sofa. "It says she wasn't a patient there."

"There must be a mistake," Anna says, reaching for the discarded letter.

I jump to my feet, banging my knee on the coffee table. The pain doesn't register. I grab my phone and find the hospital's number, following the prompts to speak with the medical records department. Thirty minutes and four transfers later, a woman with a nasal tone apologizes and tells me there is no record of my mother ever attending Massachusetts General Hospital. I'm so lightheaded I barely hear her lengthy explanation about misplaced records during the digitization process seven years ago.

"Is there anything else I can help you with?" the nasally voice asks. "Hello?"

"No. Thank you."

"Have a nice day."

The phone cuts out, and a heavy silence rings in my ears.

"What did they say?" Anna asks. She's hovered close by for the whole ordeal.

"Either she wasn't a patient there, or they've lost her record," I say, biting my lip. *I need to do something. But what?* "I'm going back to the hospital," I say.

✧

"Ma'am, if you don't calm down, I can't help you," the receptionist at the hospital front desk says. "I'm going to give you a form to fill in—"

"No." The backs of my eyelids burn with unshed tears. "I'm not filling in another form and waiting another month. I want to speak to someone about my mother. Now." I unclench my fists and blood rushes back into my fingers.

"I can see you're upset. I'm going to give you the email for our complaints department. Send them an—"

I scrunch my eyes shut, blocking out the low-grade hum of people ambling past and the squeaking of wheelchairs. A barista froths milk at the busy coffee cart to our right, hospital chairs scrape against vinyl, and a woman scolds her children for misbehaving. "You're not helping me," I snap.

The woman leans back in her chair, taking me in. "I'm trying to help you," she says. "You'll receive a case number via email when the complaints department receives your ticket." The woman pushes a business card through the rectangular gap at the bottom of the glass.

I snatch it up and storm past the desk, my feet carrying me along the hospital's bare labyrinth-like walls. It's been ten years since I walked these corridors, but my legs complete each step from memory. Ahead of me, a nurse opens a pair of security doors and I slip in behind her, marching toward a desk in the middle of the ward.

"Can I help you?" asks a blonde, middle-aged nurse in navy scrubs.

"I want information on Evelyn Adams. She was a patient here ten years ago, but the records department lost her chart." My palm hits the counter with a smack, and I slide the letter toward her. "I need to know what happened to her," I say between heaving breaths. "I was told she killed herself here."

The nurse picks up the paper, and I scrutinize her face as she scans the letter. Am I imagining the perspiration on her brow? The slight dilatation of her pupils? Did this woman know my mother? She passes the letter back to me. "Even if we had her file, I can't give out confidential information, sweetie."

The tears I've been holding back spill onto my cheeks. "Please," I beg, splaying my hands on the desk. "I'm her daughter. Please just look her up and tell me how and when she died. Please?"

"You said ten years ago?" she asks, and I nod. "Even if I wanted to help you, we didn't have electronic records back then. I'm not even sure the hard files of deceased patients are kept on the premises. You'll need to check again with the records department on level four."

"The medical records department won't help me." The level of my voice has crept up, my words rebounding off the walls.

"Calm down," the nurse says in a soft voice.

"Don't tell me to calm down when the hospital *lost* my mother's record," I yell.

"I understand you're upset, but you're disturbing our patients."

I follow the nurse's gaze to a number of patients in hospital gowns, watching from their open doorways. I catch an elderly nurse with silver hair staring, and she averts her eyes.

I tug at the front of my sweater, the scratchy fabric sticking to my skin. "Never mind," I say, storming away from the desk.

Rectangles of fluorescent light reflect off the hospital floor, and I count them instead of meeting each patient's unapologetic stare. Arms clutching my chest, I follow the signs back to the foyer and duck into a small public washroom. I hurl open the door, and a strangled sob escapes me. *I wish my mom was here. Or Anna. Or Parker.* Silas's name flitters through my mind and my stomach shrivels. Tears gush down my cheeks as I enter the first cubicle and shut the door.

"You don't need me anymore."

I grit my teeth. *No. I don't.*

I drop onto the toilet and stifle my cries in my knees. I've dreamed of my mother every night for weeks. She was well. Healthy. She wanted to come home. To take care of me. She wouldn't have killed herself.

Behind my wet eyes, I see the memory of my mother, peering through her bedroom curtain. Was she in danger? Is that why she sent me to boarding school? To keep me safe?

I wipe the tears from my face. *I need to see her death certificate.* I'll go down to the records department and *force* them to find it and show it to me. I fumble with the cubicle lock and hurl the door open, catching my reflection in the mirror. My eyes are red and puffy, trails of black eyeliner bleeding through patches of lingering foundation from last night. I lower my face toward the sink and splash handfuls of freezing water over my skin, scrubbing at the makeup until my cheeks feel raw.

I'm smothering my face with a paper towel, palms pressing into my eye sockets, when a shiver races down my spine and the hairs on the back of my neck prickle. My head whips from the three empty cubicles in the mirror's reflection, to the closed bathroom door. "No one's watching you," I mutter at my reflection with the vigor of a mother scolding her child.

I storm out the door and almost collide with the elderly nurse I caught staring in the mental health ward.

"Didn't mean to startle you," she says in a deep, croaky voice. Her wrinkled face breaks into a knowing grin. "You look like her."

My breath catches in my throat. "You knew my mother."

She extends a weathered arm toward me. "Walk with an old lady during her tea break?"

I link my arm through hers, and she urges me toward the main foyer, limping with every second step. We exit the hospital in silence, and part of me wonders if this is a ploy to move me away from the hospital doors.

"Who are you?" I ask once we're halfway across the green front lawn.

"My name's Marg. We've met before. But you were much younger then. You look more like her now."

My cringe is second nature. I've spent my life to date wanting to be the furthest thing from my mother. I even enrolled in psychology to try to diagnose her, to stop myself from following in her path. *Has it all been for nothing?*

"What's your name, girl?" Marg asks.

"Mariella."

Marg smiles, filling her face with deep crinkles. "Mari," she says, and I wince. "That's right. I worked nights while your mother was here."

"Do you remember all of your patients?" I ask.

"No," she says with a laugh. "But your mother was . . . *unique*."

"How?"

"She had the highest number of escapes in the ward's history. And she was only with us for a short time. Couldn't count the number of times the east wing went into lockdown while they tried to find her." Marg lets out a blunt, gravelly laugh. "She was smart, too. She talked about you a lot." We walk past an elderly man in a wheelchair watching his grandson dig in the garden.

"Were you working the night she died?" I ask.

Marg's voice drops. "No, but I remember it was Christmas Eve. Broke my heart, knowing she left you behind."

I stop walking and turn to face her. "Do you believe she killed herself?"

The woman's forehead crinkles. "I was told she did."

"But did you believe it, at the time? Did she seem unwell enough to do it?"

The woman shakes her head. "It's been so long. The mind has a way of selectively remembering some things and forgetting others. But I remember the change in her on the days you visited. You and that handsome fellow."

"What?" *A man visited my mother? Was it my father?* "Who was he?"

"Couldn't say. But the way the nurses would stare when he came in . . ." Her creased face tilts to the sky, and she lets out another harsh laugh. "A face like that doesn't come along very often."

"What did he look like?" I ask, tracing every wrinkle as if they might hold the clues I desperately seek.

The woman shakes her head. "I don't remember, darlin'. Tall, dark and handsome?"

"Well, how old was he? Around her age or . . . ?"

"Too old to be her son. Too young to be her lover."

My shoulders drop. Not my father, then.

"Why are you here? Waving that around." Marg dips her head to the letter clutched in my hand. "No mother would want their daughter suffering so many years past their death."

"I don't think she died here." It's the first time I've spoken the words aloud, and it loosens the band of tension wrapped around my chest for the past ten years, my lungs expanding a little easier with each breath.

The hospital doors open, and two security guards step outside. Holding them off with a stern glance, Marg encourages me to keep moving. "Mariella, your mother wanted the best for you, as any mother would. Don't waste your life here searching for answers you already have."

"But I don't have answers. I haven't even seen her death certificate. I'm going back to speak with records on level four." I try to pull my arm from hers, but her iron grip tightens, her sharp gaze flashing to the front entrance.

"You step inside that hospital again and those security guards will be all over you."

We reach the bus stop, and Marg turns to face me, wrapping her wrinkled hands around my own. "I've watched too many people wither inside those walls. Your mother's gone, but you can live the life she didn't. Don't come back here." Marg pats my hand. "Goodbye, Mariella."

"Goodbye," I say.

Marg limps across the yard and reenters the hospital, swatting at one of the security guards holding out his arm to help her.

I sit on the cold metal bench at the bus stop and stare at the empty street. Vacant faces drift past as I sift through distorted memories of my mother, muddled by time, and compare them to my vivid dreams. I need to know what happened to her, and if the hospital won't give me the information I need, I'll find someone who will.

I pull out my phone and enter a number from memory, with trembling fingers. The call goes straight to voicemail, as always.

"Silas, it's me. I need a favor."

18

Mariella

The sun has set by the time I return to Bromley House, and Anna's sweater is doing little to combat the chilling evening breeze. I'm a few yards away from the door when shadows shift beside the building, and I freeze. Heart racing, I squint through the darkness at the figure moving toward me. Parker steps from the shadows with labored steps, carrying Rose in his arms. His body's fading and reappearing, like a flickering lightbulb about to burn out.

"Parker?" I run toward him. Dark red blood is smeared over his and Rose's bodies. "What happened?"

He looks past me, scanning the perimeter before one of the hands supporting Rose holds out a tattered book. He grunts with the movement. "Take this," he says. "Keep it safe."

I tuck the book against my chest and enter the code at the front of the building. Parker tenses with every step on the staircase, but he doesn't stop moving until we're inside their apartment. I place the book on their tiny dining table and follow Parker into the bedroom.

"Where's all the blood coming from?" I ask.

"It's mine," Parker says, laying Rose on her bed. He turns toward me and my stomach drops. Slick, dark red blood saturates his shirt. The fabric's torn over the left side of his rib cage like a jagged window to the mangled skin beneath.

Lowering his head, he peels up the wet fabric and I shudder. His tan skin is split, tainted by the blood oozing down his torso. "It's just a bullet graze," he says.

Just a bullet graze? "You need to put pressure on that." I reach for him, but all I meet is air.

He steps away from me. "You can't do anything to help me, so please, help Rose." His lips turn upward as he feigns a smile that doesn't reach his eyes.

"You're losing too much blood. You need stitches," I say.

"I'll be fine," he grunts, and his body fades to a new shade of translucent.

I turn back toward Rose, blood smeared across her forehead. A sweaty sheen coats her olive skin, which has taken on a grayish hue. Underneath her closed lids, her eyes race back and forth.

"What happened?" I ask over the broken, incoherent sentences pouring from Rose's mouth.

"She traveled, and when we came back, she was like this." Parker runs his hands through his hair and flinches. "I tried to stop her, but she wouldn't listen." He leans down, brushing a strand of damp hair off her face. "You're safe now, Rose. You did so well," he says in a low voice.

I avert my gaze to the carpet. "Is it normal to be unwell after time traveling?"

"No. Not like this." Parker straightens. "But normally you aren't staying for extended periods of time while carrying another person. She's never been this bad before. I don't know if it's exhaustion or something else." Parker's gaze darts to Rose as she draws a stilted breath.

I edge toward her and press my hand to her forehead, while Parker steps back to give me room. "She's burning up," I say. "We need to cool her down." I remove my now blood-stained leather jacket from Rose's body. *Now I know where it went.* My mother's necklace is no longer around Rose's neck. Did my future self really part with it? Where is it now?

I find a washcloth in the bathroom and place it over Rose's forehead. Parker sits on his bed and slips a hand into his pocket with a grimace.

"She takes about eight of those a day, so she'll need something stronger than paracetamol," Parker says, when I pull painkillers from my handbag.

"Eight? What for?"

"Headaches. You need to remember, time travel isn't exactly normal. I mean, traveling to a place and back is fine, but extended stays make you sick. And we've been here for seven months."

"Why so long?" I ask.

"Rose hated traveling with a passenger at Neurovida. The first time we tried to come here, she accidentally took us back five years from now. I knew she was exhausted, but she wanted to try again. The second time, we were closer, but still six months off from when McGregor started work here on campus, and he's the reason we came here." His face falls. "She needed to rest for a week. Then the migraines started, and we decided it was easier to just wait. But holding me in this time for so long . . ."

He searches Rose's face with drawn brows and there's no mistaking his guilt. I hate that he blames himself for Rose's poor health and the situation they've found themselves in.

"I've never seen her like this," he says. "I think she's losing her grip on reality."

Rose's haunted look in the restroom at Tilly's flashes across my mind and I shudder. "She must be getting better at it—traveling with you, I mean. I only saw you last night."

"I think it's different now that she has a tether to this time." He shakes his head. "I'm not sure."

I fiddle with the painkillers in my hand. "What does she usually take when she's unwell like this?"

"Take your pick." Parker gestures to a small bag hidden beneath Rose's bed that I missed this morning.

I grab the bag and rifle through packets of painkillers and sedatives. I read the information on the back of each packet and settle on one. "These should reduce her fever." I sit beside Rose and ease her head onto my lap. "Rose, I'm going to give you some medication."

She mumbles something and Parker winces.

"She's confused," he says.

I pour water into Rose's mouth and feed her the tablets one at a time. "We should take her to the hospital. They'll be able to do more for her there."

Parker shakes his head. "No. It's too dangerous."

"We can go to the police," I say, easing Rose back onto her pillow. "My friend works undercover. We can go to him and—"

"No. If we talk to the police there will be records, which make us traceable. Nowhere's safe. Not from the kind of people looking for us."

"Do you mean other time travelers?" I hesitate. "What will happen if they find you?"

His face hardens, and he looks away.

"Why are they chasing you?" I ask, staring at the side of his face, wishing any of this made sense. "What do they want?"

Parker swallows, the corners of his mouth tense. "I can't tell you."

"*Why?*"

His defeated gaze locks with mine. "Because I don't want to scare you."

"I'm already scared, Parker. Someone shot you, and you look like you're about to disappear." I turn to Rose, muttering against her pillow. "Rose is unconscious, and I have no idea how to help her. I don't even know what's wrong with her."

"We'll be okay," he says, running his hands through his hair for the fourth time since we entered the room.

Beside me, Rose's body tenses and she lets out a strained cry. I look to Parker and gasp; his body is so faint I can barely see him.

He jumps to his feet, staring at his translucent hands with wide eyes.

"What's happening?" I ask, meeting him in the middle of the room with my heart in my throat.

"I don't know." His gaze flickers to Rose, and he's biting the inside of his cheek as if he's deciding something. "But I think you might be able to help."

"How?"

"There's something I used to do at Neurovida—to help someone along when they were struggling. To sort of anchor them. It might not work, but seeing as you're from this time . . ."

"I don't understand," I say.

"You can use your powers to anchor her in this time. It might give her mind and body respite."

Power? I don't *have* any power. "Parker, I—I don't know how. I can't." I take two steps away from him, tugging my sleeves over my hands.

Parker follows me step for step. "You can," he says, and I want to turn and run from the blind faith brimming in his eyes.

Rose stutters and Parker's body disappears and reappears.

"Parker," I scream. I need to do something. *Now*. Before he vanishes to a place I can't reach. "Tell me what to do."

"Quick, grab her hands."

I drop to the floor at Rose's side and clutch her tense hands in mine, the rough carpet burning my knees.

Parker's immediately at my side. "Think about the electricity you feel when you wake from your dreams. Focus on Rose. See if you can feel it in her hands."

I press my fingertips into Rose's palms, her skin cold and clammy. "I can't feel anything."

"Keep trying," he says, his voice smooth and even.

I close my eyes and concentrate on the warmth growing between our skin, but there's nothing. I adjust my grip and wait, but I don't know what I'm waiting *for*. I ignore the blood draining from my arms, and the numbness in its wake. Maybe there's a reason nothing's happening? Maybe Parker's made a mistake, and I don't have special skills. I'm just Mariella. The weird girl who can't speak out in class. The loner who's more alive when she's absorbed in a book than in real life. Tears build behind my closed eyelids but I scrunch them tighter and concentrate. Another five minutes pass before I drop Rose's hands. "I—I can't do this."

Parker's golden eyes are ablaze, as if lit from within. "Yes, you can."

"I can't, Parker," I cry. "Nothing's happening."

He kneels beside me, only space where our shoulders should be brushing. His amber eyes lock on mine. "I *know* you can, because I've seen you do it before. I've seen you push yourself to breaking point. I've seen you get knocked down time and time again, and never once did you give up. You need to stop running from what you are. You have no idea how much power you have. You can do this, Ella. Now focus."

Drawing in a deep breath, I clutch Rose's hands, focusing on the tips of my fingers. I imagine the layers of skin, blood and bone separating Rose's from mine, searching for anything beyond my racing pulse. I'm about to give up when the tiniest spark licks my finger, so small I might have imagined it. I tense but grab hold of it, and it happens again, a flicker of warm energy, humming against my fingertips.

"I feel it," I say, not daring to open my eyes.

"Good," Parker says in my ear, his tone warm with approval. "Now imagine that current is a string you're pulling through her body to yours."

I nod and envision the energy at my fingertips flowing into me. And like the flicking of a light switch, fiery, crackling electricity races up my arm and into my chest, pooling beneath my sternum. "It's working."

Rose groans, but I keep my eyes clamped shut.

"Okay, Ella," Parker says. "I want you to send it back the other way. *Now.*"

I focus on the energy swirling in my chest and envision it flowing down my arms and back into Rose. Power ignites in my chest and that familiar ball of unstable energy bursts to life, pulsing against my rib cage.

I immediately force it away and energy gushes from me, through every skin cell coating my body. I push what I can toward Rose, but the moment the current passes through my fingertips, a band of tension clamps over my head. I double over, as if the air's been ripped from my lungs. Scrunching my eyelids tighter, I will the energy to flow into Rose, who's now silent on the bed. She draws in a deep, steady breath, and her rigid hands slacken.

"That's it. See how long you can hold it," Parker says.

It won't be long. Within seconds my limbs grow heavy, and the power inside my chest dims. I need to let go, but the memory of Parker's fading form has me gritting my teeth, shutting out every thought except pouring energy into Rose. The band of pain around my head tightens, pressure building inside my skull.

Gasping for breath, I release one of Rose's hands and sink back onto my feet. My sweaty, pounding forehead presses against the mattress, but I don't dare break contact with Rose.

Parker's voice is a warm caress against my shaking core. "Let go. You've given her enough."

The energy is dwindling, but I keep drawing on it, willing every ounce into Rose. Sharp, stabbing pain rips through my head, but I cling to her hand like a drowning swimmer to a lifebuoy, ignoring Parker's panicked pleas for me to stop.

Rose has spent months sacrificing her mental and physical health for Parker, and if this is my one chance to ease the burden, I need to give it everything I have.

I hold on until each breath is a gasp and my body feels lined with lead. Warm liquid trickles from my right nostril.

"Ella!" Parker yells.

Without warning the current breaks, leaving nothing inside my weary chest but a sluggish heart and burning lungs. I have nothing more to give, and there's relief in the knowledge I can let go. The hand holding Rose's falls to the floor. I open my eyes, but the room spins and I collapse, Parker's voice a distant call as I plunge into darkness.

19

Mariella

I wake on the floor beside Rose's bed, pressure lingering over my temples. Parker's sitting beside me, no longer translucent, but vivid and whole. My heart stutters at the sight of him, his blond brows drawn in, a bloody hand pressed over the wound on his torso. He lets out a breath when our eyes lock, but the tension in his body lingers.

I push myself into a sitting position and lean against Rose's bed frame. Every muscle aches like I've run a marathon. "How long was I asleep?"

"Over an hour." His mouth tenses and he averts his gaze, but then it's back on me. "Why didn't you stop?" he asks. His nostrils are flared, the back of his neck red. "Your nose was bleeding."

I touch my fingers to the dried blood on my face. "Are you . . . angry with me?" I ask.

He turns away as if he can't stand to look at me. "I'm angry at myself. I never should've put you in that position. If something happened to you—"

"I'm fine. And it was my decision to try."

He shakes his head, still avoiding my stare, but I dip my head and force our eyes to meet. "Parker. I'm fine."

He studies me for a moment, and I offer a closed-lip smile to emphasize my point.

His shoulders drop. "Never do that again."

"Promise." I eye his blood-slicked hand, still gripping his oozing wound, and my throat constricts. He must be in agony, but all I can do is sit here, uselessly watching him bleed until Rose wakes. When will that be? Did I do enough to help her? Why is she still unconscious?

A beat of sweat rolls down Parker's temple, his golden skin paler than before. "How are you?" I ask. *Please let him be okay.*

"Still here." He smiles, suppressing his wince when he stands.

I crane my neck. "And Rose?" She's curled on her side, sleeping soundlessly.

"She looks terrible because of the blood, but she'll be alright. Thanks to you."

I press my hand to her forehead. "Her fever's broken." The touch rouses her, but she slips back to sleep, her forehead smooth and full lips parted. "I've never seen her this peaceful. She's normally kind of scary," I whisper.

Parker stares at me flatly. "What are you talking about? She's a placid dream."

I laugh into the back of my hand, my heart swelling when he laughs with me. "I'm going to clean some of the blood off of her."

Standing on wobbly legs, I slip into the bathroom and wash the blood from my face. When I return to the bedroom with supplies for Rose, Parker is sitting on the edge of his bed. I slip off Rose's jeans and black, long-sleeved shirt, leaving her in a cropped tank top. The tip of a tattoo extends beneath the elastic.

Parker sits in silence as I wipe the blood from Rose's body, but my skin tingles with awareness under his heavy stare. When I'm finished, we leave Rose to rest and move into their tiny living room. The book he asked me to keep safe remains on the dining table, his blood soaked into the leather.

"Must be important," I say, tilting my head toward it. I pull up a chair and Parker leans against the table beside me.

"We're hoping it holds the answers to getting my traveling back. It's what we left for."

"Where did you go?"

"Five years from now," he says casually, as if it's *normal* to travel to another year.

I'd meant my question literally and was expecting a place, not a year. Frankly, with all of Parker and Rose's secrets, I'm shocked he answered at all. I can't comprehend anyone being able to jump between one year and another, let alone *five*. I trace Parker's line of sight outside the kitchen window. "Has much changed between now and then?"

"A bit." His mouth pulls to the side.

"Did you see me?" I ask before I can stop myself.

Parker's eyes widen and he sits a little straighter. "No."

My chest sinks. He and Rose have been here for six months, yet he returned to his time and didn't see me. Was our future relationship simply an amicable one?

"*Nothing memorable.*"

The words still sting.

"Why not?" I ask.

"Well . . . we were there for such a short time, to get

McGregor's journal, so we didn't see anyone." He shifts his position and flinches.

"I wish there was something I could do to help you," I say. "If only I could touch you, I could put pressure on your wound or at least bandage it. Give you painkillers. You really need stitches."

The corner of his mouth pulls into a cheeky grin, tugging on my heart, and lower in my abdomen. "You're not worried about me, are you?" He leans toward me, irises the color of warm honey. "If I could touch you, the last thing I'd be concerned about is the wound on my chest."

My breath hitches in my throat, and I spend a moment lost in those eyes. "Why is it you can touch Rose and the book, but you can't touch me?" I clear my throat. "Or open a door?"

"I can touch Rose because she's holding me here, and the book because it's from my time."

"But you can lean against this table?" I gesture before me.

He runs his hand along the light pine surface. "Yes, but I can't move it or feel the texture of the wood." A drop of blood falls from the hand pressed against his wound, disappearing before it hits the wooden floor.

I swallow, coaxing moisture into my mouth. "What happened?"

"We were caught stealing that journal." He inclines his head toward the blood-soaked book. "Rose traveled us away, but the bullet had already hit. I'm sorry, Ella, I shouldn't be dragging you into this."

"It's okay. I'm glad I was here to help Rose. Can subconscious travel affect someone in the same way as normal time travel?"

Parker frowns. "I don't think so. Subconscious travel happens when you're sleeping and your brain's relaxed, so it exerts little energy. It *can* make you tired and give you a headache if you're traveling multiple times a night. Plus, emotionally charged memories draw you in, and the echo can be intense."

"What does that mean? The echo?"

"When you travel into your past, you—and anyone you've brought with you—feel an echo of the emotions you experienced in that moment in time. It can be strong for some travelers, and not so much for others. Neurovida teaches you to dull it down, but if the memory is emotional, the echo can be hard to suppress."

Flashes of my dreams rush through my mind. My joy when I'm in my mother's warm embrace or the nervous excitement flooding me when I kiss Parker. My cheeks heat, my heart falling into that flustered rhythm only he can evoke. Does he know how he consumes my nights, like a thief holding my subconscious hostage? "Before you knew about time travel, did you subconsciously travel?"

"Yes, but I thought I was dreaming. And you can call it *sub-t*. That's what we all called it at Neurovida."

I peer over at him. "Did you ever sub-t and see me?"

"You've never asked me that before," he says, a hint of surprise in his voice.

I sit back in my chair. "This is so strange. You talk to me as if you've known me for years, but we've only just met, and I still know nothing about you."

Parker eases back against the table, surveying me with a gleam in his eye. "What do you want to know?"

I want to know everything about you. The thought

hits me at once. Every tick, habit and mannerism. Where did he grow up? What was his life like before Neurovida? Before he was running for his life? I want to watch him wake up in the morning and put himself together, glimpsing those private moments no one else gets to see.

I study the sloping curve of his top lip, the cocky crinkle beside his eyes. "Will you answer truthfully?"

"What are you insinuating?" he asks, feigning offense. "I'll answer your questions. As long as I'm not telling you anything that will get me into trouble with Rose later."

"Fine." I cross my arms and lean them on the table. "How old are you?"

"Twenty-four," he answers immediately.

"And how old were you when you were recruited?"

"Twenty-one."

I worry my bottom lip as we stare at each other for a beat, his amber eyes heating when they flicker to my mouth. "Had you seen me in your sub-t before we met for the first time?"

He groans. "Thought I'd dodged that question. No, it wasn't until after we'd become Alphas that I saw you in my sub-t."

I mask my disappointment. Obviously, my unhealthy infatuation with Parker isn't reciprocated. "Alphas?"

He glances at the bedroom door again. "It's the name of our group at Neurovida. Alpha because we were the first group of our kind."

"Alpha, huh? Sounds a little pompous."

Parker's golden eyes dance with amusement. "That's what you said when we thought up the name."

It's unnerving that he's met a version of myself I'm yet

to become and has recollections of conversations I'm yet to experience. "When we met at Neurovida, did I ever mention any of this? You and Rose showing up and asking for my blood?"

We both ignore the chime of my phone.

"No. As far as I knew, we'd never met before your first day at Neurovida."

I imagine meeting a younger version of Parker for the first time, and a smile plays on my lips. "What's your last name?"

"It's just Parker," he says with a shrug.

"Parker who?"

He rubs the back of his neck. "When you get recruited, you pick a name, and mine's Parker."

My mouth drops open. "Parker isn't your real name?"

"No," he says, his gaze dipping to my hand fiddling with the charm on my necklace. A haze passes over his eyes, but he blinks and it's gone.

"Well, what is it? Is it—Jimmy?"

A brief laugh escapes him. "No. *Please* never call me that."

"Then why does Rose call you Jimmy?" Does she know his real name, or does he keep secrets from her too?

Parker groans, tilting his head to the ceiling. "Because she's a monster. Look, it's a term of . . . endearment, for lack of a better word. It might not make sense now, but when you get recruited, you pick an alias, take the oath, and everything in your life before that moment becomes a secret."

"Why?" I ask.

"To protect yourself. To guard your past. To—"

"Stop time travelers showing up and asking for your blood?" I joke, but Parker doesn't smile.

"Yes! Neurovida erases all records of your former life.

Birth certificates, school report cards, everything. Even your electronic footprint vanishes. We glimpse each other's pasts during training, but eventually Neurovida teaches you to conceal every detail."

What would it be like, getting to know someone with so many rules and stipulations? "If we couldn't tell each other anything about ourselves, how did we get to know one another?"

Parker shrugs. "We told each other things, just nothing with *identifying details*. No names, dates or places. It's not as bad as it sounds. Besides, you aren't completely dictated by your past, are you?"

"I don't know," I wonder aloud. "But if you don't know about my past, maybe you don't know me as well as you think."

Parker cocks an eyebrow. "You're quiet, but it's not because you have nothing to say. You're constantly mulling things over in your head, but you never have an ulterior motive. You're forgiving and selfless and smart. You have a small, triangular birthmark on your left leg. When you're determined to do something, you won't let anyone get in your way, including me. Nothing gets you riled up like injustice, especially toward the people you care about. Your favorite book's *The Night Circus*, and you'd pick reading over TV any night of the week. You're right, I don't know everything about your past, but I know you . . . better than I know myself at times."

I'm speechless. He isn't bluffing. Does he know the intricacies of all the members of Alpha or am I the exception?

My cheeks flush. My birthmark is high on my inner thigh, only visible if I'm wearing just swimmers or underwear.

My heart skips a beat. *Has he seen me naked?* I take a deep breath. "What are we to one another in the future?"

A stillness washes over him. "Next question."

"That's not fair."

"It's not, but I can tell you firsthand there's no fun in living if you know how everything's going to turn out. Knowing things you shouldn't isn't healthy."

"But there's so much power in having that kind of knowledge. Say the world was ending. I'd want to know so I could do things before it happened."

An intrigued smile crosses Parker's face. "Oh yeah? Like what?"

I laugh, and Parker's gaze tracks my hand as it covers my mouth. "I don't know." I pause. "I think . . . maybe I'd live life a little more spontaneously? I'd go out more with Anna—and meet her friends." A slow grin creeps across my face. "Start ticking off my bucket list. Buy a plane ticket last minute and live in another country. Travel the world. Throw caution to the wind and see where life takes me."

Parker's staring at me with wide eyes, the ghost of a smile playing on his lips. "What?" I ask.

"I like this side of you," he says.

I scrunch my nose. "Am I different to my future self?"

Parker pauses, his mouth tugging to the side. "A bit. In the future you're more—" His eyes narrow. "Shy isn't the right word. Reserved, maybe?" *Reserved?* The dream version of myself seems anything but. "Once you got to know me, it didn't take you long to speak your mind." The corner of his mouth kicks up. "Or call me on my shit. You were intelligent and beautiful, of course, as you are now."

My cheeks warm.

"And you almost *never* blushed," he adds. "You should do it, you know? Start living your life."

I roll my eyes. "Just because I won't give up my responsibilities and party every night doesn't mean I'm not living my life."

"No, but for the time we were watching you, there weren't any classes missed or crazy nights out with Anna."

"There was *one*," I say with a scoffing laugh.

"That was after." Parker leans toward me, and every cell in my body tingles with a nervous energy, like water simmering in a pot. "I mean it, start living. Do all those things you just said you would. You only live once, so you should live every day without regret."

I eye him. "I'll work on it." Sheets rustle in the bedroom, and Rose sighs in her sleep. "What was Rose like when you first met her?"

Parker laughs. "Exactly the same as she is now. Argumentative, opinionated, angry at the world," he says, and though his words are unkind, the light in his eyes betrays him.

I rest my head on my hand and stare up at him. "And what about you?"

"What about me?" he says with a lazy smile.

"What were you like when you got recruited?"

Parker barks out a quick laugh. "Young and dumb."

"What's changed?" I ask with a tiny smile, and Parker feigns offense.

"Fair call. It did take me a while to see what was right in front of me." He stares at me with a molten thirst in his eyes, as though he won't make the same mistake again.

My breath hitches. "What name do you call me in the future?"

"Next question."

Damn it. "If you don't tell me, I might pick a different name when I get recruited. What if you being here changes my decision and I'll never know?"

Parker laughs. "I thought you weren't going to Neurovida."

The smile on my mouth falls. "I'm not," I say.

"You are. And your name won't change."

"How can you be so sure?" I lean forward. "Have you ever tried to change the past?"

"Next question," he says, and I huff, shrugging off the twitchy feeling in my arms.

"Isn't it disconcerting calling me Ella after calling me something else for so long?"

Parker leans forward, his body tense, and an emotion I can't read flickers across his face. "Yes."

Am I making him nervous? I smile, brushing my fingertips over my lips.

Parker tilts his head, watching me with furrowed brows. "You did that in the future, too. Hid your smile. I always wondered why."

I shrug, glancing at my hands. Why does he drag his hands through his hair when he's at a loss, or tuck his hands into his pockets when . . . okay, I'm still figuring that one out.

"Look at me," he says, a hint of anguish leaking into his tone. I glance up, and his honey-hued eyes lock with mine, holding me in place. "Your smile's beautiful. Don't hide it."

His gaze drops to my mouth and my breath catches in my throat. "I don't understand. If it's *my* name, why can't you tell me what it is?"

Parker sighs. "Why can't you enjoy what you have now? Live in the moment. If you spend too much time focusing on the future, you might miss what's happening here in the present." My phone chimes again, and I pull it from my pocket. An unread message from Silas illuminates the screen.

"Do you need to get that?" Parker asks.

Shaking my head, I place the phone face down on the table. "It's my—a guy I used to know. We're not friends anymore."

"I don't mind," he says, tilting his head.

I pick up my phone and read the message from Silas:

About to leave for work. Message when I'm back.

I roll my eyes. He's always had a way with words. I type a quick reply and put my phone in my lap.

"All good?" Parker says.

I search for a hint of intrigue or jealousy, but I find none in his earnest gaze. "We're planning to meet up for the first time in a while and . . . I'm kind of terrified."

"Why?" he asks.

It should feel strange talking about Silas with Parker but *somehow* I know I could talk to him about anything. I look down at my fingers, curling the edge of my phone case away from the screen. "The last time I saw him, I thought he was going to ask me out but instead he cut me out of his life." A hard mass forms beneath my ribs, and I let out a deep breath. "But that was months ago. I'm fine."

"It's okay if you're not," Parker says.

"No, I am. It's just—he was the first person to . . . see me, you know?" I peer up at Parker, that pained expression still creasing the corners of his eyes.

"Was he the first person to see you, or was he the first person you let in?"

I exhale. "I don't know."

"Well, he's an idiot," Parker says. He has a talent for making my problems blow away, like dry leaves in an autumn breeze. "And I know I can't tell you much, but seeing as I know *everything* about you, I can tell you that you're much happier without him."

I roll my eyes. "I thought you weren't supposed to tell me things about my future."

"You're right, I shouldn't." His eyes light, a roguish smirk on his face. "But I'm slightly biased on this one. Poor old Glenn."

"*Ha.* Maybe you don't know as much as you think. His name is Silas," I say, and Parker's brows twitch. "What?"

He searches my face. "When I first met you, you said you'd recently broken up with a guy called Glenn. You said you got together at the start of college."

"Well, I'm sorry to disappoint, but Silas and I were never dating, and there's definitely no Glenn. I will keep an eye out for this mysterious stranger, though."

"Maybe you go through a few before you get recruited," Parker says, imitating sincerity.

I'm tempted to slap the wide, dimpled grin off his face. "What are you implying?"

"Nothing," he says, holding his hands up in the air. "Like I said, you don't want to have any regrets."

I blow out a breath. "You make Neurovida sound like a life sentence."

"Not at all. I loved it there, and you will too. But things change when you get recruited. You'll spend every minute mastering time travel. There isn't time for anything else."

Every minute? "What—" My hands still. I'd thought

of Neurovida as an extracurricular activity, but the way Parker's talking about it now . . . "Was I not studying psychology while I was at Neurovida?"

"No. Like I said, Neurovida's a full-time gig. Even if you have a degree, you sign it away before you walk in the door, so there'd be no record of it."

My hands shift to what feels like a growing mass of concrete inside my stomach. Until this moment, I was toying with the idea I might attend Neurovida, meet Parker, *and* continue my studies. But with Parker's words, he's killed that fantasy. I'll need to choose—Neurovida and time traveling. *Him.* Or clinical psychology, my plan since I was fifteen years old.

"I'm sorry. I shouldn't have said anything," Parker says. "This is why knowing things about your future isn't good." His eyebrows draw up. "What's wrong?"

"I just—never considered the possibility that I'd do anything with my life besides psychology."

"You know, you can be a time traveler and still help people. Look at what you just did for Rose, and your powers aren't even at full strength."

I shake my head, pressing my palms into my eyes.

"Please talk to me," Parker says. "Tell me what you're thinking."

I drop my hands from my face. "It's stupid, but I'd convinced myself if I became a psychologist, I might finally be *normal.*"

Parker's irises darken to a burnt bronze, dragging from my fingers, twisted within the fabric of my sleeve, and up to my face. His eyes dart back and forth between mine, as if looking for something beyond them, and he releases a slow breath. "But Ella, you're not normal. You'll never be anything short of incredible."

Heat crawls up my neck, and I force myself to hold his stare. "It doesn't feel that way."

"Doesn't make it any less true." His hand flexes, as if he wants to reach out and touch me. As if he's forgotten he can't. "I wish you could see what I do," he says, and with a forced exhale, his hand drops to his side, curling into a tight fist. "I hate being stuck like this. With no control over my life. I don't want to sound ungrateful to Rose for everything she's doing for me, because I *am* grateful, but,"—his jaw tenses—"I want my traveling back."

How differently we view time travel. He'd kill to have his powers back, while I'd pay for someone to take mine away. And if interacting with the past has no influence on the future besides altering memories—

"Why?" I ask.

"Why wouldn't I?" he asks, tilting his head to the side.

"Because time travel's the source of all your problems. Without your powers, you'd have a normal life. You wouldn't be different anymore."

Parker shakes his head. "These powers don't make us different, Ella. They make us special. We can literally jump through space and time. Plus, being a time traveler lets you relive *any* memory you want. It's a gift."

I let out a self-deprecating laugh. "Living each day once is more than enough for me."

He searches my face. "Can I ask you a question?" he asks, and I nod. "When we first met after McGregor's lecture, why did you get upset about me calling you Mari?"

My stomach twists. "It was my nickname as a kid."

We sit in silence, and my skin crawls.

"Ella," Parker says softly, but I can't bring myself to look at him.

"I'm afraid if I tell you, it'll change the way you see me," I whisper.

"It won't," he says.

"You say that now, but maybe it's only because the rules at Neurovida didn't *let me* tell you about my past."

"Ella, when we met, I was a mess. I was so wrapped up in my own depression, I didn't care who I hurt. You saw every ugly side of me, and you forgave me. Repeatedly. I wasn't worthy of you then, and I'm not worthy of you now. But it kills me to know you'll go to Neurovida and keep secrets from me." He runs another hand through his hair. "And being here with you now, before you're recruited . . . I know it's wrong. But it's made me realize . . ." He tilts his head to the ceiling, as if offering a silent prayer.

"What?" I whisper, my heart in my throat.

He turns his body toward me, golden eyes filled with grief as they lock with mine. "I want to know everything about you, Ella," he says, echoing my earlier thoughts. "Your dreams for the future and your favorite childhood memories. Once you get recruited, most of your life becomes a secret."

My fingers are tangled in the fabric of my sleeve when Parker's hand settles above mine. My heart sinks because I'm desperate to feel the weight of it, for the touch of his fingertips and the warmth of his skin.

"Please trust me?" he begs.

"I do trust you," I say, and truer words have never left my mouth.

His voice thickens. "Then tell me," he says, his voice raw,

and it feels as if I'm standing at a precipice. If I take this step, something will change. Between us and within myself. Something I won't come back from. But that's the thing about Parker, he makes me want to be brave. To be seen. He makes me want to jump.

I suck in a deep breath. "My mom used to call me Mari. She was my favorite person in the world. Every weekend we'd go to the pier and read by the ocean. When I started school, I couldn't understand why no one else loved books as much as me . . . But she did." I let out a sad laugh and wipe the silent tears off my cheeks. "When she got sick, she sent me to boarding school. She said it'd only be for a little while." The words tear at the dormant scar scorched across my heart. "The kids used to sneak around at night and play games. In my first week, they dragged me out of bed to use a Ouija board. I felt so sick. One minute I was in the library, and the next I was outside, naked. It was like I blacked out, or something. Things got worse after that. Some girls made it their mission to torment me."

A cold shiver races up my spine. I can still feel their hands on me. Holding me down, covering my mouth to stifle my screams. The crunching of the scissors as they hack the hair from my head. "They cut holes in my uniforms, snuck into my room and ripped the pages from all my books. Vandalized the walls of my room." The curling, red letters of *Mad Mari* are burned behind my eyelids. Their eyes were always on me, waiting for their next chance to taunt me. Goosebumps blossom over my arms. "They started calling me Mad Mari, and the nickname's still a trigger for me."

"Ella," Parker says, pulling me back to the present. "That

night at school, I don't think you blacked out. I think you time traveled."

My gaze snaps to his. "What?"

"When we first learned to travel at Neurovida, everyone left pieces of clothing behind. It took one guy in the group over two months to learn to keep anything on when he traveled." Parker laughs. "I couldn't tell you the number of times I had to watch him run naked from the room. And he was an adult. As a child, you'd have no control at all, let alone enough to travel your clothes with you. It's rare to time travel at such a young age, but it's the only reasonable explanation. Normal kids don't just black out and come to, naked."

"But I'm not normal, Parker," I say, shaking my head. "Sometimes I get paranoid I'm being watched, and it worsens by the day."

"I used to get that too, especially at Neurovida. I think it stems from watching yourself in your sub-t."

The blood drains from my face. For as long as I can remember, I've been afraid. Of my past and my paranoia. Of ending up like my mother, standing out and being different. But time travel readily explains my strange electrical symptoms and vivid dreams. Could it really explain my paranoia too? I study the square of night sky visible through the kitchen window. "So, you're saying . . ." I stare at Parker with wide eyes. "That nothing's *wrong* with me?"

Parker's brows rise, a smile tugging at his lips. "Well, I mean—you have *terrible* taste in men."

A laugh bursts from my mouth. "I've spent my whole life believing something was wrong with me . . . that I'd never belong anywhere."

The smile on Parker's face falls. "You belong at Neurovida, Ella." His voice softens. "With me."

His words tug at a hidden, sealed part of my chest. Is Parker right? *Do I belong at Neurovida?* With him, and the other Alphas? Even Rose?

"Why do you act differently toward me around Rose?" I ask, surprising myself with the directness of my question. "And when you and Rose first told me about time travel, and I recalled my dream, my sub-t I mean, why did you act as if nothing happened?"

"Isn't it obvious?" he says, his gaze searching mine.

"No." Parker and Rose's relationship is unusual, but it's obvious they care for one another. The heartbreaking concern on Parker's face when Rose was unwell couldn't be faked. Neither could the tenderness in his hand as he brushed the hair from her forehead. An icy burn prickles my chest. "Is it because you have feelings for her?"

"What?" Parker stills, his face scrunched. "Rose and I are—friends, and I didn't rehash your sub-t in front of her because that memory is *ours*. And it's private." He finishes in a raised voice.

The sudden silence rings in my ears. "I—I'm sorry," I whisper.

He stares at his large hands. "I don't want you to be sorry," he murmurs. "None of this is your fault, and I shouldn't be getting defensive. Not with you." His dark blond brows crease, and he looks across at the empty space where a sofa should sit. "It's—Being a time traveler gives you access to a vault of your best memories in perfect detail. I've lost that, and now it feels like those memories are slipping away. If I'm being honest, I'm struggling with it."

My heart sinks. What I'd give to take his pain away. "They're not gone. They're still in your memory."

The corner of his mouth lifts into a sad smile. "It's not the same thing. The most endearing qualities of a person lie in the small details. Their unique mannerisms, the way they pronounce certain words, or the way they—" His gaze darts to my mouth, his voice dropping to a whisper. "I don't want to forget."

"You won't, and as soon as you get your powers back, you'll be able to jump in and out of them whenever you want."

He leans back on the table. "I hope so," he says, more to himself. "I'm sorry if I've been acting weird around Rose. I guess when she's not here, it's so easy to forget—" He exhales, struggling to find the right words. "It's too easy to slip back into the way things were. With you." He shakes his head. "The truth is, I promised Rose I'd stay away from you, and when she's around, I'm reminded of that promise."

"Why does she want you to stay away from me?"

"For your safety. And so our memories don't split when we go home. It's also part of the oath we took at Neurovida. Rose will be furious when she finds out how long you were here." He rubs the back of his neck, thoughts spinning behind his unfocused gaze.

After a moment of silence, the realization dawns on me. "You want me to leave," I state.

He looks up at me, his pleading eyes piercing my soul. "No. That's the thing. I want you to stay. Too much. And every second I spend with you, I'm reminded that if I don't get my powers back I might—" His voice cracks, tension rippling through his body. "And I can't even hold you."

Pressure clamps around my heart. "I'll go," I say, standing and slinging my satchel over my shoulder. Parker edges off the table with a soft groan and walks me to the front door. "Can I come back in the morning to check on Rose?" I ask.

Parker's gaze softens. "Of course."

I offer a tiny smile and open the door. "I'll bring bandages for your chest."

"Thanks. And Ella?"

I halt with my hand on the door handle. "Yes?"

"Please don't mention the whole *anchor* thing to Rose. She doesn't like accepting help, and she doesn't know I used to do it at Neurovida. She'd kill me if she knew I—"

I hold up my hand and offer him another smile. "Parker, it's fine. I won't say anything."

He releases a breath. "Thanks."

We stare at each other for a moment, unspoken words hanging between us. What would he say if he hadn't promised Rose to stay away from me? What would he do if he hadn't lost his powers? If he *could* hold me? I want to ask him, but every second I stay, I'm forcing him to choose between me and keeping his word to Rose, so I turn and let myself out.

20

Rose

My eyelids are weighted, my arms too weak to lift. *Get up.* I propel myself forward, but I barely move. A cold sweat breaks out over my brow. I'm trapped. Defenseless. *Get up.* I sense someone hovering over me and my breathing quickens, adrenaline soaking every aching muscle. *Get the fuck up!* Gritting my teeth, I try again, pushing past my excruciating headache. A choked groan rips from my throat, and a large, familiar hand slips into mine, soothing me like a hit of nicotine. I release a breath and slump back against the mattress.

Since I was a kid, I've wanted to be alone. Safe. In my world of revolving foster homes, the darkness of sleep was my only reliable embrace. Parker's like a comet, tearing through my bleak night sky, garish yet mesmerizing.

"Rest," he says, his temple warm against mine. "I'm here. You're safe."

But I'm not. Not if Matthews finds us. And here I am, bedbound, useless and barely holding on.

Parker gives my hands a squeeze. "Rest," he says again.

Oblivion's steadfast hold slithers through my bones. I fight against it, the shaking of my head nothing more than a pitiful jerk. I need to tell him this is too much.

Darkness engulfs me, one tiny, golden thread winking at me in the far distance, like a star about to burn out.
I need to tell him.

✧

The pounding in my head's so relentless I must still be in the past. I bite the inside of my cheek, longing for my own time, where I'm untethered. Headache-free, my mind clear.
But not safe.
Nowhere's safe.

I push myself into a sitting position and bitter saliva pools in my mouth. I swallow it down and wait for the nausea to subside. How long have I been unconscious? Parker's asleep on the floor beside me, back slumped against my bed. Reaching toward him, my fingertips hover an inch from his short, blond strands.

What I'd give for another life, where we don't spend every waking second running. I drop my hand into my lap and pick at my nails. We have McGregor's journal now. It's almost over. He'll restore Parker's powers and I'll be free from the bars of my own cage.

I contemplate the gentle rise and fall of Parker's shoulders. Would he sleep as peacefully if he knew the damage we've done? The second we appeared in our time at Neurovida, my memories had shifted. Blurred. Tainted. A large debt repaid for the short time we've spent here, and our fleeting interactions with Ella. Fragments of memories race through my brain, the old and new blending together like paint on a canvas until I can't differentiate the two. I bite the inside of my cheek. What will Parker say when his powers are restored, and he returns to the future to find his precious memories spoiled? He'll hate me. Us. What we've done.

I need my vape.

"Parker," I say, my voice weak and croaky.

He jerks awake and cranes his neck to stare at me. Eyes momentarily closing, he lets out a slow exhale. "You had me worried there."

"How long was I out?"

"About twelve hours." He pushes himself from the floor, hissing as he straightens.

My gaze drops to the blood drenching his shirt, and my stomach plummets. "*Fuck*," I whisper. Twelve hours he's sat beside my bed suffering.

"It's nothing," he says, easing down onto the bed opposite and rubbing his eyes. "Just a graze."

"What—" Memories from last night punch through my mind's blurred haze. Guards storming McGregor's office. Parker thrusting me behind him, using his body to shield my own. The mild power whirring through my veins had amplified to a raging inferno, a silent word echoing with every pulsing particle. *Protect. Protect. Protect.* But it hadn't been enough. Why would he put himself between me and a bullet? The world *needs* people like Parker, not pessimistic outcasts like me.

My nails bite into my palms. "Why did you do it?" I ask in a strangled whisper.

"Because you're my family," he says without hesitation.

The words sit heavily on my chest, like I'm buried in wet cement.

"*You're my family.*"

"*I'm here. You're safe.*"

"Everything will be okay, Rose."

A jolt races through me, an unnerving tightness growing in the center of my chest.

How did we get here? Parker and I aren't friends. We barely tolerated each other at Neurovida. And when he gets home and his memories change, he won't want me anywhere near him. He won't stare at me the way he does now, a silent plea in his gaze.

I can almost hear the whispered words, floating through my own head. *Stay. Stick together. Fight.* Dangerous thoughts. I let Flame in. And Matthews. They're the reason I'm in this mess. They are the mistakes I can't make again. *Stick with the plan. We restore his powers, and I'm free.*

"Let me see how bad it is," I say, gesturing to Parker's abdomen. He stands and lifts his shirt, prying back the fabric stuck to his wound with a hiss. I shudder at the crimson streak. "Jesus, Parker."

"It's fine." He lowers his shirt and eases down onto the edge of my bed. "How are you feeling? Honestly."

"Like shit." I rub my temples, memories from our field trip to Neurovida flashing through my mind. "Matthews knew we were going to be there . . . and the way he moved . . . I've never seen anything like it."

At Neurovida, Matthews excelled in time and date accuracy. He was the only Alpha who could jump into the past and return within the space of a second. Even after years of training, none of us could match his precision. The only traveler who rivalled him was Flame. A shudder works its way down my spine at the memory of her standing in Neurovida's dim training room. Pupils racing behind her closed lids, blood streaming from her nostrils. That ominous hum of power and lightbulbs shattering . . . There were times I found the power she possessed truly terrifying.

No wonder Matthews wanted her help. And after his show in McGregor's office—

"He's been training."

"It wasn't that impressive," Parker says under his breath.

I'd forgotten about the fierce rivalry between him and Matthews at Neurovida. "Are you kidding? He traveled directly into the room and skipped through moments in time *by the millisecond*."

Parker suppresses an evil grin. "Did you see the paperweight hit him in the face?"

I smirk. "I think you broke his eye."

"Breaking every bone in his face wouldn't be enough," Parker says with a sneer.

No, it wouldn't. Matthews deserves far worse for what he's done. "He's obviously still working with Neurovida?"

"Looks that way."

I gnaw the inside of my cheek. "I don't understand. If he wants us dead, why doesn't he travel back to the days we were at Neurovida and kill us there?" *Why did he betray us in the first place?*

Parker shakes his head. "I don't know."

I still don't understand what happened the day we fled Neurovida. One moment we were in session like any other day, and the next Matthews was accusing us of being traitors to Neurovida. "If Matthews finds out we're here, we're fucked," I say.

"Maybe." Parker scoffs. "He didn't even have both shoes on last night."

I'd forgotten about Matthews' one pitfall—his inability to consistently travel with all his clothing. Neurovida seems like a lifetime ago. I close my eyes and see the faces of the other recruits—Flame, Bandit and Axis.

"Remember the time we had to travel back one month, and Bandit ended up a year off everyone else?" Parker says, and I laugh but it turns into a cough.

"Or the time you came to class so hungover you vomited on the floor. You were a mess. No wonder she broke up with you so many times."

The grin on Parker's face falls. "I know."

"I miss it." The words are out of my mouth before I can stop them. I miss training and the sessions and the recruits. I miss Bandit and Axis. But I miss Flame the most. She was the binding to our messed-up group, holding us all together, and she didn't even know it.

I wish I'd never gone to Neurovida. The thought sits like a black hole in the center of my chest, threatening to suck me into its impenetrable depth. I'll spend the rest of my life knowing what it was like to have a home ... and what it's like to lose one.

"I miss it too," Parker says, his warm voice filling the room.

I clear my throat. "At least we have McGregor's journal now. Soon you'll have your powers back and we can split." Parker slips his hand into his pocket, our plans to separate hovering in the air between us like thick smoke. "What date is it?" I ask.

"October twenty-six. We were gone for less than twenty-four hours." A shit-stirring grin creeps across his face. "You might finally be getting the hang of this."

"Imagine how good I'd be if I wasn't carrying your massive head with me." I laugh again, and my entire body aches with the movement. "Where's McGregor's research?"

Parker gets to his feet and retrieves the journal from his bed. It lands in my lap with a soft thud. "Lucky it's from our time and I can hold it, or it'd be on the ground outside."

I clutch the book in my trembling hands, as precious to me as the air I breathe. Our last hope.

"We should take it to McGregor," Parker says. "Now."

"We need to sort out your wound first. Find a first-aid kit and—" My bare legs brush against crisp bedsheets, the cool morning air kissing my exposed arms. My head snaps up. "Did you take off my clothes?"

"No." He presses his lips together, gaze dropping to the floor. "Ella was here."

I slump back against my pillow. *Of course* she was. "Parker, when I traveled us to Neurovida, my memories split. Spending time with Ella will only make it worse. You *know* this."

"My memories didn't change," Parker says.

"Because you don't have any powers. Only a time traveler's memories can split, remember?" I exhale and lower my voice. "Parker, the more you interact with her, the worse it's going to be when we go back. You need to leave her alone. *Please.* You're putting her in danger," I say, pointing at him. "Stop using every excuse to spend time with her."

"Excuse?" Parker says, his mouth hanging open. "You really have no idea, do you?" He purses his lips and stares through the open doorway. "I didn't know what to do last night. You were incoherent, covered in blood, and I couldn't help you." His voice breaks on the last few words, the memories of last night reflected in his pinched brows. "Without Ella, we wouldn't have made it through that front door. You owe her a massive thank you."

I pick at my nails. Of course Parker sees it that way. People will tell themselves anything to sleep at night. "Where's my fucking vape?"

Parker tries to snatch my jeans from the floor with a silent wince, but his hands pass through the fabric. "Fuck, Rose," he says. Closing my eyes, I exert more energy to allow him to interact with his surroundings, and my brain protests in piercing jabs. He tries again, pulls my vape from the back pocket of my jeans and slams it down on my nightstand. "You're welcome," he says bitterly as I bring it to my lips.

My shoulders drop at the first inhale. "Go take a shower. You stink." Vapor curls from my mouth. "I'm going to look through McGregor's journal before we give it to him."

Parker stops in the doorway, his posture stiff. "Why?"

"In case there's information about why Neurovida turned on us," I say, opening the old book.

Parker shrugs. "Because of Matthews. McGregor had nothing to do with it, but suit yourself."

"I will," I state to his back as he saunters out of sight.

Exhaling, I scan the first page of McGregor's journal, but his messy, looped handwriting is near impossible to read.

E2360—Sedative

E1007—Catalyst

E2409—Inhibitor

What does it mean? There are pages of mathematical formulas, diagrams of chemical structures, medications and drug reactions. I can't say half of them aloud. I press the heels of my palms into my eyes. I'm not equipped for this.

"Can I ask you a question?" Parker asks, reappearing shirtless in the doorway.

"Fuck off, Jimmy. I'm reading."

"You're hilarious. Do you remember the name of the guy Ella dated before she was recruited?"

My jaw tightens. Why does it matter? Here I am, killing myself so he can have some sort of future, and all he wants is to focus on Ella. I close my eyes. "No," I bite out.

"What about how long they were together?"

I thrust McGregor's journal onto my lap. "Honestly, I don't remember any boyfriend, okay?" I lift the journal and reread the page. How do I know it's safe to give McGregor his research if I can't understand it? It may as well be written in another language.

"She told me last night his name was Silas."

I want to scream. "It doesn't *fucking* matter." The pounding in my head intensifies. Why can't he get it through his thick skull that this version of Ella doesn't matter? That this part of her life's already been lived? Doesn't he want his powers back? Doesn't he want to return to the future?

He does, doesn't he? Or does he want to stay here ... with her? I suck on my vape and roll my shoulders. I don't care.

I don't.

And the second Parker's powers are restored, he won't be my problem anymore. *Focus on the book. One step at a time.*

I shake my head. "Stay out of her life, Parker. We're only here to get your powers back, and then we're gone. Now can you leave me in peace for five minutes to read this fucking book?"

"But it doesn't add up."

I clutch my hands to my head. "Then lucky it's not your job to count, so leave it."

"Fine," Parker says. He worries his bottom lip and edges forward. "There's something else I need to talk to you about. I tried before we went to McGregor's—"

"Parker," I yell. "I swear if you don't fuck off in the next two seconds, I'll send you home and go on vacation."

Parker scowls and exits the room, finally leaving me alone to read. I spend another five minutes inhaling deeply on my vape before the words have any impact. I pore over McGregor's book, searching for hints he or Matthews were going to betray us, but the combination of his messy handwriting and the extensive scientific jargon leaves me understanding very little. I have no choice but to hand McGregor his journal. He's our last hope. Besides, Parker and McGregor were close at Neurovida. *"Like a father,"* Parker said.

But if Parker and McGregor were so close, why did McGregor develop a chemical weapon against him?

21

Mariella

Nothing is wrong with me. The thought bounces around my head the next morning as I return to Parker and Rose's apartment with two cups of soup and supplies to bandage Parker's wound. My heart jitters at the thought of seeing him again. It hasn't resumed its normal pace since I woke this morning with a light chest and my head full of whimsical ideas about what my life could be like at Neurovida. *With him.*

When no one answers my knock, I awkwardly let myself in and cross the tiny living room, a trail of absconded soup dripping in my wake. Rose is sitting up in bed, scowling at the blood-stained journal open in her lap. Escaped strands of hair frame her narrow face, the dark circles beneath her eyes more prominent than ever. She inhales on her vape, blowing apple-scented vapor toward the empty, unmade bed on the other side of the room.

"How are you feeling?" I ask from the doorway.

"Sore," she says without glancing up. A silent moment passes between us before she spits out, "Thanks for your help last night."

"You're welcome." I step into the room and place one of the soup cups on her nightstand. "I figured it might've been a while since you ate."

Rose draws on her vape with glazed eyes, as if her mind's somewhere else entirely.

I place the bandages and Parker's soup on the desk separating the beds, sit on the swivel chair, and twiddle the charm on my necklace. My muscles tighten as we sit in silence, words building in the back of my throat. "I brought bandages for Parker," I say, moments before he saunters shirtless through the doorway, navy chinos slung low on his hips.

"Is my shirt in here?" he asks, head bowed to button his pants. He pauses when he sees me, a grin creeping across his face. "Morning."

Heat floods my cheeks as I take him in, momentarily lost for words. I spare one second for the wound on his upper abdomen, which looks less severe now the dried blood's washed away. Then my gaze wanders over his bronze skin, glowing in the morning sun.

Mouth dry, I trace the veins decorating the prominent muscles of his forearms, the swell of his deltoids, and the muscular hollow below his pecs. I look lower, down each perfectly ribbed abdominal muscle, to the deep grooves in his lower abdomen forming a V that disappears beneath his pants. Anna calls them *sex lines* but, until this moment, I've never entertained the thought.

Rose hasn't looked up, her nose still stuck in the leather-bound book. Has she become desensitized to the sight of Parker half-naked before her? *How?*

"I brought bandages," I mumble, and he steps closer, stealing my breath as he towers over me. He leans down, remnant beads of water glistening on his skin.

"Thanks," he says. He grabs a clean shirt from the bed beside me and turns to Rose. "Anything good in there?"

I bite my lip, dissecting the defined muscles in his upper back and the strong ridges of his shoulder blades. I want to trace the long, muscular indent that runs over his spine, down to—

The blood drains from my face. Parker has a tattoo on his skin, partially concealed by his pants. It looks like the sketch of the strange clock I found in my mother's journal.

"Your tattoo," I whisper.

"Parker, cover up," Rose says with a sigh.

He turns to catch me staring. "Living up to your name there, stalker."

Warmth flushes my cheeks, and my eyes shoot to Rose's chest, to the concealed tattoo I glimpsed last night. "You have it too, don't you?"

Rose and Parker eye each other, and Rose shakes her head.

"Please, tell me. I've seen it before." I glance between them. "What does it mean?"

"We call it the Mark of the Time Traveler," Parker says. "Every member of our group at Neurovida had it."

"Okay, Parker, you've said enough," Rose says through clenched teeth.

My heart stops. The Mark of the Time Traveler. And my mother had a copy in her journal. "Who designed it?" I ask.

Rose and Parker exchange another glance, and there's a small crease between Parker's brows when he turns to face me. "You did," he says. "You—"

"Parker," Rose yells.

He tightens his lips and reaches for his soup, sulking at Rose when his hand passes through the mug.

"Can I see it?" I ask Rose. I'd ask Parker, but only a

quarter of the clock is visible above his waistline, suggesting the rest sits indecently low.

Rose hesitates for a moment, then lets out a loud breath as she scowls at Parker. "I guess you've seen it now." She leans back, lifting the front of her shirt to reveal the same tattoo in the center of her chest, extending underneath her black bra. "Hurt like a bitch."

I'm ambivalent about tattoos, but there's something beautiful about Rose's. The subtle rise and fall of the clock with each breath, as if it's in motion. I study the intricate design, its curving lines and swirling clock with its six unique hands. Vines with beautiful flowers and sharp, deadly thorns climb upward, over a backdrop of the sun setting over the ocean. Far more detailed than the sketch I found in my mother's journal.

Parker steps beside me. "What is it?"

"Are you *sure* time travel isn't genetic?" I ask.

Parker nods. "We studied theory of time travel with McGregor at Neurovida every day for years. If it was genetic, we'd know. Why?"

A heaviness seeps into my limbs. "I found a sketch of your tattoo on a scrap piece of paper in my mother's journal."

"Okay?" he states.

"Why would she have it unless she was a time traveler, or she knew something about Neurovida?"

"Maybe in the future, *you* draw the clock and put it in your mother's journal yourself."

"I didn't draw it." Neither did my mother. Whoever drew the clock used a heavy hand and thick, hurried strokes to craft the circumference of the clock. Nothing like my mother's precise, delicate penmanship.

"I think you need to entertain the possibility that you've got this around the wrong way," Parker says. "Maybe you designed our tattoo based off the picture from your mother's journal because it had sentimental value?"

"Maybe." Another question to ask my mom when Parker takes me to see her.

"Plus, you designed the tattoo specifically for us," Parker adds.

"Parker," Rose warns.

"That's why there's little symbols—"

Rose throws the journal down. "Jesus Christ, Parker," she cries. "Stop breaking your oath."

Parker leans backward. "I'm not."

"Yes. You are. And you're being fucking careless about it. The Alphas would be ashamed of you."

Parker hurtles to his feet and strides toward Rose. "You know what, Rose? The oath is a joke. It's a set of rules Neurovida made up to control us, and the longer it takes you to realize that, the longer you'll be living in ignorance."

"How can you say that?" Rose demands. "The oath is to protect us."

Parker's laugh lacks its usual warmth. "And how safe have you felt these last seven months?"

"You're unbelievable. It's not about Neurovida, it's about the Alphas. Respecting each other's pasts. Protecting our memories. We took the oath together. *All of us.* It binds us, and you're going to throw that away?"

Parker flings his hands out in front of him. "Throw what away?" His voice breaks. "There's nothing left. And as soon as I have my powers back, you're going to make sure of it."

My back hits the wall beside their bedroom door. "I'm going to go," I mutter, startling Rose.

Her eyes widen. "No. You stay, I'll go," she says, cringing as she swings her long, bare legs out of bed. "You can sort out his wound."

I stare at her. "But I can't touch him."

Rose's dark gaze snaps to Parker. "Wow, there's something you didn't tell her? I might die of shock."

"Rose can let me interact with things," Parker says. "It's how I eat, and shower—"

"And stay alive," she barks. "And it takes an extreme amount of mental exertion, which is why I can't do it all the time. Maybe you should act a little more grateful." She turns to me and says, "You can sort it out, Ella." Her narrowed gaze slides back to Parker. "I don't want to waste the energy." She storms into the bathroom, slamming the door shut behind her.

Parker releases a heavy breath and slumps onto the edge of his bed, dragging his fingers through his hair. It's grown in the weeks since he cut it, and the motion leaves dark blond strands sticking out at odd angles. He remains with his head in his hands, the muscles in his neck taut. After a moment, as if remembering himself, he lifts his head and his gaze flickers to me.

I swallow the lump in my throat. His lips are pressed together, tugged up at the corners into an apologetic smile. My gaze snags on the freckle above his top lip and my chest tightens. Mouths shouldn't look like his—thought-dissolving, heart-melting, tongue-tying. One glance at that sexy smirk and my mental capacity plummets. I couldn't string a sentence together if I tried.

I want to ask him more about Neurovida. But the words disintegrate on my tongue when I see the mattress indented under him, the weight of his body pressing into it. My stomach flutters, my heart rate spiking. I can't believe it. I can *finally* touch him.

"Do you want to sit?" he asks, his voice rougher than before.

Cheeks on fire, I manage a small nod and move the bandages from the desk to beside him on the bed. I roll the desk chair forward and I sit, tucking my quivering hands in my lap.

I can't bring myself to make eye contact. Not when he's half-naked and the only time we've touched is in my fiery dreams. *Especially* not when hours ago I awoke from one of those dreams, discontented and wanting, my cold bed a stark contrast to his heated body pressed against mine moments before.

What would he say if he knew in those waking moments how embarrassingly often my fingers slip between my thighs, fantasizing about our tongues colliding and his hands pulling my body against his?

His words from last night fill my mind: *If I could touch you, the last thing I'd be concerned about is the wound on my chest.*

His eyes are glued to me, as if he's waiting to see what I'll do.

I nudge my chair forward, and the brush of our knees sends a burst of energy up my thigh. I suck in a sharp breath.

"Ella, it's just me. Don't be nervous," he says, as if I've known him for years. As if we touch frequently.

I drag my gaze to his, and I'm startled by the intensity swirling in his bright amber eyes. He's staring at me as if he can see right through me, and it does *nothing* to quell my rapid heart rate or the energetic flutter in my stomach.

He starts forward and hesitates, an internal battle raging behind his eyes. Then he reaches out to take my trembling hand and presses his palm to mine.

If the graze of his knee was static electricity, the caress of his hand is lightning, jolting my heart into a frantic rhythm. His skin is warm, his palms lacking the rough calluses from my dreams.

His thumb caresses the inside of my palm, tracing a slow, endless circle that winds me tighter with each loop. I shiver. How can one touch make me feel so alive? Ten seconds in and I want his hands all over me. I need something to distract myself. To give me purpose. I'm here for a reason, aren't I? Frozen under his stare, his thumb still drawing lazy swirls in my palm, I'm having trouble remembering.

His wound!

I tear my hand away and grab a packet from beside him, fumbling with an antiseptic wipe. *Smooth.* As I clean the wound, the muscles in his abdomen tighten.

"Sorry," I whisper.

The corner of his mouth curls as he leans toward me. "Still worried about me, Ella?"

"A little," I admit, placing gauze over the wound. He raises his arms, and I secure it with a bandage. "I still think you need stitches."

"I'll be fine," he says, as if the deep gash is a mere paper cut. "I don't know what we'd do without you, Ella." He reaches for my hand, taking it in his. "Thank you."

Painfully slowly, he lifts my palm to his lips. His gaze flickers to mine before he kisses me, right over the imaginary circles forever etched into my skin, and I feel it *everywhere.* In my lungs, working overtime to produce each breathless exhale, in my heart, hammering against my rib cage, and in every nerve ending firing beneath my skin. I can't believe it. *He's touching me.* The thought reverberates through my mind. This can't be real. I'm terrified if I close my eyes for even one second, I'll find myself back in my bed, having just woken from the most wonderful dream. And yet his hand is still wrapped around mine. Warm and solid and *real.*

He turns my hand to the side, staring at my wrist with a slight frown. "That scar. When did you get it?"

I withdraw my hand, tracing the pale mark with my thumb. "I broke a bone in my wrist almost four months ago and I had to have surgery. It's been a bit of an ordeal. Sometimes it aches so badly I can't draw. Why?"

"I've never noticed it before."

"Well, maybe you don't pay attention?" I tease.

Parker's expression darkens, and when he speaks, his voice is coarse. "When it comes to you, I can't focus on anything else. Especially when you keep showing up here looking like that."

His gaze dips to my black sweater and pleated skirt—more of Anna's designer clothes—and returns to my face with hunger looming behind his amber irises. He brings his hand to my flushed cheek and I lean into his touch. My eyes flutter closed, and I breathe him in—warm cedar mixed with something fresh, like cut grass—and I realize this is the first time I've been able to smell him.

When I open my eyes, he's staring at me, lips parted, body

so still he could be frozen in time. Then, ever so slowly, his thumb sweeps down, grazing my bottom lip until he plucks it like a string.

I focus on that freckle, perfectly positioned above his lip. My personal homing device. Would he taste as sweet as in my dreams? Would his intimate caress ignite the same fire within my bones?

His gaze dances across my lips and he draws in a deep breath. He's looking at me as if—

Wait. Is he going to kiss me?

Whispering my name in an exhale, he tips his head forward to rest his forehead against mine. "You're so young," he says in a pained voice, and my heart plummets—I've been here before.

I search his face. "Does it bother you . . . the age gap between us?"

I brace myself for the letdown.

The excuses.

The lies.

And yet, when Parker's gaze locks with mine, there's a hint of sadness, but it's wrapped in fire and want.

"Age and time could never change the way I feel about you," he says softly, then he closes the gap between us and brushes his lips against mine.

There's a gentle restraint to his kiss, softer than a light breeze tickling my skin. But it's over before I can savor it. Parker breaks the kiss and I nearly slip off my chair. Off the face of the earth. And before I fall, before Rose returns and this moment's stolen from us, I plan to make the most of every second I have with him.

I grasp his face and kiss him again, slipping my tongue

into his mouth, just as I have every night in my dreams. He responds in kind, as if we've done this a thousand times before. In an instant, time shifts from slow motion to fast forward, and the invisible cord holding us back is severed.

Arms wrapping around my waist, he pulls me onto his lap. As my weight shifts, he groans, his body tensing. I lift myself, but he growls in disapproval, holding my body to his.

His large hands move to my face, through my hair and down my back, as if he wants to trace my whole body at once. He grabs the bottom of my sweater and pulls it over my head, resuming his exploration of the exposed skin not covered by my tank top. His touch leaves a path of fire in its wake like a brand igniting me, fueling my racing heart and the rocking of my hips against his.

His unyielding body flush against mine, every powerful thump of his heart mirrors my own, like two drums building to a crescendo. He explores my neck with tongue and teeth, and I close my eyes, savoring the sensation of his lips on my skin and the warmth of his body transferring to mine. He moves to the upper swell of my breast and shivers dance down my spine, a throaty moan escaping my lips. The sound startles him, and he pulls his lips from my skin to capture my gaze with his, as if to check I'm still here. That this is real.

The desire burning in his eyes has turned them the color of molten honey and they bore into mine as we hold one another, our breathing quick and uneven.

"I've been waiting for over six months to hold you again," he whispers against my lips.

So, we are *together in the future?*

I thread my fingers through his hair and tug his face back toward me, needing his mouth on mine. When our lips touch, he's smiling at my unspoken command, no doubt two gorgeous dimples set in his cheeks.

Then he devours my mouth like he's an addict and I'm his next hit. There's no coming back from a kiss like this. I'll die with the memory of his taste on my lips. His hand brushes my knee, gliding up the bare flesh of my thigh and disappearing underneath my skirt, his thumbs recommencing their torturous circles. My breath hitches. His finger toys with the elastic of my underwear—

The rattle of the bathroom door handle jolts me back to reality. Pulse pounding and body aching, I unravel my limbs from Parker's waist, leap back onto the desk chair and catapult away from him, praying my poker face is better than my restraint.

Parker's piercing stare remains glued to me as Rose barges through the bedroom door, clad in her usual black attire.

"Parker, let's go," she barks, snatching the journal off the bed and turning to stare at him expectantly.

"Now?" Parker says, slipping his shirt back on.

Rose's lethal gaze locks on me.

"I should go," I say, grabbing my discarded sweater.

"Ella, wait." Parker follows me to the front door with Rose at his heels. He runs a hand through his hair, glancing between Rose and me. "Rose, can you—"

"You know as soon as we restore Parker's powers, we're leaving and not coming back, right?" Rose says, her voice cold.

Flustered, my body still burning from Parker's touch, I open the door and stumble into the corridor.

"Take care, Ella," Rose murmurs and slams the door in my face.

22

Rose

I slam the door and turn toward Parker. Does he think I'm stupid? That I don't know he's just had his tongue down her throat? That I was oblivious to the fact that his plans changed the *second* he saw her?

The truth pools behind his cunning eyes. Once Parker's powers are restored, he isn't going home. He's going to stay here with *her*. He's tried to tell me for days, but I haven't wanted to hear it. Because deep down, part of me wanted to buy his family bullshit. *He's a liar. I'm better alone.* I *like* being alone. At least I did, until Neurovida ruined me.

"Did you tell her?" I ask him, my forearm clutching McGregor's journal against my chest. The corner digs into my ribs.

He spends a moment taking me in. "Tell her what?"

"About *Flame*."

"*Shh*, keep your voice down," he says, leading me away from the door.

I yank my elbow out of his hold. "She has a right to know, don't you think?"

He studies me for a moment, his blond brows furrowed. "You were the one who wanted to keep that information between us."

"To protect her," I say with a snarl. "Not play fucking house in the past and repress what happened."

"That's not what I'm doing."

I laugh. "Could've fooled me."

"What's going on, Rose? You're not yourself."

I hate the way he keeps his voice level, as if he's reining me in like a wild animal.

"How would you know?" I spit. "We spend every single second focused on *you*." I inhale on my vape, gripping the plastic stick so tightly my fingers ache.

"Where's this coming from?" he asks, moving toward me.

I dodge his touch and pace the room, randomly changing direction without purpose. I never should've let Parker talk me into coming here. Six months I've been stuck here, living with this relentless headache, losing my mind. *Fuck Parker.*

I jerk to a halt. "I want to travel the book to McGregor. To when he first agreed to help us. It'll save time."

Parker steps in front of me. "No way. You're not traveling again. You need to rest."

"I'll rest once he has his journal," I argue, holding it up.

Parker's jaw flexes. "If we're taking it back to when we first met him, it won't matter if we go now or in a week or two."

I slam McGregor's journal down on the dining table. "You're stalling so you can spend more time with her," I yell.

"Are you kidding me?" Parker asks, his face scrunched. "I'm *stalling* because I don't want you to travel so soon after last night. At one point, you nearly lost your hold on me."

I laugh at the ceiling. "So, this is about you?" *Surprise, surprise.*

"I'm worried about you. Your clothes are hanging off you. You barely eat, or sleep for more than three hours straight.

Every day, you become more distant. I don't know how to get through to you anymore."

"Get *through* to me? As if you've ever tried. You'll never be able to see past her, will you? Never be able to see what's right in front of you."

"See past her?" Parker squints, his lips pressed together. "What are you talking about?"

I storm into the kitchen, shoving my shaking hands into my hoodie.

He releases a breath and sits at the dining table. "Rose, come and sit down for a second. Please?"

I pace the short distance between the front door and the kitchenette. *How could I be so stupid?* I promised myself I wouldn't let this happen, but somehow Parker crept in, settling under my skin like a splinter left to fester. *Cut him out*, snarls a dark voice. *Leave him, before he leaves you.*

He stands and approaches me slowly. "Look, it's been a tough twenty-four hours, for you more than me, and I know that's because you're the one doing all the work. But I'm worried about you. You're not thinking clearly."

I storm past him, continuing with my pacing. "Don't pretend to care," I throw behind my back.

"Of course I care." I turn around and he grabs my shoulders, stopping me in my tracks. He dips his head so I'm forced to meet his gaze. "Rose, I fucking care."

His fingers press into my shoulders, and my pulse spikes. "Get your hands *off* me," I scream.

He yanks his arms away as if I've burned him. "Why do you do that?" he yells back. "You think I can't feel it because Neurovida taught you to block it out, but you're so unwell, you don't even realize . . . I've felt it for *months*."

Now he's gaslighting me. Telling me I'm not thinking clearly. Making me believe I'm the one who's crazy, so he can call the shots. He's a fucking monster. I size him up. "Feel what?"

"Your echo. That tightness in your chest, the burning in your gut. The pain. The anger. I feel all of it, and nothing I do makes it better. You *hate* me. Being stuck with me. This burden I've put on you."

His words are like an injection of icy water through my veins. "I—" I fumble for a response. I had no idea he could feel my echo. Here I was thinking I'd been so *clever* suppressing it. I stop avoiding his stare. His pupils are dilated, his eyebrows drawn up at the center. Guilt bubbles in my chest at his tension-lined face.

What the fuck is wrong with me? Parker isn't a monster. He literally took a bullet for me, and he's right. I'm *not* thinking clearly. "I don't hate you," I say.

He steps toward me, so close his woody scent envelopes me. "Then why can I feel it? Every time you look at me. Every time I touch you." He presses his fingers to his chest. "This explosive hatred, right here."

"I don't hate you, Parker," I repeat, my body trembling.

"What is it then? Tell me what I can do to make it better."

I stare out the kitchen window as my shaking limbs turn heavy. Leaning against the sink, I close my eyes. "There's nothing you can do."

"There must be. Tell me." He's beside me now, taking up too much space. Too close. Eyes too bright.

I turn toward him, chewing on the inside of my cheek. He raises his brows—he won't let this go. My shoulders drop.

"Come on, Parker. It's not hate, it's—" I sigh. "I hate . . . the way I feel about you."

His brows furrow. "You—" His eyes widen, his mouth slackening. I've never seen Parker speechless before. And the sadness in his eyes is crushing. "But you like women."

"I mean, not *exclusively*. After what happened, I didn't think I'd ever . . ." Parker's shoulders tense, and I trail off. He's seen more than enough of my memories at Neurovida to understand.

He leans against the sink beside me and runs a hand through his hair, gaze darting around our half-furnished apartment for an answer that isn't there. A way to fix this massive problem that is *me*. I study his profile, the tension in his strong jaw, the movement of his Adam's apple as he swallows. "Let's just—"

"It's fine, Parker." I rush to the dining table and pick up McGregor's stolen journal. "Let's take this to McGregor. There's no point wasting any more time." I check my watch and plant my hand on his shoulder. Our bodies tremble, the throbbing in my head a vicious stab.

"Rose, wait. You're my *best friend*. I owe you my life. And you know how I feel about you." He grabs my hand, gripping it to stop me from pulling away. "But it's like you said . . . I'll never be able to see past her. She took up so much space. I'm not sure there will ever be room for anyone else."

"I know," I whisper, slipping my hand from his. And I really do know. But what Parker fails to understand is how much I don't want to feel this way about him. I don't *want* him to make room for me in his heart. I don't want my chest to palpitate every time I close my eyes and see his tilted grin. I need to make it stop, to give myself a break.

My aching heart. My pounding head. My worn out body. I've spent the last six months putting Parker before myself, but I can't do it any longer. Something's going to break, and I can't let it be me.

Heart sinking, stomach too tight, I hold my hand out to him and put on a firm voice. "I'm taking this book to McGregor, and I'm going with or without you. Decide."

He shakes his head but mutters, "Fine," and takes my hand. "But after this, *promise* me you'll rest."

"I promise." I close my eyes and push the volatile energy swarming my chest into Parker. My body heats from the inside, every cell in our bodies vibrating. "Please don't forget everything I'm doing is for you. To get your powers back."

He gives my hand a squeeze. "Never."

Pain rips through my head, and my power whips through our bodies, carrying us forward through time.

"Goodbye," I whisper, but with the blood whooshing through Parker's ears, I know he can't hear me.

23

Mariella

I cross the corridor and return to Anna's apartment, fumbling with the lock. Once inside, I fall back against the door and press my fingertips to my tingling lips.

"Hey," Anna says, appearing in her doorway wearing a blood red, strapless gown that clings to her hips. "You remember my girl, Emma?"

Her friend Emma appears beside her, wearing an equally gorgeous silver dress with a 1920s edge.

"Hi," she says with a smile.

"You both look beautiful," I say.

"*Duh*," Anna says, beaming, while Emma offers a humbler, "Thank you."

"So, where have you been?" Anna asks, leaning against the door frame.

I want to tell her about Parker. How when he pressed his lips to mine, every thought in my brain flitted away, along with the ground beneath my feet. That by opening up to him, the crushing weight I've been carrying on my shoulders for the past decade has lifted.

That I am a time traveler.

A wide smile spreads across my face, faltering a little because I can't tell her any of it. "I was with Sarah."

"Nice. You should invite her to the ball," Anna says. She disappears into her room and returns with another dress bundled in her arms. "What do you think?"

The navy silk fabric falls from her arms like cascading water and, as she readjusts her hold on the hanger and lifts it higher, my response catches in my throat. The fitted, V-neck bodice is covered in tiny crystals, sparkling against the dark fabric like stars in the night sky. From the waist, the fabric plummets to the floor, the dense crystals dwindling into delicate streaks resembling falling stars.

"I—it's gorgeous."

"Right?" Anna's hand snakes around my wrist, and she yanks me into her room. "Get in here and try it on."

My instinct is to pull away, to retreat to my bedroom and hide. But Parker's words echo in my head. *You should do it, you know? Start living your life.*

We spend the next hour trying on dress after dress, Anna hurling matching shoes and accessories at Emma and me with the fervor of a shop assistant working on commission. Anna settles on an emerald dress with side cut-outs, while Emma opts for a fitted, curve-accentuating lavender dress. Of the dozen designer dresses I haul over my head or shimmy past my hips, none compare to the floor-length, navy dress Anna originally selected for me.

"I'm starving," Anna says after we've rehung each dress and tucked them back into their bags. We leave her bedroom and collapse onto the sofa.

"What should we get for dinner?" Emma asks, tucking her feet underneath her.

In the last hour, I've learned she's pre-med, has the same fervor for fashion as Anna, and isn't half as scary as

I assumed she would be. How many days like this have I missed out on?

"Ahh, sushi?" Anna says.

"Tarogashi's started delivering last week," Emma says, fingers flying over the keys on her phone.

"Yes," Anna exclaims, and they both turn to me.

"Have dinner with us?" Emma asks.

My gaze slides from her kind smile to Anna's ecstatic grin. "Sure. I'd like that."

✧

I step forward into silvery wisps of light spiraling around me, longing for the comfort of Parker's touch. His easy smile. That look he gets about him when he wants something and is about to take it.

I wait for my echo, the nervous thrill I've come to associate with seeing Parker in my dreams, but a cold shiver twists through my body. The pervasive, bright light doesn't repel away from me, but fades to black, enveloping me like a stale blanket. I press a shaking hand to my chest, right over the resounding thump of each staccato heartbeat.

I need to move. Now.

I'm stumbling through the darkness when off-tune music begins. Goosebumps rise over my skin, followed by a rush of adrenaline. My heart rate intensifies, but my legs grow heavy and unresponsive, as if I'm trapped in waist-high mud. My breathing becomes labored, each exhale a deathly rattle.

A warm voice fills my ears, "Stay with me," and I cling to it, a light in this endless tunnel. The darkness seeps into me, sucking the life from my body, clipping short every beat of my racing heart. Something booms in the distance, and the sound is instantly upon me. I squeeze my eyelids shut.

You're dreaming. Wake up.

The sound intensifies, resembling a freight train ringing in my ears.

"Wake up," I yell, the words drowned by the ear-splitting grumble vibrating through my body.

The pressure inside my chest increases as if I'm being crushed from the inside out. I can't breathe. I gasp for oxygen, but with each inhale, less air enters my lungs. The fiery burn of skin scraping off my knees hits me as I crumble to the floor. I take my last shallow breath, and my heart explodes in my chest.

I'm thrown into silence.

I'm floating through quiet darkness, numb and mute, when a deep voice fills my head. "I love you, Mariella." *The words are anguished and raw, as if they've been ripped from the speaker's throat.*

✧

I wake in my bed, clutching my throat, my chest heaving as I gasp for breath. My limbs are live with surging current. I flick it away, willing the electrical buzzing to stop, but I'm shaking so badly my body won't cooperate. My heart is racing, the familiar voice ringing in my ears.

"I love you, Mariella."

How bittersweet the words are, a perfect ending to a terrifying nightmare—

I sit up. What if it wasn't a dream? What did Rose say about subconscious travel? *"It's always within a . . ."*

A fist pounds on my bedroom door. "Ella?" Anna's voice is high and panicked.

Did I just glimpse my future? My pounding heart stutters.

The banging on my door continues, and yet it sounds far

away, as if I'm still in that cold, dark room. *What's going to happen to me?*

I throw off my blankets and hurl open my bedroom door.

"*Ella*," Anna says, searching my room for some unknown threat. "Are you okay? You were screaming."

"I'm fine. I have to go," I murmur, racing past her. I need to speak with Parker.

"Ella, what—Where are you going?" she calls behind me. "Your phone's been ringing."

Storming past the kitchen table, I grab my phone and slip it into the pocket of my pajamas. I'm out the door and across the corridor in two strides, fists aching as I pound on Parker's door.

"You know, as soon as we restore Parker's powers, we're leaving and not coming back, right?"

I bang harder, but no one answers. Parker and Rose have McGregor's journal and the sample of my blood. How long until Parker's powers are restored and they leave? Have they already succeeded? *No.* Parker would come and say goodbye. And he promised to take me to see my mother. He wouldn't lie to me.

Flashbacks of my nightmare race through my mind: the oxygen being sucked from my lungs and the stutter of my sluggish heart. Goosebumps rise along my arms. The same nightmare haunting me since I was seven years old.

My phone vibrates, and I pull it from my pocket, squinting at the harsh, artificial light. Fingers still live with current, I tap a trembling finger on the unread message from Silas: *I'm back.*

24

Rose

I wake to the sound of approaching footsteps. I roll onto my back and stare up at McGregor's ugly face.

"Rose," he says.

He knows who I am. *Good.* My timing isn't too off. Ignoring his extended hand, I stagger to my feet and brace myself against the wall outside his office. My head's pounding, but it's nothing compared to when I was carrying Parker.

Parker.

It feels like something's pushing on my chest, crushing my heart and lungs from the inside out. I place my hand over the aching spot and clamp my eyes shut.

"Where's Parker?" McGregor says.

My stomach clenches. "What's the time?"

McGregor reads the time from his watch, and I adjust my own.

"When did you last see me?" I ask.

"Yesterday, when you disappeared from my office." McGregor gestures to the book in my hand, his beady eyes wide. "Is that it?"

Yesterday. Parker's right, my precision is improving.

"Where's Parker?" McGregor repeats, and my body heats.

"Does it matter?" I snap. "Do you want your research or not?"

I hold his journal out to him, my fingers gripping the blood-stained leather. Am I making a mistake? I'm breaking the oath I swore to uphold at Neurovida, for a man I don't trust. I pass the book over to him, but before I let go, my gaze locks with his.

"I want to help him, Rose," he says. "I want to help both of you. And if I don't hold up my end of the deal, neither will you." His voice is hoarse. "There's much at stake for me, too."

"Good," I say. "Because if you use this book to betray us, I'll go back to the day we met, and I'll kill you."

25

Matthews

I stride down a dim office corridor lined with doors. A halo of light frames the door at the end. They're already inside, waiting for me. My hand hesitates over the handle. I take in a deep breath, compose myself, and enter the room. Besides the single desk and two chairs, it's empty, as if it's been set up for this one, brief meeting.

The hum of the air-conditioner fills the silence, blowing stale air thick with mildew into my face. I don't recognize the bald man sitting behind the generic metal desk. They change seasonally. But they always hire different versions of the same suit—old, clueless men, forever in a hurry and wanting the job done yesterday.

"Sit," he orders, gesturing to the metal chair in front of his desk.

I sit, placing a hand on either knee. I keep my body relaxed, ensuring I don't fidget or adjust my position. The neutral expression I slipped on in the corridor remains in place, a familiar mask slowly melding to my face these past twelve months.

"I'm informed you had the opportunity to catch your targets, yet you were unsuccessful?" His mouth twitches, and he peers at me over the top of his glasses.

"The correspondence from your department wasn't clear," I reply, matching his stare with a trained intensity.

"Apparently not," the man says. "Do you have anything further to report?"

"No. As I've mentioned to your colleagues, these meetings not only waste time, but compromise our position."

"I will be the one to decide what is, and what is not, a waste of time. Have you forgotten what's at stake?"

There's something about this man, perhaps his quiet air of authority, his linguistic style, that screams power with minimal exertion, and has me leaning back in my chair. The metal chills my spine. "No," I answer.

"I'm pulling you from this case. We need results, and you've failed to provide any. Your time will be better spent here."

"What? No." I jerk forward, my façade momentarily slipping before I school it back into place. I've spent twelve months eating, sleeping, and living this case. I've sacrificed everything in my life for it. They can't let me go yet. A bead of sweat runs down my temple. "That would be a mistake. The targets are close. I just need more time."

The man folds his hands together and rests them on the table with an air of boredom. "Your time is up."

"I have a new lead." I'd hoped to keep this information to myself, but I can't be dropped from this case.

The man raises his eyebrows. "Withholding such information is a breach of contract. Why are you only reporting this now?"

"I was looking into it when I received your correspondence. If I'm correct, I hope to have the case closed within a few months."

The man stares at me for a moment. "What lead?"

I clench my hands into fists.

"Don't waste my time, boy," the man says through gritted teeth.

"I've been tracking a member of Alpha . . . in the past."

"Why?" the man demands.

I swallow, but it gets caught in my throat. "I believe the others have communicated with her and will again soon."

"*You* haven't been stupid enough to make contact?" he asks, eyes bulging.

I square my shoulders, keeping my tone light. "Of course not."

The man stands. "You have two months, and if Parker and Rose aren't dead, the deal's off. Now get out of my sight."

I get up and walk toward the doorway, my heart slamming against my rib cage.

"Wait," the man calls. "Which Alpha are you tracking?"

I force my breathing to steady, but bile rises in my throat. "Mariella Adams."

26

Mariella

My hand hovers over Silas's wooden front door. I should've asked him to meet on neutral ground, at one of the college cafes or the local mall. Standing here on his porch, our past conversations waft in and out of my head with the cool afternoon breeze.

"You don't need me anymore."

"Don't you need me?" I push the words past the sob building in my throat. A subtle shake of his head is enough to tear my heart open.

"Not enough, Mariella."

The words sting far less than before. I rap firmly on the door and it swings open, as if Silas was hovering on the other side. He's wearing his favorite long-sleeved soccer jersey, dark gray sweats, and a solemn expression.

"Mariella." My name sounds like velvet on his tongue.

I often forget how tall he is, and after our time apart, I'm struck by the size of him. I tilt my head for our eyes to meet, his gray-blue gaze scouring me from head to toe. I used to love being at the center of his scrutiny . . . Not anymore. Silas moves toward me and, like muscle memory, I mimic the movement. But before we touch, we both pull up short.

I step away from him, and Silas stares down at me with shadows whirling behind his irises. Clearing his throat, he stands aside. I slip into his cottage, wrapping my arms around my chest as if to ward off the scent of *him*, magnified tenfold in the absence of my medication.

"How are you?" he says, closing the door behind us.

Should I tell him I'm a mess? That I'm barely sleeping and, when I do, my nights are plagued with strange dark dreams, and the two people capable of explaining it all have literally vanished?

Last night I woke to Anna hovering above me, her hands gripping my shoulders, and eyes wide with terror. This morning her perceptive gaze tracked my every move until I left.

I scan Silas's aged wooden floorboards, the pairs of shoes neatly aligned by the door. So much has happened since we last spoke. So much has changed. Silas used to be the person I told everything, willingly. Now I don't want to tell him any of it. "I'm . . . fine. And you?"

"I'm alright. Keeping busy." We stand in silence, until he clears his throat and gestures along the corridor. "Come in."

I lead the way to the living area and sit at his dining table, while Silas moves into the kitchen. After a few minutes, he places a mug of coffee before me and slides into the chair opposite mine, holding a mug of his own. It's as if we've slipped back in time, sitting together at his table, coffee-scented steam rising from my mug. I don't need to take a sip to know he's used my favorite beans and added just the right dollop of milk.

"I'm sorry about your house," he says. We exchanged a few messages in the lead-up to my visit, so he knows about the fire and my new living situation. "What happened?"

I take a sip and recall the events of the fire. Silas stares into his drink as I speak, the mug encased between his large hands.

"I'm sorry," he says when I finish, and his gaze flickers to mine.

"Me too." I clutch the charm on my necklace. "Still feels strange not living there."

"How's living with Anna?"

A smile tugs at my lips. "She wants to party all the time, and she's really hard to say no to. But it's good." I hesitate. "Her friends are nice, too. How's work?"

His mouth pulls to the side, landing somewhere between a smile and a grimace. "Awful."

"I'm sorry."

"It's not your fault." He gives me a small smile, but the tension doesn't leave his eyes. "In your voicemail, you said you needed something?"

That's Silas, always straight to the point. I take another sip of coffee and release a breath. "I'm trying to find a copy of my mother's death certificate."

Silas's dark brows furrow, his eyes abruptly lifting to mine. "Why?"

He already knows everything about me, so there's no point in lying. "I found one of her old journals after the fire and the entry dates don't line up. There's no public record of her death, and the hospital lost her chart. But then I thought— the police have access to those sorts of records, don't they?"

A look of pity crosses his face. "Mariella, your mother killed herself," he says softly.

My fingers tighten around my mug. "But what if she didn't? What if she wasn't mentally ill? I need to know, before I waste my whole life trying to diagnose her."

"Waste?" he says, tilting his head. "Becoming a psychologist is your dream."

It *was* my dream, back when I didn't think I had a choice. Before I got a taste of what life might be like without the weight of my mother's disease hanging over my shoulders. Before I knew about time travel and Neurovida.

Before I knew about Parker.

"I don't think it is anymore," I whisper into the dregs of coffee at the bottom of my mug. I feel Silas's gaze like a cool chill on a winter's night, and I glance up at him. He's sitting impossibly still, his expression unreadable. A closed book since the day we met.

"Since when?" he asks, his voice taut.

I bite my lip and lower my hands into my lap, curling the sleeve of my sweater around my fingers.

Silas leans forward, the table creaking under the weight of his tense arms. "You're making a mistake. Don't throw all your hard work away on a whim."

I sit up and place my hands on the coarse surface of the table. "Like you threw me away?"

He leans back in his chair, dark brows raised as he scans the forest outside his living room.

"Why did you do it?" The words slip out before I can stop them, small and fragile.

"Mariella," he warns.

"Please, Silas. I need to hear it."

He exhales through his nose, frowning at his large fists, white-knuckled on the table. "I told you. I was holding you back," he says, his deep voice laced with regret. "You'd turn down invites from Anna and come here instead. And even when I was away, you'd only leave the house to go to class or work. And look at you now." He gestures across the table. "Living on campus. Going out. Making friends. The way it should be. I *knew* without me you'd have a better life."

His throat moves in a forced swallow, his gaze averted to the rough grains in the tabletop. "You're lying," I say. "You pushed me away, and the least you can do is tell me why, Silas. You owe me that. Why wouldn't you let me in? Why wasn't I enough?"

He slams his fist down on the table with such force my mug rattles. "Because you're a *child*. You're eighteen and I'm—We're in different stages of our lives. When we met, I took pity on you, Mariella." His voice breaks and he clenches his jaw. "You needed help and I gave it to you. But like I said, you don't need me anymore. You haven't for a long time. You need to move on with your life."

I get to my feet, tears sliding down my cheeks. "I wish I'd never met you," I whisper. The words don't seem to surprise him; the crease in his brow only deepens. "I feel sorry for you. I think you want to be alone and miserable. I think you're punishing yourself for some messed-up reason, and you justify your actions as noble and selfless. But the reality is you led me on, Silas."

He takes every word I throw at him. I'm not sure he's drawn a breath. Then his stormy blue gaze lifts to mine, and it's as if I'm looking through a window he's always kept shut. "I never meant to hurt you."

But he did. And I'm glad, because never again will I let anyone treat me like he did.

"I have to go."

Silas gets to his feet, his eyes glassy. "Wait. Please." He clears the emotion from his throat. "There's something I need to ask you." He disappears into his bedroom and returns with his shoulders set and a cold expression. He's slammed that window shut, locking his feelings away, nestled among the hundreds of secrets and lies he keeps inside.

"I know it's poor timing, but . . . there's been a development with a case at work. I believe two of the fugitives I'm tracking might be on campus." He places a black-and-white photo on the table before me. "Have either of these people ever tried to contact you?"

I step toward the table, and my blood cools. The figures are unmistakable—Parker and Rose.

"Mariella," Silas says, his voice low. "Have you seen them before?"

"No," I say. "Why would I?"

"They were spotted on campus a few weeks ago at a bar called Tilly's. College security cameras place you at the scene. I need to find these people, Mariella. Do you understand?"

I nod, but I don't understand because none of this makes sense.

"Are you sure you've never seen either of these people before?" Silas asks, his steely gaze holding me in place.

I study the image of Parker and Rose, a screenshot of them running down a corridor. My heart squeezes at the sight of Parker. Is this why he left without saying goodbye? Where is he now? Is he safe?

"Mariella," Silas says.

I can't bring myself to meet his stare. "I said no. Tilly's is always packed with students and I'm not exactly social."

He nods. "If you do, call me straight away. I know things are rocky between us, but I *need* to find them."

"What have they done?"

"You know I can't tell you," he says. It's confidential, like everything else in his life. My skin crawls from the intensity of his gaze, as if he's trying to read my thoughts.

"I have to go," I say, moving toward the front door. "Anna will worry."

He follows me, speaking to my back. "If those people contact you, call me."

"I will," I lie, reaching the front door. I abruptly turn, remembering the reason I came here in the first place. "And you'll find my mother's death certificate?"

"I promise to try," he says. He passes me the photo of Rose and Parker I didn't know was in his hand.

"Goodbye, Mariella," he says. The words sound sad and final.

I step out onto his porch with the photograph clutched in my hand. The door closes behind me, and I stare down at the image. Blinking, I pull the pixelated picture closer. I glance back toward Silas's closed door with my heart in my throat, wondering if he noticed Rose wearing my favorite brown leather jacket.

27

Rose

"It's time you learned the purpose of your recruitment," Nickol says, scanning the recruits before him. His eyes breeze over me, and I stiffen. He's always been my least favorite instructor at Neurovida.

He presses the space bar on his laptop, and a video begins to play. Two men stand in Neurovida's library, their backs to one another as if they're waiting for something. The air swirls on their right, and a dark shape materializes.

I lean toward the screen. The figure is moving around the room so quickly the image is nothing more than a blur. One of the men calls out. The other's hand has barely brushed the gun strapped to his leg when he crumbles to the ground. The other follows half a second later.

McGregor closes his laptop, but the image of the men unmoving on the library floor is burned into my brain. "Meet Fan," he says. "A rogue time-traveling vigilante who kills any traveler who crosses his path. And I want you to stop him."

✧

I yank out of the memory and scan McGregor's cluttered office. I'm sitting cross-legged beside his desk. McGregor's balding head is lowered, scrutinizing every inch of his stolen journal. I replay my memory again while the pendulum of metal balls swings back and forth on his desk, each *click* echoing through my mind. It's been over three months since I gave him his journal, yet he's no closer to finding a cure for Parker than the day he started.

Parker.

I rub the aching spot over my chest. I'm trying to stay positive, but with each day that passes without progress, the pain deepens. At least my pounding migraines have dimmed to nagging aches. I'm still having trouble regulating my emotions, but my body feels lighter. More *me*. I want to bring him back, but I always stop myself at the last moment. It's better this way. I can't take the physical toll of carrying him with me again and I can't risk losing my sanity. I won't bring him back until McGregor has the antidote. Then we'll fix his powers, and I'll say goodbye.

For now, I spend my days alone. Ashamed. Pulling myself back together, debating and reasoning. Justifying to myself that leaving Parker was for the best. I've moved out of our apartment, so I'm not constantly reminded of him. I'm now staying in a tiny dorm closer to McGregor's lab. When I'm not resting, I spend most of my time traveling back to watch over my last few weeks at Neurovida, trying to figure out how everything went so tragically wrong.

McGregor slides a granola bar along the desk toward me without looking up from his reading. "Eat."

I stare at the journal lying open before him and clench my jaw. He's getting nowhere. At this rate, Parker will never get his powers back, and I'll be stuck here, wasting away, waiting. I stand and slam my fists on his desk. "Tell me what I can do to help. Put me to work."

McGregor removes his glasses and stares up at me. "Go home. I don't know why you insist on being here. I've told you time and time again, I'll let you know once I find something."

I bite the inside of my cheek. We both know why I'm here; I don't trust him. But also—

"I don't have anywhere to go," I mumble.

McGregor remains silent, focused on the journal before him. Is he ignoring me? I press my palms into my eye sockets, failing to calm the rage bubbling in my chest. It's become a permanent part of me, pressing on my lungs, exacerbated by every second I sit in this office hopelessly waiting. Is this some of what Parker could feel?

I stretch my legs and circle McGregor's tiny office. What if Parker never gets his powers back? He'll spend his life in danger. Sweat prickles the back of my neck. How long until Matthews catches up with him? I grind my teeth and glance back at McGregor.

Is he even trying? If anyone can figure this out, it's him, right? It's *his* journal, for fuck's sake. If my pulse would stop pounding in my ears, I could help McGregor with *something*, instead of lingering here like an idiot.

Who am I kidding? I'm not a scientist. I didn't even finish school. I'm useless.

Useless. Useless. Useless.

And when Parker dies, it will be my fault.

I grab a trophy from the bookshelf and hurl it across the room. It damages the wall, hitting the floor with a resounding clang. McGregor doesn't even look up.

I storm toward him with my hands on my head, fingers tugging at my roots. "Let me help," I demand. "Give me something to do."

McGregor throws down his precious fountain pen. "Fine. Get me another blood sample."

"Something else," I say through my teeth.

"If you want to help, that's what I need," he says.

"Why can't you use the sample I already got you?"

"It's too old," he says, retrieving his cardigan from the back of his chair and sliding his arms through the sleeves. "I'll need much more over the coming year if I'm going to figure out how to inhibit time travel and then reverse it."

He may as well have drenched me in a bucket of iced water. "*Year?* What the fuck, McGregor? I can't leave Parker for that long. He's not safe."

"Then go get him." His focus returns to the journal. "Even better, go stay with him. Rest. Check back within the month."

Not a chance. I gesture to the journal. "It's all there, isn't it? What else do you need?"

"Time," he states, removing his glasses and rubbing the bridge of his nose. "This journal contains a sliver of the findings gathered from years of research into a subject which is exceedingly complex. It is therefore up to me to fill in the gaps." He leans back in his chair. "I also don't have access to the technology my future self has, *and* I need to figure out what was done to Parker to take his ability away before I can develop the antidote. And to do that, I'll need more samples." He slides his glasses back on and returns to his reading, his dismissal clear.

I push away from his desk and hover by the doorway. Is McGregor really having as much trouble as he says he is? Or is he stalling?

"Are we going to have a problem?" he asks.

I throw him a look of hatred and storm out of his office. Outside, I flip the hood of my sweatshirt over my head and cross the yard toward Ella's apartment building, snow crunching beneath my boots.

How long has it been since I last saw Ella? How am I going to explain Parker's absence? I shake my head. I'll keep the details to a minimum and ask for her blood outright. She's helped us before.

She helped Parker before, not you.

So that's how I'll frame it. I'll make it all about Parker.

Because isn't it always?

28

Mariella

"Ta-da," Anna says, pushing me in front of the full-length mirror in her living room.

She's spent the last hour tweezing, curling and styling, all to prepare me for tonight's psychology ball. A transformed girl stands before me. My beautiful navy dress plunges indecently low on my chest, loose curls falling around my face, makeup contoured to perfection. My blue-brown eyes are enhanced with smoky eyeshadow, my lips a creamy pink. Anna's even managed to hide the bags under my eyes.

"Well, what do you think?" Anna asks.

"I love it. Thanks Anna."

"No problem, babe. I'm going to put my dress on," she says, ducking into her bedroom.

Laughter in the corridor draws my attention to our front door, my mind jumping to Parker and Rose's door opposite. During the first two weeks of their absence, I occasionally knocked on their door in the hope they'd returned. Now, resigned to disappointment, I don't bother. It's been months since I've seen either of them. Thanksgiving and Christmas came and went. Why didn't Parker say goodbye?

I'm desperate to talk to him about my conversation with

Silas. I knew Rose and Parker were in trouble, but I never found out *who* they were running from.

I yawn while I wait for Anna to dress. She's stopped asking about my nightmares, even though my screaming wakes her every other night. My vivid dreams have intensified in Parker and Rose's absence, playing on repeat during my sleeping hours. My mother by the ocean, Parker kissing me, followed by my nightmare—the violent booming and suffocating darkness before an unsettling silence descends. I wake with my heart pounding in my chest and electricity racing through my body. That smooth, deep voice ringing in my head, "*I love you, Mariella.*" Those emotion-laced words echo through my mind as Anna returns in her dress.

"Anna, you look stunning."

"I know," she says, beaming. "Hey, it's not a big deal, but did you go through the closet in my room?"

"No, why?"

"A few things were in the wrong place." She waves her hand. "It was probably me last night. I was pretty drunk." She eyes me up and down with a knowing smile. "You ready?"

✧

"Drink," Anna screams, pointing a black fingernail at Emma's date, a tall, red-haired guy in a velvet suit. We're on the third round of a drinking game in our apartment common area, waiting for our limo to collect us for the ball. The group is borderline drunk, and almost no one notices the tall, temperamental woman dressed in black who storms past. She disappears down the corridor, leaving a trail of white, apple-scented mist in her wake.

"I'll be back," I tell Anna, springing up to follow Rose. I step out into the corridor and scan the empty space for Parker. Rose stands alone outside my apartment, her long, dark brown hair tied back in a messy low ponytail.

"Can we talk inside?" she asks.

"Sure." I let her in and shut the door.

Her tired, onyx gaze slides over me. "You look . . . nice. Or whatever."

My hands wrap around my bare arms. "Thanks. There's a ball on tonight."

Rose nods and checks her watch. We stand in awkward silence, avoiding each other's direct line of sight. I have so many questions I want to ask her. "Where is he?" I blurt.

Rose tucks her hands into her hoodie and turns toward the sofa, taking in the colorful items of clothing draped around Anna's living area. "Parker isn't with me anymore."

The energy within my stomach dissipates. "I don't understand. Did he get his powers back?"

"That doesn't concern you," she says coolly.

"Yes, it does," I fire back. "He promised to take me to see my mother. To find out if she was a time traveler."

Rose whips around and strides toward me, the tendons in her neck taut. "Time travel isn't genetic. Leave the past alone and accept you won't see Parker until you're recruited to Neurovida."

I study her butchered nails and the dark rings under her eyes. Is she trying not to shake? "Is that his decision or yours?" Rose scoffs, and I step toward her. "What else aren't you telling me?"

"There's a difference between lying to you, and not telling

you things you don't need to know," she growls, straightening her spine.

"Well, now I need to know. Because you and Parker disappeared without saying goodbye, and I've had police interrogating me."

"What?" she blurts.

"They're looking for you."

She grabs my shoulders. "Ella, listen to me. That wasn't the police. They don't know Neurovida exists, or anything about time travel."

"I promise you it was the police." I storm into my room and return with the photo Silas gave me. "The officer showed me this."

Her face stills as she takes the photograph from my hand. "What did you tell them?"

"Nothing. I've been waiting to talk to you first because I don't know what to believe."

"Thank fuck. Never tell anyone we were here."

I throw my hands up in the air. "Great. So now that I'm lying to the police for you, I need answers. I've been having this dream, and I think I'm sub-ting." I shake my head. Dark visions flash before my eyes and goosebumps rise along my skin. "Something about it is *wrong*, Rose. What happens to me?"

"Nothing," she says, a little too quickly. Judging by the firm set of her jaw, she'll never give me the answers I'm looking for.

I sigh. "What do you want?" The words have far less fire than I'd intended.

"I need more of your blood," she says.

I laugh. "You're joking. Why should I help you if you won't even be honest with me?"

Rose closes her eyes and exhales through gritted teeth. "Because if you don't, Parker might die. Don't you get that? Without his powers, he's in danger, Ella."

So, he doesn't have his powers back. Then where is he? "Why? Why are the police after you? I don't understand—"

"Which is the way it should be. *Jesus*, Ella. Wake up. People have come here questioning you, which means you're being watched," she says, and the hairs on my skin prickle. "Not knowing could save you. Fuck, can't you see I'm trying to protect you? If anything happens to you or Parker—"

She abruptly turns away from me, pressing the back of her shaking hand to her lips. "Fuck," she whispers. "It's this." She gestures around herself. "Traveling, I mean. It's not *normal* to spend so much time in the wrong year. It's messing with my head. I wake up, and I don't know where I am anymore. I can't get more than an hour of sleep at a time because my sub-t is out of control. It's always worse when you're in the wrong time. I have nightmares all night long and when I wake, I'm in a different kind of hell, and there's never any break."

Rose is killing herself for Parker, but with her hard exterior, it's so easy to forget. "Wait here."

I duck into my room and grab the sleeping pills I found at Silas's place. "Maybe these will help?" I say when I return to the living area and hand them to Rose.

She rotates the bottle to read the label. "*E2409. Take once at night.* What are these?"

"Sleeping pills. It's a long story, but my friend Silas booked me in with a psychiatrist. He misdiagnosed me with a sleep disorder. Drowsiness is obviously a side effect, but it also stops my sub-t. They'll help you sleep."

"I don't want them," she says, wiping her eyes.

"Take them," I insist, stuffing the pills into her hand. "Even if you only take one every now and then—to get a good night's sleep."

She smiles, offering me a glimpse through her rock-hard exterior. "You know, the only reason I agreed to help Parker was for you? Because of what he meant to you, or will mean, in your future. You were the first true friend I ever had."

"She doesn't like accepting help." The words Parker spoke when Rose was unwell. But all she does is help Parker. When was the last time she put herself before the needs of others?

"We might not be besties yet, but I'm still here for you, Rose. And so is Parker. He'd want to be with you."

Rose shakes her head. "I can't carry him with me anymore. And it's better this way. It will be easier for us, when—" She draws in a sharp breath. "When we split."

"What do you mean?"

"I mean . . . after Parker gets his powers back, we're going our separate ways," she says, keeping her gaze low.

I step toward her. "I don't understand. Did you two have a fight?"

Rose stares at me with wide eyes. Her voice lowers. "Not yet." She shakes her head. "We always planned to go our separate ways, and when Parker realizes the damage we've done . . . It's not good, Ella. He'll leave."

"How can you say that? He loves you, Rose."

She shakes her head. "He doesn't."

"Of course he does. Every time you were sick, he would barely step outside your bedroom, let alone leave you." I let out a humorless laugh. "I may know nothing about you, but I do know Parker, and so do you. He'd never abandon you. Have a little faith. Has he let you down before?"

Rose grimaces. "Can you just let me take your blood? McGregor says he needs it."

I exhale. "Fine. But don't get any blood on my dress or Anna will kill me."

Rose grabs her bag, and we sit on the sofa while she takes six vials of my blood. When she's done, she pulls the needle from my skin and I wince.

"Thanks," she grunts and shoves the vials of blood into the pocket at the front of her hoodie. Troubled thoughts tumble around in her bleak onyx gaze. "Get on with your life. And stay away from those police." She storms toward the front door and halts, frowning at the handle. Her sharp gaze flickers to mine. "I'll need to travel from here. Now that you're being watched . . ." She shakes her head, cursing under her breath.

Silence stretches between us. "Will you at least tell me where he is?" I ask, and she stiffens.

"Somewhere he can't hurt you."

"Parker would never hurt me," I state.

"Every second we spend with you, in a time that isn't ours, *we are hurting you*." Squaring her shoulders, she closes her eyes and lowers her head, drawing a deep breath past her full lips.

I rush toward her. "I don't believe that." I *can't* accept I won't see Parker until Neurovida. "Rose, wait. When am I recruited? Please tell me. Just this once, *please* give me a straight answer." I grab her forearm. "Please?"

Rose studies me for a long moment, chewing on the inside of her cheek. "Two years. You won't see him again until then." With a sad smile, she closes her eyes and disappears, my medication bottle forgotten on the hallway table behind her.

❖

On the way to the ball, the limousine stops intermittently along the river as planned. Anna pulls me into a few photos with the rest of the group before I slip away and stroll beside the frozen river, the city lights twinkling in the distance.

Two years.

Two years until I'll need to decide. Psychology or Neurovida. Two more years of waiting, as I've spent my adult life to date. Waiting those agonizing years to leave the toxic environment of boarding school. Waiting for Silas to let me in. Waiting to start college. Waiting to become a psychologist. To find out what happened to my mother. Waiting to be recruited to Neurovida.

And then? When am I going to stop waiting and live my life? Really live it, without fear or hesitation? How many times have Rose and Parker told me to live my life to the fullest? How many times has Anna?

I can't keep waiting. I *need* to make a change, and it needs to be now. I won't spend the next two years waiting for Parker, or Neurovida, consumed by dreams and nightmares. If I want a chance at a normal life, I need to start now.

I spend the night drinking, dancing and laughing with Anna. By the end of the night, my feet are aching from hours of assault in high heels. After sitting at a table watching Anna make out with a random guy on the dance floor for three songs, I grab my coat and stroll home alone.

29

Rose

Four months later

I stay in bed all day, unable to muster the energy to get up. To eat. To travel. To do anything other than stare at my ceiling and drift in and out of sleep. Once the sun's set, I travel to the tiny broom closet that shares a corridor with McGregor's office, cutting my palm on something sharp while scrambling for the light switch.

"*Shit*," I mutter, wiping the blood on my sleeve.

I stride past a row of closed office doors to McGregor's lab, expecting to find him in his pompous white coat and oversized safety goggles, extracting antibodies from Ella's blood. Or scribbling indecipherable notes into the margins of his journal. But his shiny lab sits remarkably empty, his equipment covered and tucked away. Continuing along the hallway, I reach McGregor's office and frown at the fountain pen snug in its leather stand and the closed journal in the center of his desk.

"Rose," McGregor says, slipping on the beige cardigan habitually draped across the back of his chair.

I stride forward, scanning him for hidden injuries. "What's wrong?"

"I can't work tonight," he says, sliding the stolen journal into his suitcase.

"What?"

"I have a life outside of these walls, Rose," he says in a flat voice. I don't mention the fact that we worked through Thanksgiving, Christmas and Easter.

"The fuck you do. We had a deal. I get you the journal, you find the cure. You promised."

"I promised to help you, not chain myself to this office every night for the rest of my life." His blue gaze slides somewhere behind me, the twinkle leached from his irises. He exhales and his eyes close momentarily. "I'll see you tomorrow."

"Where are you going?" I force myself between him and the door. One night away from his desk means another night Parker's without his powers.

"I have plans," he says, his wide stare imploring me to move.

"Cancel them," I say, my feet glued in place.

"No. We don't all share your craving for a melancholic existence."

"Fuck you." *And fuck his simple, easy life.* I pick up the faded fabric chair I've sat in every night for seven and a half months, and hurl it across the room. It smacks into the bookcase against the wall, remaining infuriatingly intact as it clatters to the floor. This is how it begins. At first it's just a night off, but then it becomes two. Then three. McGregor will continue with his life, and I'll be stuck here, alone, waiting for a promise that will never come. I'm powerless to stop it.

I wrap my arms about my chest and hold my breath, containing the scorching pressure in my lungs. The same pressure that's built every day since Matthews threw us into this mess. Tears sting the back of my eyes, and I clamp them shut, blocking out McGregor still standing uselessly before me. Dropping into a crouch, I shove my face into my knees and stifle the guttural cry that rips from my throat.

McGregor wraps his beefy arms around me, squeezing the air from my lungs. He doesn't say a word, but his steadfast embrace remains while I break apart, gulping down air laced with coffee, musk and dust. I cry away the unbearable tension I've carried since the day we fled Neurovida, only stopping once my chest is numb and my voice a hoarse bark.

"I'm alright," I say, shrugging McGregor off.

He releases me and pats me curtly on the back, as if I've just got a C in a quiz or failed my first driving exam. "It's the anniversary of my son's death today," he says, and clears his throat. "I'm visiting his grave."

"I'm sorry."

He nods his appreciation. "We'll get back to it tomorrow," he says, a rare softness in his voice. "I promise."

I follow him out of his office and leave him to lock up, my sluggish steps carrying me toward my favorite supply closet. McGregor halts me with a hand to my shoulder. "Rose, wait." He pauses for a moment. Exhales. "I pushed everyone in my life away after he died. Buried myself in work. Destroyed my marriage. Don't end up like me. You're too young to be alone."

"I want to be alone." The words roll off my tongue.

"For someone who wants to be alone, you're spending a hell of a lot of time trying to get Parker back." I can't stand the weight of his sharp, blue eyes. Shifting on my feet, my gaze wanders past his burly shoulder, searching for purchase, but the corridor behind him is dark and empty. He sighs again. "Goodnight, Rose."

I return to the supply closet and travel to my empty apartment, collapsing onto my bed. McGregor's parting words circulate around my head like the annoying jingle of a cheesy commercial.

Clamping my eyes shut, I slow my breathing and prepare to travel. But every time I conjure a memory from Neurovida, the emptiness inside my chest expands, the faces of the Alphas flashing through my mind.

Matthews' face appears, and I grit my teeth. I wish I'd never gone to Neurovida. I wish I'd never befriended Ella's future self enough to care about her or felt indebted enough to her to help Parker. I wish I'd never opened up to Matthews, become so close that his betrayal still stings like an open wound. I wish I'd never become an Alpha. I was better off on the streets.

The memory of the biting January wind breezes through my brain. I blink and I'm standing on a street corner, watching my past self sleep. Huddled in a closed shop entranceway, she tucks her blackened feet beneath a blanket so dirty it's difficult to tell what color it once was. My hand aches, fingers cold and stiff around the pocketknife clutched in my palm. Down the street, a trash can crashes to the ground, and rubbish scatters across the pavement. My past self jerks awake, her head snapping toward the group of rowdy men moving in her direction.

My heart rate kicks into a gallop, each beat hammering in my ears. Any wisp of warmth contained within that dingy, concrete entranceway is lost as she flees down the alleyway beside the building, torn between her safety and the tattered blanket she's left behind.

I jerk out of the memory, my heart rate slowing the moment my room appears, but the whispers of my echo scratch beneath my skin like razor-sharp claws. I'd waited for two hours in that alley before I'd gathered the courage to return to my sleeping place for the night, starving and freezing, lacking the energy to muster tears.

I rub my hands over my face. I hadn't been living; I'd been scraping by. How quickly I'd forgotten. The fear of being attacked, the craving for a safe place. By the time I was recruited to Neurovida, I was too terrified to get comfortable, ready to be back on the streets at a moment's notice. Why did I take every second at Neurovida for granted? Why didn't I realize what I had and the family I was creating? Why did I spend every second pushing Parker away?

Now I have what I've always wanted. A small fortune from my salary at Neurovida. Housed and safer than I ever was on the streets. And I'm alone ... just like I've always wanted. Alone and *miserable*. The emptiness in the pit of my stomach swells. McGregor was right. I've spent every minute fighting to get Parker back. And not just for the person Ella will become. *For me.*

"You're my family."

I was too stubborn to accept it. To believe I could be anything to him. But if the last few months have taught me anything, it's how much better life is with Parker in it. But until McGregor uncovers Parker's cure, I'm stuck.

I sit up, swinging my legs off the edge of the bed. I need to get Parker back. But how? Bringing him back here will only make things worse. I stand and pace my room, hacking at my nails. "What do I do?" I cry to the empty room. *What would Parker do?*

If he were here right now, he'd slip his hands into his pockets with a nonchalant shrug and tell me not to worry. *Blasé motherfucker.* Hell, the world could be burning to the ground, and he'd pour himself a glass of whiskey on the rocks and tell me to have a little—

My mouth falls open. *Faith.* Ella's advice the night of the ball comes crashing back to me: *You need to have a little faith.*

Parker would tell me to have faith. To trust. Trust myself. Trust McGregor, who's spent the past seven months working every night to help us.

"What else do you need?"

"Time."

Time. The one thing I have to my advantage, that I can bend to my will. Closing my eyes, I slow my breathing. Fire erupts within my chest, racing into my abdomen and along my limbs, heating my entire body. I open my eyes, and I'm standing in the cleaning closet, the air warm and stuffy. I sprint to McGregor's lab, bile rising in my throat. I release a breath when I find him, standing in his white lab coat, goggle-covered eyes glued to the Petri dish in his hand.

"Rose," he says, without looking up.

If my timing's right, he hasn't seen me for over a month. But he's here, working toward Parker's cure. Just as he promised he would.

"I—I'm sorry I didn't trust you. And sorry I never thanked you for helping us . . ." I scratch my forearm. "And for every moment since."

He nods and returns to his work, as if I've just told him today's weather forecast. "Blood collection kit's above the sink," he mutters, tipping his head to the cupboards on his right. "I'll need new samples of blood every time you visit."

I walk over and open the wooden doors, finding what I need. "What's the date?" I ask.

"July seventeenth," he says, sliding liquid along a horizontal metal column until it melts. He records something in his notepad, smiling down at the page. "You finally figured it out?" he asks, without looking up.

Faith. Trust.

"I think so." I walk out the door, McGregor's voice echoing along the corridor.

"Another four weeks should do it," he says.

✧

Blood whooshing in my ears, I open my eyes and I'm standing on a rolling hill with a solitary, crooked tree. Memories rush through my head, old and new twisting together like a strangler fig smothering its host. I clutch my temples and draw in a deep lungful of humid air. The longer we spend in the past, the worse it will get. My stomach shrivels and I trudge across the grass toward the crooked tree. *What if he's already left?*

Thunder rumbles beyond the hillside, the mountains in the distance hazed in menacing clouds. I reach the tree and smirk at the small Alpha symbol carved into its base. I plonk down onto the lush grass and lean against the tree. Lightning flashes in the distance, those ominous clouds drifting closer. I hack at my nails and wait, the light spatter of raindrops cooling my skin.

"Rose," a warm voice calls behind me. My eyelids flutter closed, and I release my first free breath in months.

I stand and turn toward Parker, who's crossing the quiet country road at the edge of the field. Shame swirls like lava in my stomach, but I force my legs forward to meet him. *He'll forgive me.* Sporadic raindrops plop onto my skin, each gust of wind tugging strands from my braid. The sky's darkened in the short time since my arrival, the clouds now rumbling directly overhead.

Parker meets me in the center of the field with a wide grin. He yanks me in for a hug and I relax in his arms, breathing him in. My heart twitches. *Traitor!*

After a moment, he pulls away, holding me at arm's length as he searches my face. "What happened? Are you okay?"

"I'm fine. I just needed some time."

His smile falters, the light behind his eyes dimming. "Some time? What are you talking about?"

Thunder booms, and the clouds above us relent, drenching us both.

"Let's get out of here and I'll explain," I call over the torrential rain.

Parker's eyes narrow. "Explain it to me now."

I cringe. He wants to have it out here. "I wasn't well, Parker. You know that. Holding you with me was getting to be too much. I needed to put myself first for once." A bolt of lightning flashes across the sky and I flinch.

"So . . . you left me here?" His despondent tone claws at my insides.

"Don't look at me like that. I knew you'd be safe here. You need to understand—"

"Understand? I've been waiting here in this field all day," he calls over the storm.

"It's been a little bit longer than a day." I clear my throat. "For me."

His face scrunches, and his narrowed gaze shoots to mine. "Are you serious? How long?"

I bite the inside of my cheek, and a coppery tang fills my mouth. "You felt my echo. You *know* I—"

"How long, Rose?" his voice raises.

Lightning strikes at the same time thunder booms, the sound reverberating through my chest. The storm's now directly above us; water pools in my Docs. "Long enough for McGregor to develop a cure." Parker scans the cloud-hazed view, the skin around his eyes pinched. The silence eats me alive. "I want to take you to him right now."

"How long *exactly*?" Parker yells, and I wince.

"Almost ten months," I say, so softly I'm surprised he hears. He draws in a sharp breath. "It took McGregor much longer. I've been jumping forward a month or so at a time, checking in and tracking his progress. Giving him blood." Mariella's blood, but Parker doesn't need to know that. "I want to take you to him now." His frown eases as my words sink in. "Parker, if this works, McGregor says you'll have your traveling back tonight."

His eyes flash, but he keeps his arms crossed. "Fine," he mutters, stepping toward me.

We stare at each other for a moment as the downpour eases. His strong jaw flexes, the glow in his eyes lacking their tint of amusement.

"I missed you," I say.

"Obviously not enough," he grumbles.

"If it's any consolation, it's been a brutal year. And no matter what happens after this, I don't want us to go our separate ways." The words spill out of me. I'd planned to wait until his powers were restored, but what if it doesn't work? I need him to know, no matter what, he can trust me the way I trust him.

"What?" he says. His wide eyes search mine.

I wipe the dark, wet strands of hair from my face. "My parents abandoned me as a baby, so I've always thought . . . I was meant to be alone. Like some fucked-up part of me thought it was what I deserved. Then we went to Neurovida and I got comfortable, and Matthews screwed us over, and Flame—I couldn't let anyone in and risk being abandoned again. I thought being alone would be easier . . . I was wrong. I'm sorry for pushing you away. And . . ." I force the last words out, low and rushed. "You're my family too."

He's silent for a moment, his light brown eyes boring into mine. He tilts his head, cocking a wet brow. "You haven't turned soft, have you?"

A smile tugs at my lips. "I mean, if I'm begging to have you back, my situation's obviously dire."

"Obviously." The corner of his mouth kicks up into a smirk, one I've deeply missed, but it fades. "Rose, there's something I need to tell you."

"Okay." I'm ready. Whatever Parker's plan is, I trust him.

"When I get my powers back . . ." He runs a hand through his hair. "I want to reunite the Alphas."

Warmth rushes through my chest. He wants us all together again. It might not be the same as before, but—

"Yes," I say. This is far better than anything I'd anticipated. I was expecting Parker to tell me he was staying in the past with Ella or had some crazy plan to bring her with us back to our time. But this? It's a dream come true.

"*All* the Alphas. Besides Matthews," he adds. "And I want to go back to Neurovida."

"But—they shot at us, Parker. They think we're traitors. We can't go back."

"We'll expose Matthews before he turns Neurovida against us," Parker says, his eyes wide. "Before *everything*."

"What?" I stare at him.

"I want to change the past," he says.

And there it is. The secret he's kept from the moment he saw Ella. The heat in my chest dissipates. "You can't. It's impossible."

"We don't know that," he argues, stepping toward me.

"Yes. We do. It's the first thing we learned at Neurovida," I say.

"But what if they were wrong?" His eager eyes search mine. "I believe there's a reason we have this gift, Rose, other than to sit around and rewatch our lives. A reason each time traveler has special skills that are unique only to them."

"What if there's not? How many memories are you going to damage before you accept defeat? How long are you going to spend playing God?"

His voice lowers. "As long as it takes to save her."

My stomach drops with my exhale. "Parker—I'm fucking tired. I just want to go somewhere that feels remotely safe and *exist* for a while. I don't want to spend the rest of my life meddling in the past." I turn away from him. "I'm not cut out for it."

"I'll carry you," he says, placing a hand on my shoulder. "You won't have to travel anymore. I'll do it for you. You can rest."

I shake my head. "What you're asking . . . it's a pipe dream."

Parker's jaw tenses. "It's not a pipe dream. Before we left

Neurovida, McGregor was doing research, and he believed it was possible." He lifts his chin. "And so do I."

I shake my head. "And if it's not?"

"Then we'll figure it out." He steps closer. "Rose, I don't want to do this without you. Please help me?"

I should say no. But what's the point? Once Parker gets an idea stuck in his head, nothing will change his mind. We either stick together and I help him, or we go our separate ways, like I'd always planned. I stare into his light brown eyes, and my decision is made for me. I want him with me. Even if it means spending the rest of my life in the past. I don't care if every time I look at him my breath hitches in my throat. *I don't care* if my feelings for him never completely fade. It's a small price to pay. I can't explain why or how, but somehow, I know, our lives will be forever intertwined.

I cross my arms over my chest. "Fine. I'll help you." The faces of the Alphas flash through my mind, and something dangerously close to hope swirls in my chest. "But we find Axis and Bandit first."

Parker's eyes dart back and forth between mine, a slow smile spreading across his face. "Really?"

"Don't get your hopes up. I don't believe changing the past is possible, but if any privileged asshole is going to do it, it'll be you. And I sort of owe you one for leaving you."

The corner of his mouth kicks up. "Just one?"

"If anything, Jimmy, you owe *me* for carrying your intolerable ego for all those months." I hold my hand out to him, electricity spiraling through my fingers. "You ready?"

"Almost." He rubs the back of his neck. "I want to talk about what you said the day you brought me here."

I groan and cover my face with my hands. "Can we not?"

He pries my hands away. "I'll say it once, then we can never talk about it again."

"*Ugh*, fine. Get it over with."

"I love you,"—another mortified groan from me—"and it might not be the way you want me to, but we're family and I'm not going anywhere. And I'll always be here for you, no matter—"

"Parker, I know. We're friends and nothing will change that. Now are you done?"

He looks upward, mouth pinched to the side as he torments me. Then his eyes return to mine, and a goofy smile crosses his lips. "Yep."

"Thank fuck. Let's go." I check my watch and grasp his shoulder.

✧

Parker's weight presses against me as I search for the door handle in the dark. We both stumble out of the small cleaning closet near McGregor's office.

"Jesus, Rose. Couldn't you have picked a larger area?" Parker grumbles, rubbing his elbow. "Good work on your accuracy, though."

I rub my pounding temples. I can't believe I put up with this for months. *McGregor's antidote had better work.*

"Every time I come and go, it's from here. Neurovida knew we visited the past. We can't risk being seen," I say, surveying the empty corridor.

"How did they find us?" Parker asks. "Is it Matthews?"

"*Shh*, keep your voice down." I lead the way to McGregor's office, leaving streaks of rainwater on the floor in our wake.

"All I know is someone posing as a police officer found Ella and showed her a picture of us."

"What? Is she okay?" he blurts.

I roll my eyes. "No, I left her in an interrogation room and said *good luck*." I scoff. "She's fine. She's smart, so she didn't tell them anything, but we need to be careful. The sooner we get out of here, the better."

Our steps echo along the corridor toward McGregor's office, the bare passage seeming to narrow with each stride. Everything we've worked toward comes down to this moment. If it doesn't work—

"Welcome back," McGregor says as we enter his office. He greets Parker with a firm handshake, then grabs some old towels from a cupboard and hands me one with a nod of his head. "Rose."

"Thanks," I say, drying my face. We may not be each other's biggest fans, but we've come to understand one another since I stopped spending every second breathing down his neck.

He turns back to Parker. "Before we start, I need you to know this drug has only been tested on cells in a Petri dish, but I've followed the research in my journal, and I'm hopeful it will work."

"Only one way to find out," Parker says, stepping toward McGregor.

I wish I shared his confidence. My eyes are glued to McGregor as he attaches a needle to a syringe and draws clear liquid from a glass vial. *Please God let this work.*

McGregor removes the needle and attaches another, the light reflecting off the pointed tip. I hold my breath as he plunges the antidote into Parker's muscular biceps and withdraws the needle.

"Now what?" Parker asks, pulling down his sleeve.

"The antidote works by interacting with your immune cells, which will take time," McGregor says. "So, now we wait and see."

"It'll work," Parker says. "And then I'm taking you to see your son."

McGregor dips his head, hiding the tears shining in his eyes. "Let's see if it works first," he says, his voice taut.

✧

I glance at my watch and sit behind McGregor's desk, swiveling back and forth in his chair. He's conducting tests on Parker, who's spent the last hour attempting to travel without success. With every minute that ticks by, my body grows warmer. I hack at my nails and check my watch for the hundredth time. This *needs* to work. I can't carry him for an extended period and risk losing control again. I pull my vape from my pocket and slam it down onto the desk. McGregor will berate me if I take one puff inside this building.

Needing something to do with my hands, I open the stolen journal lying on the desk before me. I turn the page and pause on a highlighted sentence. *E2409—Inhibitor.*

"McGregor, what's this?" I call.

He walks over, adjusting his glasses. "It's a drug that inhibits time travel. Interestingly, it has a similar chemical structure to the drug that removed Parker's powers."

E2409. Where have I heard that before?

"Rose," Parker yells, and at the same time I crumple over the desk, intense pain shooting through my head.

It feels like someone's playing a ruthless game of tug-of-war with my brain. I clutch my hand to my head, where beads of sweat are forming over my temples. My eyes shoot to Parker, and I jump to my feet. Parker's body is blurring. My head throbs again as if it's being pierced with a sharp object, and I stumble forward.

"Let go," Parker insists.

Of course. I'm holding him here while he's trying to leave. It's no wonder my head's protesting. I ease my hold on him, expecting him to become translucent, but Parker's appearance doesn't change.

His face lights up. "Release it completely."

"Are you sure?" I hesitate. "It might not be safe."

"Please," he begs.

I take a deep breath. "Okay, get ready."

Parker glances at the tan skin of his wrist where his watch once sat and lowers his head. His hands clench into fists at his sides.

I ease my hold on him. My mind and body relax, and my headache eases. I sigh, yet uncertainty flashes across Parker's face.

"That's all you," I say, moving around the desk until we're facing. "Touch something?"

Parker reaches toward the desk, his hand hovering above McGregor's fancy fountain pen. The room turns silent. He plucks it from the leather stand, eyes unblinking and mouth quivering. His eyes flicker to me, and a wide, disbelieving smile splits his face.

"Fuck," I whisper. "He did it."

Parker charges toward me and hauls me against his chest,

lifting me off my feet. He laughs and McGregor slaps his desk in triumph.

"Thank you," Parker says to McGregor as he places me down.

I try to step away from Parker, but he holds me against his chest. "Thank you," he says, holding me in a bear hug, his breath warming the shell of my ear. "I owe you everything."

My heart flips and I push him away. "It's not over yet. We still have work to do."

"I know. But first I want to double check my traveling abilities." He turns to McGregor. "Then I'm taking you to see Henry." He lowers his head, and his arms fall to his sides, hands clenched into fists. His body begins shaking, and a hint of a grin creeps across his face.

"Parker, wait." The blood drains from my face. "When you return to our current time, your memories will split."

He shakes his head. "I'm not going forward, I'm going back."

"Where?" I ask.

"To say goodbye," he says, his body blurring.

I sigh. "She went to a ball on the night of February twenty-first. Might be a good time to visit her." *I hate being a good person.*

"Thanks, Rose."

"Be careful," I yell, but he's already disappeared. I shake my head. He hasn't traveled for an entire year, but I'm willing to bet he'll appear minutes off his target. *Talented ass.*

I turn to McGregor. "Don't worry, he'll be back."

Then our real work begins.

30

Mariella

I pull my fur coat across my chest and dawdle home beside the river. Snowflakes drift around me, the towering elms dusted in white. I cross the road, and a shadow stirs in the corner of my vision. Whipping around, I track the movement with a racing heart. Seconds ago, I could've sworn the street was empty. Twenty meters away, a silhouette steps toward me and I freeze.

I'm going to be murdered just as I've started to live my life.

The figure moves closer and, as I prepare to kick off my heels and make a run for it, a man steps under the glow of the nearest streetlight.

"Parker," I whisper.

He crosses the street and strolls toward me, hands tucked into the pockets of a tuxedo. He's always been gorgeous, but with the triangle of bronzed skin at his open collar, the sliver of white cuff at his wrists, and the bulge of his muscles beneath the fitted fabric, my breath catches in my throat. My fingers tingle with a burning need to touch him, and my chest aches with the reminder that I cannot.

A slow smile builds as he closes the distance between us, a dimple creasing each cheek. He tips his head.

"I can't believe you're here. How did you—" My words dissipate as he reaches out and tucks my hair behind my ear, his hand lingering over my temple. I gasp, butterflies swarming my stomach. "Wait, you can touch me? Does that mean . . ." I bring my hand to his, and our fingers entwine.

"I would've been your date and danced with you all night if circumstances were different." He lifts my hand to his lips and presses a kiss to the back of my knuckles, his honey-hued eyes fixed on mine.

I laugh. "You mean if you weren't from the future and on the run?"

He shrugs, the corner of his mouth tugging up into a cheeky grin. "Something like that." His eyes stray to my ball gown, down the deep neckline visible beneath my open coat. "Besides, I wouldn't have been able to hold a conversation with anyone when you look like this. Dance with me?"

I nod, and his hand slips beneath my coat to my waist, pulling me toward him. I breath him in: warm cedar, cut grass, and something distinctly *Parker* that heats my body from the inside out. My head rests in the space between his neck and shoulder, and with his other hand laced with mine, he leads me in a slow dance, snowflakes catching in our hair.

"Rose said I wouldn't see you again," I whisper.

"Did she?" he teases.

I peer up at him. "Are you okay? Where have you been?"

"Rose took me on a little field trip." His amber eyes burn with intensity. "I came to see you as soon as I got my powers back so I could do this."

He lowers his head, and I glimpse his mouth curving into a smile before he brushes his lips against mine.

I've spent months daydreaming about our last kiss—the softness of his lips and the sweep of his tongue, my body's reaction to his closeness. The mere thought of his mouth on mine was enough to reignite the throbbing heat that had coursed through my veins.

I was convinced it wouldn't be the same the second time around. That the fire behind his kiss would wane, or the tingling shudder that raced through my chest to settle between my thighs wouldn't stir. Yet, when his lips meet mine, his kiss is as intense and staggering as I remembered, and for a moment I forget myself.

The chilling night air turns stifling, and every thought in my nervous brain evaporates. Everything I am, smell and feel is this intoxicating man holding my body to his, lips pressed against mine.

He wraps his arms around my thighs and hitches me up until our chests are pressed together. I bring my hands to his face, cradling his smooth jaw as I open my mouth and slide my tongue against his. His grip on my legs tightens, but he pulls back, leaving me hollow when our lips part.

My brain is dizzy and my body burns with want as Parker lowers my feet to the ground, every nerve ending aching where every inch of him touches every inch of me. My mind catches up and nervous energy flashes through me. Parker has his powers back. He can touch me. And for the first time, we're alone together. *Truly alone.* No Rose to watch our every move or burst in at any moment. There's nothing holding us back from being together. So why aren't his lips still on mine?

"You're freezing," Parker says, his voice gravelly.

I can't be freezing, because he's replaced the blood flowing in my veins with something searing and volatile. I bring my icy fingertips to my flushed cheeks and flinch.

"Feel my hands," I say, pressing the backs of my fingers against his cheeks. He groans and grabs my hands, tucking them into his pockets. My thumb brushes a familiar metal. I pull the chain from his pocket, and my necklace dangles from my fingertips. "My necklace?"

He hesitates, scratching the back of his neck. "Yeah. I sometimes have it." He clears his throat. "That's a lie. I always have it. I promise I'll keep it safe."

"Thank you. It was my mother's ... I'm guessing you already knew that?"

He shakes his head. "I didn't. I always presumed it was yours because of the inscription."

I drag my thumb over the metal. *Let the current carry you.* "She always loved the ocean. Like you."

I hand him the necklace, and he slips it back into his pocket, the muscles in his forearm shifting. I recognize the movement, him turning the charm over inside his pocket as he's done from the moment I first spotted him in my lecture. The thought flitters across my mind and realization dawns on me—Parker and Rose have achieved what they set out to do. Parker has his powers back and there's nothing tying him to this time.

"You're leaving," I say.

He nods. "After I take you to see your mom. But first, I want to show you something." He extends his hand toward me, and I stare into his mischievous, golden eyes. I would let him take me anywhere. Past, present or future. I would give hours of my life to have seconds in his.

So I reach out and take his hand.

The moment we touch, a wave of electricity brushes my fingertips, warmth flooding up my arm to congregate underneath my sternum. Within seconds, my whole body's buzzing.

I don't ask where we're going. I trust him, just as my future self trusted him with my most treasured possession: my mother's necklace. And if, after this moment, he's going to leave, I'll seize every stolen second I have with him now.

My pulse skitters. *I'm about to time travel.* I close my eyes and suck in a deep breath as that unstable ball of searing electricity explodes in my chest. The cool night air presses against me, every cell in my body quaking. I suck in airless breaths, my heart thrashing against my rib cage. I step into Parker, gripping his shoulder with my free hand. Just as the bizarre sensations threaten to overcome me, they vanish, and a warm, humid breeze sweeps across my cheek.

Head spinning, I open my eyes to complete darkness. "That felt different to when I sub-t," I admit, remnant electricity sparking between our fingertips.

He squeezes my hand. "I'm sorry. I should've warned you. It's more intense when your body actually travels. Are you okay?"

I nod and slip off my coat, waiting for my eyes to adjust. *I can't believe it.* I've just jumped through space and time. It's *impossible*, and yet the tangy aroma of salt and seaweed hangs in the air. I crane my neck, and my breath hitches at the sight of the Milky Way stretching across the night sky in clusters of stars so dense they could be mistaken for fluorescent clouds.

"I've never seen the stars look like this."

"The city lights drown them out, but not out here." He tugs me forward, but my heels catch. I slip them off, my feet sinking into soft, cool sand. Parker takes my heels and leads me through dense bushes that tug on the fabric of my dress as I pass. I rely on him to guide me—even with a sky full of stars, the path before us is unusually dark. The shrubs give way, and we come to the edge of a dune. Parker shrugs off his jacket and sits, staring out at the shimmering ocean, gentle waves lapping the coastline.

I could be in one of my dreams, alone with Parker by the beach, underneath a constellation of stars. I sit beside him and his shoulder brushes mine; it's surreal after months of being unable to touch him. My hand finds his, tingling where our skin touches. "Where are we?"

"Broome, Australia. My family vacationed here when I was a kid. Have you visited before?" he asks, his eyes focused somewhere in the distance.

I shake my head and squint at the ocean. A tiny orange blob spots the horizon, warm tones of light skipping across the water. "What is that? Is it the sun?"

Parker wraps his arm around my shoulder, drawing me toward him. "Wait and see," he says in a mischievous tone.

The globule is growing, taking on the shape of a semicircle: the moon, rising over the ocean. A beautiful, golden-orange reflection runs vertically along the water's surface, linking the moon's rising point all the way to the shore.

"It's called the Staircase to the Moon," Parker says. "My uncle lived here. He used to take us to watch it all the time when we visited."

I smile. "Do you and your family still visit?"

Parker's silent for a moment. "Everyone in my family is dead," he says, still staring out at the ocean.

My heart breaks for him, this small admission reminding me how little I know about him.

"I'm sorry," I whisper. "I know what it's like to be alone."

Parker shakes his head. "You're not alone, Ella. You have me, and the second you become an Alpha, you'll have a family full of misfits who'll love and support you. Plus, you'll be able to drop in and see your mom whenever you want."

"Do you visit your family?" I ask, searching his face.

"Yeah. Sometimes it helps to talk to them. The people from your past. Even if they don't talk back." He squeezes my shoulder. "You taught me that."

Flashes of my dreams skitter through my mind. My mother beside the ocean, and my dark nightmare. "Sometimes I wish my sub-t would stop. I love some of my memories, but others scare me."

"When I first started at Neurovida, we used early memories with strong emotional ties to hone our skills. I hated it, so instead of staying in them, I'd find an out. Locate a door and leave the room or walk away. Anything to put distance between myself and the memory." He laughs. "Sometimes I'd just hold my shield until the allocated time had passed."

"I don't know what that means," I say.

"The barrier between you and your timeline." His mouth curves into a smile, a memory dancing behind his wistful eyes. "Yours was light."

I think about the blinding light blocking my field of view every time I dream. "How do you hold it?"

"Instead of focusing on what's past it, draw it toward you." He shrugs at my skeptical expression. "It's easier than it sounds."

Is putting distance between myself and my past what I need? It breaks my heart to think of Parker shutting himself away from the pain of his memories. "I'm sorry you had to do that . . . escape your past."

Parker shrugs. "I used to see it as a burden, like you do, but that'll change."

I draw my legs up to my chest and wrap my arms around my knees. We stare out across the ocean as the full moon rises in the sky, casting shadows on the surrounding dunes.

"Are you okay?" I ask when Parker becomes unusually quiet.

He turns his body toward me, running a hand through his hair. "Ella, I brought you here to tell you something . . . while I have the chance." His eyebrows crease together, chest expanding as his eyes search mine. "I need you to know that every second I'm not with you, I'm thinking of you. And what I'm about to say might sound intense because you don't know me well, but I know you *so* well." He takes my hands in his and brushes my knuckles with his thumbs. "I don't need the details of your past to know how kind and selfless you are. I know people think you're withdrawn because you aren't always the first to speak up, but it's only because your beautiful, intelligent mind's ticking away. And behind that guarded front, you're the bravest person I've ever met. It kills me to think you've spent your entire life believing you're different and you don't fit in. But I'm telling you, it's everyone else who should want to fit in with you, because you're the most incredible woman I've ever met in my life—"

"Parker—" I interrupt him, but he continues to speak, desperate to convey his thoughts as if the words might vanish from his mind, or he'll miss the opportunity if he pauses for even one second.

"And I don't want you to say it back, but I fell so stupidly in love with you at Neurovida, and now I'm kicking myself for not telling you sooner. You deserve to be told, every day, how loved you are. And incredible and funny and special." Tears well in his eyes despite the smile on his face. "You're the best person I've ever met. And in case I never get the chance to tell you again, at least I'll know I told you now. I love you, Ella."

His words hit me in the center of my chest, right over the hole I've been mending since my mother died. The hole Silas widened when he discarded me, deepened each night I spent at home alone, believing I was different and unlovable.

Parker sucks in a breath. "And I—"

I grab his shirt and crash my lips into his. He immediately clasps each side of my face and kisses me back greedily. Goosebumps rise over my skin. His hands trail down my neck and over my breasts to settle on my waist, his strong muscles flexing as he lifts me, pulling me into his lap without breaking our kiss.

There's nothing slow about the way we explore each other, clutching and pulling, filled with a burning, agonizing need to be closer. To touch and taste and smell, knowing we may never have this chance again.

I fumble with the buttons of Parker's shirt, dying to feel his bare skin against mine. I've undone the first two when electricity races through me. The temperature shifts, and we materialize on Parker's bed inside the apartment opposite Anna's.

His lips never leave me, worshiping every inch of exposed skin. I undo the rest of his buttons and push the fabric from his shoulders, running my hands over his warm skin. My fingers move lower, tracing the pink scar on his abdomen from the bullet graze. He shudders, his mouth buried in the crook of my neck. His tongue sweeps along my skin, tasting me, pinching it between his teeth. I sigh and his head shoots up, his bedroom eyes meeting mine.

"That sound. It's one of the things I was worried I'd forget." He runs his hands over the curve of my backside. "The shape of you." He presses his mouth to the fabric over my nipple, and my heart falters, a shiver racing through me that doesn't stop until it hits my throbbing core. "The way you taste. I could travel back to this moment one thousand times over just to hear you moan and never tire of it."

His mouth returns to my neck, trailing kisses lower until he reaches the fabric covering my breasts and he groans in mock frustration. His hand finds the zipper on the back of my dress, sliding it down until the fabric is gaping. He guides my arms upward, dragging a finger up the sensitive flesh on the inside of my arm before he slips my dress over my head.

Left in my underwear, I blush under his heavy stare, roaming my near naked body as I sit in his lap. I resist the urge to wrap my arms around myself. I want this. I want him. His hands all over me, touching my most intimate parts.

I bring my lips to his and lean forward, pushing him back onto the bed so I'm lying on top of him. He grabs my thighs and flips me onto my back, and the air whooshes from my lungs. My hands roam his muscular back and arms, tracing every firm line. He grinds down into me, guiding my legs to wrap around his waist so there's no space left between us. His hard length presses against me, and a jolt of nerves races through me at the thought he might ache for me in the same way I do for him.

His lips pull at the skin of my neck, and his hand finds my breast, his fingers closing over the tip of my peaked nipple. I arch into his touch, the deep aching below my navel almost painful now. I want him to touch me, but I've never been with anyone like this before. Does he know?

He shifts above me, and his hand trails lower, palm gliding down my stomach, tracing my skin without hesitation, with a confident familiarity that comes from years of intimacy. I want more, but I don't need to speak—his finger slips beneath my panties, moving straight to my throbbing core to circle me. Trembling at his touch, my head falls back against the mattress, my body too hot, every exhale breathless.

The same talented finger moves lower, slipping inside me before returning to circle me again, drawing those dizzying rings that make my body so tight it's hard to breathe.

Parker touches me as if he magically knows what I want and how I want it. And somewhere in the back of my mind, through the clouded heat of his body over mine, his scent in my lungs and his scorching touch, a voice murmurs, *because maybe he does?*

Does Parker know what I like because he's slept with me before, in my future I'm yet to live? Has he been with me many times? My breathing quickens for another reason altogether. Does Parker know I've never had sex before? Does he want me to touch him? My throat tightens. I don't know how to pleasure a man. I've barely seen one naked. What if I don't live up to his expectations?

"Parker," I say, my voice husky and wrong. "Wait."

He stops kissing my neck, pulling away when our eyes lock. "Did I hurt you?" he asks, searching my face.

I sit up and cover my bare chest with my arms, and it's as if the temperature in the room has plummeted.

"Here," Parker says, grabbing his dress shirt and placing it around me.

I slip my arms into the sleeves, breathing in his masculine scent. *What am I doing?* I force my next sentence out. "Have we done this before? I mean, in the future, have we had sex?"

Parker sits on the edge of the bed and runs a hand through his hair. "Well . . . Yeah. I thought you knew?"

I shake my head, unable to verbalize my thoughts. But he's right. Of course I knew. My intimate, heated dream—not a dream at all, but a glimpse of our future together. How do I explain that I don't want to compete with my future self? That I'm worried the experience might fall short for him? I stare at him, all bronzed skin and defined muscle, sitting half-naked on the bed. My bottom lip trembles—our last time together and I've blown it.

He buries his head in his hands. "I'm sorry, Ella. I got carried away."

"No, stop. Please don't. I want this, it's just—" I want to crawl into a hole and die. "I've never—" I take a deep breath. "I've never been with anyone before."

Parker's jaw drops, and his body stills. "I thought you and your ex . . ."

I shake my head, and he gets off the bed. I've only seen him this angry once before, on the night I helped anchor Rose. How did things change so quickly? I wish I could time travel back five minutes and still be in his arms. "I'm sorry," I whisper.

He tenses. "I would *never* want to take that experience from you."

I draw my knees into my chest. "So, when we're together, after I'm recruited, I'm not—I've already—"

"The first time we were together, it wasn't your first time," he says quietly, staring at his empty hands.

I twist the button on the cuff of his shirt. How is it possible I'll sleep with someone else while feeling this way about Parker?

He sits next to me, his mouth pulled to the side in a grimace. "Please tell me what you're thinking."

I'm unable to meet his gaze. "I want my first time to be with you, but you said when we have sex in the future, I'm not a virgin, so—" I suck in a breath. The room seems too quiet, my stomach too tight. I rush the words out. "If we do it now, what if it's not what you expect?" I peer up at him with my heart in my throat.

Parker's leaning away from me, his brows drawn up. "*That's* what you're worried about?" A tentative smile builds on his lips. "Those things don't matter."

I don't see how. Parker exudes confidence . . . and *experience*. "Really?"

He laughs. "Of course not." He puts his arms around me and draws me into his chest. "Our time will come, and when it does, it's"—he shakes his head—"everything."

He guides me back down onto the bed, shifting so my

back is flush against his warm chest. With his arms wrapped around me, I close my eyes, and the tension leaches from my body with each steady thump of his heart.

✧

Parker stirs behind me, and I wake from my sleep. I turn to face him, his legs tangling with mine.

"Still feels like a dream, being able to touch you," he says.

I press my lips to his. His kiss is slow and gentle, lacking the urgency of our previous encounters. We break apart and my heart sinks—he's kissing me goodbye.

"I don't want you to go," I whisper.

"I promised I'd take you to see your mom," he says. "When you're ready."

"I'm ready," I say, despite my quickening pulse.

We stand from the bed, and I immediately miss Parker's warm, reassuring touch and the scent clinging to his dress shirt as it slides from my shoulders. I pass it to him, a flush creeping up my neck at his dilated pupils, his bronze gaze hovering over my exposed skin. I step into my dress, struggling with the zip at the back.

"Let me," Parker says. He steps up behind me, heat radiating from his body. "Ella, I want you to prepare yourself for the possibility your mother wasn't a time traveler," he says, dragging my zipper up. His knuckles brush my bare back, igniting a shiver over my skin.

I nod, my reply hitched in my throat.

Parker makes quick work buttoning his shirt and holds his palms out toward me. "You'll have to help me," he says. "As long as you can recall the memory, I'll be able to take you to it."

I slide my hands into his, and his fingers wrap around mine. "How?"

"Do you know what memory you want to enter?" he asks.

"Yes."

"Close your eyes and imagine you're in it now. Replay it in your mind, slowly, taking in every detail."

I shut my eyes, the memory of my mother beside the ocean vivid in my mind. Waves rush against the shore, and the sun warms my back. My mother's fingers are cool against my skin as she fastens her chain around my neck.

"What stands out the most from that memory?" Parker asks.

My mother pulls me into her, and the air rushes from my lungs. I can almost feel her arms wrapped around me. I was safe. Loved. And I wasn't alone. "The way I felt in her arms," I say, my voice wavering.

Electricity bursts to life between our palms, flowing up my arms until it's lapping at my chest, like warm, rising water.

"Focus on that feeling," Parker says, and my body begins to pulse.

I can't believe it. I'm going to see my mother. Tears well behind my closed eyelids. I have so many questions for her. About our life before she died, and the handsome stranger who visited her in the hospital. I draw in a deep breath, fighting the vibrating air inside my lungs.

I wait for the feeling to overcome me, for the temperature to shift or the ocean breeze to hit me. But nothing happens. Parker's grip on my hands tightens, and another strong wave of his power floods through me. I keep my eyes closed, centering all my attention on my mother.

"Pick a different sense," Parker says through gritted teeth after another minute has passed.

"Okay." I breathe in, remembering the salty ocean breeze, the sweetness of coconut sunscreen, and my mother's fresh, citrus scent.

"Good. I can smell it," Parker says, his voice swelling with pride.

The surrounding air presses against my skin, every cell shuddering. Parker releases my hands and my eyes snap open.

My stomach drops. We're still standing in Parker and Rose's apartment. "What . . ." I trail off at the confusion on Parker's face.

"Something's wrong," he says, slightly out of breath. "I can't access the memory. It's as if . . . there's a wall blocking me."

My shoulders fall. "Is it me? Am I doing something wrong?"

"No. Both times I could feel your echo." His golden eyes scour the room. "Let's try a different memory?"

He retakes my hands, and I focus on the memory of my mother in our apartment, peeking through the curtains. I stood by her bedroom door, feet bare against the cool wooden floor. Parker's power rushes into me, but the room stays whole around us.

"Different sense," he says between gritted teeth.

Canned laughter hums from the TV, and cars fly past on the street below.

"Another," Parker says.

My mother's olive dress brushing her slender calves. The fabric swishes as she shifts her balance from one foot to another.

Parker's grip is tighter than before, his hands clammy against my skin. We go on like this for another half hour, swapping between senses and memories, until Parker is panting, sweat beading down his brow. He breaks away, bending forward to plant his hands on his knees.

"Something must be wrong with my powers," he says, straightening and re-extending his palms toward me. "Try picking a memory without your mother."

My gaze slides from the hands reaching toward me to his heaving chest. "Should you take a break?" I say.

He shakes his head. "What do you think we did at Neurovida all day long?"

My stomach knots at his cold tone, but I retake his hands and shut my eyes. Drawing in a deep breath, I search the void behind my closed lids for a memory. The darkness seems to stretch forever, like a black, infinite tunnel. The booming sound comes easily, intensifying until it's hitting me from all sides. A cold shiver skitters through me.

Parker's grip on my hands tightens. "What are you . . . ?" he mutters under his breath, his energy rushing through me. The room presses in on me, as if I'm a square being squeezed through a tight, circular space. The sensation eases, a gust of cool air conditioning igniting pebbles across my skin. My heart rate accelerates, my breaths now quickened, adrenaline-fueled pants. The silent space surrounding me is thick with tension.

We're no longer in Parker and Rose's apartment.

A bloodcurdling scream pierces the air.

"Fuck," Parker yells, yanking his hands from mine. Electricity erupts beneath my skin, and the bedroom reappears. Parker stumbles away from me with a gaping mouth.

"What was that?" I ask, my heart thrashing against my ribs.

"Why did you do that?" Parker's face is pale, his eyes squeezed shut as if he's in pain.

"What was it?" I ask again, but Parker remains silent, running a hand through his hair. "Please, Parker. I need answers. That was a dream I've had since I was a little girl. What happens to me?"

Parker slumps onto the edge of his bed, and I perch beside him. He's silent for a beat with his head hung, then he turns to face me. "I think . . . that was the day I lost my powers." His voice turns raspy, as if each word scrapes against his vocal cords. "You were hurt, Ella. But now I have my powers back, Rose and I are going to stop anything from happening to you."

"Why didn't you tell me?" I sit up beside him. "Why keep these things from me?"

"Because I'm selfish. And it's easier when you're *you*, not a time traveler or an Alpha, and you're here and safe." He cups my cheek, rubbing his thumb over my cheekbone. "I want you to live in the now. Knowing things about your future will drive you crazy. Please trust me, everything's going to be okay. I'll make sure of it."

I nod, wanting to believe he's right.

He stretches his hands toward me. "Let's try visiting another memory of your mother?"

"Okay," I say, resting my palms on his.

I repeat the same process as before, focusing on the darkness behind my eyelids before recalling the warmth of my mother's embrace beside the ocean, but the seaside park doesn't appear.

Another thirty minutes later, Parker groans. His hair's sticking up at odd angles from the excessive number of times he's run his hands through it. "I don't understand why it's not working. There must be something wrong with my powers. I'll go and speak with McGregor. Maybe there's something in his journal about losing skills or—"

"It's okay, Parker," I say, despite the fierce ache in my chest.

"No," he says, his voice breaking. "I promised I'd take you to see your mom."

"I guess I'll have to go and see her myself . . . once I learn to travel at Neurovida." I don't know when I made the final decision. I guess deep down, a part of me always knew. I can't explain it, but something is pulling me toward Neurovida.

Parker stills, his eyebrows furrowing as if he's heard me wrong. Then his mouth pulls into a wide, dimpled grin, and he rushes toward me, lifting me off my feet. He holds me against his chest, engulfing me in his scent.

"I'm going to miss you," he says into my ear, and he lowers me to the ground.

His hands slip into mine and my fingertips tingle, as if they have their own burning need for his touch.

"When will I see you again?" I ask.

"At Neurovida, when you're recruited." He smiles, but no dimples appear.

My heart sinks. It isn't fair. Our time together has barely begun. I bump my shoulder against his. "But I'll never see *you* again."

"It'll still be me. I'll just be younger." He laughs. "And dumber."

It might still be him, but his past self won't remember me. He won't know me the way Parker does. He'll be a stranger.

Parker reaches up and brushes the tears from my cheeks. "I know this is hard, but I can't keep showing up and disappearing from your life. It wouldn't be fair to you, and you've seen what being here for so long did to Rose. Little by little, you lose pieces of yourself. I don't want that to happen to me. I need my mind clear for what's ahead of me."

I nod, but inside, my heart's breaking.

"I'll travel from here," he says, his amber eyes dim. My heart rate doubles.

This is it. I'll never see *him* again. I'll never have the chance to ask him my questions, to learn about his life before Neurovida, his fears and his dreams, to love him the way I want.

He tucks my hair behind my ear. "Promise me you'll live your life to its fullest until Neurovida?"

"I will," I say, pressing my lips to his. He cups my face in his hands and kisses me tenderly, as if his touch might shatter me into one hundred tiny pieces. When he lets me go, his brows are drawn, a sudden coldness about him. "Rose will kill me for telling you, but you need to know. We were betrayed by a man named Matthews. He was one of us. Or at least, we thought he was. He turned Neurovida against us. When you meet him in the future, don't trust him."

I nod. "I'll see you in two years."

He presses a kiss to my forehead, his warm gaze filled with an emotion I can't place. "Goodbye, Ella. I love you."

Hands balled into fists at his side, he lowers his head, and his body blurs. Then he lifts his head—and there's that roguish smile that still makes me weak at the knees. "Hey,

Ella? Before I forget, when you meet me at Neurovida, go easy on me, okay?"

"What do you mean?"

"Like I said, I was an idiot," he confesses, and before I have the chance to blink, he's gone.

31

Mariella

I reread the current page of my book, the words trickling from my brain like water through a sieve. Eventually I toss the book on my nightstand, switch off my lamp, and lie back on my pillow. After Anna and I turn in each night, my evenings are spent like this, lying in bed, daydreaming about Parker and my first day at Neurovida. Meeting his younger self. Falling in love.

The light from my phone cuts through the darkness, Silas's name appearing on the screen. We haven't spoken since the day he showed me the picture of Parker and Rose. He's sent an attachment, with a message underneath:

I'm sorry.

I jerk upright, flick the light back on, and click on the attachment. My mother's black-and-white death certificate fills my screen. It's only one page, the typed contents bearing the speckled markings of a photocopy. Under *Standard Certificate of Death* is my mother's name.

The date and place of her birth.

Our home address.

My deceased grandparents' names.

I read on. The certificate names *Massachusetts General Hospital* as the place of death, with an inpatient box checked and the name of the cemetery where her body was taken. Beneath are the signatures of the funeral service licensee and the attending doctor. I continue reading.

The report lists December twenty-fourth as the day my mother died. Suicide is stated as the immediate cause of death and, below this, *bilateral vertical incision to ventral surface of wrist*. The report lists the underlying causes as schizophrenia, psychosis and post-traumatic stress disorder.

"*What?*" I whisper at the screen and reread the report. *It must be wrong*. My mother didn't kill herself. She wouldn't leave me. At this point, I'm not even sure she was sick. Maybe she was in danger and had to flee, like Parker and Rose?

I blank my screen and lie back in bed. Neurovida will have answers, I know it. At the minimum, I'll learn to time travel, and I'll visit my mother.

I'll uncover the truth if it kills me.

✧

Brilliant white light dances around me, easing backward with every step.

"Mari, come here." My mother's voice drifts through the waning light, and I rush forward until she's within my circle of clarity.

I suck in a stilted breath.

She's standing at the end of the hospital corridor, her frail arms reaching for my younger self, like two bony twigs lined with scars. Her sack-like hospital gown engulfs her malnourished body, the lilac color a cruel complement to the purple rings under her eyes.

Recollections of this day inundate my brain. Memories suppressed and faded by time.

"No," I whisper.

My younger self runs toward my mother, the green linoleum squeaking beneath her feet. "Mommy," she squeals, and she catapults into my mother's arms.

My mother almost tips from the impact. Clutching her daughter against her chest, her head whips back and forth along the empty corridor before she lowers the girl to the ground and drops into a crouch. They huddle together in the tiny space between the hospital corner and a mobile laundry unit overflowing with bleached-white sheets and well-used cotton blankets.

"I need you to listen to me, Mari," she whispers into the ear of my younger self. "Are you listening, darling?"

"Yes," she replies in a small voice.

I edge forward and crouch beside them. My mother's eyes are two wide, unblinking beacons, holding us both in place. "I want to show you something." She holds her hand up into a fist, her thumb poking out between her index and middle finger. Fresh, angry marks line her wrist. A bitter taste fills my mouth. "This means safe. Can you do it too?"

The little girl mimics the gesture, and my mother's smile transforms her face. The hollows in her cheeks fill, and her eyes sparkle. "I'm going to teach you another one." She crosses her index and middle fingers over one another, like a child telling a fib. "This is how we can tell there are people around us who are dangerous."

"Evelyn, how did you get out of your room?" a nurse calls from the other end of the corridor.

My mother's eyes widen, and she leans toward my younger self, fingernails digging into the girl's tiny shoulders. "We can use these to communicate with each other. Our little secret, hmm?" Hospital staff in navy scrubs stride toward us, and my mother stands, thrusting the girl behind her. "You're not safe, Mari," she screams. "They're going to kill us."

Two nurses approach, speaking under their breath. "I found a stash of pills in her bedroom. She hasn't been medicated for over a week," one says.

"Explains the hallucinations," the other says.

A younger man in black scrubs steps past the nurses and approaches my mother. "No one's trying to kill you, Evelyn. We're here to help you."

Another nurse reaches for my younger self's hand. "Time to go, Mari."

My mother straightens, staggering backwards into the laundry cart. "This isn't real," she screams.

"We're real, Evelyn," the man in black scrubs says calmly.

A burly staff member clamps his arms around my mother, her bare feet lifting off the ground.

"Get off me," she screams, and it sounds as if the words are being torn from her throat. "No. They're trying to kill me."

I jerk awake to the rumble of a garbage truck and the clatter of breaking bottles. My heart's racing from my dream, my mother's unhinged face fresh in my mind. Grabbing my phone, I open Silas's message containing my mother's death certificate. *Bilateral vertical incision to ventral surface of wrist.* Tears spill onto my cheeks at the memory of the fresh, raised cuts on my mother's wrists and her high-pitched wail as she was dragged back to her room.

Schizophrenia, psychosis, post-traumatic stress disorder.

Did reading my mother's death certificate somehow trigger a memory trapped within my own subconscious?

Electric sparks lick at my fingertips, and I shake my hands, hurling the energy away like it's toxic.

I read the report again, each inhale more restricted than the last.

"Time travel isn't genetic."

"We studied theory of time travel with McGregor at Neurovida every day. For years. If it was genetic, we'd know."

A shiver races down my spine, and my gaze jumps from the closed bedroom door to the sliver of night visible between my drawn curtains. *No one is watching you.* I creep toward the window and glance down at the empty street. A cat scampers beneath a parked car. A memory flashes through my head: my mother standing by her own bedroom window, fingers curled into her cardigan as she peered down at the street. "Shh," she whispered, eyes glued to the front lawn. "Someone's out there."

My hand rises to my mouth.

Oh, God.

Time travel isn't genetic. My mother killed herself. And there were warning signs. Her secret hand signals and lying about her medication. Her paranoia about being followed, just like mine.

There's a knock on my door. "Ella, are you in there?" Anna says.

I cross the bedroom on numb legs and turn the handle, my thoughts scrambling. Anna's hot pink lips are pressed together, her brows scrunched.

"What's wrong?" I ask, seeing the subtle tic in her jaw.

She shifts on her wedges, arms crossed tightly against her chest. "I was at dinner with my father last night, and he ran into an old rowing friend and his daughter. Sarah Walker." The blood drains from my face. "I told her it was really nice to finally meet her, seeing as she's your *best friend*."

"Anna—" I say, cringing.

The smile on her face sends chills down my arms. "She says she hasn't seen you in years. Says you weren't even friends at school. She only knew who you were because she said your mother killed herself when you were in elementary school." Tears brim in her narrowed eyes. "Ella, you told me your mom died from a heart attack. Did you not think you could trust me? That I would want to be there for you? And I know you went through my closet again."

"What?" I ask.

Anna shakes her head and picks something up from the floor. She places my sketchbook into my arms. "I found this in there."

My head snaps to the desk next to my bed, where my sketchbook usually sits. Why was it in Anna's room?

"Where have you been all this time, when you said you were with Sarah?"

I stare down at the book clutched in my hands, wishing it would suck me into its blank pages. "I don't know what to say."

"Try the truth," she says, her voice trembling. She pulls

a bottle of pills from her jacket—the half-empty container I tried to give Rose. "What are these?"

I shake my head. I don't know what to say without lying. How do I tell her I took them to stop time traveling in my sleep? *I can't.* How did I get myself into this mess? I never should've lied to Anna about my mother's death.

Black, mascara-infused tears streak Anna's cheeks. "Ella, if you can't be honest with me, then are we really friends?"

I press my lips together. Even if I did tell her about time travel, I don't have any proof. It would only sound like far-fetched lies. I lower my gaze to the floor, as if I might find a piece of my heart on the thick sage rug. I can't bring myself to tell Anna another lie, but I also can't give her the truth. My bottom lip trembles. "I'm sorry—I can't."

Mouth tense, Anna tosses my pills onto the bed and strides to her own room, her thick wedges clunking on the floorboards. With one last disappointed glance, she slams her door closed, locking our friendship away with it.

✧

The porch stairs creak as I climb to my front door, satchel in hand and the past twelve hours ringing through my head. Three lines of police tape cross the doorway, one obstructing the four locks my mother installed. Another sign of her paranoia—the beginning of her disease progression. My skin crawls and I whip around, scanning the few parked cars on the street. My fist closes around the charm on my necklace, right above my racing heart. This is more than the familiarity of watching myself in my sub-t. My paranoia's real. And it's worsening. *I'm already following in her footsteps.*

I flash back to my mother in that hospital, screaming. My mother who couldn't differentiate fact from fiction. My mother who killed herself.

I can't end up like her, locked up while my mind slips away. My stomach hardens. Silas was right. I can't throw away my lifelong plan on a whim. I need to finish my studies and learn about my mother's disease. Book back in with Dr Williams. I need to fight for the safe, normal life I've spent the last twelve months building.

The ache in my chest feels like a tangible thing. No Neurovida. *No Parker.*

When I break the tape and open my front door, I'm hit with the thick, bitter scent of smoke and burned plastic. I trudge across the living room and collapse on my faded brown sofa, the half-empty bottle of pills rattling inside my open bag. I miss Anna and her constant chit-chat. Her revolving door of guests and outfit changes.

I lie back and close my eyes, but they tug back open. If I go to sleep, I'll dream of my mother and the trauma ahead of me. Of my future with Parker that will never be. The blood drains from my face, and my heart aches fiercely. *I'll never see him again.* I reach into my bag and pluck out my medication. Tipping the bottle, I shake two pills into my open palm.

I don't want to dream . . . I want to forget.

32

Mariella

I fall into a dreamless sleep, waking the next morning groggy with a heavy fog blanketing my brain. I sit up and rub my aching neck, pausing to stare at my hand. The familiar electrical tingling is absent, replaced with a systemic numbness. I can't smell the lingering smoke clinging to every surface of my house. I can't smell anything.

I grab my phone and check the time. *11 am.* I've slept through my morning class. *At least I can ask Anna for her notes.* A painful jolt sears through my chest. I can't ask Anna for anything. I've lost her. And Parker. And the future family he'd promised would await me at Neurovida.

I take two more pills, pull the moth-eaten blanket over my head, and shut my eyes.

✧

I wake disoriented and starving. When did I last eat or take my meds? I drag my feet into the bathroom and splash cold water on my face. Catching my reflection in the bathroom mirror, I flinch. A cool sweat breaks over my skin. I edge forward until my nose is an inch from the mirror. Wet strands of brown hair cling to my pale face, a haunting emptiness whirling behind my mismatched eyes. The spitting image of my mother in that hospital corridor. Alone and confused. *Just like me.*

I dry my face and make instant noodles on the stove, but they taste like bland cardboard. *Get dressed. Go to class. You're falling behind.*

I lie back down on the sofa and close my eyes.

✧

White light dances around me, easing as I step forward. Waves break on the shore, the scent of ocean and sunscreen filling my nostrils.

"Mari, come here," my mother calls to my younger self through the waning light, unaware that the same girl will watch this memory far too many times to count, hanging off her every word with silent tears streaming down her cheeks.

The light continues to recede, but I draw it back toward me, ray by golden ray, until I'm submerged in blinding light, just as Parker told me I could. I don't want to spend every night haunted by my mother's end. By what I will one day become. I hold the barrier of shimmering light around me, like a memory-retardant blanket, and wait until I wake and can take my medication.

"Open the door," a faraway voice calls.

"Go away," I mumble.

✧

I rouse to a heavy pounding on my front door, electricity surging through my body. Tears well in my eyes and I shake my hands, pushing the energy away.

"I'm not going away until you talk to me." The voice is closer now. Clearer.

Anna's voice registers, and my eyes snap open. Dragging my feet, I cross the living area and open the door. It's odd, Anna standing on my dingy porch in her designer clothing and studded stilettos. I curl my hands inside the bottom of the same oversized top I've worn for the past three days.

Anna pushes her way inside, heels clicking on the scuffed floorboards. "I've been trying to—" Her mouth drops as she looks around my mother's house and back at me. "Call you."

"My phone died."

She exhales and passes me a tote bag, the sequins on her dress swishing. "You left these at my place. You didn't need to move out."

I peer into the bag, filled with my mother's journals. "Thanks," I say, placing them on the dining table.

"I didn't read them," Anna says, pursing her dark red lips. "If you were wondering."

I nod and, for the first time in our friendship, an awkward silence hangs in the air between us. I flick away the current jumping between my fingertips.

Anna takes a step toward me, rolling her shoulders like she's preparing for battle. "Why did you lie to me?" she asks. "I thought we were friends."

The waver of her voice hits me like a jab to the heart. I've hurt her, and after everything she's done for me . . . She's better off without me.

Anna's wide, glassy eyes don't stray from mine. "Did you not think you could trust me?"

The stabbing sensation worsens. "Of course I did," I say.

"Well then why?" she cries, searching my face for answers I can't give her. After a moment of silence, she turns toward the door.

"Wait," I blurt. I need to give her something. So she knows this is all on me. That she's been nothing but a wonderful friend who deserves better. "I lied because you were the first friend I'd ever had, and I wanted you to think I was normal."

She tilts her head, her nose scrunching. "You are normal."

"But I'm not. I haven't been my whole life. At school, I never fit in. Then my mother got sick, and it became so much worse . . . I was the girl whose mother 'went crazy and killed herself'. Every single day was hell, and when I started college, I made a decision to do everything I could to blend in. Build a normal life. I changed the way I dressed, and I never drew attention to myself in class. I didn't even plan on making any friends, but then you sat next to me, and you kept sitting with me . . . and we became close."

"So why didn't you tell me then?"

Tears pool in my eyes. "Because I was afraid you'd push me away, like Silas. I opened up to him about my life and my past, and he—I couldn't risk losing you too."

"You should've trusted me," she says, smearing black tears across her cheeks and storming to the door. She grasps the handle, her manicured fingers white. Her shoulders creep up, then she drops her hand and her face whips to me. "You know, Ella, when we met, you were awkward and quiet, sure, but what I liked most was that you didn't judge me. My whole family—and many of my friends—think I'm a joke, but everything they teased me about, who I am and the way I live my life, you looked up to me for."

She takes a deep breath and shakes her head. "I liked you from the start because I thought you weren't like all the other fake bitches I knew. You never judged me. Even *after*

I sat next to you for an entire lecture calling you the wrong name." Her bitter laugh is like a stab to my gut. "I guess the joke's on me. I was dumb enough to fall for your act." She eyes me up and down, mouth twisted like she's ingested something stale. "You wanted to fit in and be like everyone else? I think you'll be fine." With one last resigned glance, she steps onto my porch and shuts my front door.

Tears rolling down my cheeks, I stand by the door on numb legs. I'd always wondered why Anna kept me as a friend. It wasn't because I was trying to be something I wasn't—it was because I gave her the freedom to be herself. But now she's hurting, because of me. Because I didn't reciprocate her trust.

I'm reminded of the many occasions Anna invited me to go to her family dinners and hang out with her friends.

"I'd love someone to take the attention off me."

All this time, I thought she was just being nice. But she wanted backup. And I let her down.

I yank open the front door, current buzzing down my legs, and storm across the front lawn toward Anna's Jeep. I don't care if she thinks I'm crazy, or different. As long as she doesn't believe I share similarities with the people in her life who've hurt her. All that matters is proving I was worthy of her friendship.

"Anna, wait," I call.

Tears spilling onto her cheeks, she gets into her car and slams the door with such force, the faux lipstick hanging from her mirror swings. I open the passenger door and jump in. "I don't think you're a joke."

She turns to me, hands clutching the steering wheel. "Is that why you created a fake friend, so you had an excuse not to spend time with me?"

"Of course not." How can I prove to her it's the opposite? That I've always looked up to her, with her bold opinions and the way she's uniquely herself. That deep down, a part of me has always wished to have one ounce of her confidence. "At first, when I said I was with Sarah, I was here, alone. It wasn't *you* I didn't want to be around, it was—all the other people. Groups scare me, okay? And the thought of hanging out with you and more than one other friend was overwhelming."

"And after you moved into my place?"

I promised Parker and Rose I wouldn't tell anyone about the time we spent together. So how do I tell Anna I was with a man from my future? That I'm a time traveler?

"Get out of my car," Anna demands.

"Wait!" I grab her hands. Even if I tell her, she won't believe me. But maybe I can show her. "I don't know if this will work but just—wait." I close my eyes and draw in a slow breath, focusing on the current jumping between my fingertips. And for the first time in my life, I don't immediately push it away. I call to it. It flurries in response, as if it's waiting for me, simmering beneath the surface. The energy concentrates in my hands, heat warming my palms from the inside out. I pull my second memory of Anna.

She'd come to class, just as she had the week before, and plopped down next to me, a whirlwind of accessories and color. A spike of adrenaline rushed through my veins. Had she made a mistake for a second week? Heart thrumming, I spent minutes mustering the confidence to tell her I loved her earrings. She launched into conversation, information spilling from her like an overflowing fountain. After class, she clutched my hands and told me she'd known we were destined to be friends. My reply lodged in my throat; why would this flamboyant, courageous person want to be my friend?

The sentiment fresh in my mind, I force the warm current pooling within my palms toward Anna, just like when I anchored Rose. Volatile energy ignites within my chest and tears down my limbs. Euphoria floods my body, but it's fleeting, pouring out of me, yanking the buzzing current with it. Photons of bright white fly toward us, like thousands of shooting stars engulfing us in light. Anna's hands stiffen in mine, her acrylic nails digging into my skin when the tunnel of white expands.

I'm staring at our past selves sitting in the lecture hall on that second day. The vision is fleeting, like a flash of lightning across a dark night sky, but my echo lingers: my churning stomach and racing heart. The exhilarating prospect of becoming Anna's friend.

Pain slices through my skull, and I'm thrown from my visions, my chest heaving. Temples damp with sweat, I release Anna's hands.

Her eyes are wide, her mouth slightly agape. "What—what was that?" she whispers, staring at her hands as if she might see electrical sparks dancing along her skin.

"Did you see anything?" I ask between breaths.

"I saw . . . *myself*." Her brows draw together, and she presses her hand to her chest. "But it felt like, I wasn't—myself."

"That's because you were feeling an echo of how I felt in that memory. Ever since I was a kid, I've had vivid dreams. And when I wake—" I glance up at Anna. Her eyes are fixed on mine, her expression unreadable. "—I have these strange symptoms, like there's electricity running through me." I clutch my heart-shaped charm between my fingertips.

"Those pills you found? They're sleeping pills, prescribed by my psychiatrist to make it stop. I spent years thinking there was something wrong with me. But this year, I met people like me. They told me I wasn't dreaming; I was time traveling. I can't tell you much more than that." I search her wide eyes and slack mouth.

"That's where I've been every time I said I was with Sarah—since I moved in with you. I'm sorry I lied to you. And that I made you question yourself. You're the best friend I've ever had, Anna, and I think the world of you. Please forgive me?"

Anna finally closes her gaping mouth, her vacant gaze looking outside. When her head swings back to me, her bottom lip is trembling. "Oh my God!" she screams, bursting into tears. She wraps her hands around my shoulders and yanks me toward her until we're awkwardly hugging over her central console.

"So, you can, like—see into the past?" Anna asks, finally letting me go. I nod, and her green eyes light. "Oh my God," she says again. "What else can you do?"

"Nothing. There's a place that trains people to time travel, but I'm not going."

"Why not?" she demands.

Emptiness spreads through my chest. "Because I'd have to drop psychology."

Anna scrunches her button nose. "Okay? So, drop psychology."

I shake my head. "I can't."

"Ella, you've been given a gift," Anna says, grabbing my hands. "Don't throw it away."

I pull my hands from hers. "I've already decided."

"Why?" she says.

My arms snake around my heaving chest. "Because I'm terrified of ending up like my mom. Studying psychology is the only way I—" Tears sting the back of my eyes. "If I can understand her illness, I can prevent it . . . Stop it from happening to me."

"You're not going to end up like her," Anna says softly.

"I finally got her death certificate. It listed schizophrenia and psychosis as contributing causes. We're products of our parents, and mental illnesses have genetic components. Schizophrenia is highly inheritable. Last year I started getting paranoid that I was being followed, and it's only getting worse. That was how it started for my mother. She and I are so similar, even our mannerisms are the same." Both introverted homebodies who'd prefer to sketch the world around them than actively participate. "You even said yourself how much I look like her."

Anna's face falls. "You're not your mother, Ella. Just because she got sick doesn't mean you will."

"You don't know that. She seemed fine. Then she deteriorated over the course of three months, and there was no trigger. She didn't drink or take drugs. We were happy. It makes no sense."

"Sometimes mental health disorders don't. Sometimes there isn't always an answer."

"I need there to be an answer." I'm giving up too much for there not to be.

"Ella, you just said your mother was well her entire life until she got sick. You said you were happy."

"So?"

"*So*," she mimics with wide eyes, "maybe you can't control what's going to happen to you. But you can control your life now. If you're going to inherit your mother's illness, the disease obviously hits later in life and has a rapid onset. And it sounds like you already know her medical diagnoses. So, learn the warning signs and have regular sessions with your psych. It doesn't mean you need to throw away your chance at something great."

"But what if I'm making a mistake?" I say, my voice small.

"Let the current carry you," Anna says, and my eyes lift to meet hers.

"I don't know what that means," I say.

"Isn't it obvious?" Anna stares at me earnestly. "It means trust yourself, Ella. Follow your heart." She shifts in her seat, turning so her legs are angled toward mine. "Close your eyes." I give her a look. "Just do it, ho," she orders. "Close your eyes."

Exhaling, I do as she asks.

"What do you see?" she says, her gentle tone coaxing me to search the darkness behind my lids. "What do you want?"

Parker's beautiful golden gaze flashes before my eyes.

"These powers don't make us different, Ella. They make us special. Being a time traveler lets you relive any memory you want. It's a gift."

I want to believe him. I want to make memories I'm desperate to relive. And I want him to be in them.

I open my eyes. Anna's brows are raised, a knowing smile on her dark red lips.

She's right. I can't control my genetic predispositions. If my mind's going to fail me, like my mother's did, I need to enjoy my life now. And I won't be alone at the end, because I'll have created memories worth being lost in. Exciting memories as a time traveler, at Neurovida. With Parker. And Rose. As an Alpha.

"What do you want?" Anna asks again, shrugging her shoulders as if she's asking the simplest question in the world. Perhaps she is.

"I want to be a time traveler," I say, my mouth splitting into an open grin.

"*Duh*," she says with wide eyes, and angles her head toward my house. "Now go get your shit."

"What?"

Anna starts her car, and a pop song blares through the speakers. "You can't stay here, babe." She slips on a pair of oversized black sunglasses and angles the rearview mirror to study her own reflection. "You're coming home."

✧

Rays of white light bounce around me, shimmering in my periphery like the midday sun on the surface of the ocean. I'm standing in the mental health ward, my mother and younger self crouched before me.

The hospital staff move toward my mother.

"Get off me," she screams. "No. They're trying to kill me."

The wall of bright light edges toward me, readying to carry me into another time, another memory, but I push against it, demanding it wait until I'm ready. It's time I stop running.

I follow the hospital staff dragging my mother back toward her room. The tunnel of white is closing in, a sphere of light and pressure pushing against me. Gritting my teeth, I try to hold it back, but only my mother and her bed are now visible within the dazzling light.

She's injected with some sort of sedative and left prone over the crisp white bedsheets. The bolt on the door clicks after they leave. Unable to move, my mother's gaze drags to the far corner of the room, focused somewhere past the wall of white.

"I'm sorry this happened to you, Mom," I say aloud, even though she can't hear me. I step closer to the bed and reach for her, my hand moving through hers like a lost ship drifting through mist-coated water. What I'd give just to hold her. To let her know she wasn't alone. To thank her for the wonderful memories she left me with. I want to tell her that reliving them in my dreams is the greatest gift a mother could give their child.

My vision blurs, and I blink away tears. "I'm sorry for forgetting what it was like before you got sick. For blaming you for sending me away. For spending my life wishing I wasn't like you. You told me all along I was special. I believe it now. And I know I am who I am today because of you. Because of how much you loved and cared for me when you could." I sink to my knees beside her bed, head bowed, tears blotting my light blue dress.

"I know you're there," my mother mumbles, and my head snaps up.

"Mom," I cry, my heart lurching into my throat. "Can you hear me?"

My mother's head turns, and my heart stops as her haunted gaze drifts into the shimmering light behind me.

Hairs rise on the back of my neck, and I get to my feet, slowly turning to face the wall of light.

Then I sprint directly into it.

I'm saturated in white, the only sound my quickened breath. The light bounces backward, and it feels like my stomach is being crushed from the inside out.

I must be losing it. Because what I'm seeing can't be real.

It can't be Silas standing in the corner of the room.

33

Mariella

I unlock Silas's front door and bolt down the hallway to his living area. "Silas? Are you here?" I storm toward his office and yank the locked door handle. "Silas," I yell at the wooden door. I race into his bedroom and open the top drawer of his nightstand, rifling through the mound of half-empty pill packets to find the brass key resting at the bottom.

The office door unlocks with a satisfying *pop*, and I hurtle into the dark room, tripping on a stray shoe. Asynchronous ticking fills my ears, surrounding me from all directions. I flick on the light and breathe in Silas's fresh, minty scent.

There's a single bed pushed against the far wall, a large desk, and a metal, industrial-looking filing cabinet against another wall. Numerous clocks are positioned around the room, a mix of digital and analogue, all displaying the exact time, day, month and year.

But it's not the clocks spiking my adrenaline, or the collage of photographs, documents and profile shots neatly lining the walls by the desk. It's not the maps, or the dates and times labeled on every document. And it's not the two large profile shots of Parker and Rose staring back at me from the center of the wall.

It's the far wall above the single bed that has me speechless, backing away on shaking legs. Because this wall also has photos, but only of one person.

Me.

Every aspect of my life's mapped out, documented in an immaculate timeline extending well past the current year. Heart racing, I study the pictures of myself in my school uniform before we ever met, working in the library, and walking between classes with Anna. There are copies of my school and college schedules and my sketches displayed among childhood photos, each marked with handwritten dates and times.

I retreat further, and my back presses against something warm and solid. My scream hitches in my throat.

"Silas," I gasp, whipping to face him. There's only one way he could've been in my sub-t, watching over my interaction with my mother all those years ago. "You're a time traveler."

He closes the door, trapping me inside. "Yes," he murmurs. He steps forward, his gray-blue gaze locking me in place. "How long have you been in contact with Parker?"

Heat surges through my chest. "You knew about my paranoia of being followed. You let me believe I was crazy. That it was all in my head." I swallow the cry rising in my throat, looking over the wall displaying my life and intimate memories as though I'm at the center of a crime investigation. I'm reminded of all the times I passed lone figures on campus, feeling like I was being watched. "This whole time, it was you. Spying on me, before we even met."

He shakes his head. "I wasn't spying on you. I was looking for *him*." He pulls something from the top drawer of the filing cabinet and places it on the desk. "When did you meet him?"

I stare down at the paper, my drawing of Parker from so many months ago, torn from my sketchbook. A wave of disgust rolls through me. "You went through our apartment. Why did you leave my sketchbook in Anna's closet?"

"I'm sorry. Anna came home while I was there. I was forced to leave it."

"Why were you even there? What else are you hiding from me?" I suck in a breath, the blood draining from my face. "Did you start the fire at my house?"

A muscle tenses in his jaw, and his eyes darken to a murky gray, like the surface of the ocean on a stormy day. "How could you think that? I pulled you *from* the fire." He drags a hand down his face. "Where's Parker, Mariella? What's he told you?"

"Nothing," I snap.

His lips part. "I can't believe after everything, you don't trust me."

A bitter laugh bursts from me. "I *did* trust you. It was you who refused to trust me." *And now I know why.* "You were lying to me this whole time."

He gestures to the wall of photos. "To stop you from finding out about any of this. To keep you safe. And I've spent the last twelve months looking for Parker and Rose so I can help them."

I straighten my spine. "Help them with what?"

His cold gaze gives nothing away. "I think you know."

I shake my head, my lips pressed together.

He steps back and lifts the bottom of his shirt.

"What are you doing?" I ask.

He pulls down his sweats and there, on his muscular right quad, etched into his gleaming skin, is a tattoo. The same tattoo Parker and Rose have. My sketch, the Mark of the Time Traveler.

"You know what this tattoo is. What it means," he says, pulling his pants back up.

I slump onto the office chair. *Silas went to Neurovida.*

"We were recruits together," he says. "I came back here to keep you away from Neurovida. Everything I did was to stop you discovering anything about it."

"Why? What happens to me if I go there?"

He swallows, brows drawn as he spits out, "If you go to Neurovida, you'll die. Did Parker tell you that?"

His body is trembling, every visible muscle taut. I stare into those gray-blue eyes, dark shadows swirling like smoke. How many times did I fail to imitate them in my sketchbook? I can finally put my finger on the emotion hovering in the background, an emotion he's so carefully masked from me until now.

Fear.

Silas is afraid for me.

"You're lying," I whisper, but as I say the words, an icy chill curls down my spine.

Silas rummages through the drawers of the filing cabinet. He pulls out another picture and slams it onto the desk before me.

He turns away from me, leaving me to stare at the photo of myself. My stomach hardens. My skin is sickly pale, and dried blood coats my face. Bile rises in my throat at my lifeless form, eyelids half open and mouth agape.

He's telling the truth, displayed blatantly in front of me. The nightmare plaguing me since I was seven years old brought to life.

A sour taste fills my mouth. Every time Parker mentioned

me at Neurovida, he always spoke in the past tense. *Parker knew.* I get to my feet and stumble away from the desk.

Neurovida's the place I'll die.

"This is what happens if you join Neurovida," Silas says, his voice breaking.

Tears well in my eyes. Why didn't Parker warn me? My back hits the wall filled with photos of Parker and Rose. I turn and mindlessly take it in. A damaged Polaroid sits in the middle of the wall, so small I might have walked by it. Six people huddle together, wearing the same black smartwatch on their left wrists. Parker grins in the middle, his arm wrapped around Rose's shoulders as she pushes him away. Silas and I are on Parker's other side, flanked by two people I don't recognize.

The Alphas.

Beaming in triumph. Some of us holding up clothing to reveal dark tattoos surrounded by red skin. Even Rose is smiling.

I turn back to Silas, sitting on the bed and watching me with a clenched jaw. When he speaks, his voice is soft and smooth. "Mariella, I have a plan in place to prevent you from ever going to Neurovida." He rests his hand on his knee, a plastic cylinder in his open palm.

"What is that?" I ask, edging backward.

He turns the needle over, and his defeated gaze rises to me. "Your chance at a regular life. An opportunity to finish your psychology degree. No more dreams. No more symptoms or pills. This is safety. Normalcy. It's what you've always wanted."

I stare at the syringe in his hand, held out to me like an offering. *He wants to remove my powers.* "I don't want that."

"You're building a life here. Don't throw it away." He looks down at the syringe in his hand. "This medicine is a cure. If you don't take it, you'll be recruited to Neurovida, and you'll die. I've tried to stop it so many times." He stands and steps toward me. "This is the only way."

Keeping my powers doesn't guarantee I'll go to Neurovida, but taking the drug in his hand would ensure I'll never see my mother again. Or Parker. My heart shudders.

Silas's large form looms over me, like a dark thundercloud blocking the sun. I can't think. *I can't breathe.*

"I need some time to think."

His control snaps. "What's there to think about?" he yells, a vein pulsing in his neck. "It's this or your death, Mariella." He's upon me with lightning speed, forcing the glass cylinder into my hand. When his fingers brush my skin he tenses, yanking his hand away. He pulls an empty pill packet from his pocket, the muscles in his jaw twitching.

He told me he took medication for stress headaches, but now I reflect on his behavior since we met. He's become more unhinged and irritable. His body's shaking. One wrong move and his guarded façade will crumble. Just like—

Rose.

I'm reminded of her bag, overflowing with medication, just like his bedside drawer. "Staying in the wrong time's making you sick," I whisper, twisting the tie at the front of my dress around my fingers.

"I'm fine." His eyes stray to the closed office door and he brushes his hand over his sternum. "I just need to take something for this headache. I'll be back." He strides from the room and closes the door behind him.

I turn back to the faded Polaroid of the Neurovida recruits and locate Silas, the only recruit not grinning. He hasn't aged a day. He has the same striking features—defined jaw, straight nose, strong cheekbones—but less tension lines his face. His eyes are sparkling, his forehead smooth, partly covered by a tousled lock of dark hair that's fallen forward. He's so beautiful it almost hurts to look at him.

I'm scanning the wall for more photos of him when he returns, eyes distant and posture rigid. When did he lose that magnetic shine to his eyes? How startling to compare his now cold and serious demeanor with the exuberance radiating from his picture.

"What name did you go by?" I ask.

He shakes his head, as if his mind is elsewhere. "What?"

"The name you picked for yourself when you were recruited."

"Matthews," he says, his voice thick.

"We were betrayed by a man named Matthews ... Don't trust him." Parker's words echo through my mind. I lean toward the Polaroid. My future self's head is turned to the side, her arm slung around Silas's broad shoulders. I squint at the hand hanging off his shoulder and the subtle cross of her index and middle fingers. My heart rate kicks up.

"This is how we can tell there are people around us who are dangerous."

My body turns numb. I need to leave.

Now.

"Silas, I—"

His strong arms clamp around me, forcing the wind from my lungs and locking me firmly against his chest.

"I didn't want it to come to this," he says, and I struggle against him, but it's useless.

I can't escape his hold.

I can't stop him taking the syringe from my hand, or plunging the needle deep into my biceps.

"I'm sorry," he mumbles against my ear.

34

Rose

We appear in a deserted park surrounded by tall pine trees, Parker carrying Ella's future self in his arms. He lowers her to the ground and yanks a small syringe from the side of his neck, his gaze never leaving her blank face.

I keep waiting for her to blink. To draw breath. But her body remains still, her unfocused gaze tilted toward the insultingly blue sky. The metallic scent of blood fills my nostrils and I keel over and dry retch into the grass.

Parker presses his fingers to her neck and whispers, "She's gone." He closes her eyelids and cradles her against his chest. Head bowed, he shakes as he sobs, at first quietly, then louder, until he's gasping for breath between each cry.

The guttural sounds tear at my insides. I turn away, clamping my eyes shut, as if it will erase the image of my dead best friend burned into my mind. I should do something. Cry? Scream? But I'm numb. I half sit, half fall onto the wet grass beside Parker and just breathe.

"Rose." Parker's hoarse voice startles me.

"Where are you going?" I ask, jumping to my feet. He's fading, as if he's about to travel.

"I don't know. It's not me," he says, staring at his translucent hands with wide eyes.

"Well, fight it." I don't understand. Five minutes ago, Parker traveled three of us at once, without touching me.

He lowers his head in concentration, yet his body continues to fade. "I can't. I think I'm losing my ability."

I point to the needle mark on his neck. "They shot you with something."

Parker's face pales, his hand ghosting over the puncture site. "You have to hold us here."

"I can't travel three people at once," I cry. "I struggle with two."

Parker's eyes meet mine. "Try, Rose. You can do this. Focus."

I take a deep breath and kneel beside him, placing one hand on his shoulder. Taking Ella's cold fingers in my other hand, I focus every part of my being into holding them in this moment with me. Sweat breaks out across my brow, yet slowly, they reappear.

"How long can you hold it for?" Parker asks.

Pain rips through my head. "Not long." I gasp. "A minute at most."

Parker lays Ella's future self down on the grass and kisses her on the cheek. My head pounds in warning, and their bodies fade.

"I need to let her go," I say.

With silent tears streaming down his face, he unfastens her heart-shaped necklace and tucks it into his pocket. "Goodbye," he says, his voice breaking.

I place her hands over her still chest and let go. "Goodbye," I whisper, and she disappears.

"Take my watch off," I say, holding out my hand. The other still clings to Parker's shoulder. "It could be a way for them to track us."

Parker removes the black smartwatches Neurovida gave us in silence, any trace of emotion leached from his face. I keep my concentration on him, placing my free hand on his other shoulder. "Are you ready?"

I push through the pain, waiting until Parker's bloodshot, empty eyes reach mine. He nods, and we disappear.

✧

I return to my body, resting on my bed, and drop my head into my hands.

The bed dips beside me. "It's okay, Rose," Parker says, wrapping his arms around me, and for once I let him hold me.

Parker hoped reliving Ella's last moments might provide insight. Details we'd missed, like what happened to the other Alphas or why Matthews betrayed us. None of those questions were answered. Reliving my past has only highlighted the lack of time I've had to process her death. We've been running from the moment we left Neurovida, focused on saving Parker's life and what comes next.

I piece myself together and pull away from Parker. "No, it's not okay. She's gone. Nothing we do will change that. It's hopeless."

He sits beside me. "I don't think it is," he says, his voice lifting.

"What do you mean?" I ask, wiping my nose on my sleeve.

"Did Ella's future self ever tell you she broke her wrist before Neurovida?"

"Yeah of course. It hurt her all the time. Especially during fights."

"And *after* we stole McGregor's journal and your

memories split? Did you lose or gain any memories involving her wrist?" Parker asks.

"I don't think so?" I filter through my hazy, split memories. "No. Why?"

Parker runs a tense hand through his hair. "When Ella bandaged my chest, I noticed a scar on her left wrist."

"Okay," I state. "That's nothing new."

"But what if it is?" He stands from the bed and paces, something I've *never* seen him do. "Because before that day, I thought I'd never noticed it before, or it was hidden beneath her watch," he says. "So tell me why, in my memory of her death, there's no scar on either wrist."

"I'm not following Parker."

"Why do you have memories of her with a sore wrist at Neurovida and I don't?" He strides toward me. "Don't you get it? Something changed in Ella's past, *before* we showed up, and it's only altered *your* memories, not mine."

"Because you haven't been back to our time since you regained your powers. Your memories haven't split yet."

"But neither have yours," Parker says.

"I—" I go to argue and slam my mouth shut. If something changed in her past, and it involved her wrist, I would have gained new memories, in addition to my existing ones, but I haven't. And those memories would be split. Blurred together. I wouldn't know which were real. But my memories surrounding Ella's broken wrist remain intact. "How is that possible?"

"It's not," Parker says. His shoulders drop.

"Fuck," I say, straightening. "Okay, if what you're saying is right, what other inconsistencies have you noticed between Ella in the past and Ella at Neurovida?"

Parker halts. "Her ex-boyfriend, Glenn."

He mentioned this before, but at the time, the information seemed trivial. "No. She never had a boyfriend before Neurovida," I say.

"Yes, she did. His name was Glenn and they met at the start of college, but when I brought him up, Ella said she'd been hanging out with someone called Silas. She never met Glenn." Parker groans in frustration. "Can't you see—" He plonks down on the bed beside me. "So many of the memories she used to enter at Neurovida involved Glenn. You trained with her every day and yet you have no memory of Glenn, not even split ones."

"What are you fucking saying?"

"Rose, your memories aren't split because *they've been replaced*. And the second I go back to our current time, mine will be replaced too."

I stare at the off-white wall opposite my bed and my stomach turns. "There's something else." I hesitate. How has it taken me so long to put this together? "Ella told me she has medication that stops her sub-t. Completely."

"What?" Parker yells. "And you didn't say anything?"

I press my palms into my eyes. "I'm so stupid. She said they were sleeping pills, so I didn't think much of it. And I saw the same drug in McGregor's book, *E24* . . . something, and it sounded familiar, but then you got your powers back and—"

"Did she say who gave her the pills?" Parker asks, running a hand through his hair.

"I can't remember. No, wait." I want to kick myself. "She said her friend Silas got her in with some psychiatrist."

Parker's face pales. "We need to see Ella. Now."

35

Mariella

I clutch a hand to my stinging biceps and stagger out of Silas's grip, the empty syringe falling to the floor.

"How could you?" I cry, detesting the quiver in my voice. Detesting *him*—and myself, for coming here in the first place. For trusting him, even though I knew he wasn't being honest with me. Why did I barge in here like a fool, putting myself in danger despite learning he was a time traveler?

In one thoughtless action, I've let him take away my past and my future. My choice.

"I'm sorry, Mariella. I can't let you go to Neurovida," he says, body trembling.

"That wasn't your decision to make."

There's a sudden shift behind him. The air is distorting, swirling, like melted sugar whirling in a pot. Parker and Rose materialize, Parker pressing a silent finger to his lips.

I try not to react, but from the spike in my heart rate to the heat flooding my veins, my entire body responds to his presence. And I want to grab hold of those sensations and throw them away, because I shouldn't feel this way about someone who's been lying to me.

Silas's eyes widen, and he begins to turn, but Parker lurches forward and shoves something into his arm. Silas slumps to the floor.

"Holy fuck," Rose mutters, taking in the document-lined walls.

Parker secures Silas's arms behind his back with a cable tie. "Rose, help me," he says, and they struggle to shove Silas's unconscious body into a sitting position against the wall.

"What did you give him?" I ask Parker.

"A sedative. He isn't who you think he is. This is *Matthews*," Parker says, stepping toward me.

"He told me," I say, and Parker's brows rise. "He said if I go to Neurovida, I'll die." My lip trembles. "Tell me it isn't true."

He's staring at me, his mouth downturned and pain burning behind his golden eyes.

"That's why Rose made you promise to stay away from me, isn't it? So you wouldn't get too close to me. So all your secrets and lies wouldn't unravel."

"I never lied to you," Parker says, his gaze unwavering. "Please let me explain."

I step away from him, my eyes burning. "Did you tell me anything real, or just enough to take my blood and get your powers back?"

"I only wanted to get my powers back so I could save you," he whispers, and Rose stiffens in the corner of my vision.

"Why should I believe you? You've kept things from me since the day we met. You're as bad as he is," I say, gesturing to Silas.

Parker's mouth falls. "I'm *nothing* like him."

"He changed your past," Rose says, still standing by the wall adorned with photos.

I turn to Parker, my hands snaking protectively around my chest. "You told me that wasn't possible."

"We were told it wasn't, but there's no other explanation," he says. "Before Neurovida, you never broke your wrist, and you were in a relationship with a guy named Glenn."

"And those pills you've been taking aren't sleeping pills," Rose adds.

I frown. "I got them from a doctor."

"But Matthews set up your appointments, didn't he?" Rose says, and my stomach clenches. "You never would've been recruited while you were taking those pills."

How could Silas do this to me? How was I so wrong about him?

"McGregor confirmed it," Rose says. "In small amounts they stop your sub-t and dampen your abilities, but a large dose of this drug will remove your powers altogether. He convinced you to take the pills so you wouldn't find out the truth."

I shake my head, searching the countless names, faces and dates covering the paper-lined walls. It feels like they're pressing in on me, inching closer with each rapid breath. "What is the truth?" I whisper. "Why didn't you warn me?"

Parker looks as if something inside him is breaking. "I didn't want to tell you until I knew I could stop it. Telling you would've felt like acceptance."

"We were protecting you," Rose adds, her voice solemn.

"You sound just like him," I say, gesturing to Silas.

"That man betrayed all of us," Rose says, jabbing her

blood-crusted nail at the man on the floor. "He's the reason you die."

"If that's true, why did he spend the last thirty minutes begging me never to go to Neurovida, so I'll live?"

Parker and Rose exchange a glance. "That doesn't make any sense," Parker says.

It doesn't. The used syringe that stole my powers lies forgotten in the corner of the room. I should tell Parker what Silas did. That power no longer runs through my veins. But something is holding me back, an unexplainable nagging low in my gut. Parker will want to go to Professor McGregor and get me the antidote. *And then what?* Would I take it? The nagging sensation deepens. Parker has opened my eyes to a life I've only dreamed of and, without the antidote, that part of it will end.

I uncoil my arms from around my chest and lift my chin. "I want to see what happens to me in my future," I say, keeping my voice stern. "I need to know the truth."

Parker's body tenses. "No."

"Parker, it's the only way to get her to trust us," Rose says. "Travel and show her that Matthews is a lying piece of shit."

Parker shakes his head. "I won't put her through it."

"I've experienced it in my sub-t, but it's always dark," I say.

"Because you're untrained. With Parker, every sense will be incredibly clear. If you want to know the truth, this is how," Rose says.

Parker's silent for a moment, turning the idea over in his head. "If I take you into my past, you'll see everything from my point of view. It'll be different from your sub-t. With my abilities, every detail will be as clear as the day I lived it. You might also experience an echo of what I felt in that moment, but I'll do my best to block it from you."

Rose shakes her head. "Parker, you're wasting time, she said—"

"Just wait, Rose," Parker says with a raised voice. He turns back to me. "Before we do this, I need you to know . . . what you're about to see will *never* be a reality. I'll die before I let it." He extends a tense arm toward me, his eyes searching mine. "Are you sure you want to do this?"

"I need to know the truth," I say again, taking his hand, and sparks of electricity ignite where our skin touches. Parker leads me to the single bed. I pause, looking up at him. "I don't understand."

"There's a difference between watching a memory and physically entering one. Our bodies will stay here," he says, tugging me to sit next to him. "This way we can't interact with anyone and cause split memories." He glances at his watch, one I've never seen him wear before, and takes my hands.

Rose stands silently beside Silas, gnawing on her nails. "Make it quick. He could wake up any second," she says, but my body's already flaring with warmth, every cell vibrating with energy.

When Parker last traveled us, I clamped my eyes shut. This time, I keep them wide open, electricity roaring up my arms and building within my chest. I suck in a deep breath to combat the pressure crushing my lungs.

Rough sandstone walls materialize before my eyes, encasing me and obscuring Silas's office. I stiffen, my heart rate jumping. Is the unease clawing against my rib cage my own emotion, or Parker's echo as he lived through this moment?

I blink, and the walls have crumbled, a grand home cinema appearing in their wake. Plush leather sofas fill the three tiers, centrally divided by crimson, carpet-lined stairs. The cinema is mostly empty, occupants seated only on the sofas on the lowest level.

Professor McGregor sits facing the audience on a wooden chair at the front of the room, his back to the screen and an antique wooden box clutched in his hands.

Parker wasn't lying when he said this memory would be different through his eyes. My visions of this memory are clouded by darkness, leaving me to rely on sounds and primitive feelings such as fear. With Parker, every aspect of the room is so real I'm having trouble believing I'm in his past. The rich, oaky smell of leather hangs in the air, mixed with a softer floral scent I cannot place.

Ivory half-moon lamps line the room, domes of soft light accentuating the red and gold patterns in the walls. Parker's younger self is lazing on the sofa to McGregor's left, furthest from the door. Rose and Silas sit on the other sofa, Rose picking at her nails while Silas leans forward, his covered forearms resting on his knees. They're all wearing the same square smartwatches and strange black uniforms, made of an unusual fabric that fits snugly against their bodies.

Professor McGregor winds a lever on the back of the box, each flick of his wrist producing a series of sharp clicks.

Parker groans. "Please, not again," he says, tilting his face toward the decorative ceiling and stretching his arms above his head. "I'll be hearing that creepy tune in my sleep tonight."

"Then *focus*," McGregor says, and the clicking halts.

"Concentrate on the sound of the music or the rotation of the ballerina, and see if you can slow it down."

Parker glances around the room with an indifferent expression, and yet another jab of apprehension fills my chest.

"This is a waste of time," Rose says. "It's impossible."

"We don't know that," McGregor snaps, scanning the three recruits before him. "Now concentrate. All of you."

"Why are we getting punished for showing up on time, when Nickol and the rest of the Alphas aren't even here?" Rose asks.

McGregor ignores her question and places the wooden box on the floor before him. "We're going to try this again. Remember your training. Find your focus before you begin."

He leans down and flips open the lid. A miniature ballerina pops up in the center of the box, its paint faded with age. The ballerina rotates, and I flinch at the off-key, high-pitched melody of Sleeping Beauty's "Once Upon a Dream". I try to step backward, but my body is still planted on the bed back in Silas's office. My feet push back into the bed base, every muscle straining. I'm trapped inside Parker's past, and the only way out is to finish watching it.

Parker and Rose stare at the music box, eyes glued to the rotating ballerina, but with each passing second, my heart rate quickens.

Something's wrong.

Silas jumps to his feet a second before my older self barges into the room, pale-faced and short of breath. "We have to go. Now," she orders, freezing before the spinning ballerina. Her trembling hands rise to her mouth.

I don't need an echo to feel her heart racing in her chest

or the terror flooding her body. I've felt it every night since I was seven years old. I'm living my recurring nightmare in perfect detail.

A middle-aged man with short, dark hair enters the room behind her, flushed and breathing heavily. "You need to come with me," he says to her, straightening his tie. An armed man appears behind him.

"Nickol?" Professor McGregor says.

My future self twists to face the man—Nickol—and backs away from the door. "Stay away from me."

"I just want to have a quick chat in my office," he says.

The room's silent besides a few lingering, off-key notes as the music box runs out of rotations.

"I'm not going anywhere with you," she says.

Nickol nods to the security guard, who pulls a handgun from his holster, and the room erupts into chaos. Everyone rushes to their feet. Rose and McGregor are yelling, and Parker and Silas storm forward.

Emotions flicker through me—confusion, disbelief, betrayal—but the moment they reach me, they vanish, as if Parker's plucking them from my body. I wonder why he doesn't shield me from the silent rage simmering beneath the surface, like a dark snake slithering under my skin, preparing to strike.

Silas reaches my past self first, wedging himself between her and the gun aimed at her head.

"Wait," she yells. She reaches for Silas, a sudden wave of calm in the room's pandemonium. Her hand touches the middle of his back. His body tenses, and she closes her eyes for one fleeting second before Parker breaks the group apart, ramming the guard away.

Everything happens at once. I don't see Silas take the gun, but suddenly it's aimed at my future self, a dark fury in his gaze, and the gunshot is ringing in my ears. She crumples to the ground, a circle of dark red blood blossoming over her chest.

Parker roars, rushing forward to take her into his arms. "*No!*" he yells, his voice breaking. "Stay with me."

Silas gestures to Rose and Parker. "They're working with Fan," he says to Nickol.

"Liar," Rose screams, tears streaming down her snarling face.

There's no blue left in Silas's narrowed gaze, as if the pigment has washed away, leaving behind a cold, cloudy gray.

After everything he's done, deep down a part of me still believed there was good in him. Even when he took away my powers, he did it to protect me. *But this?*

Tears wet my cheeks, and my heart aches fiercely, as if the dormant chamber reserved for him has been torn from my body. It's as if I've slipped into yet another nightmare, where *my* Silas—the first person I trusted after my mother died, whose chest I wept on while divulging my past—turns into something else. Someone else.

Matthews.

My attention snaps to my future self. She's dying. *I'm dying.* I need to stop thinking of her as someone else, because it's *my* limbs twisted on the floor. *My* blood pouring from my body. *My* life about to end.

Parker's emotions gush through me, adrenaline, terror and distress overwhelming my senses. I'm struggling to focus over the roaring in my head, my racing heart, and the uncontrollable tremor seizing my body.

"You're a dead man," Parker growls at Silas, and I feel his raging promise from the top of my head to the tips of my toes. He lowers his head, and warmth spreads through my body.

"He's trying to travel," someone yells.

"Stop," Nickol yells. It's then I notice the strange-looking gun with a long, narrow barrel in his hand. "You leave this room and you're as good as dead. We'll send people after you. You'll never stop running."

Parker doesn't respond. Body shaking and head bowed, energy erupts within his chest, the thrumming power mirrored within my own body. He doesn't react when Nickol fires his gun, or when a small syringe embeds in his neck, but I flinch as if the needle's pierced my own skin. Another gunshot rings in my ears, and I'm thrown into my own memories.

The darkness.

My heart struggling to complete its final beats.

The oxygen dwindling in my blood.

This is it. My spirit's about to leave my body.

I am seconds from death.

I close my eyes, and every single emotion Parker felt in that moment pummels my body, knocking the air from my lungs. Emotions so strong and pure, no amount of training could suppress them. His fear and desperation inundate me, his burning need to protect my future self and his eternal promise to undo what's happening to her.

To change his past and save her life.

Above all, I feel his blinding, unconditional love for her. *For me.* And I know without any doubt in my mind that Parker would *never* do anything to harm me.

Wet tears spill onto my cheeks. My mind's in this dim room, but back in Silas's office, Parker pulls my body toward his, as if he needs to be closer. As if my touch might ease some of his debilitating grief.

Our chests press together, warm cedar and freshly cut grass igniting my senses as he draws my face toward his. "I'll save you," he says into the shell of my ear, voice trembling with emotion. "And I'll kill Matthews for what he did to you." And through the death, the darkness, and the despair, his lips find mine, a silent vow promising revenge.

My skin buzzes, the electricity pulsing through me, far stronger than when Parker brought me into his past. He opens his mouth, tongue tangling with mine in a desperate, fervent kiss. Parker's energy continues to course through my body, accumulating until the pressure in the rooms shifts. His grasp on my arms tightens, but he breaks away from me, drawing in a ragged breath . . . and everything else—Rose, Silas, his cottage—is gone.

36

Mariella

I'm standing inside a small cabin with wooden floorboards. "Where are we?" I ask.

"Ski cabin in Wyoming," he says over the gentle sound of burning logs crackling in the fireplace.

The subtle, smoky scent blends with the aroma of fresh pine. I tear my gaze from the dancing flames.

Parker's a living statue with his hands in his pockets, skin aglow from the warm, golden light cast by the fireplace. His honey-hued gaze meets mine and heat floods my body.

"Fuck. Those eyes," he says, his voice low and raspy. He shakes his head. "You shouldn't look at me like that."

I take in the king-sized bed sitting against the main wall of the cabin and the grand bathtub in the corner, flickering candles scattered along its edge. "Then you shouldn't have brought me somewhere like this," I say, not daring to take my eyes off him again. Heart racing, I suck in a shallow breath containing little oxygen.

He stares back at me intensely, his chest rising and falling as if he's out of breath. "You're right."

I don't know who moves first, but in a heartbeat I'm back in his arms, his mouth claiming mine. His kiss is rough and desperate, as if at any minute we might be thrown back into that dark room where my life was taken.

His hands trailing my body, our chests crushed together, he urges me backward until we're stumbling toward the bed, falling onto it with our lips locked. His body covers mine, pressing me down into the soft mattress, the evidence of his arousal firm against my stomach.

A heady need courses through my veins, and I grind against him, reveling in the deep, pained groan that rumbles from his chest. He plants fast, messy kisses down my neck and I want to stay here forever, cocooned beneath him, his consuming scent my own personal aphrodisiac. But I need his bare skin against mine.

I tug the bottom of his shirt, and he breaks our kiss, shifting his weight to reach behind his head and slide it off in one fluid movement. He tosses it on the floor, muscles rippling beneath my touch, and returns his mouth to mine.

I reach for the top button of his pants, and he pulls away from me, as if he's awoken from a spell.

"Ella," he says, and the word sounds pained. He sits up. "Wait."

"I want this," I say, sitting up beside him. I want *more* than heated glances and stolen touches. I want *him*. All of him. "The way I see it, I either don't go to Neurovida and I live, or I'm recruited and I die—"

"Don't say that," he begs. "I swear to you, I'll stop it from happening."

"—and I want to know I lived the short time I have left with you the way *I* want it. If people have been changing things in my life without my knowledge, at least with this

I'm the one who gets to choose. Please don't take that away from me."

Parker's eyes race back and forth between mine. "What are you saying?"

I lean toward him, bringing my lips to his. His hands remain by his sides, his kiss cautious, the fire behind it stifled to smoking embers.

"Touch me," I plead, my cheeks burning.

A cheeky grin creeps across his face. "I'm going to miss that," he says, brushing his thumb over the redness in my cheek. "I can count on one hand the number of times I saw you blush at Neurovida. But to be fair, all of them involved the absence of clothing."

"Don't tell me," I say, scrunching my nose.

His eyebrow twitches. "Why?"

Because it may never happen. The thought stabs at my heart. But if I take the antidote—if I go to Neurovida—I'll have *time* with Parker. The chance to fall in love with him. I shut the thought down. I need time to process everything I've learned. To sift through the truths and the lies.

Parker's still staring at me, waiting for my answer. I can't bring myself to maintain eye contact and instead stare into the fire. "I don't know. I guess I want to find those things out when I'm supposed to. It's kind of exciting . . . the thought of *you* meeting *me* for the first time."

I peer up to catch him grinning. "That's the sweetest thing I've ever heard," he teases.

"At least I'll have the upper hand."

Parker takes my hands in his, and I relish the warmth of his skin. "Ella, you *always* have the upper hand when it comes to us."

Us. Something inside me melts at the word, but it recondenses into a cold, rigid mass. In my future, we would've been together if it weren't for Silas. Now we can't unless I take the antidote, ensuring my death. Again, I push the thoughts away. Silas won't taint any more of my memories. This moment is about me and Parker, not anyone else or the impossible decisions ahead of us.

I press my lips to his, and he wraps his arms around me, drawing me closer.

"I want it to be you, Parker," I whisper into his lips.

He tips his face toward me and spends a moment searching my gaze, a small frown between his brows. "It's Liam. My real name. I don't want secrets between us."

"Liam," I repeat, and it sparks something inside of him, his eyes changing from a cool amber to a warm honey as if they have a will of their own.

He tucks a strand of hair behind my ear, knuckles grazing my cheekbone. His hand lingers by my face and my skin tingles beneath his touch. It's not enough. It'll never be enough. "Touch me," I beg.

His eyes don't leave mine as his fingertips trail downward, brushing the column of my flushed neck. My eyes drift shut, and I arch into him, silently begging. His hand moves lower, his touch like a light draft kissing the skin beneath my collarbone, skimming the swell of my breasts, ruffling the tie at the front of my dress.

He pulls at the knot, and my pulse quickens. The knot comes undone, and the material slackens, exposing my bra underneath. His pupils are dilated, his gaze locked on my breasts. I wait breathlessly as he sweeps my dress off my shoulders, the fabric pooling at my waist.

He swallows, his wild eyes roaming my body. "Are you sure this is what you want?" he asks in a gravelly voice.

I nod, impatient for his touch, and when it doesn't come, I reach behind me and unclasp my bra, leaving myself exposed. "Touch me," I repeat, lying back on the bed.

I'm about to die of shame when he moves over me, the painful longing in his eyes stealing the breath from my lungs. Holding his body above mine, he touches his hand to my jaw, assessing me, then he tilts my face up and captures my lips with his.

His kisses are no longer heated and desperate, but slow and deliberate, drawing out my pleasure with each careful stroke of his tongue. He kisses me until my breathing turns heavy, and I'm clutching at his sides, pulling him to me, desperate for the relief of his weight pressing down on me.

He finally relents, lowering his body to mine, and we both groan. We press into each other, and his lips explore my neck, trailing kisses down my skin until he reaches my chest.

"I've missed these," he says in a playful lilt, giving my breasts the same careful attention he gave my lips. He licks and bites, taking my nipple between his teeth.

Within seconds I'm a writhing mess, a fierce ache between my thighs. I want his hands on me, winding me up like he did after the ball, but he's content flirting with my chest.

"Liam," I say, and it comes out like a plea.

"You have no idea how much I love hearing you say that," he says, the two dimples in his cheeks fuel to the fire raging inside me. He returns his attention to my bare chest. "Now where were we, ladies?"

I cover my smile with the back of my hand, my laugh turning to a moan when he pinches one of my nipples and circles his tongue over the other. "I know what you're doing," I say.

"What am I doing?" he asks in mock innocence.

"You're—" I gasp as he sucks my nipple into his mouth. "Stalling."

"So impatient," he mutters, shifting to lie beside me. "There's a difference between stalling and taking my time, Ella."

Then his lips are back on mine, our tongues caressing, his heavenly scent enveloping me. He presses a splayed hand to the skin below my breast and slides it down my ribs, gliding over the crest of my pelvis and lower, between my thighs. He strokes me through the thin material of my underwear with a feather-light touch, teasing me until I'm clutching the bedsheets and my body's shuddering, the ache in my center now a throbbing heat.

I've gone this far with him before, but this time it's different. The last time we were together was intense in its own way, but the way he's kissing and touching me now is gentler. Slower. He's taking his time with me, savoring every moment.

The corner of Parker's—Liam's—mouth kicks up into a mischievous smile. "I like these," he says, fingering the lace of my underwear. He pulls them down, and I shift my hips to help him remove them, his upper body settling between my legs.

His hand trails up my inner thigh, brushing my bare flesh, and goosebumps erupt over my skin. I squirm, craving his touch and the pleasure it incites. His fingers move higher, my hips jerking at his teasing strokes, begging for that clever finger to press against my bare core.

Soft lips press against my thigh, right over my birthmark, and my breath catches. He draws the skin into his mouth, sucking and caressing with his tongue, leaving what I can imagine will be a large bruise.

"Liam," I cry, lacing my fingers through his hair. I need more. "Please just have sex with me."

He lets out a mocking laugh.

"Don't—" My words hitch in my throat, replaced with a sharp inhale as he presses his mouth to my center, setting me on fire. His warm tongue works me in measured, sweeping strokes, and my head falls back onto the mattress, chest fluttering with each clipped, quickened breath.

I won't last long, not when he changes his technique, alternating between sucking and running his tongue over me, swirling and pressing, drawing me to the edge.

I groan at the ceiling. He's going to burn me alive. I can't breathe, or think, or do anything other than hold the bedsheets in an iron grip and writhe with pleasure.

He clamps a hand down on my waist, holding me firm to the mattress, and I squirm under him, seeing stars when he slips a finger inside me.

Oh my—

"Liam," I choke out in another breathy plea.

His tongue presses down harder, and he slips another finger in, filling me, curling to press against a hidden spot inside me that floods my body with heat and kicks my heart into a gallop.

The last time we were together, I was alarmed at the way he traced my body and anticipated my needs, but now I revel in it. I can't stop the moans escaping my lips or the way my hips arch toward him as he brings me dangerously close to the edge. Pulse pounding and breathing ragged, I lace my fingers through his hair, holding him to me as the tension threatens to overcome me.

The hand clamping me down moves to my breast, pinching my nipple, and the sensation, combined with the wicked movements of his tongue and his fingers plunging inside me, sends me over the edge. I cry out, coming undone in waves of intense pleasure that whip through my body, my walls fluttering against the fingers still pumping inside me.

Liam's tongue draws out every last shudder, lapping at my core like an addict chasing his fix. After what feels like an eternity, my boneless form collapses back onto the bed, and Liam crawls over me, a cocky smile on his lips.

Traitorous heat creeps into my cheeks at what he just did, and what's still to come. I move to kiss him, but he pulls away, subtly adjusting himself where he's straining against the front of his pants.

"We don't have to—I wanted this to be about you," he says.

"You won't make me change my mind," I say, shuffling into him, but still he pulls away. I don't know how, but I want to make him feel some of what he did for me. I want to bring him pleasure and watch him come undone. I tug at his pants, ordering him to stand and remove them. As he does, I take in his naked body, the hard lines surrounding each defined muscle and the stunning, sun-kissed color of his skin, contrasted against the paleness of my own.

My gaze shifts lower, to where his body reflects the strong desire he feels toward me. I don't know what I was expecting. Certainly not for him to be so big. I should be nervous or self-conscious, but all I feel is adoration for

Liam and my longing to live every moment I have with him to its fullest.

He lies beside me, and I rest my hands on his chest, trailing them lower, over his prominent abdominal muscles, across the faded scar I tended to all those months ago, and lower still, reaching his hard length. He sucks in a sharp breath when my fingers brush him, but the sound doesn't incite confidence in my inexperienced skills.

How can I make him feel everything he made me feel if I have no idea what I'm doing? A tingling sensation sweeps across my upper body, leaving me flushed from ear to ear. I yank my hand away. "I'm sorry, I don't know how to—I've never—" I release a breath, but I can't seem to meet his gaze. "Please show me?" I whisper.

He understands, his hand closing over mine, guiding it up and down his thick length. After a moment, his hand falls away and his eyes close, head dropping back onto the bed.

It's empowering—the way his body responds to my touch, the low sounds escaping him, and soon the curl of desire returns in my body. His deep moans increase, and with each stroke, his hips lift into my hands, but all I want is to give him more. As he has for me.

"Liam," I whisper, ceasing my touch to pull his torso toward me.

He lifts himself over me, holding his body so we aren't touching. His eyes scrunch closed. "Fuck. I don't have anything."

"Anything?" I ask, searching his crinkled brow.

"Protection," he says. "Are you—At Neurovida you were on the pill."

"I am."

He brings his face toward mine, brushing the tips of our noses. "Are you sure?"

"I'm sure," I say, holding his honey-hued gaze. "I want everything with you."

Touching his lips to mine, he reaches a hand between us, and his shaft nudges my entrance. I close my eyes and try to relax as he eases himself inside me.

"You're—" Liam groans, and I wince.

For a moment I worry he won't fit, that it might be too much, but my body gradually stretches to accommodate him, and the discomfort lessens.

Liam swears, but stills above me, his breathing heavy. "Are you okay?"

I nod, wrapping my arms around his neck, and only then does he pull out slightly and push himself back in, his tense muscles trembling beneath my fingertips. "God, I've missed this," he says, his breath hot on my skin.

His golden gaze locks with mine, and vulnerability, safety, pain and pleasure swirl through me. I memorize every single detail of his face and body, the tender fullness of him inside me and his masculine scent, taste and touch.

If I never have the chance to be with him again, at least I'll remember how right it felt to be caged in his arms, with his forehead resting in the crook of my neck as he moves above me. He whispers into my ear how perfect I am, how much he's missed being inside me, how much he loves me.

I press my mouth to the bronze skin on his neck, and he grunts, quickening his pace.

"Fuck. I can't—" Liam's breaths are heavy, his precise movements becoming jerky and irregular. He drops his head into my neck, plunging himself deeper. I cling to him as he thrusts, until he buries himself to the hilt and every muscle in his body tenses. Then he shudders inside me, his lips warm against my neck.

I hold him to me until the tension in his shoulders eases, and his body sinks down onto mine, pressing us into the mattress. He eases himself out, trails of his seed coating my tender flesh. He rolls onto his back, pulling me with him so I'm pressed against his side.

I rest my head on his chest, his racing heart slowing beneath my ear, hands drawing swirls over my bare back. I don't want to break the silence, to breach this whimsical fantasy where we're together, alone, in a gorgeous cabin with a crackling fireplace and a bathtub large enough to fit four. How much longer do I have until Liam takes me back, and I'm forced to choose between him and my future?

"Are you okay?" he asks, his chest rumbling beneath my ear.

I peer up at him, offering a sated smile. "I'm perfect."

"I'm here if you want to talk about anything, like what happened at Neurovida," he says. His tone flattens. "Or Matthews."

My gaze strays to the dwindling fire. "He said he's tried to stop my death more than once," I whisper. "Which doesn't make sense, because I just saw him shoot me."

Liam shifts so our eyes are level. "I'll force him to tell me how he changed your past, and I'll stop him pulling that trigger." He speaks with such assurance, as if he's already done it. "*No one* is going to hurt you."

I want him to be right. But what if he can't stop my death? Liam's arms tighten around me, as if he can sense my thoughts.

"How long until we need to go back?" I whisper. When we disappeared, Rose must've been furious.

Parker presses his forehead to mine and my fear dissipates. "All the time in the world. And then I'm going to make it so we have forever."

37

Rose

The blunt ache in my skull morphs into a fierce stab. My nails claw at Matthews' shoulder as I slide onto the floor beside him, facing the space where Parker and Ella disappeared. Fucking assholes. He'd better be using this time to say goodbye. The relentless ticking has my skin crawling. It feels like the room's swallowed me whole, and I'm stuck with Matthews inside the belly of a beast of his creation.

He hasn't moved since Parker injected him, but considering his size, he won't be out long. The clock I'm monitoring flicks to nine forty-eight. Ten minutes have passed. Either Parker's losing his touch, or he's distracted. *Where are they?*

As if demonstrating his impeccable timing, Parker and Ella appear, hands clasped together. A dark determination shines in Parker's eyes, but I'm having trouble getting a read on Ella.

"You okay?" I ask her. *Who would be after watching themselves die?* She nods, but her eyes are glazed over, her fingers clutching the charm on her necklace. "She should leave," I say to Parker, snapping Ella from her daze.

"You won't hurt him, will you?" she asks, looking between Parker and me.

I have to give her credit; she's witnessed her death at the hands of this man and still requests mercy on his behalf. She's always been the better person.

"We need answers," Parker says, his eyes glued to Matthews.

"I'm staying," Ella says, lifting her chin. "You two aren't the only ones who deserve the truth."

"If you're sure," I murmur, glancing at Parker.

They sit on the bed while we wait, Ella perched by Parker's side. He's holding her to him as if reluctant to let her go. A prickling heat fills my chest. It's obvious something's changed between them. I just hope Parker knows what he's doing.

Matthews groans, and I funnel more power into him, holding him here in this time in case he tries to escape. I've been waiting for this moment for a long time. *Finally*, we will get answers, and he'll get what's coming to him.

"You ready?" I ask Parker, and he nods. The pounding in my head eases, his influence flowing into Matthews from where he sits on the bed. *Show-off.*

In his groggy and disoriented state, Matthews opens and closes his eyes a few times. He glances from Ella to me, but when he sees Parker he jerks awake, yanking his wrists against their restraint.

Parker springs to his feet. "Hey, Matthews." One side of his mouth curves into a malicious smirk, but there's no humor in his voice. "How's the eye? Looks all better."

Matthews mumbles something, but with the sedative flooding his system, the words are too slurred to decipher. Parker lunges for him and crushes his forearm against Matthews' throat. "That's not how this is going to work," he growls. "I'm going to ask you a question, and you're going to answer it. Now, tell me how you change the past without detection." Parker releases Matthews, glaring down at him while he coughs.

"Don't know what you're talking about," Matthews says, his deep voice slow and hoarse.

Parker thrusts his arm back against Matthews' throat. "Let's try that one more time. How did you change Ella's past without our memories splitting?"

I dig my nails into his shoulder. "And don't bother lying. We already know about the sleeping pills and the scar on her wrist. How did you stop her from meeting her ex-boyfriend, Glenn?"

The moment Parker lets go, Matthews throws his head forward, striking Parker with surprising accuracy. I shudder at the sickening crack of bone colliding with bone and the hunger for vengeance behind Matthews' steely gaze.

Parker falls backward and Ella cries out, moving to help him. But Parker's back on his feet, lunging at Matthews, nostrils flared and body shaking. "Why did you tell Neurovida we were working with Fan?" he asks, and I shudder at the memory of the rogue time traveler on the video, plucking those men's lives like grapes from a vine.

"To get you out of the way," Matthews mutters.

"Why?" I ask, but Matthews remains silent.

"Still not getting it, are you?" Parker says. He grabs the fabric of Matthews' shirt and wrenches him forward, his other hand tightening into a fist. "Maybe if I break your other eye socket?" Matthews doesn't flinch or pull away. He just stares at Parker, his gaze lethal beneath his drooping eyelids.

"Silas, please."

Ella's voice is like a gentle lull in a roaring storm. She approaches us hesitantly and kneels beside Parker. Parker thrusts Matthews back against the wall, but releases him. Getting to his feet, he moves away, as if he can't bear the sight of Matthews and Ella together.

"You've been lying to me for almost a year," Ella says to Matthews, her voice unsteady. "Please tell the truth now. How do you change the past?"

I nearly choke. Not only because he's done the impossible and changed the past, but he's integrated himself into her life for one whole year? *Why?*

Every tense line in Matthews' face eases as he stares at Ella. "I'm not telling them anything until I know they won't run straight back into the past and undo the changes I've made," he says slowly, his deep, smooth voice laced with sedative.

"If you're so adamant about saving her, why did you shoot her?" Parker asks, his voice breaking.

Matthews slumps back against the wall, his sluggish gaze crawling between Parker and Ella.

"Don't bother denying it," I say, jerking my head toward Ella. "She's seen Parker's memory. Why did you shoot her?"

"She told me to," Matthews says, his eyes rolling back in their sockets.

"Just like she told you to insert yourself into her past and take advantage of her?" Parker says, a humorless smile on his face.

Matthews shakes his head. "I barely touched her. I'd never stoop to that," he says, and Ella gets to her feet, chin trembling as she moves to stand beside Parker.

"What do you want, a medal?" I ask Matthews. "You *changed* her past. Replaced my memories. It goes against everything the Alphas stood for." I take in his handsome face, the harsh lines eased by the strong analgesic flooding his system. Once I thought he was a good man, with a rare decency so few possess. Once I'd looked up to him. The thought makes me sick. You don't survive on the streets without being a sound judge of character. *How was I so wrong about him?*

"She would've been ashamed of you," Parker says, fire behind every word.

Matthews laugh is low and cold. "Don't pretend like you knew her," he says slowly. "Wrapped up in your own self-pity. Drinking. High. Missing sessions. You had *no idea* what she went through before Neurovida. What happened to her."

"What are you talking about?" Parker says, turning to me. "Rose?"

I shake my head. "All my memories of Ella's ex-boyfriend are gone." *How the hell did Matthews erase them?*

"Neurovida wrote the oath to stop us getting too close to each other," Matthews slurs.

"They wrote the oath to stop our memories splitting and to keep us safe," I say.

Matthews laughs, and his eyes drift shut, the tension bleeding from his drawn, scarred eyebrows.

"Wake up," I yell. "What happened to Axis and Bandit after we left?" I demand, shaking his massive frame. "Axis and Bandit. Where are they?"

He slowly opens his eyes and mumbles, "Gone."

"You killed them," I whisper. My chest feels like it's caving in on itself. Gritting my teeth, I hold back the tears stinging my eyes. I grip the front of Matthews' shirt and pull him toward me. "Tell me how you change the past. *Tell me*," I scream into his face.

Matthews' head slumps forward. "I won't."

Pressure builds in my chest. *I want to hurt him. I want him writhing in pain for what he's done.* "If you don't tell me, I swear to fucking God, I'll kill you."

Matthews' eyelids close, and my brain splits in agonizing pain. *He's trying to travel away.* Crying out, I crumple to the floor, fighting to keep contact. Even sedated, his strength is incredible, but I grit my teeth and hold him in this time, my vision blurring.

"What's happening?" Ella cries.

Parker stumbles toward us, hands landing beside mine on Matthews' shoulders. Power surges from Parker, warm energy gushing through Matthews and returning to Parker's hands, white-knuckled beside mine. Parker's influence thrums against my palms, a silent request to be let in.

I draw it toward me, and the moment it passes my fingertips, it cascades up my arms and into my chest, gathering and melding with my own power before surging back toward my hands. Our combined influence barrels into Matthews, amplified tenfold, coursing through his body like an avalanche of power.

Matthews relents, and the searing pain abruptly ceases. I slump back against the wall, gasping for breath. Sweat shines on Parker's brow, and Matthews is breathing heavily, as affected as we are by our mental game of tug-of-war.

Parker moves away, but I can still feel his power flowing through Matthews, his influence licking at the spot where my hand clutches Matthews' strong shoulder.

"I'm done fucking around," I mutter, and I turn to Ella. "Do you have any final questions you want to ask him?"

She frowns, looking to Parker. "What do you mean, final?"

I pull out my pocketknife and press the blade into Matthews' neck.

"Rose," Ella screams, rushing toward us. Parker holds her back, and she folds into his arms, burying her head against his chest.

"Don't fuck with me, Matthews," I say through gritted teeth. "How do you change the past?"

"I'm the only one who can do it," he says. "Just like Parker can travel other people without touching them, and you can go back further than your own life."

"If you believe you're the only one who can do it, then you won't mind telling me *how*." I lean toward him, his blood beading at the tip of my knife. "Tell me before I slit your throat."

Matthews' gray-blue eyes stare into mine, his jaw set. His intentions are clear—he won't tell us a thing. Not without *motivation*.

I glance at Parker. We prepared for this, stealing enough medicine to drug Matthews for days. I know where Parker stands. We need answers, and to save Ella's life, Bandit's life, Axis's life, I'll gladly take Matthews'. My eyes dart from Parker to Ella, and Parker nods. Removing Ella from his arms, he steps toward me, his body vibrating.

"Say goodbye, Ella," he says.

Her eyes widen. "Stop," she begs, tears streaming down her cheeks. "Please don't do this."

Parker places one hand on my shoulder and the other on Matthews', his influence gushing through us both.

"I'm sorry," Parker says to Ella, his voice pained. "I need to do this to save you." He checks his watch and lowers his head, and the room begins to shift.

Ella rushes forward, fisting the material at the back of Parker's shirt. "Liam, please."

A sudden coldness hits me at my core. *Liam.* In all the time we've spent together, Parker's never disclosed this information to me. Yet he's told Ella after spending a collection of hours with her. My stomach turns at the intimacy of it. At the way he's staring at her, as if she holds the power to build or break him.

Pull it together. I turn to Parker, ignoring the crushing in my chest. "Let's go."

Parker nods, but his amber eyes are focused solely on Ella. "I'll come back for you," he says in a low voice, and he travels us from the room.

38

Mariella

I stare at the mass of documents lining the walls of Silas's office without seeing anything at all. My mind keeps jumping from those beautiful, rare moments alone with Liam in the cabin, to Rose holding Silas at knifepoint, and the unsolved puzzle that was my friendship with Silas. It all makes sense now. Silas had a plan from the beginning: get close enough to manipulate me and ensure I stayed at uni. Push me to socialize with Anna and build a life here, outside of Neurovida's walls. My pills were another piece of that puzzle. Stop my sub-t to ensure I never glimpsed my future or discovered anything about time travel. If what Rose said is correct, the pills were also a clever backup, should I still choose to go to Neurovida. Medicine to strip away any power I might possess to actually be recruited. But Parker had stepped into my world, and Silas's carefully constructed scheme had come crashing down. My brain a tumble of thoughts, I untack the hundreds of photos and documents from the office walls.

"I'll come back for you."

When? The back of my throat burns. Liam and Rose won't kill Silas, will they?

I finish clearing the walls and begin emptying the desk and filing cabinet, shoving papers into a small moving box I find in Silas's attic. It feels wrong keeping them, as if I'm prying into a time not yet my own. I'm carrying the box to the living room when Liam calls my name. My eyes momentarily flutter closed at the sound of my name on his lips.

He's appeared in the hallway behind me, and it's as if no time's passed. "Liam."

A slow grin creeps across his face, and he walks toward me, hands tucked into his pockets. "It's only been a day, but I've missed you like it's been years."

I walk into him, relaxing my head in the crook of his neck. His arms wrap around me, and I breathe in his scent.

"What did you do to Silas?" I ask, and Liam's arms stiffen.

"Nothing yet. We're still questioning him. He hasn't said much since we left here, but he'll crack with time," he says, an iciness in his voice I'm unaccustomed to.

"I packed up everything in his office," I say, gesturing to the moving box. "Maybe there are clues in there that will help you?" My voice lowers to a whisper. "You won't kill him, will you?"

Liam's silence turns my blood cold, and I pull away from him. "Killing him won't bring back the lost members of Alpha, but it will make you as bad as he is."

"Don't you think I know that?" he says.

I take in his trembling body. His pale face. "You're scared," I say.

Liam's gaze rushes back and forth between my eyes. "I'm terrified," he whispers, tilting my chin upward. "I keep thinking unless we get answers out of Matthews, I'll never see you again." He presses his forehead against mine. "And I'm afraid of the things I'll do to get those answers. I can't lose you again."

"Then take me back with you," I beg, resting my hands against his chest. "Silas will talk to me. I know he will."

He shakes his head, as if compelling his fear away, and places his hands over mine. "Ella, I came back to check you're okay. And to let you know I'll *never* stop fighting for you. And I know I've said goodbye about a hundred times now, but this is it for a while. At least for me. Until Rose and I figure everything out. Please try to understand."

Salty tears wet my lips. I want to tell him to stay. To run away with me so we can have the time together we deserve. To get to know each other without breaking oaths and the pressure of Neurovida. But that means asking him to give up on his future and saving his friends. To give up on Rose. To give up on *me*.

I take a breath and stare into his golden eyes. "I understand, but it doesn't make saying goodbye any easier."

"It's not really goodbye. Not forever." He lifts his hand to brush a stray lock of hair from my face. "Matthews has the answers, I just need to get them. And if I can't, I'll figure it out myself. Now I know changing the past is possible . . ." He smiles at me and a wide, mirroring grin pulls at my lips. "The next time I see you, I'll tell you how happy we are together in the future."

My chest swells, yet tears fall down my cheeks. I need to believe that time will come. That Liam will be in my future. That he will save my life, and we'll be together. And when the day he speaks of comes, I'll go to Professor McGregor and ask for the antidote. But until then, I'll keep my lost powers a secret. I won't add another burden to Liam's shoulders.

I stand on my tiptoes and press my lips to his. He wraps his arms around me, lifting me off my feet, and his tongue parts my lips in slow, worshiping strokes that make my heart stammer. Fire erupts under my skin. Will any length of time with him satisfy the burning ache his touch provokes? The sparkle in his eyes tells me I'll soon have a lifetime to test my theory.

My feet touch the ground, but Liam's arms linger around my waist, as if he can't quite let go. A mischievous grin plays at his lips. "There's no coming back from you, Ella. You're an addiction. The guy you'll meet at Neurovida . . . has no idea what's coming."

"I want to know *everything* about us, and Neurovida . . . and time travel."

Liam laughs. "See, that's where you're wrong. I've told you there's no fun in living if you know how everything's going to turn out."

"If you say so," I murmur.

He presses a kiss to my forehead. "Goodbye, Ella."

"Goodbye," I whisper, and in an instant, he's gone, the moving box filled with documents disappearing with him.

I move toward the office, but another noise echoes in the corridor. Smiling wildly and heart racing, I whip around. "I wasn't expecting—"

The words disintegrate on my tongue. I stand mute, staring at the man walking toward me. A man who, seconds ago, was at least five years younger. Subtle lines crowd the outer corners of his eyes, yet somehow he's more handsome than ever.

"Liam." I reach out and brush my fingers along his bearded cheek. "I don't understand. How long has it been?"

He grasps my hand long enough to draw it away from his face. "The last time you saw me, I was six years younger."

"Six years? I don't—" A heaviness settles in my stomach. Six years and he hasn't come back.

"The next time I see you, I'll tell you how happy we are together in the future."

The day never came. He and Rose didn't discover how to change my future. They couldn't stop my death. It's written all over him. He can't save my life, and we won't be together. *He's here to say goodbye.*

For a fleeting moment, I'm falling, the world spinning around me as my body hurtles toward the ground with nothing to slow my descent. The resignation on Liam's face confirms it, but I still ask, "You didn't figure out how to save me, did you?"

Liam's face twists, as if the words he speaks are agonizing. "I swear to you, Rose and I have tried. I've spent every waking minute since we left in the past, but we haven't been able to change anything."

"And Silas, he didn't—He said he wanted to save me." And despite everything he's done, I believed him. *Fool.*

"He was an exceptional liar. If he wanted to save you, he could go back and stop it from happening, just like he could erase turning Neurovida against us," Liam says.

"But if he already knows I won't survive, then why bother entering my past?" *Why push me to let him in and take away my powers?*

"We only know he came to this time looking for us. We think he knew I'd try to find you, so he needed a reason to stay close to you."

An uncomfortable tightness forms in my chest as I scan Silas's neat cottage. The dark leather sofa where I opened up to him about my past. His white tiled kitchen where he cooked us dinner, his gray-blue eyes tracking me as I studied at his dining table. Whenever our gazes locked, the tension around his eyes would ease, as if I were his salvation in a life of damnation. All a lie. A trick. To get close to me, to find Liam and Rose.

"I didn't think . . . Was it *all* fake?"

"Yes. Silas wasn't even his real name."

The pain in my chest is now a vicious stabbing, right beneath my sternum. Because of Silas, I'll never master time travel. I'll never see my mother again. My lungs are incompetent, each inhale strained. *I'll never meet Liam.*

I want to scream. Break down. Do *anything* to release the unbearable pain tearing at my insides, but I swallow the cry in my throat and hold back the tears burning my eyes. Liam's spent the past six years trying to save me, and the agony of defeat is written all over his face. For him, I need to be strong. I raise my chin. "Did you kill him?"

"Yes," he says without hesitation, his voice unrecognizably cold.

I should feel satisfaction, but the pain in my heart worsens, threatening to tear me apart. Silent tears stream down my cheeks.

Liam runs a hand through his hair, eyes glazed over as if his mind is in another place. "We couldn't let him go. Not with the power he had to change the past. He could come back here and kill us all." He shakes off his stupor, his golden gaze returning to mine. "Ella, I came back for two reasons. I hate to ask you for anything again but—"

"I want to help," I say.

Liam nods. "Get rid of everything in here. Just in case he's hidden information that will lead anyone to us."

"I will. And the second thing?"

Liam is silent, his shoulders slumping as he pulls something from his pocket, his knuckles white.

I stare at the syringe in his hand, and my heart drops. "You know?"

"Matthews." Liam's brows crease. "A lot of what he said didn't make sense, but he made it clear he was threatened by you. His plan was always to take away your powers and keep you contained." His lips press together, and he stares down at me, the light behind his eyes dim. "I don't want you to take this, Ella. The only consistent information we got out of Matthews is if you don't go to Neurovida, you'll live." He takes a step toward me. "As long as you pretend to know nothing, Neurovida will leave you alone. You can have a normal life."

A normal life. The words ring in my ears.

I've spent so long chasing normality. Afraid of being the weird girl or being singled out. I let it take over my life.

But standing before Liam, knowing I've already missed out on *six years*—that he wants to make it longer. *Forever.*

I don't want a normal life.

The realization knocks the breath from my lungs. Not if it means a life without him.

"If I don't go to Neurovida, we'll never meet," I whisper, and as the words leave my mouth more tears fall, no matter how much I try to stop them.

Liam tenses, but he doesn't reach out to touch or comfort me. His shoulders are slumped, his eyes dim. The past six years have broken something within him. "I don't want you to meet me," he says. "Not if it means your death. I want you to live a long, safe life. This is the only way I can ensure that happens. But I don't want to be another person in your life making choices for you." He releases a breath and extends the syringe toward me. "I told you I'd never keep anything from you again. It's not a promise I've kept, but at least this way you can decide for yourself."

Hand shaking, I reach out and take the antidote. "And if I don't take it, what does that mean for us?"

"I can't—" He pauses, pressing his lips together. "I need to go back, but Rose and I won't stop trying. I promised you I never would."

"It's been six years. Stop searching. Stay here with me. I can take the antidote, and you can teach me how to time travel. We can go somewhere safe."

"I don't want to hide in the past forever. You saw what being here did to Rose. The painkillers and the unstable behavior are only a glimpse of what happens if we stay too long in the wrong time. Plus, Neurovida will be watching you now, getting ready to recruit you. The only way I can guarantee your safety is by staying away."

"Can't you visit me at Neurovida and tell me when it's time to leave? Before anything happens to me?"

"Once you set foot in Neurovida, you never leave. You die no matter what."

I grip the syringe in my hand. I'm not ready to say goodbye. I'm not ready to accept I'll never go to Neurovida, never meet him, never live the life I was destined to live. "What if I find you before either of us gets recruited?"

Liam shakes his head. "It's too dangerous."

My heart's racing, as if it senses how unbearably close it is to breaking. "No. I'll find you in this time. I'll—"

"Ella, *no!*" he yells. He points to the syringe in my hand. "Throw that away and move on with your life. Finish your studies and become a psychologist like you always wanted.

Don't waste your life waiting for me." He's shaking, body half turned away as if he can't bear to look at me. "There's no future for us anymore."

His words hit me with such force that the air expels from my lungs. I clutch the charm on my necklace, fighting to stay upright. This can't be the end. I move toward him, needing to close the distance between us. I'm desperate for him to take me into his arms and promise me it will be okay, but he steps backward, and my feet come to a halt.

Tension lines Liam's forehead, and dark bags sit beneath his eyes from years of stress and hiding. Six years, to be exact. Six years of his life, and Rose's, wasted trying to change my future. They've lost so much time on the impossible. What if they never stop? They'll waste their whole lives.

Rose and Liam have continuously stressed to me the importance of living my life to its fullest, but when is the time for them to live theirs?

I force away the pain of my heart shattering and the cry building at the back of my throat. I wipe the tears from my cheeks. "Okay," I whisper, my body shaking. "I'll throw it away. If you promise to do something for me."

His eyes lifts to mine, and he nods.

"I want you to stop. Stop trying to change what happened at Neurovida and stop putting others before yourself. You've spent so much of your life concentrating on other people. Rose too. I want you to stop focusing on what you can't control and focus on what you can. I want you and Rose to be happy. Find a place where you can both be safe and live your lives. I don't want you to spend another second trying to save me."

His body tenses. "Ella—"

"Please. You need to forget about me."

"That's like telling me not to breathe," he says quietly.

The truth shines in his eyes—he won't sacrifice me for himself. Ever. Unless I force his hand. "Liam, I'll take this antidote unless you promise to let this go."

"This is bigger than you and me. There are other members of Alpha who Rose and I need to save."

"They wouldn't want you saving their lives at the cost of your own. You told me once you'd never lie to me. So, I want you to promise me. Swear it to me now. If you love me at all, you will stop trying to change your past. And even if you could stop my death, I don't want to go to Neurovida. I want to stay at college and become a psychologist. All I've ever wanted is to be normal, and this way I can." The lies burn my throat, but I hold his defeated, amber gaze. "Promise me."

Liam stares back for an eternity, his face filled with torment. Finally, he whispers, "I promise."

"Promise me you'll try to move on." I force out my next sentence, the words tasting like poison. "If you meet someone, I would . . . find a way to understand."

Liam's eyes lock with mine, so many unspoken words hanging between us. I step toward him and pull him against me. Squeezing my eyes shut, I breathe him in—warm cedar mixed with the freshness of cut grass. His arms wrap around me, but he doesn't pull me firmly against him like his younger self had.

"Goodbye," he whispers into my hair. "You're going to have a wonderful life, Ella. Don't waste a second of it."

"I won't," I say, tightening my arms around him, but it doesn't stop him vanishing for what I know will be the last time.

39

Rose

Waves kiss the side of the yacht, rocking me back and forth while I wait for Liam's return. We're still in the past, anchored off the coast of a tiny island. It's safer out here. We figure any traveler looking for us will be dissuaded, should they get their time wrong and end up in the middle of the ocean instead of on our boat. But even my renewed sense of security and the beauty of the afternoon can't soothe my nerves.

I'm picking at my nails when he materializes at the bow. He slips off his shoes and walks the length of the boat barefoot, body stiff despite his casual boating attire. He sits beside me, resting his arms on bent knees, and joins me in staring out at the horizon.

"Did she take the antidote?" I ask, breaking the silence.

"No," he says, his voice raw. I release a deep breath. "She promised me she wouldn't if I agreed to something in return."

"Okay." I study the side of his face, his golden features taut. He turns to face me, pain filling his light brown eyes.

"She made me promise to stop trying to change the past." He slumps forward and rubs his hands over his face, speaking to the deck. "I said I would. Do you hate me?"

The wind picks up, ropes tinkling against the mast. "No," I admit. I'm *relieved*. Six grueling years we've spent trying to save her, without success. I stopped believing changing her fate was possible years ago, but he needed to come to the same realization on his own terms. If anything, Ella's done us a favor. "I think . . . this is a good thing. I can't keep doing this. It's too much."

He nods, his eyes watering. "I know." He stands and disappears into the hull, reappearing with two beers in his hand. He opens one and passes it to me before he opens his own. We stare out at the sunset, the gentle lull of the ocean current rocking us.

"Do you think she has any idea what you've just done? The things you've saved her from?" *The power she's lost.*

"No," he says. "And I hope she never does."

He slips his hand into mine, and I give it a gentle squeeze before he lets go. Six years and my pulse still jumps every time he touches me.

He wipes the tears from his cheeks. "Now we look forward. We live," he says, holding out his beer. "To the Alphas."

I clink my bottle against his, my voice wavering as I say, "To the Alphas." I take a swig and rest my head on his shoulder. We sit in companionable silence, the sun disappearing behind the horizon. Now is the time to mourn our losses. To let go of our past.

But I'll never stop looking behind me.

He may have promised Ella he'd stop trying to change *his* past, but he didn't promise to stay out of the past altogether. When he told me he believed there was a reason we have these gifts, I'd rejected the thought. But lately, I've been thinking he was right.

Neurovida's going to wish it wasn't *me* blessed with the special skill of traveling further back in time than my own life. Because I don't need to change my past to get vengeance. Besides him, all my friends are dead. I never knew my family. I have no one left to lose. And when you have nothing left to lose, you have *everything* to gain.

As soon as he's ready, we're going back to Neurovida's beginning. Before we were Alphas. Before we were born.

And we're going to burn Neurovida to the fucking ground.

40

Mariella

"And can anyone remember which area of the brain is considered the 'personality center'?" asks our lecturer, glancing around the quiet lecture hall.

Anna's elbow digs into my ribs, but I'm already holding my hand high above my head.

"Miss Adams?" he says, gesturing to my raised hand. He knows me by name, as do the rest of the psychology faculty.

Hundreds of heads turn in my direction. My heart rate jumps, but I raise my chin. "The prefrontal cortex," I say, loud enough for my voice to carry to the front of the hall.

"Correct," the lecturer says, with an astute grin. "As always." He turns toward the lectern and continues his presentation.

"Show-off," Anna whispers into my ear. A wide, open smile blooms over my face. "I'm proud of you, nerd."

"Thanks, Anna."

We settle back in our seats, Anna's attention returning to our lecturer, but I let my gaze wander past our friends and peers sitting immediately around us, and across the mass of students filling the hall. I pause on the empty chair in the third row from the front, thoughts consumed by the man who once sat there with golden hair and a mischievous grin.

The man who, along with the woman sitting beside me, showed me how to live. How to fight. I twist the fabric of my sweater between my fingers. Not a day goes by that I don't think of Liam . . . or how much I'm going to miss him.

✧

"I still can't believe you're leaving me," Anna complains for the fifth time since I started packing. She plonks down beside me on my bed, the motion ruffling the contents in my suitcase. "If anyone's going to drop out, it should be me."

I lower the dress I'm folding into my lap. "I'm not leaving *you*, college just isn't for me." I don't know what is, but unless I get out into the world and experience it now, I never will.

Since Liam, Rose and Silas left, something inside me has broken free. I will *never* again be the scared woman letting others call the shots in my life. Liam and Rose sacrificed too much of their lives trying to save mine, and it won't be in vain. I may have lost my powers, but in doing so I've been given a clean slate. My life's just beginning, and I won't waste another second of it.

"Who are you, and what have you done with Mariella Adams?" Anna demands with a disbelieving grin.

"She's still here, but I want to get out and see the world. Live a little. A lot."

If the last few months have taught me anything, it's how brief life is and, if mine were to be cut short, I'd want to have experienced as much of the world as I could prior to that moment. "It's not too late for you to come with me, you know? My offer to pay stands." The money I made selling my house could support us both for years. Apparently land close to Harvard is in high demand, even with a fire-ravaged house occupying it. I raise my brows and lean toward her. "Apparently, the clubs are amazing in Europe."

Anna groans. "I *so* want to come with you, but I can't join the family business until I complete a degree, so if I drop out now, I'm on my own." She gestures to the pile of neatly folded hand-me-downs I'm yet to return to her wardrobe. "You know, you're welcome to take those."

"Are you sure?" I run my hand over the cashmere cardigan on top of the pile.

"Of course. Something to remember me by." She eyes my brown leather jacket. "When you get sick of that old thing." She places the pile of clothes into my suitcase and my chest expands.

How can I ever repay everything she's done for me? She's boosted my confidence, showed me how to let loose and have fun. Most of all, she's been a true friend. I reach out and yank her into my chest, drawing in the comforting scent of strawberry lip gloss, peonies and her sweet perfume. "I'll miss you, Anna."

She laughs, wrapping her arms around me. "You too, Ella. Make sure you sleep with plenty of hot European men for me. I still can't believe you're giving up studying to go traveling. I thought if anyone was going to become a clinical psychologist, it'd be you."

"Yeah, well . . ." Liam's words play in my mind. "There's no fun in living if you know how everything's going to turn out."

41

Mariella

Twelve months later

My limbs ache with fatigue, the muscles trembling for the past three hours. I draw in a sharp breath of fresh mountain air, laced with pine and snow. A sharp sting bites at my palm, and my clammy hand unfurls, releasing the plastic corners of the Polaroid digging into my skin. The only photo remaining from the mass of documents cleared from Silas's office and ceded to Liam two years ago.

Some would call it fate that this particular photo was missed, wedged at the back of Silas's filing cabinet between the drawer and its base. I trace a numb finger over my mother's serene face. She sits beside me on a rock wall by the ocean, face turned to the side as if catching the photographer in mid-exposure. Her top's risen with the movement, dark ink marking the sliver of exposed skin on her lower back. An unmistakable tattoo. The Mark of the Time Traveler. Why do I have no recollection of my mother having a tattoo?

Silas's messy scrawl dates the picture to three months before she died. In the photo, my mother is healthy. Happy. And the day she was taken away, my young mind struggled to comprehend how someone could deteriorate in such a short period of time. Unless my concept of that time was wrong . . .

I tuck the Polaroid into my pocket, fingers brushing the small syringe Liam left me two years ago. In that time, I've traveled as much of the world as I could, living every moment as if it was my last. I've stood, legs weary, gasping for breath at the top of the Eiffel Tower, screamed until my throat burned as I leaped from a plane in Hawaii, and lost hours partying in Amsterdam, surrounded by laughter and smoke. I've met fascinating people from all walks of life, allowing myself to interact without fear of judgment. I've been set free, and with freedom, I've gained clarity.

Throwing away the antidote in my hand will ensure me many things, including a life of safety and normalcy. But I've *never* been normal, and now I don't want to be.

I don't want to spend my life wondering *what if*? What if Neurovida was responsible for my mother's death and I was too scared to discover why? What if I live my entire life without seeing Liam again? What if I give up the love of my life before he's ever met me?

Liam said time travel's a gift, and I won't throw it away. He and Rose couldn't save me, but I am the master of my own destiny, and I *will* learn how to time travel. Liam said there was a reason Silas wanted to keep me from Neurovida once he'd interfered with my life. He was right to call me a threat. One his younger self won't see coming.

I will uncover the truth behind what happened to my mother. I will force Matthews to teach me how to change the past, and I will save myself. I will prevent the nightmare plaguing me since I was a child from becoming my reality and, if the dates in Silas's office were correct, I have three years to do it.

And if I can't? I'll still have three years to fall for Liam all over again, to experience a love so consuming that he was willing to sacrifice his entire life to fight for it.

Snow crunches beneath my boots as I walk through the white-tipped forest, rubbing my hand over the ache beneath my sternum. With each step, the burning sensation fades. I pause before two tall, wrought-iron gates, and close my eyes.

"Let the current carry you," I say softly, clutching my mother's necklace between my fingers. An icy chill breaches my thick coat, creeping under my skin and into my muscles, like phantom hands urging me forward. Calling to me. Whispering that this is where I was meant to be.

This is my fate.

Hauling off my coat, I yank the neckline of my top past my bare shoulder, pull the protective plastic cap off the needle, and plunge it deep into my arm. Biting back a cry, I pull the needle from my skin and scan the imposing mansion casting me in shade.

Neurovida.

✧

"I want you to listen to me carefully, Miss Adams," says the middle-aged woman sitting across the desk from me. She lowers her fountain pen and delicately clasps her hands atop the marble surface, inclining her head to peer at me over her black, rectangular glasses.

She never offered her name. I knew better than to ask.

"The second you walk through that door"—her eyes flicker toward the door at the far side of the room—"you are no longer Mariella Adams. That name does not exist to you. You have no past, no present, and no future. You must pick an alias. No first or last name, no titles. One word." The woman pauses. "This is for your safety. Do you understand?"

"Yes," I reply, my voice strong despite my racing heart.

She unclasps her hands and retrieves her pen, head lowered to the papers before her. "As soon as you've decided, you can join the others. Do you need some time?"

"No, thank you." I move toward the door, one hand trembling over the handle, the other clutching the heart-shaped charm on my necklace.

"Well?" the woman asks, looking up from the mass of legal papers I've just signed.

I take a deep breath. "It's Flame," I say, opening the door and walking straight through it without looking back.

Want more? Keep an eye out for book two in the Mark of the Time Traveler series, coming in 2026.

Acknowledgments

This book would not be what it is today without the support and guidance of many incredible people.

First and foremost, my sister, Katharine. Thank you for reading every single draft of this manuscript (numerous times). I'm sure your eyes are bleeding at this point. Thank you for your brutal, hilarious comments, and for supporting my silly little dream from day one. I wouldn't be here without you, and I'm forever grateful for every line you've read, every "WTF" comment, and everything in between. Words cannot describe how grateful I am for the time you've spent helping me with this book. I love you. Also, please write a book! You'd be an incredible author.

Mum. Thank you for always reinforcing that I could do anything if only I set my mind to it. I never thought that would entail anything as creative as writing, but you gave me the confidence to chase this dream, and for that I will be forever grateful. I love you.

For my girls, Emilie and Charlie. I love you both more than anything in the world. I hope I give you the courage to chase your dreams no matter how farfetched they may seem (just like your Nanny did for me).

My husband, Chris. Thank you for being a wonderful

father to our beautiful girls and helping me make this dream come true. It took you a while to get on board but we're here now so buckle up, baby, because book two is bigger.

Annie. Thank you for being my positive little rock and always being in my corner. Thank you for trying to "get me", even when I'm being a closed book, and for never judging. I love you.

Emily. Thank you for all your love and support, and for always being my cheerleader, even across the country.

To my beta readers: Renae, Kez, Kelly, Gabby, Matt, Zali, Kirsty, Dominique, Jeff, Georgia, Devon, Tessa, Brooklyn, Hannah, Amelia, Odhette, Lauren, Flo and Emma. Thank you so much for taking the time to read this book and giving me your thoughts. Each and every one of you helped shaped this manuscript, and I am so grateful for you sharing your time to help me.

To my wonderful cover designer, Libby. Thank you for your hard work and the time you spent perfecting my cover. Thank you for your patience and kindness. You're an incredibly talented woman, and there is no doubt in my mind how far you will go.

To my agent, Tara. Thank you for taking a chance on me and for your patience (when answering one thousand questions about publishing). I'll be forever grateful for everything you have done for me.

To Anthea and the team at Atria. Thank you so much for all your support and for helping me make my dreams of being a published author come true.

To Andy and Charlie, my artists. Thank you for all your hard work with the design of the clock. You are both incredibly talented. Thank you for bringing my vision to life.

To my editors, Brooke, Kelly, Celia and Kate. Thank you for your gentle guidance and wise advice. I've learned so much from each of you, and you've not only helped improve my manuscript, but strengthen my writing. Thank you!!!

To all my fellow writers with the Romance Writers of Australia. Joining this group has connected me with many brilliant, dedicated writers who I'm now incredibly humbled to call my friends. Thank you for being there as I embark on this terrifying, exciting journey. Thank you to every person who made me feel welcome at conferences, shared their stories with me and gave me writing tips. Thank you for swapping excerpts with me and sharing your work.

To my fellow aspirers (especially Selina), thank you for our monthly Zoom chats, and for cheering me on, for pulling together through the highs and the lows. I'm incredibly grateful for every single one of you.

To the Bookstagram community. Getting this book out into the world would not have been possible without you. Thank you to every single person who supported me and cheered me on, who shared my posts, quotes, and cover. Most importantly, thank you for welcoming me, sharing my passion for reading romance, and for contributing to my never ending TBR.

And finally to you, the reader. Thank you for taking a chance on my book. I'm willing to bet you love reading as much as I do, and I hope you enjoyed *Within the Space of a Second* enough to stick with me for the second book in the Mark of the Time Traveler series. In the meantime, happy reading. Love, Elise. <3

About the Author

Elise is a radiographer who lives in sunny Queensland, Australia with her husband and two daughters. She wrote *Within the Space of a Second* while juggling full-time work, pregnancies and caring for her two under two. When Elise isn't parenting or writing, she's either in her head watching characters and storylines come to life, or curled up at home with a glass of wine in hand, reading romantasy or contemporary romance. Elise loves connecting with readers and writers. For more, please follow Elise on Instagram at @elisehelliwellauthor or visit www.elisehelliwell.com to sign up to her newsletter.

Content Warning

Within the Space of a Second is intended for readers over the age of eighteen. Content warning for this book includes vaping and vaping addiction, mention of sexual abuse, off-page torture, mention of self-harm and mention of suicide, off-page death of a parent, discussions surrounding mental illness, unprotected sex, stalking, off-page forced separation of a mother and child, depiction of a lock-in mental health ward, house fire, school bullying and prescription drug abuse.